GW01444947

THE SECRET
YEAR OF
ZARA HOLT

Also by Kimberley Freeman

Duet
Gold Dust
Wildflower Hill
Lighthouse Bay
Ember Island
Evergreen Falls
Stars Across the Ocean

THE SECRET YEAR OF ZARA HOLT

KIMBERLEY FREEMAN

hachette
AUSTRALIA

hachette
AUSTRALIA

Published in Australia and New Zealand in 2025
by Hachette Australia
(an imprint of Hachette Australia Pty Limited)
Gadigal Country, Level 17, 207 Kent Street, Sydney, NSW 2000
www.hachette.com.au

Hachette Australia acknowledges and pays our respects to the past, present and
future Traditional Owners and Custodians of Country throughout Australia
and recognises the continuation of cultural, spiritual and educational practices
of Aboriginal and Torres Strait Islander peoples. Our head office is located on
the lands of the Gadigal people of the Eora Nation.

Copyright © Kimberley Freeman 2025

This book is copyright. Apart from any fair dealing for the purposes of private study,
research, criticism or review permitted under the *Copyright Act 1968*, no part
may be stored or reproduced by any process without prior written permission.
Enquiries should be made to the publisher.

NATIONAL
LIBRARY
OF AUSTRALIA

A catalogue record for this
book is available from the
National Library of Australia

ISBN: 978 0 7336 3356 0 (paperback)

Cover design by Christabella Designs
Cover photography courtesy of Natasza Fiedotjew / Trevillion Images
Author photography courtesy of Louis Valenti / Shuttercraft
Typeset in 12/17 pt Minion Pro by Bookhouse, Sydney
Printed and bound in Australia by McPherson's Printing Group

FSC
www.fsc.org

MIX
Paper | Supporting
responsible forestry
FSC® C001695

The paper this book is printed on is certified against the
Forest Stewardship Council® Standards. McPherson's Printing
Group holds FSC® chain of custody certification SA-COC-005379.
FSC® promotes environmentally responsible, socially beneficial
and economically viable management of the world's forests.

The Secret Year of Zara Holt is a work of fiction. Many of the characters are based on real people, but the way I've drawn them, made them speak or think, or react to the real or fictional events in their lives is entirely imagined.

FOR SELWA

The grave's a fine and private place,
But none, I think, do there embrace.

ANDREW MARVELL, 'TO HIS COY MISTRESS'

PROLOGUE

She wakes (had she slept?) to the familiar sound of the shower running. Relief floods her body, warm and liquid. She turns on the lamp next to the bed and reads the clock. Three in the morning.

'I knew you'd be back,' she says as he enters the room, a towel wrapped around his waist, his silvery chest hair damp. 'I said to Vieve, it feels as though he's going to walk in the door any moment and have a laugh at us all for crying.'

'I always come back to you. You know that.' He sits on the bed, picking up her hand.

'Why all the fuss then? I was beside myself. There must have been over a hundred people looking for you.'

'I'm tired. The world is with us all the time. I'm done with it.'

'You must let me call the children. They're devastated.'

He shakes his head decisively. 'No-one can know. Just you and me.'

She doesn't push the point. He's right – this can't work otherwise. The boys were adults now anyway; they had their own lives to be getting on with.

'Come to bed,' she says. 'It's late.'

'Early,' he corrects her, smiling. The towel is on the floor and the lamp is extinguished, and it's just the two of them in the dark.

1

She curls against his warm body, hand across his upper arm, trying not to hold too tightly. That's the trick with him; it always has been.

'What will we do?' she asks.

'We will work it out in the morning. You're clever. You'll figure out a solution.'

'The whole country's in uproar. This will be impossible.' The weight of the task ahead is suddenly too much for her. Her imagination can't support it.

He rests his finger gently across her lips. 'In the morning,' he says. 'I'm tired.'

She kisses his finger. 'I'm sorry,' she says.

'So am I,' he replies. 'You know how sorry I am, don't you?'

She has never needed him to say sorry; she always finds a way to forgive. She sees past his betrayals to his gentle heart, his blazing intellect, his good soul.

'No more of that,' he says, as if reading her mind. 'I am back and nobody knows except you, and if we are to keep it secret then there can be no other women.'

She says nothing.

'I'm tired,' he says again. 'Tired of all of it.'

'Tired of me?' she asks, hearing her voice waver.

He kisses the top of her head. 'Never tired of you,' he replies. 'Never.'

Sometime around dawn, on the day they run away, she drifts back to sleep.

PART 1

CHAPTER 1

MELBOURNE, 1927

The night I met Harry I was wearing a dress I had designed and made myself. White organdie over a short black slip, black embroidery around the yoke and the hem, and a crimson taffeta sash tied in a huge bow on my hips. It was early December and the summer flowers smelled like Christmas. Party season, as all the college boys from the university celebrated the end of exams before they returned home to families in the countryside. Daddy and Mum had restricted me to one party a week . . . they were old-fashioned and worried about my reputation. Truly, I did love boys. I loved dancing with them, flirting with them, exchanging furtive glances with them, but it was a game to me. Nothing serious.

I waited on the front veranda of our little house in Kew, eyes on the road for Norman's Morris. I heard the front door behind me open and Mum's light footsteps.

'Who are you going out with tonight then?' she asked in her lilting Scottish accent.

'Norman.'

'Again?'

'Mm-hm.'

'And who is bringing you home?'

I turned to her and smiled. 'Norman,' I said firmly, though I didn't blame her for asking. Going out with one boy and coming home with another had become a habit of mine.

'It's serious with him? That's been a whole month to my reckoning.'

'Six weeks,' I replied.

'You be careful,' she said, and I knew what she meant. A girl my age, two doors down, had been forced through a hastily organised and teary wedding just two weeks before.

I wanted to tell Mum that I didn't need to be 'careful', that I knew what kind of kissing I liked and didn't like and was forthright enough to stop a boy who went too far. Also, that I had no intention of swelling up in the middle with a baby when I had spent most of the year dieting strictly enough to have visible hipbones. My natural figure and the most fashionable dresses that year did not flatter each other. But I could never talk to my mother about such things, so instead I feigned innocence.

'Norman is a perfect gentleman,' I said, though of course this wasn't true. He was a rakishly handsome party-lover who danced like a fiend and told the most scandalous dirty jokes.

Norman's dark green Morris Roadster puttered into view, saving me from further conversation. 'Bye, Mum.'

'Don't be home too late,' she called after me – vainly, I suspected.

Then I was cosying up next to Norman on the long bench seat, headed for St Mary's Hall, where most of our dances were held. Nobody had any money, so every week a different group of us decorated the hall, brought along a gramophone, provided the punch (none of us could afford gin to make it *interesting* punch) and stayed to clean up afterwards.

'Wrong turn,' I said to Norman.

'I have to pick up a friend and his girl.'

I eyed the remaining room on the seat. 'Where are they going to fit?'

'We'll squash up. You can sit on my knee and steer if you like.'

We were heading up towards the university. Norman was studying law, so I presumed his friend was a classmate. I watched the late-afternoon shadows out the window, the back of my head leaning against Norman's hard shoulder. I felt the week fall away from me – the dreary paper-shuffling and envelope-stuffing of my job at the local parish office – and imagined a weekend of walks with Norman, afternoons stretched out on my bed drawing, baking with my sister Genevieve in our cool kitchen.

The car pulled up and I looked around. Leaning in the driver-side window was a dark-haired, bright-eyed young man. Behind him was a slender young woman in a black beaded dress.

'Harry, Vera,' Norman said. 'Jump in.'

'There isn't room,' Vera noted.

'Beg to differ,' Norman said, and gestured them around the front of the car to the passenger door, which I opened for them. 'This is Zara.'

'Pleased to meet you,' I said, squeezing up onto Norman's lap. The steering wheel dug into my thighs. 'Norman, I'm not sure this will work,' I muttered.

'I'll never fit. I'm so fat,' the impossibly slim Vera said, making her my instant enemy.

'This won't do,' Harry said. 'I'll ride on the hood at the back.'

'It will be fine. We'll all just breathe in,' Norman said. 'Zara, can you shift your weight so you're not digging into me?'

I felt suddenly all wrong in my body, as though I was the problem. The reason we couldn't all fit. I slid off Norman's lap and said, '*I'll* sit on the hood. Then you'll all fit.'

'I'm not letting a woman sit on the hood while I take the seat,' Harry said.

'It's my choice,' I said, pushing my way out of the car and gesturing Harry and Vera in.

'Then I'll sit with you,' Harry said. 'Vera, you can ride with Norman.'

I hitched myself up on the hood, my shoes resting on the spare tyre. 'There's really no need,' I said, but Harry was already sitting next to me, smiling down at me. His eyes seemed to twinkle and his lashes were very long.

'Your lipstick is the precise colour of your sash,' he said.

'Yes,' I replied, shocked that a man would notice such a thing. Norman certainly never did. 'I bought the taffeta on purpose for that reason. It's my favourite lipstick.'

The car shuddered into life, making me lose my footing. Harry grasped my wrist and held it until I was secure again.

'Steady now,' he said. 'I'd never forgive myself if you dashed your brains out on the road all because I'm too poor to own a car.'

'I've ridden the hood loads of times,' I replied, gesturing at the view.

'Is that so?' He sized me up in the fading light. 'Good god, I like a woman with a spirit of adventure.'

I couldn't hide my smile. 'It's the only way to see the world. Backwards, with the wind in one's hair.'

'The wind in one's hair, eh?' He took off his Panama hat, but his hair was too slick with brilliantine to be much moved.

Impulsively I grabbed his Panama and pressed it onto my head over my dark curls. 'Look at me,' I said, in a deep voice. 'I'm Harry and I'm going to be a lawyer and then I'll be rich and buy as many cars as I like.'

'Oh, I'm going to be more than a lawyer,' he said.

'What are you going to be?' I asked.

'I'm going to change the world.' He had flipped so quickly from light-hearted to serious it made me blink.

'You are?'

'Watch me,' he said with a smile that creased the corners of his eyes.

And that was it. I *did* want to watch him. I never wanted to take my eyes off him.

———

Whoever decorated the hall that night had done it cursorily at best. A few sad crepe-paper chains hung from the rafters, and the long table for the bowls of punch and the enamel cups was bare of any doilies or garlands. Still, we had good music, a roomy dance floor, and a hall full of young people determined to have fun. I danced with Norman for two songs, spending most of the time glancing around for Harry and Vera. She was so tall and elegant – taller than Harry – that she stood out, and the knot of jealousy in my stomach grew ever tighter. Vera didn't look to me as though she had a 'spirit of adventure'. I wondered if Harry had told her he was going to change the world, and if she believed him. I believed him. I believed him with my whole heart.

Harry caught my eye and smiled over Vera's head. The corners of his mouth went all the way up when he smiled, as though he was filled with boyish delight. I felt my own lips curve up, not the coquettish smile I normally used with boys I like, but something genuine and irresistible.

Norman saw my expression and looked around. 'Why are you grinning at Harry Holt?' he said.

'I'm not grinning,' I said, as Norman spun me so my back was to Harry.

His eyebrows twitched but he said nothing more.

Later, I gathered with a group of my girlfriends out on the back steps of the hall. The air smelled like cut grass and jasmine. Eloise and I smoked, though I didn't care much for cigarettes. Betty was in the middle of describing to us how to use a fork to make perfect pleats when a shadow blocked the light from the door and I looked up to see Harry.

'Hello,' I said, beaming.

He joined us on the stairs. 'Am I interrupting something?'

'No, not at all.' I extinguished my cigarette under my shoe. 'Girls, this is Harry. A friend of Norman's from university.'

My friends introduced themselves one by one, and he was charming with all of them, but then turned to me and said, 'I haven't had a dance with you yet, Miss Dickins.'

Something about the way he said it, with a deep promise in his voice, made my heart stir. A ragtime piano tune came on the gramophone inside. I loved a foxtrot.

He took my hand in the light from the doorway and tugged it gently, leading me out onto the lawn. 'There's more room to dance out here,' he said. The music was faint, but audible enough to hear the rhythm. He pulled me up against him – I could smell the sharp, slightly mineral scent of his hair cream – and we danced in the balmy evening air.

I suppose that's when I fell in love with Harry, though in some ways it felt as though I had always loved him and had simply been waiting for him to arrive. He was not half the dancer that Norman was, and yet when the music ended and he let me go, I ached for more. We returned to the stairs, and I realised his girl, Vera, had joined our little gang. If she was perturbed by me dancing with Harry, she didn't show it. And of course we all danced with each other all the time – nobody was expected to dance with the same boy all night. But that dance felt different from any dance I'd danced before. The heat and the power of his body were imprinted on all my senses. I felt giddy.

Harry disappeared back into the hall, but Vera stayed with us. She was funny and friendly, despite being thin, and in no time she was making up dirty lyrics to a song with Eloise. It was only when we were heading inside for some punch that Vera gently grasped my elbow and held me back.

My heart thudded in my throat. Why did I feel guilty?

'He does this,' she said.

'Does what?'

'Woos other girls. All the time.'

'He wasn't wooing me,' I said lightly, shrugging her off. 'It was just a dance.'

She sniffed. 'He won't be any more faithful to you than he is to me. Or the last girl or the one before.'

'It was just a dance,' I said again. 'But thank you.'

I didn't dance with Harry again that night and in fact I didn't see him leave, which made me feel terribly deflated. I had thought he might seek me out to say goodnight, but he didn't. Those few magic moments dancing with him had clearly meant more to me than to him. Norman brought me home at eleven. We sat in the car a few minutes kissing, but then he got a little too bold with his hands and for some reason tonight I couldn't tolerate it. I firmly pushed him away and said it was late. I waved him off from the patio where Mum had left a hurricane lamp burning for me by the door. His car disappeared down the street and I listened to its engine recede. Then I turned to go inside.

'Zara?' A harsh whisper.

I spun round. Emerging from the shadows of the high rose hedge that bordered our garden was Harry.

'Harry?' Puzzled. Thrilled.

He walked towards me, spreading his hands, hat loosely grasped. 'I hope you don't mind.'

'How do you know where I live?' I asked as he ascended the three stairs to our patio.

'I didn't until I asked Eloise,' he said in a soft voice. No lights were on inside and neither of us wanted to wake my parents. 'I'm sorry I left without saying goodbye. Vera's parents expected her home by ten.'

'So how long have you been waiting for me to come home?'

He shrugged. 'Doesn't matter.'

I stood, gazing at him in wonder for a few moments, then remembered myself. 'I can't invite you in, but we could sit here for a while?' I gestured to the wicker settee by the door.

'I'd like that,' he said, and took my hand so we sat down together, close. Again, I experienced the heat of him, the warm magnetism of his presence.

Both of us looked straight ahead. A few moments of silence ensued, but they weren't awkward. I could hear the crickets, the soft breeze in the very tips of the trees, the faint *shush* of the hurricane lamp. Then he shifted in his seat so he could face me, and I turned too. He was smiling.

'Why did you come here?' I asked him.

'I'm going away tomorrow,' he said. 'London. I'll be gone until the middle of next year.'

The distance my heart fell surprised me. 'Oh,' I said.

'I couldn't leave without seeing you,' he said. 'Asking you if . . . well, I think I know.'

'Know . . . ?'

He tilted his head. That boyish grin. 'You feel it. How can you not? It's too hot and bright for me to be imagining it.'

I opened my mouth to play the coquette, play hard-to-get. *Feel what?* But with Harry, I wanted to be simple and true. Instead I said softly, 'Oh yes, I feel it.'

He picked up my hand, rubbed his thumbs slowly up and down the length of my fingers. Electricity flared in all my nerve endings.

'Be my girl and wait for me?' he asked.

Good sense kicked in. I wasn't a green little girl. Six months was a long time. 'Harry, we've only just met. I know nothing about you.'

He withdrew his hands. 'Well, then. I will tell you all there is to know, and then you'll be my girl.'

I laughed. 'Go on.'

He told me the facts: his mother dead, his father living in London where he worked in the theatre trade, his younger brother Cliff also pursuing a career in entertainment. But it was the small changes of expression in his face, the tone of his voice, and his shifting between expansive and terse that told me the most about him.

Summers at his grandfather's farm were covered in detail. The dislocated loneliness of arriving at boarding school at twelve were reframed in the reasonable tone of a man looking back embarrassedly on childish things. Missing his mother's funeral was skipped over in a clipped sentence. And when the facts were exhausted and he started talking about his thoughts and feelings, he invited me to share mine too. Hours passed as we agreed and disagreed violently with each other, our voices sometimes becoming too loud, which resulted in us shushing each other and giggling. We wove magic between us with our words, soul to soul, and when the sun cracked the horizon he kissed me goodnight and promised me he'd write as soon as he arrived in London.

'You won't,' I said, feeling the morning cold. 'You'll forget me.'

He stood up. 'You'll see,' he said. 'We belong to each other now. Always will.'

I shook my head, smiling. 'I don't know what to make of you.' I picked up his hat, which he had rested on the back of the settee. 'Here, don't forget this.'

'You mind it for me,' he said. 'That way you know I'll come back for it. Besides, it looks prettier on you.'

I placed it on my head and blew him a kiss.

'Prettier than a rose,' he said. 'My Zara.' Down the stairs, looking over his shoulder. 'I'll write.'

'And I'll write back.'

'You'll have to break it off with Norman.'

'And you with Vera.'

'Already done. I'm no two-timer.'

I didn't tell him that Vera had said differently.

I watched him until he disappeared around the corner then sat on the settee, eyes gritty with tiredness as the sun came up over the laurels.

Christmas passed, and New Year's, and no letter came. My heart didn't break. Sometimes before I went to sleep, I'd do the maths of the situation in my head. Six weeks for him to get to London, perhaps two weeks for a letter to get back via air mail. And when I thought of that exotic route – the aeroplane stopping in places like Persia and Burma – it seemed highly likely something so inconsequential as a letter would get lost along the way. Then again, perhaps he had sent his letters via sea mail, which would mean an even longer wait.

Or perhaps he hadn't meant it when he said we belonged to each other. Or he had meant it at the time but his regard for me dissolved as the ship left the shore. So I kept seeing Norman, though the shine was dulling when we danced and kissed.

My best friend Betty started work at a construction company office on the northern end of Russell Street, and found me a job in the secretarial pool with her, so I leaped at the chance to work in town and felt quite the grown woman on the tram every morning with my new tooled-leather handbag over my wrist. I had plenty on my mind, and by February I couldn't remember Harry's face all that clearly anymore.

It was only when I woke before dawn that a deep sense of loneliness washed over me. As though something important was missing, as though a glittering opportunity had been within my reach and I'd failed to grasp it.

———

Betty and I sat together in a pod of three desks in the secretarial pool, which was very poor planning on our head secretary Mrs Bloomsbury's part, as we spent a good deal of the day gossiping over the clatter of typewriters. I loved to draw dresses and Betty loved to sew, and that meant a lot of our conversation was about clothes, and of course which shoes and lipsticks and hairstyles went best with them. Irma, the thin-mouthed secretary who sat at the head of the pod, clearly disapproved of our obsession with appearance (though Betty and

I had commented many times that she had the *perfect* figure for a drop-waist shift). *Dresses won't get you far in life*, was her favourite thing to say to us, but I suspected she was wrong. Being a secretary didn't get you far, or at least only as far as a marriage because no woman could possibly support herself on a secretary's wage.

So we started playing a secret game with Irma. Every Friday, I would hand a dress sketch to Betty and over the weekend she would make it. Betty's aunt had passed on her old sewing machine as a Christmas gift, and she hoarded fabrics and lace, sometimes taking apart an old dress to make a new one. On Monday, she would wear the dress and tell Irma she'd bought it on the weekend at Manton's or even Georges, and Irma never once suspected they were our designs. Instead, she usually complained that Betty spent far too much money on clothes, given some people were too poor to eat.

I became bored with the game after a few months because the dresses I liked to sketch were evening gowns with beads and sequins, velvet and chiffon. Not even a glamourpuss like Betty could get away with wearing those to work, at least not without being mistaken for a lady of the night. But the game was the start of us thinking about what it might be like if we opened our own dress shop. Would we simply gossip all day and go out of business in a month? Or would working at something we both deeply loved keep our 'heads down', as the head secretary liked to tell us?

We talked about it idly, dreamily, but I was aware that Betty's boyfriend Tom Ramsay was likely to propose soon, and that would be that for dreams of single ladies running a dress shop. I had no desire for Norman to ask me to marry him. Things had changed between us too much since I met Harry. He annoyed me more readily now. He seemed clingy, perhaps because I was impatient with him. And I could hardly let myself think about Harry as a potential husband, given that he had come into my life in one bright moment then disappeared like a phantom.

Once a week, Mum caught the tram into town with a picnic from home. Ordinarily I didn't eat, keen to preserve my figure. We walked down to Fitzroy Gardens and Mum would spread out a checked cloth for us to sit on. It was nothing fancy – just sandwiches and a flask of tea, and sometimes jam tarts if she had made them – but I spent so much time ravenous that it seemed a joyous treat.

On this particular February afternoon, unusually hot, I had a mouthful of cheese sandwich when Mum reached into her handbag and pulled out two letters.

Two.

I knew straight away what they were, though I waited for Mum to pass them to me.

'These arrived this morning, both from the same person. London address. Do you know a Harry Holt?'

I tried not to be too eager snatching them from her. 'Yes, I met him a few months ago.' The envelopes were both thickly stuffed. My heart swelled. I slid them into my handbag and fastened the clip, then tried very hard to concentrate on what Mum was saying.

My mother was beautiful, and this had been a great source of pain for me since I reached my teenage years. She was tall and slender where I was five feet two and well-covered with a soft layer of flesh. She had wide-spaced eyes and a strongly defined jaw and cheekbones, whereas I had a round face and a small mouth. I watched her hands as she poured us tea into two enamel mugs: they were elegant with rounded nails. My hands, by comparison, were small and doughy with nails most often bitten down to the quick. I had seen among my friends that a moment always came when their own beauty blossomed and surpassed their mother's. I didn't believe that moment would ever come for me.

I found it difficult to engage with our usual lunchtime conversation because my mind was most determinedly elsewhere. If Mum noticed, she didn't say anything. She loved to talk – something I *did* inherit from her – and filled me in on all the latest about our neighbours (who fought savagely and audibly every Sunday after church), about how she was certain Genevieve's boyfriend Jack was going to propose any moment, about how my two younger brothers had muddied the sheets on the line this morning playing in the garden before school. I nodded and tutted and smiled exactly where I should, but my heart was off with Harry.

Where it would be all my life.

CHAPTER 2

We wrote to each other with force and fire, crushing pen tips and burning pages with our fervour. After those first two letters – one of which had been delayed somewhere along the route, the other full of reproaches that I hadn't responded – they kept coming. Great wads of paper covered in his looping, flowing handwriting. So little of what he wrote was of the day-to-day life in London with his father. Rather, he wrote to me about the ideas he had and the dreams he was nurturing, or he wrote about things that had happened in his childhood, and how boarding school and his mother's death had affected him. He gave me his future and his past but very little about his present. By contrast, I felt my letters were mundane and full of details of secretarial pool gossip and complaints about my brothers. So I embellished them with tiny drawings in the margins and corners, mostly pixies and fairies, which I had always been fascinated by. They all had cupid's bow lips (like me) and tiny waists. Harry loved them, and asked for more of my art, but I had never considered my pictures art. So sometimes I would include a few sketches in the envelope, and he was delighted by them. He was delighted by me. I had never known a boy to be so interested in me, not as a pretty girl, but as a person.

Of course, I imagined him coming home and asking me to marry him, perhaps with a ring he bought on the way in Ceylon, which I understood had the most beautiful sapphires in the world. I dreamily drew wedding dresses on my bed in the evening, concoctions of flowing satin, chiffon and rose-point lace. But his letters also made me want to imagine other things. He spoke openly of his desire for me, and I responded in kind. I had not forgotten the irresistible physical draw of him, and at night before I went to sleep, I imagined over and over being with him. Kisses at first, then touches, and over time it all grew more intimate and feverish in my head, until some nights I couldn't get to sleep for the violence of my body's reaction to such thoughts. More than once Mum found me in the kitchen drinking milk from the ice chest at midnight, and when she asked me why I couldn't sleep I would never have been able to answer her. *Lust, Mum. I am full of burning lust.* All the cold milk in the world could not extinguish it.

While my thoughts were always turned towards Harry – imagining encounters with him, making note of things to write to him, reading books he'd recommended (usually not my style) and so on – he didn't exist in a real way in the world, and that's probably why I didn't do as he'd asked and break it off with Norman for quite some time. I had a real life to live and, as a young woman, that involved parties and dances. Getting dressed up and arriving on a dapper man's arm was part of that.

Around the middle of April, as the weather was obdurately turning towards winter, Eloise had her nineteenth birthday and threw an enormous party at her godfather's house in Toorak. While Eloise's family was an ordinary middle-income one like mine, her godfather was, in her words, 'richer than Croesus', and his house boasted a small ballroom with a parquetry floor and an arched ceiling. The room was lit softly and shadows shifted across the walls. A live swing band played on the low stage, and it was so much louder than a gramophone that the only way to talk was to head out through the French doors onto the tiled patio overlooking the tulip trees.

After the warmth of the ballroom, the chill of the patio was welcome and I stood out there with Betty, as we often did, dissecting every dress we'd seen, enthusing over some and shuddering with horror over others. Betty's Tom came and fetched her to dance, and I was by myself a few moments before Norman joined me at my side.

'Have you seen the size of the birthday cake?' he asked.

'No.'

He held his hand at hip height. 'They just brought it out. I dare say they'll be cutting it shortly. Want to head back inside?' He took me gently and pulled me against him in foxtrot-ready stance. 'I'm not done dancing with you yet.'

I laughed and gently extricated myself. 'Not now.'

I was expecting him to shrug it off as he usually did, but something had changed with him and he grabbed me with force. 'Not now? Then when, Zara? We come to parties and dances, and you give me one dance. I drop you home and you give me one kiss. I can't live on one dance and one kiss a week.'

I shrank back but he held me firm. 'Norman, let go of me.'

'You know I fancied myself in love with you?'

'I'm sorry, Norman, I don't feel the same.' I said it all in a rush, guilty.

He released me so roughly that I stumbled and had to reach for the stone balustrade to steady myself. 'It's a dangerous game you're playing, Zara. Leading a man on like this.'

'I hadn't meant to lead you on,' I said, forcing a smile, lightening my tone. 'We have a good time, don't we? We're young. Nothing needs to be so serious.'

He shook his head, and the sadness in his eyes sent a sharp pulse of guilt through my chest. 'I thought we were serious. I'd started saving for a ring.'

Words stuck coldly in my throat.

'Zara, I know,' he said.

'What do you mean?'

'I overheard you and Vieve talking at last week's dance. Harry Holt's been writing you love letters, hasn't he?'

My furtive romance with Harry was so secret I hadn't even told Betty. But Mum and my sister knew because they saw the letters arrive. 'He's been writing to me, yes,' I said. 'And I write back. But I barely know him and we're only friends.'

'Ha!' Norman said with a bitter shake of his head. 'I should have known better than to introduce him to you. There's not a woman alive who can resist him if he puts his mind to it, apparently. It's not the first time he's decided he wants what's mine.'

I fell silent. I couldn't bear angry men; they frightened me.

He drilled a finger into the soft part of my shoulder. 'You're welcome to him. In fact, you are welcome to each other. A pair of two-timers. He will lead you on a merry dance and, when it's over, you'll realise what you lost. And I wouldn't have you back for all the tea in China.'

I tried to stammer out an apology but he stormed off. I was so relieved that I sagged against the balustrade and took deep breaths. He was right to break it off with me. I should have done it myself, months ago. After the first letter. No, even earlier – after dancing with Harry. There was no other man for me from that moment on, so I should have admitted it to myself and to Norman.

A few minutes later, Betty emerged. 'Oh my, Zara, what have you done to Norman? He's raced off in his car and I think he was crying.'

The very idea that I made a man cry cut me deeply. I confessed everything to Betty, who comforted me and told me I'd done nothing wrong, but Norman's words stayed with me. *A pair of two-timers.* I knew it was true of me, and more than one person had now told me it was true of Harry. What had I gotten myself into?

There were six of us in our house in Kew, so quarters were a little cramped and Genevieve and I shared the smallest bedroom at the front of the house. On a clear day, if you tilted your head at just the right angle, you could glimpse the Yarra River in the distance over the violet farms that dotted the hills. John and David, my younger brothers, had another room, and my parents had the largest, facing the garden with its tidy lawn and beds of hyacinth. In the middle of the house was Daddy's dark little den, where Vieve and I had lessons with a governess until I was twelve. After that, my parents had sent me to school, with barely any skills for coping with the intensity of teenage-girl friends or enemies. For a slightly round young woman like myself, who enjoyed nothing more than dreamily sketching pictures of fairies, school had been hard and I'd managed a sterling record of second-bottom of the class in most things. Thank god for Betty James, and thank god for Vieve who was the best sister a girl could wish for.

I was kneeling on the bed next to Vieve pinning her dark hair into finger waves, though not particularly neatly – when Vieve pinned my hair it always looked fantastic; I was rarely capable of returning the favour – when Mum knocked at the threshold and said, 'Zara, there's a telephone call for you.'

I looked up, my heart ticking hard.

'It's Harry Holt,' she said. 'Ringing from Fremantle.'

I dropped everything and shot to my feet. Vieve bounced and clapped for me, and Mum was smiling broadly. I'd known he was on his way back but hadn't expected to hear from him until he arrived in Melbourne.

Our telephone was in the storage cupboard off the hallway with no light inside. But I didn't want anyone to listen in so I shut myself in the dark and said a breathless, 'Hello?'

'Zara, I'm on Australian soil,' he said, and his voice sounded crackly and far away but it was still *his voice*. He wasn't a character in my imagination anymore but an embodied creature. He was real.

'I'm so glad to hear your voice,' I said.

'Same. I'd forgotten how sweet you sound. Like clover honey.'

My heart swelled. 'When will you be home?'

'They're telling us Saturday. So I called to ask you to go out with me on Saturday night.'

'Yes!' I squealed, and the thought that I would be with him in only five days overwhelmed me so much I had to crack the door of the cupboard open to breathe. 'What shall we do? A dance? Dinner?'

There was a pause. 'Just you and me,' he said. 'I've no money for fancy dinners and no heart for crowds. Just you and me, somewhere pretty.'

He sounded a little embarrassed, so I stopped myself from saying I'd happily pay for us to go to dinner. No man wanted to have a girl pay his way, especially not on a first date. 'That sounds divine,' I said. 'As long as we are together.'

'I can't wait to see you,' he said, and then a woman's voice came on the line, the operator saying he was out of time on his trunk call.

'Goodbye, Harry,' I said, desperate for even one more second of his voice. 'See you on Saturday.'

'See you on Saturday,' he echoed. 'Goodbye –' The call cut off abruptly, but I thought I'd heard him start to say 'darling'. Or perhaps it was just 'Zara', but I closed my eyes for a second and conjured his voice. *Goodbye, darling.*

I hung the receiver back in its cradle and emerged into the hallway. Mum was in the kitchen rolling pastry.

'So, he's real then?' she said.

'He's real,' I sighed, and a warm flutter of excitement rose through me, all the way to the roots of my hair. As though my life – my real life – was just about to begin.

———

At our first tea break the next day, I prattled on to Betty about Harry's return, and she mm-ed in all the right places as a good friend would. We were walking with purpose down Swanston Street because Betty had told me she wanted to show me something. The spires of the cathedral were nearly finished, though the scaffolding still surrounded them, making them look as though they'd been drawn then crossed out vigorously by a disappointed artist. I was mid-sentence, talking about what I was going to wear for my date with Harry, when Betty stopped.

'Here,' she said.

We stood outside an empty shop with soaped windows, directly across from the cathedral.

'What is it?' I asked.

'Our dress shop,' she said firmly. 'I saw this on my walk up from the station and I thought, Zara and I could rent that. We could make dresses and sell them.' She grinned. '*Expensive* dresses.'

I stared at the shop windows, and in my mind's eye the soap was gone and I could see mannequins draped in gorgeous dresses. Excitement shivered through me, and every inch of me wanted to shout, 'Yes!' but the word that came out of my mouth was, 'How?'

'Daddy says he'll loan me two hundred pounds, and if your father says the same, we'll have enough for the first few months' rent, the fabric, the furniture . . .' She trailed off as she saw I was shaking my head. 'No?' she asked, her voice suddenly forlorn.

'Even if my father had two hundred pounds, I couldn't ask him for it,' I said gently.

'You couldn't?'

I also wanted to say that I didn't think this a good location for a dress shop – not the kind we would want to run anyway. Bracketed by an insurance office and a leather warehouse, across the road from a cathedral . . . when would stylish women happen upon us? And the more I thought of it, the constant rattle of cars and trams would ruin any peaceful ambience we wanted to create. No, this was not a good place for our dress shop.

I slid my arm around Betty's waist. 'I'm sorry,' I said. 'But I will save every penny I can from now on if you're serious about a shop.'

'I am,' she said. 'I don't want to be a secretary until I marry. I want to have *done* something, Zara. And your designs are so good, it's criminal to waste them.'

I squeezed her. 'Not to mention your needlework. And I bet you'd be good at keeping the ledger. Lord knows I wouldn't be – I can barely add up.'

Betty giggled. 'Yes, but you would know how to decorate the store, and what to call it.'

'Oh yes, what would we call it?'

'Zara and Betty's?'

'Two Typists?'

'Lovely Dresses?'

'Zara and Betty the Two Typists' Lovely Dresses?'

We made up longer and longer and more improbable names until we fell on each other laughing, and our laughter helped distract me from the ache of ambition that had arisen in me; I had imagined it now and it wouldn't go away. We laughed all the way back to our desks in the secretarial pool, which is where girls like me, I feared, were destined to stay.

———

The week crawled and I drove my family mad. My brothers got tired of hammering on the bathroom door in the afternoons after I'd locked myself in for too long fussing over my eyebrows (ever since Betty had mentioned in passing that I reminded her of Loretta Young in *Laugh, Clown, Laugh*, I had become fixated on having precisely her eyebrows), or just gazing disconsolately at my face and imagining Harry looking at me and finding me wanting. I couldn't concentrate on anything, was off in a dream when Mum asked me to pass the salt at dinner, and went to bed early every evening so

I could lie there for hours before sleep, creating elaborate fantasies about Harry and me.

Not all of these fantasies were thrilling though. Sometimes my mind went down a dark path where all I could imagine was him rejecting me, then taking up again with Vera or some other beauty and marrying her, and me somehow being invited to the wedding and having to sit in the back pew breaking my heart . . . My imagination always had a way of getting out of control like that.

My greatest fear that day though was that he wouldn't show up at all. I had no idea how to find out if his ship had arrived because I hadn't done anything nearly so practical as asking for the name of the vessel. He hadn't specified a time for our date, so I was ready stupidly early, waiting on the front veranda in my heels and red wool dress. Fashion's silhouettes were slowly becoming more forgiving for those of us with curves, and this dress had a bias cut and a waist where my actual waist lay. I had changed my mind a million times about what to wear. My heart wanted to wear an evening gown, but Harry had been explicit that we weren't going anywhere fancy. So instead I had embellished this day dress with sequins spilling down one arm. I sparkled with a rhinestone hairclip and Vieve's favourite glittery drop earrings, which she had grudgingly let me borrow.

And so I waited. Knees together, hands in lap, eyes fixed on the road. Wished I had pressed Harry for more details. Did he own a car? He mustn't, or else he wouldn't have had Norman pick him up the night we met. Did he have to walk all the way from his college? Was he even off the ship yet?

In my fast-beating heart, it felt as though hour upon hour passed and the sky grew dark. I waited, like 'patience on a monument' as Shakespeare wrote, hoping and hoping and hoping that he would come, that he would see me and not think it a terrible mistake. My stillness belied a terrible storm of feeling under my ribs.

In fact, Mum pointed out later that it was only forty-five minutes before she heard his footsteps advancing up the path.

The first sight of him, walking purposefully up the street with a calico bag over his elbow, had me leaping to my feet. He didn't seem real, as though I were seeing a movie star in the flesh. He took off his hat and hurried his steps, and a few moments later I was in his arms.

'There you are,' he murmured into my hair, and I fell against him and my heart was perfectly happy.

The sound of the door opening behind us reminded me that I was at my family home, so I stepped back demurely and turned to see Mum and my nine-year-old brother David looking out curiously.

Harry stepped forward extending his hand. 'Mrs Dickins? I'm Harry,' he said.

I saw my mother fighting a smile and knew that his charm had worked on her. She allowed him to take her hand and gave him a decorous nod. 'Harry, we have heard a lot about you.'

'Likewise,' he said. 'Your accent is beautiful. What part of Scotland are you from?'

I swear she blushed. 'Ah well. Thank you. I was born in a wee village just outside Aberdeen. Come along inside. Mr Dickins is very keen to meet you.'

'Of course,' Harry said smoothly.

Mum took his coat and gestured him ahead. I couldn't take my eyes off him and nearly tripped over the threshold. David made a gooey-eyed expression at me behind Harry's back and I kicked him in the shins, rather harder than I should have. His freckled face screwed up in anger.

Daddy was waiting in the sitting room in the big green chair none of the rest of us was allowed to sit in (but where Domino our cat was always welcome). He closed his book and put it aside, climbing to his feet to pump Harry's hand in a firm shake. Then Harry and I sat on the settee. Harry set down his drawstring bag and it made a slight clink. Mum insisted on making tea, and David disappeared after shooting me an unsettling smirk.

My father was very protective of us girls, but even his aloof exterior melted quickly with Harry, who had spotted immediately that Daddy was reading *The Bridge of San Luis Rey*, and launched into an enthusiastic discussion about it and about American literature more generally. They were deep in conversation when Mum came back with the tea, while I sat dumbly. My taste in literature ran to scandalous stories about girls falling in love with rakish cousins and so on.

Over tea, Daddy asked Harry about his studies and other things designed to judge his value and prospects. I suppose he and Mum must have realised I was head over heels for Harry, and Daddy read the news every day about the stock market situation in America, which he was sure would throw the whole world into ruin if it fell over. Harry was due to finish his studies at the end of the following year now he'd had his term in London.

Daddy made impressed noises about Harry being on a full scholarship at Queens College, that he represented the university in football *and* cricket *and* debating. But for my father, there was an important question that needed answering.

'And do you work at all, lad?' he asked. For my father, working was a sign you were a worthwhile human being.

'Mondays and Wednesdays,' Harry said. 'Delivering briefs around the city.'

Daddy nodded, satisfied.

'It's unpaid,' Harry admitted. 'But my father is in London, and anyway I know nobody in the legal profession so I have to build my networks somehow.'

'Working for nothing?' Daddy said, and I could tell he didn't know if this was very impressive or the complete opposite. Harry had already charmed him though, so he came down on the side of impressed and said, 'Enterprising!'

'Harry wants to go into politics,' I said, knowing Daddy would like that.

'You do, eh? You'd do a finer job than a lot of the fellows suck-ling at the public teat,' Daddy said.

'Sydney, enough with crudity,' Mum said to him. 'Who's after more tea?'

David appeared then, hands suspiciously tucked behind his back, very still and gazing at Harry.

'Hello, boy,' Harry said with a friendly grin. Lord, how I loved that smile. 'Are you all right?'

'Getting a good look at you so I can tell Vieve what you look like,' David replied. 'She's dead curious, but is out with Jack.'

Harry tilted his chin up, turned his head this way and that. 'How's that? Seen enough?'

'Question is, have you?' David asked, and the imp then pulled out one of my sketchbooks from behind his back.

I saw immediately what he was going to show Harry. He had the book bent back to a page where I'd drawn a wedding dress on a model that looked suspiciously like me.

'Did you know my sister was such a fine artist?' David said, but his eyes were on me, flinty about that kick in the shins I'd given him earlier.

'Harry doesn't need to see my silly drawings,' I said, standing and reaching to snatch the book from him.

But it was too late. Harry had taken the sketchbook and was leafing through. There were rather a lot of wedding dresses, and I was in all of them. 'I did know,' Harry said, and smiled up at David. 'She illustrated all her letters to me. She's very talented, though I don't know much about dresses.' He closed the sketchbook and handed it back to David with a twinkling smile. 'But thank you for showing me.'

'We should let you two get away,' Mum said. 'Off to a party?'

'Of sorts,' Harry said, picking up his mysterious bag again. He helped me to my feet and offered me his free elbow, which I took happily. With a round of goodbyes and a promise to be home by ten, we left.

It was early evening, clear but cold. I did hope we would be indoors somewhere soon as my nose was getting runny. I expected he had in mind a small coffee house nearby (or at least that's what my fantasy of the evening had involved), but we walked in the opposite direction and down the hill. His little calico bag clinked, so I asked, 'What's in the bag?'

He smiled, and shook it a little. 'Do you like it? I made it myself. Not as clever as you with the needle and thread, but a man needs a library bag.'

'It doesn't sound like there are books in there.'

'Perhaps there aren't.' He hooked his elbow a little closer to his side so I was pulled against him. 'Do you like me when I'm mysterious?'

'I like you all the time, Harry,' I said, and it came out rather more breathless and yearning than I'd expected. 'Where are we going?'

'You'll see. It's such a beautiful night. Look at the stars, Zara.'

I looked up. The stars formed pale clouds. My breath fogged in the air. I heard a distant car fading to quiet. 'It really is a beautiful night,' I said, 'though I expect I'm ruining it by speaking.'

'Your voice is part of the starlight,' he said, perhaps more breathless and yearning than he'd expected.

We took a turn down the unsealed road to the violet farm. 'Harry?' I asked.

He stopped and set down his library bag, loosened the drawstring and pulled out a hurricane lamp and a box of safety matches. Crouching near the ground, he lit the lamp and closed the bag again, which he handed to me.

'Have you ever had a starlit picnic in a violet field?' he asked.

'Never,' I said. 'I didn't even imagine there was such a thing.'

Holding the lamp in front of him, he grasped my hand and pulled me gently towards the entrance to the farm. 'Come along then.'

'I don't think they'll let us in,' I said. 'We usually have to pay threepence to enter and they are only open on Sundays.'

'Trust me,' he said.

We moved along the road, our shadows long beside us. The fence was high, made of wood and wire. When we got to the gate we found it was, indeed, locked. A *No Trespassing* sign hung off the post for good measure.

Harry turned to me with a smile that looked a little sinister, lit as it was from underneath by the hurricane lamp. 'Trust me,' he said again.

'The more you say that, the less I trust you.' I laughed.

The gate was about six feet high, made of horizontal wooden planks with an inch between them. He handed me the lamp and climbed up, then sat on the top reaching down.

'Harry, I'm not climbing up there.'

'Hand me the lamp.'

I stretched up to give it to him.

'Come on,' he said. 'It's easy. Plenty of hand and foot holds.'

I glanced around, sure I was going to get in some kind of trouble. 'I'm wearing a skirt,' I said. 'How do you expect me . . . ?' I trailed off, because he was gorgeous up there, grinning boyishly down at me.

'Oh, all right,' I said, and made sure his library bag was hooked firmly in my elbow crook before placing one toe carefully in a gap and reaching up. Hand over hand, and then Harry had my fingers in his and was pulling me up. There was no delicate way to throw my leg over, but I did my best not to reveal anything more than the tops of my stockings.

'Wait here,' Harry said, handing me the lamp again. He climbed down, landed and reached for the lamp, which he placed on the ground before helping me down.

His hands on my waist were very warm.

'You see? We're fine.'

'We have to get back over later – without getting caught.'

'Nobody will catch us.' He held the lamp aloft. 'This way.'

We made our way down between the dark rows of violets, careful not to trample them.

'I love the smell of violets,' I said. 'They smell pale blue and rainy for a moment, and then the smell disappears.'

'As though hiding their scent, yes,' Harry said, taking my hand.

I wore gloves, he didn't, and I wondered that he wasn't turning as blue as the violets. I said as much, and he told me he rarely felt the cold, and then waxed forth for a while about his love for the outdoors, for wild spaces, for nature untamed . . . but then we arrived at a long wooden bench. I recognised it as a place where elderly people might sit while visiting the violet farm if they found the path back up the hill too taxing. Harry shrugged out of his coat and laid it carefully over the bench, inviting me to sit. The hurricane lamp sat at our feet and he gently took the library bag from me and opened the drawstring.

'For my beautiful Zara,' he said, and took out a Stanley bottle, two enamel cups and a cake tin, which he prised the lid off. 'Warm cocoa and fruit scones. Baked fresh this afternoon.'

'You made this?'

'Who else?' He poured a cup of cocoa and handed it to me. 'Sorry there's no jam for the scones, but there are dates in them. They should be sweet enough.'

I took a bite. 'This is delicious.' I had never met a man who cooked. Daddy would rather die than bake scones. 'I like baking, but I can never get the consistency of scones right.'

'You're good at other things. Designing wedding dresses for example.' He was grinning at me good-naturedly in the lamplight.

'Oh, my wretched brother. I hope you don't think . . .' I didn't know how to end that sentence, but he caught my meaning nonetheless.

'I thought nothing, Zara, just how clever you are. But I feel, while we are on the topic, that I should say something.'

My heart picked up a little, and probably some foolish, very young part of me actually thought he was about to go down on one knee.

Instead, he turned his eyes away from me and towards the dark river in the distance. 'I can't marry, not for a long time. I need to be established if I want to support a wife, possibly a family. Any girl who loved me . . .' He paused here, shot me a glance then quickly fixed his gaze in the distance again. 'Any girl who loved me would have to wait.'

I couldn't tell if it had grown colder or if I was simply disappointed. Either way, I pulled my coat around me and babbled something about what a sensible fellow he was, but in my mind I was doing the sums: eighteen months until he'd finished his studies, then a junior role somewhere . . . What did he mean by 'established'? Would it be years?

And what did that mean for me? How many years in the secretarial pool? I felt small under the sky. A little lost, a little desolate, though the bright nonsense coming out of my mouth hid it well, as I quickly pivoted the topic away from the future and into today. How long did it take him to bake the scones? Did he still feel as though he was on the ocean? Was it strange to be back in his room at the college? He answered happily, and we ate and we drank our cocoa, and it never grew warm enough for me to take off my coat and show off my sequinned sleeve, but I didn't mind so much. It was clear he was delighted by me, sequins or no.

'And so,' he said at last, when the conversation trickled away and the food was finished. 'Now I have to ask you something important.'

'Go on,' I said, intrigued.

'May I kiss you?'

I bit my lip so I wouldn't smile my face in half. 'Yes, please!'

He grasped my chin in his right hand and touched my hair with his left, and watched me for a moment.

'Are you going to kiss me?'

'I'm savouring it,' he replied.

'Oh. Very well. Carry on.'

He laughed and swooped in, his lips still turned up as they touched mine. I responded, and a feeling of such *rightness* came over me, like a last piece falling into place in a challenging puzzle. He slid his tongue into my mouth, and a silvery heat flushed up through me. I had been kissed before. Kissed badly, kissed well, kissed to bruises by Norman. Nobody had ever kissed me like Harry did, as though we had been designed by God to fit together perfectly at the lips.

We kissed for what seemed like an age, stopping occasionally to talk and laugh, then kissing some more. I could have gone on like that forever, but Harry became mindful of the time and soon enough we were packing up and climbing back over the gate again. This time I tore my stocking but I was too happy to care.

Outside my door, he gave me one last, chaste kiss on the cheek. 'I'll ring you up tomorrow evening.'

'I miss you already.'

He smiled at me. 'You know I love you, don't you, Zara?'

'I didn't know that.'

'Well, now you do.' He turned to leave and I seized his wrist, and the bottle and cups in the library bag rattled.

'I love you too,' I said. 'Madly. So madly.'

'It's the same for me,' he said. 'If love isn't mad, it's not love.'

It wasn't the last time he would say those words to me.

———

I'd like to say things proceeded blissfully for a while. Perhaps they were blissful, or perhaps hindsight colours them that way. Nonetheless, we settled into a pattern. He rang me every night – he on the telephone outside Queens College, me in the hallway cupboard in the half dark – and we spoke until one of us was ushered off by other students who wanted to use the telephone, or my mother or father expressing impatience that they'd barely seen my face all day. Then we'd spend the weekends together from just after breakfast on

Saturday right through to Sunday lunch, when Harry would suddenly grow anxious about an exam he hadn't studied for or a paper he hadn't started. Every Saturday night I'd return home at ten o'clock as promised, but Harry and I would sit on the front veranda for hours – often until dawn – talking and talking, and kissing when we were sure my parents had gone to sleep. By the end of the first month there was nothing I didn't know about Harry. I was deep in mad, mad love.

Winter passed. I probably ignored my friends, except for Betty who must have grown sick of me prattling about Harry all the time at work. Sometimes, if Harry was nearby in the city delivering his briefs around lunchtime, he might pop in and take me to the park, where we would sit and neither of us eat. Me because I was determined to stay thin; he because meals were free at his college so he couldn't countenance paying for them throughout the day. No matter. We were too in love to care about food.

It was one Monday in September, a crisp but clear Monday after a week or more of rain, that he arrived at the office but not in his usual good cheer. He barely smiled as he pushed open the door, and Mrs Bloomsbury looked at the clock pointedly. It was eleven. Nowhere near lunchtime. I smiled up at him, but got barely more than a twitch of the corner of his lip in return.

'Hello, Harry!' Betty called, barely glancing up from her typewriter.

I stood and reached for my handbag. 'Would you mind if I took an early lunch today?' I asked Mrs Bloomsbury. I became aware that Harry had not yet said a word, and a low sort of fear stirred in my guts.

'Are the letters for Mr Garrett finished?'

'No, but I will finish them by one. You'll see.' I could type like the wind if I had to.

'Very well,' she said.

Harry had already headed out the door and I hurried after him, the door swinging shut behind me with a firm thud.

'You're early today,' I said, faking a cheeriness I didn't feel.

'Needed to talk to you,' he said gruffly, still three paces ahead of me, descending the stairs at a clip.

'About what?'

'Here's not the place.'

A hundred thoughts tumbled through my imagination as I followed him: he had to go away again, he had an incurable disease, he had failed his studies and we would never marry . . . Whatever it was, this news was so very bad he couldn't even look at me. My stomach felt like water as he led me up to Carlton Gardens, where finally, under the shade of a turkey oak, he stopped and turned towards me.

And then I saw it. He wasn't here to bear bad news. He was angry. He was *furious*. With me.

'Harry,' I said, startled. 'Whatever is it?'

'Norman told me everything.'

I scrambled to think what Norman would have to say to him. Norman hadn't even crossed my mind since that night I'd made him cry (allegedly). But then I remembered I had taken quite a long time to break it off with him.

'I broke it off with Norman ages ago,' I said.

'You were writing me love letters but still seeing him.'

The deep, deep shame I felt then. It was true. I had two-timed him. 'I'm so sorry,' I said breathlessly. 'I didn't know where we were going, what would happen. You were so far away . . .'

He made a fist and pushed it into his solar plexus. 'You are killing me, Zara.'

'I broke it off as soon as I –'

'You broke it off when he found out you were writing me love letters. If he hadn't found out, perhaps you would still be seeing him now.'

'No, Harry. No.'

He ground his fist further under his rib cage. 'It's like . . . burning.'

'I'm sorry. I'm sorry, my love.' I tried to push myself against him but he stood back, raising his hands to avoid touching me.

'I want you to feel this pain,' he said. 'So I will tell you that while I was in London I was seeing a beautiful woman. More beautiful than the dawn. Her name was Evie. There. Now you know how it feels.'

Oh, I knew how it felt all right. Shame upon shame. I would never be more beautiful than the dawn. I was little and dumpy, and I felt it all the way to my ugly marrow. I could not speak.

'I thought you were my girl,' he said. 'But you're just *a* girl. Goodbye.'

He brushed past me roughly and I had to steady myself against the tree. I was sure I was going to be sick, but I hadn't eaten yet that day and so nothing came out.

Just a girl. Just a stupid, ugly, shameful girl. He had seen me at last. I was finished.

I ran home. I locked myself in my room and wouldn't come out, wouldn't let Vieve in until she swore not to ask me what was wrong. Spent the next day in bed, but by Wednesday had hatched a plan.

On my lunchbreak, I would simply hang around on the route he always took between law offices. And he would see me and forgive me.

So there I was, staring in the window of a hat shop, when I saw him appear in the reflection behind me.

'Zara?' His voice had its usual, tender tone.

I turned and he gathered me in his arms, and he pressed me so hard against him that I thought he might suffocate me. We sobbed our regret and shame to each other, we vowed undying love – mad love – and after that everything was back to normal.

Until the next time we fought.

And so on. For forty years.

CHAPTER 3

To say our first year together had its ups and downs is more than an understatement. The highs were like the Matterhorn, piercing the clouds where the air was so thin it made us breathless. The lows were dank pits impossible to climb out of. The worst of it was that Harry was so easily able to shut off his feelings. He often told me that after our worst quarrels he'd go home and tidy his desk and get on with some study, while I would cry on my bed with a storm in my heart, replaying our argument in my mind and parsing every word and gesture.

But I never stopped loving him. If anything, the intensity of the reunions deepened how we felt about each other. We savoured that powerful smashing together, the hot promises that this was the last time we'd fight. It imbued our kisses and caresses with a kind of desperate passion. It was exhausting, but addictive.

The rest of the world had receded for me. I knew that Daddy's worst predictions had come true and the stock market had crashed, and everywhere there were people without jobs or money. I never saw the soup kitchens with my own eyes, but I heard terrible tales of families who had to eat grass or kill rabbits they found in parks because they were so hungry. Daddy's business struggled on, thankfully, though Mum had started to ration everything just in case – not just meat and coffee, but soap and toothpaste. I took to making my own soap out of scraps and hiding it in my drawer so the boys couldn't use it. I contributed what I could from my secretary pay cheque, and forwent most indulgences.

We were lucky that Daddy's uncle, who lived in India, passed away and left us a small amount of money. Genevieve leapt on the opportunity, and on the same day Harry finished his last exams, my sister came home to announce she was getting married. With Christmas approaching and all of us feeling such goodwill, Daddy agreed to an engagement party.

———

Genevieve came to me to design a dress for the party. Given the financial situation and Daddy spending so much on the wedding, she didn't want to ask for anything else, but she longed to have a sapphire-blue frock in the absence of the sapphire engagement ring she had coveted; her fiancé Jack had scraped together enough for a pearl, but a lot of women were making do with amethysts and citrines.

We sat on my bed together – like we used to when we were little, shoulder to shoulder with our feet tucked under the covers against the evening chill – while I sketched rough silhouettes for her. I was a little obsessed with bustle-like bows falling at the back of gowns, below cinched waists. I drew deep V-neck and V-back lines, pointed seams and twisted shoulder straps. But Vieve was not an adventurous wearer of fashion, and insisted on flounced sleeves, curved seams and a skirt that fell in a soft bell shape. When we were happy with the design, I stood her up to measure her.

'Zara?' she asked warily, arms spread while I ran the tape measure from her shoulder to her wrist. 'Can I ask you something?'

'What is it?'

'Do you think you could ask Betty to sew it? I don't mean to sound ungrateful but . . .'

I had to laugh. 'I can't say I blame you. I am somewhere between dreaming and rushing the whole time I sew,' I said. 'Let me ask her for you.'

'You used to talk about opening a dress shop together,' Vieve said. 'It's such a good idea. Look how happy you are when you do this.'

'It's money,' I said. 'We're not rich. I can't ask Daddy for anything, and I can't start a business without a shop, furniture, fabrics . . . Also, is anyone buying dresses at the moment? The whole world seems so poor.'

'Not everyone is poor. Some people stayed rich, and they need dresses.'

I moved to measure her waist.

'I have an idea,' Vieve said, 'but I don't want you to take it the wrong way.'

'That sounds ominous,' I said, reading my sister's waist measurement and finding it caused me actual physical pain. She was much tinier than me.

'Daddy's spending up big on my wedding. Tell him you want the same amount of money for your business.'

I looked up at Vieve. 'And if I want to get married?'

She met my gaze quite coolly. 'Is he going to marry you?'

'One day.'

'When he's "established",' she said.

'He's finished his studies now.'

Vieve didn't say another word because she didn't have to. I had told her everything. Harry and I happily imagined buying a house, having a baby and so on, but if I ever tried to pin him down he would say, 'I'll probably never make much money. Money isn't important to me.' I knew, as did Vieve, that it was his way of saying he had no plans to marry me.

Vieve touched my cheek gently. 'Now you look sad. I didn't mean to make you sad. I want you to be as happy as I am.' She spread her arms. 'I'm getting married!'

I leaned in for a hug. 'I *am* happy, Vieve. Don't you worry about me.'

———

Betty loved my design for Genevieve's gown and agreed to sew it for her, and it was the most beautiful gown that Betty and I had ever made. Betty even sewed a satin tag, embroidered with our initials wrapped around each other: *ZB*. Zara and Betty.

It was strange to see our family home turned into a venue for an engagement party. All the furniture in the lounge and kitchen had been moved to the edges of the rooms, and we had cleaned it until it gleamed like a pin. Outside on the veranda, clusters of lamps lit the cool dark evening. A gramophone played inside and the younger people were dancing, while the older ones gathered in the kitchen and drank coffee with whisky my father had bought for the occasion.

Harry was by my side of course, pleased with himself because that week he had rented his own place – a room so tiny there wasn't enough space for him to kneel and pray next to his bed. But the boarding house was clean and not too far from me, and we had an outing planned for the weekend to find furniture for his brand-new office in the city, where he hoped to start taking his own briefs.

After Daddy made his speech, and Jack made his, the music grew quieter and some of the older guests started leaving. A woman in her fifties approached me and took my hand.

'You're Zara?' she asked. 'Genevieve's sister?'

'Yes.'

'I'm Jack's Aunt Maddie. So I suppose I'll be your sister's aunt-in-law . . .' She shook her head, laughing. 'She can call me Aunt Maddie and so can you.'

'That's very kind,' I said, puzzled, but drawn to her soft eyes nonetheless.

'I hear you made the gown Genevieve is wearing?'

'Ah, yes. I designed it and my friend Betty is the gifted seamstress.'

'It is a splendid gown. Just splendid. I worked for many years at Bon Marche in Sydney, buying fashion for them. Those years are well behind me, but I know a gifted designer when I see one. And I'm looking at one right now.'

I was almost smiling too broadly to speak. 'Thank you!' I said.

'Goodnight, Zara.' With that, she disappeared off to find her coat.

Harry gave me a proud squeeze. 'There you are then.'

I looked up at him. 'Wouldn't it be mad if you and I went into business at the same time? You in law. Me in fashion.'

'It wouldn't be mad at all. Here we are – young, hungry, terribly good at what we do.' He gave a self-deprecating grin. 'Well, you are at least. What I am good at is yet to be seen.'

I told Mum about my encounter with Aunt Maddie many hours later as we were cleaning up after the last guest. I would have left the clean-up for the morning, but Mum insisted she couldn't go to bed while there was still such a mess about. The boys had already gone to bed, of course, and I couldn't ask Genevieve to mop floors after her own engagement party, so it fell to Mum and me.

'What do you think, Mum?' I asked. 'I'm tired of being a secretary. Do you think I could be a fashion designer?'

Mum flinched a little, almost as if she was embarrassed that I had said it out loud. 'I don't know if people like us become fashion designers, sweet pea. Seems as though it's not a real job.'

'Somebody has to make dresses,' I bit back, immediately sorry for the heat in my voice.

She stopped and leaned on her broom. 'I suppose you're right, but I have never known a person who makes dresses. Not for a living. That's not to say you're not good at what you do, but you're also a very good secretary.'

'Mum, I'm a *terrible* secretary. I'm off with the fairies, always late, my shorthand is abominable.'

'And yet, you must be good at it, because you've been working there for so long now and they haven't marched you out.' She shrugged. 'I don't know what to say, Zara. But I'd hate for you to invest too much of yourself in a pipedream. Harry will want to marry you eventually, and then you'll want to give up work anyway. Take the path of least resistance. Stay in the secretarial pool.'

I clenched my jaw and got on with washing cups in the sink.

'I must say, love, don't spend too much longer with Harry if he won't marry you. Genevieve and Jack held out long enough . . . If a man loves you, he'll make you his wife.'

'He loves me,' I said.

'Then there's nothing to worry about. If you are right.'

———

The desire to make my own way grew every day. When we moved furniture into Harry's new office – I did my best to polish the battered bureau and shampoo the faded rugs for him – and he sat behind his desk with his first brief, I felt a stab of ferocious jealousy. Harry started working long hours and so I filled my time with drawings of dresses; it became like an obsession. I burned through sketchbooks, and started using the backs of old letters or documents destined for the dustbin at work. My job became unbearable, a torture.

Harry was surviving on twenty-five shillings a week, and most of our dates were at a tiny, noisy Italian place on Bourke Street where a half-crown bought us two three-course meals. When Harry got his first big cheque, he wanted to splash out and take me to the Wattle for high tea.

We arrived just after two, and waited in the palm-filled foyer before being ushered through to our table. I wore a dark grey Canton-silk dress with a bow tied loosely at the collar. I had originally designed it for Betty, but she took one look at the design and said it would suit me best, on account of the sharp waistline. Harry pulled out the chair for me and I sat. I found myself facing a round mirror hung on the pale blue wall. Fresh gerberas – yellow and red – filled a vase on the crisp linen tablecloth. A waitress in a blue and white smock dress approached and handed Harry a menu. While he read it, my eyes went to the mirror, which reflected the tall windows behind me. I watched a woman in a red hat pass on the street. It caught my eye so I turned to look.

That's when I saw the shop, and a *feeling* came over me. I can explain it no better than that.

The shop was empty, its windows soaped. A *FOR RENT* sign rested on the sill. Unlike the place Betty had shown me, this was on Little Collins Street, where stylish ladies were in abundance, on their way to and from shops and tearooms.

'What is it, Zara?' Harry asked.

I turned back, and saw him peering at me curiously over the top of the menu. 'Order me what you're having,' I said. 'I'll be back in a moment.'

I pushed back my chair and slipped past the waitress, my heart beating hard. The feeling of rightness, of destiny, was bright and hot in my heart. I crossed the street and put my hands against the glass. Through a gap in the soaping, I could see the interior of the shop. Wooden floorboards. Pretty glass light fittings. A long wooden counter. But nothing else. Empty enough for me to fill with my imagination.

Harry, of course, had not waited for me inside. He was at my elbow, and his hand came to rest on the small of my back. 'Care to explain?' he said, a smile in his voice.

'I have a feeling about this place,' I said, although I knew he was not fond of my 'feelings' about things. He was far too rational for that.

He seemed about to say something, perhaps something cynical or even disparaging, but he held his tongue. He blinked a few times, those long lashes dark. Perhaps half a minute passed, and then he said, 'Well, then. You'd better do something about that feeling, Zara. Because you are the cleverest girl I've ever met.'

———

That evening, I waited until after tea when Daddy was in his favourite armchair with a book and his pipe, soft music playing on the wireless, a cloud of tobacco aroma around him – Havelock Aromatic; I had bought it for him at the shop dozens of time. I could hear the boys being rowdy in their bedroom, and willed them to be quiet so my father wouldn't grow exasperated and refuse to listen to me.

'Daddy?' I said, coming to kneel next to him, my hands on the arm of his chair.

He laid his book flat on his lap and patted my left hand. 'What is it? You've a look on your face I've not seen before.'

I smiled up at him. 'What kind of look?'

'Hmmm . . . I would say *hungry*, but I'm fairly sure you're hungry all the time given the tiny amounts you eat.' He gazed at me, tilting his head to one side. 'Hungry in the heart, maybe? Have you come to ask if I'll pay for a wedding?'

I shook my head quickly. 'No. No, that's definitely not it. Though it does involve money.'

He took a puff of his pipe. 'Go on, then.'

'You know that I love to design dresses. And Betty loves to make them. We have talked a few times about opening a dress shop.'

'I see.'

'At Vieve's engagement, Jack's aunt told me I should go into fashion. She used to be a buyer for Bon Marche.'

'I don't know what that is.'

'A very, very famous dress shop, Daddy, where rich ladies spend lots of money.'

He nodded. One of the boys – it sounded like John – had started shouting at the top of his lungs, some kind of ape noise. Daddy's eyes flicked away from my face and I realised I had to be quick.

'I'd like you to give me the money you would have used for an engagement party or a wedding. I'd like to start my own business. I need two hundred pounds.'

'I see. And what if you then decide to get engaged or married?'

'It seems I am in little danger of either of those things happening.'

His eyes grew soft. He stroked my hand. 'You're a good girl, Zara. You deserve a happy marriage.'

'Perhaps one day I'll have one, but for now I want my own fashion business. I have found a shop. Luckily for you, Harry stopped me from foolishly signing a lease for it on the spot.' He'd sat with me over our high tea with his notebook and pencil, and worked out the cost of setting up. Diligent and thorough. Not once had he tried to dissuade me, instead earnestly ensuring I would be sensible.

'Harry's a good fellow,' Daddy said, leaning back in his chair, eyes going heavenward as though looking for inspiration. 'It's a pity he can't do the right thing and make you his wife.'

'He will one day. When he's on his feet. But until then, I have such big ideas, Daddy. I burst with them.'

Another puff on his pipe. The crackle of tobacco burning. 'All right then, Zara. You may have your two hundred pounds and one day, *when* you marry, you'll have no right to ask for more.'

'I wouldn't,' I said, with a little swirl of regret. I had been imagining my wedding abstractly all my life, concretely for the last year. But I told myself that when I was a successful fashion designer, I could pay for my own wedding if I chose to have one, and that thought cheered me, and made me feel quite the independent young woman. I stood and kissed Daddy on his bald spot. 'Thank you.'

'I hope neither of us regrets this,' he said, almost in jest, but I heard the warning.

'I hope so too!' I said merrily, and hurried out before he could change his mind.

I went directly to the telephone cupboard to ring up Betty. Her mother answered, and I waited like what seemed ten minutes for Betty to get to the telephone.

'Sorry,' was her first word. 'I was in the bath and didn't hear Mum calling me.'

'I found our shop,' I said.

'What do you mean?'

'I found our shop, and I have the money, and I have such a feeling about this, Betty. But I can't do it without you. Do you still want to go into business with me?' I needed Betty. I would drop stitches and add up bills all wrong.

Betty was already laughing. 'You mad hen!' she said. 'I thought I'd never get you to commit.'

'So that's a yes?'

'Of course it is. No more typing pool? No more Irma and Mrs Bloomsbury? How soon can we start?'

'Tomorrow,' I said. 'I'll get Harry to take me down to the letting office first thing.'

Betty started singing, some silly made-up song about Zara and Betty going into business making dresses, and I couldn't remember a time I felt more excited and happy. Our dream of a fashion business was going to come true.

CHAPTER 4

Betty and I were too young to know that running a business would be difficult. We picked up the keys to the empty shop one Monday morning on the way to work, and over the next week, powered by the mad enthusiasm only a pair of twenty-year-old girls could muster, we turned it into a dress salon. *Our* dress salon.

Mind you, all of this had to be done in the evenings after work in the typing pool. We gave our notice, but Mrs Bloomsbury insisted we finish up the week as there was so much work to do, and hiring two new secretaries would take time. The days dragged by, but the evenings were full of industry and bright feelings of joy.

First, we bought furniture from a second-hand shop in Fitzroy. For one pound and twelve shillings, we acquired a cedar desk, a round table, and a twenty-year-old couch with pears and hummingbirds carved into the walnut and a threadbare patch in the upholstery that would have to be covered with an artfully placed cushion. Mum and Dad gave me a wardrobe from their bedroom – a tall foreboding-looking thing that I'd been afraid of as a child – and Betty's parents gave her a large rectangular rug in dark blue and gold. We had to pay another shilling to have all of this collected and delivered to the shop, and the load arrived on the Wednesday night as Betty was sweeping the floor and I was cleaning the soap off the window.

The door swung open and a surprisingly thin man stood there, his face half in light from the shop and half in shadow. 'Misses Dickins and James?'

'That's us,' Betty said, propping up her broom.

'I have your furniture. Is there nobody here who can help me get it down from the truck?'

'We paid a shilling,' I said. 'Could you not have hired somebody to help?'

He shrugged. 'I suppose I'll just take it all back where I got it from then.'

I leapt straight to anger, but Betty was cool as always.

'If we'd have known, we could have asked Harry and Tom to come and help,' I whispered harshly to her.

'Never mind. He's here now, and I am dead keen to set it up.' She turned back to the delivery man. 'We will help,' she said.

'A pair of girls?' he replied, clearly amused.

This was fuel on my fire. 'Yes, a pair of girls,' I said. 'Show us the way.'

Much to the detriment of our soft hands, well-kept fingernails and probably our spines, Betty and I helped carry the furniture into the salon. The old wardrobe was the hardest, being both immensely heavy and awkwardly shaped, its doors flapping open as we tried to manoeuvre it under the threshold. The delivery man, true to the character he'd already revealed, refused to stay and help us try the furniture in different parts of the room. Rather, he left it all crowded near the entrance and disappeared without even a thank you.

'Our first lesson,' Betty said. 'Don't hire the first rogue you see. Here, help me with this.'

We tried the wardrobe by the window, then at the back of the room, then decided we would take the doors off, but we had the wrong-sized screwdriver so that took longer than anticipated. Then the couch – we moved that into a dozen different positions before settling on the first place we tried, under the window. By now we were both perspiring (my mother said never to use the word 'sweating', so I will just say 'perspiring *rather heavily*'), and dust from the furniture was sticking to our faces and hands. We thought we'd found the ideal place for the desk before we realised that we needed to leave room for a curtain rail so there was a private dressing area, and for Betty's sewing machine, which we would move in on the weekend. It had been running hot the last week, making up samples.

It was nine o'clock before we had everything in place, cleaned and polished. Betty and I sat on the rug rather than the couch, not wanting to get it dirty. I opened the tin of MacRobertson's chocolates we had been saving for the occasion.

'It looks almost like a real salon,' Betty said.

I gazed around. There were so many more things I wished we could do. New wallpaper. Different light fittings. But this is what we had, and it would have to do until we started making money. A shiver of doubt washed through me.

'What if nobody buys our dresses,' I said in a small voice.

Betty picked out a chocolate and shoved it in my mouth. 'Don't even say it. You'll jinx us.'

'Do you never have doubts?'

'Zara, as long as I've known you, you've had the most overactive imagination. Put it to use for good, not bad. Go on. Imagine our opening day.'

I giggled, chewing on chocolate. 'All right, then. Close your eyes.' And when she did, I continued. 'It's a cool, sunny Saturday. Bolts of cloth in gorgeous colours and textures are spilling from the wardrobe. You're out back running the sewing machine, and I'm at the desk cutting a pattern. Wealthy ladies are looking at the samples we've been working on. You're right, Betty, it could be glorious.'

Betty opened her eyes. 'It could be hard work.'

'Glorious hard work.'

'What are we going to call our salon, Zara? We still haven't come up with a name.'

'I thought maybe Z&B? Or ZaB?'

'Zab is a word already,' Betty said.

'No, it's not.'

I should have known better than to argue with Betty about words. She was the fiercest Scrabble opponent you could imagine. 'It is. It means to blab, or go on and on. I don't know if I want it associated with our dresses.'

'I'm sure you think every word is a Scrabble word,' I said, taking another chocolate. 'We'll never find a name.'

Betty narrowed her eyes. 'Actually . . .'

'Actually what?'

'The other night I was playing with Tom's family, and his father played the word "magg". M-A-G-G. And it's not a real word, he was just trying to get a triple-word score with the extra G. But I quite like it, don't you? Sounds a bit like "magazine".'

'Or "magnificent".'

'"Magnetic"! But with the extra G it sounds a bit special.'

At that moment, the door to the shop opened and I glanced around – guiltily, perhaps, as it wasn't particularly ladylike to sit on the floor eating chocolates with grimy hands. It was Jack's Aunt Maddie.

I leaped to my feet, wiping my hands on my skirt. My first thought was that something bad had happened to Genevieve. 'Aunt Maddie,' I stammered.

Betty was also on her feet, furiously chewing a caramel to get it down so she could speak.

'I was told I'd find you here,' Maddie said, glancing around the room. 'I rang you up, Zara, but Genevieve said you were working late. At your salon.'

'Welcome to Magg,' I said, and the name felt just right. I gestured around. 'Apologies for how we look. We've been moving furniture.'

I was very aware of her immaculate, fur-trimmed wool suit. It was white – the worst colour to wear near our sweaty, dirty bodies.

'You're lucky I met you before this evening,' she said. 'Or I'd think you were a vagrant.'

Betty and I exchanged glances. I noticed there was a tiny smear of chocolate on Betty's top lip.

'I have exciting news for you, girls,' Aunt Maddie said. 'Genevieve has been keeping me informed of your venture, and I spoke to a friend of mine at *Ladies' Letter*. You know, the women's magazine that comes in *The Argus*?'

Oh yes, we knew. Anyone interested in fashion knew about *Ladies' Letter*. I nodded.

'Well,' Maddie continued, 'they have agreed to run a feature on you.'

'On us?'

'Yes. Two young girls, only twenty, opening their own dress salon? It will make a marvellous story. They want to take your photo too, in something glamorous that you designed and made.'

All of the doubt and weariness left my body. A glamorous photograph in *Ladies' Letter*! It appealed to both my vanity and my hope that fashionable ladies would learn about our salon and come in to spend their money.

'This is wonderful news,' I said, and I reached out my hand to grasp Maddie's but she cautiously snatched her fingers away.

'Oh, no. You can thank me with a hug and kiss *after* you've had a bath, Zara.'

Betty was laughing, giddy. We both were. Maddie gave us the photographer's telephone number, then we showed her around the salon and told her all our plans. The shop never seemed as brightly lit as it was that night, with our spirits on fire.

———

In all, it took three weeks for us to prepare Magg for opening. A lot of that time was in waiting. Waiting for our account at the textile merchant to be approved. Waiting for my father to sign cheques for us; as we were both underage and banks were very cautious with the Depression, if we wanted to pay somebody, we needed a thorough-going adult to sign *everything* for us. And, yes, waiting for Betty to make up more samples. Betty was a perfectionist; I was not. Of course, it was important that she had every seam and hem perfect, but sometimes I just wanted to shout at her, *We need more dresses!* I could design and cut them quickly, but Betty only knew how to sew carefully and lovingly.

The morning of the opening, Harry came to pick me up in the yellow Summit he was borrowing from his uncle. On the seat lay a copy of *The Argus*, which he had collected at the paper shop.

I squealed when I saw it. 'Have you looked yet?' I asked, shaking the newspaper so the skinny *Ladies' Letter* magazine fell out.

'I have not,' he said with his patient smile. He left the car idling and leaned into me. 'Go on, find it.'

Hands clumsy with excitement, I thumbed through the maga-zine and there we were: Betty standing behind a wooden banister, eyes cast down, two glass-bead ropes around her neck and in a pale chiffon gown – semi-fitted bodice, pointed seams and long flowing panels – while in the photo beside it there was me, sitting with my back to the camera, looking over my shoulder. My gown, in a floral-print chiffon, revealed most of my back before draping at the waist and falling in a train that curved around my shoes. We looked beautiful. I looked beautiful. My face grew warm; I felt suddenly exposed to the world.

'My goodness, Zara,' Harry said, and moved a little closer to peer at the picture. 'You look like a film star.'

I turned my eyes up coquettishly to laugh off his compliment, and saw something I had seen in Harry's eyes before, but not quite so intensely. Raw, unhidden desire.

Now, I was no ingenue. Harry and I kissed and cuddled and explored each other, and he tried for more as all boys do, and I stopped him as all girls do. But this was different. He looked at me as though I was both prey and beloved, and I found this expression beyond thrilling. For a moment I forgot it was a mild Saturday morning, with my parents on the patio twenty yards away with a clear line of sight into the car. In my heart it was midnight and we were alone. A flutter of heat shifted through me, and it must have reflected in my expression because Harry's gaze deepened and he said, 'I must not kiss you, because if I did I wouldn't stop.'

Before I could answer, he returned his attention to putting the car back in gear and pulling out into the street. I kept my eyes focused on the magazine on my lap, and then the hot moment passed and Harry was telling me something amusing about a client with a glass eye who made endless jokes about it.

We parked two streets from the salon and I practically ran through the door brandishing the magazine, only to find Betty also holding it high, and we embraced and said stupid, giddy things to each other. Harry and Tom headed off to find a cafe to escape from us. I nearly made a joke about how they could spend their time talking together about why neither of them had proposed to either of us yet, but I didn't. Because at that moment, I loved being single with Betty and being the newly minted proprietress of a dress salon.

At ten o'clock, we solemnly unlocked the front door and waited. Aunt Maddie came in at ten minutes past the hour and bought a silk scarf for five shillings.

Then the long silence. The long, long, unbearable silence.

'But we were in *The Argus*,' I moaned to Betty at midday, when nobody had even slowed outside our door.

'Hush, Zara. Wait and see. It is only our first day.'

By three, two more friends had come in, then Mum, then Betty's mum, then Aunt Maddie came back to check on us and tell us it might take a while to build the business, and that she would tell all her friends about us. Then Harry and Tom returned and they'd both been drinking, which made me furious and made Betty go quiet and tight around the lips. Then it was five and then it was six and that was it. We'd made five shillings (the scarf we sold to Maddie), had two tipsy boyfriends and opening day was over.

I believe the word is *anticlimactic*.

I tried not to go too far down, but I had always been a creature who succumbed to the sunless end of the swamp. Tom waltzed Betty off for a congratulatory dinner, but of course Harry couldn't afford that so I stayed back and reconciled our minuscule sales, then switched off the lamps and locked the shop.

Harry took my hand and led me back to the car. 'So how did it go?' he asked.

'Terribly. Nobody came.' How I wanted him to take me out to dinner. How I wanted him to make today right by heaping love and extravagances and compliments upon me.

'Nobody? Not one person came in?'

I explained about family and friends, and Aunt Maddie, and he nodded as he opened the car door for me and closed it gently. 'Well, that's not nobody,' he said, ever practical.

I waited until he'd joined me in the car. 'No real customers,' I wailed. 'There's a difference.'

He turned to me, his arm resting on top of the steering wheel. 'Zara, you rarely acknowledge how good things are for you.'

'What is that supposed to mean?' Steam built behind my eyes. Not only had our opening been a flop, not only had he not taken me out for dinner, not only had he not recognised that I was feeling dejected . . . but also he was taking the opportunity to give me a lecture on gratitude?

'You are so used to your privileges that you don't even recognise them,' he said with no malice or unkindness, which somehow made it worse.

'What privileges?'

'The kind of privilege that means Daddy can give you two hundred pounds for a dress shop. The kind of contacts, like Maddie, who will no doubt tell all her wealthy and fashionable friends to come and buy clothes from you. Zara, you do realise that some people have to eat at soup kitchens? Live off ration cards? Catch mice for food?'

I experienced such a complex mix of rage and shame that I thought my heart might explode through my rib cage. Every instinct screamed at me to get away from him before I tore his calm, reasonable face off. I threw open the car door and climbed out.

'Zara, where are you going?'

'You're drunk. And mean. You've ruined my day.'

He shrugged. 'Seems to me you'd already ruined it yourself. Get back in.'

'No. I'm walking home.'

Harry, of course, did not plead with me. He calmly drove off, leaving me standing there with stupid tears of rage in my eyes, feeling utterly bereft of any joy.

———

Perhaps it was one week we didn't speak after that, perhaps two. I was depressingly accustomed to the cycle of highs and lows with Harry. I knew no different, so I went around with a stone in my belly until he called again and told me he missed me, and my heart felt light and it was all forgotten. Except it was never forgotten, not really. Forgiven, yes. But my body seemed to hold on to all the little hurts until some days I felt as though I had no skin on.

Luckily I was busy. Not as busy as I'd have liked at first. Three full days passed before we had a real customer, but then we began to attract one or two a day easily. We made absolutely no money. In fact, we owed money because it turned out that rich ladies didn't always pay their accounts swiftly, and neither Betty nor I were particularly persuasive in demanding money from them. Our fathers helped us with the bills, and I felt such guilt and shame about it. What Harry had said was true. We weren't as brave and clever as we thought. We were simply lucky enough to have rich daddies.

The shame, though, drove me. I figured I couldn't shake off my privilege, but I could work like the very devil. By the sixth week, most of the fashion set in Melbourne had heard about the two young fools who had opened a salon in the depths of the Depression. Curiosity brought them into Magg, and our designs and handiwork convinced them to stay. I never stopped. There wasn't an evening I didn't bring home designs to refine, fabric samples to work with, neglected ledgers to finish (though these were usually Betty's purview, given my appalling ability with arithmetic).

Betty worked hard too, of course. The soft steady beat-and-rattle of her Singer became the background noise of my life. I remembered how much time we'd spent in the typing pool chatting to each other; now we barely had a chance to say 'boo' to each other, and any conversation we did have was about fabrics and threads, or bills and ledgers.

I can't speak for Betty, but it was easily one of the happiest times of my life. I grew in confidence by the hour. I could look at a woman and judge in seconds what would and wouldn't work on her body, how to make her shine in a gown even though she might have fought a war her whole life with a thick waist or unrelenting bosom. I also developed a sixth sense for fabric – its colour and its texture. Once a month I visited a textile merchant out at Richmond. I was in love with the smell of the place – there was something stuffy yet faintly floral about it. The shuttered warehouse had tall wooden shelves from one end to another, with bolts of cloth arranged along them under dim electric lights to protect the colours from fade. Vermilion silks from Korea, pinstripe and herringbone suiting fabric from Italy, midnight-blue satin from France, yellow-gold cashmere from India, half an aisle of ribbons and lace on spools, and of course acres and acres of gorgeous Australian wool. Any I wanted to see closer I could take to the long counter, where elderly Miss Fanshawe – the owner's spinster aunt, I believe – would switch on a bright lamp for me. But I didn't buy on how much they delighted my eyes, or even my fingers. I bought on instinct. More and more, I just *knew*.

By the time winter started to bite, we catered to half a dozen of the richest families in Melbourne and were so terribly in debt that one morning Miss Fanshawe would not open the warehouse door to me. I stood with my back against it, staring down the lane in the weak sunshine. Across the road, I could see a family – a man, his angular-faced wife and a child of about seven – sitting under the eaves of another warehouse, about a hundred yards away. My heart felt so heavy for their misfortune, especially the child. It was entirely wrong that children should live without houses or enough food. Harry and I spoke about it all the time, and I asked him was there not something he could *do* about it with the political club he was involved in. I'd like to say it put my problems in perspective, but unfortunately I was still young enough to feel sorry for myself too. The business would soon grind to a halt if we didn't get on top of the paperwork, but honestly, all the rows of numbers were simply so boring to me that I couldn't focus on them for more than a few minutes at a time.

I knew what had to be done, so I began my walk back to the salon, deliberately passing the family, stopping to give them a shilling I couldn't afford and wishing them better luck. The mother and father nodded wearily, but the child beamed up at me with such sunshine in her face that it nearly prompted me to tears. Hope.

Betty and I wrestled over my idea – to hire a bookkeeper – because she was adamant we had to know exactly where the money was going, so we settled on hiring another seamstress who could also help with some of the paperwork. Because times were so hard, we had fourteen young women apply for the position. Like a pair of idiots, we hired with our hearts instead of our heads. Elsie was a widow with a ten-year-old son and she needed the money badly. She was a marvellous seamstress, but practically innumerate.

While her mother minded the child, she would come to work for us, and Betty would sort the books and call in all our debts.

So it was that Betty was not even in the salon on the day the film star came in.

It was Elsie's third day. She was quiet but worked hard and carefully, and only glanced up when the door opened. When she did, she let out a little gasp.

For a moment I stared at the woman, wondering what it was about her that was so arresting. Huge eyes, heart-shaped face, soft perfectly arranged curls. She was so beautiful that I would have noticed her whoever she was, but then Elsie said her name and I realised where I had seen her before.

'You're Lotus Thompson,' Elsie said, then put her head down and added, 'I do apologise.'

Lotus laughed lightly. 'Oh, don't be silly. Yes, of course I am she. I'm flattered you recognised me.'

Oh, the charm that oozed from her. The sheen and lustre of her. She seemed out of place among us ordinary women, especially here in Melbourne. To my knowledge, Lotus Thompson had moved to Hollywood. That's where she made the cowboy films she was probably best known for. I had only seen one, with Harry. *Crimson Canyon* it was called, though I recollected little about it except that she seemed to need to be rescued quite a bit. Today, she wore a dark grey cloche over her red-brown curls, dark red lipstick in perfect peaks and a dark grey satin bias-cut dress with bishop sleeves.

'Welcome to Magg,' I said, aware of my own voice sounding small and girlish compared with hers. 'How may we help you?'

'Oh, I'm in town for a few months. A little bit of trouble back in the States.' She grimaced self-deprecatingly, but even in a grimace she was gorgeous. 'And somebody told me, "Lo, you have to see these girls and buy one of their gowns." So here I am.'

'Well, I'm delighted,' I said. 'I'm Zara, and my business partner Betty is off' – I nearly said 'chasing debts' then realised I needed to sound more professional – 'at the bank,' I finished. I gestured to starstruck Elsie. 'This is Elsie, one of our seamstresses.'

But Lotus was less than interested in our names. She had begun to make a slow circle of the salon, eyeing the samples. 'My, you do beautiful work.'

'We like to think so.'

She stopped in front of one of our dress dummies, which wore a red satin evening gown. 'Do you think something like this would suit me?'

I joined her. 'I think the cut would do nicely, but I wouldn't have all these ruffles around your shoulders. You're so tiny, you might look as though you're drowning. What if we had a simpler sleeve, and if you want some detail, we can have a contrasting bow on the back?'

'A bow?'

'Large and loose, maybe even flowing down into a train.'

'I do like a train.' She smiled at me, and I took far too much joy in noting she had a spot of red lipstick on her perfect white teeth.

'With your height, I'd taper the skirt at the knee and flare at the hemline too.'

'And the colour? Everyone says red isn't for redheads.' She made an exaggerated pout. 'They all say green, but I've always thought green was bad luck.'

'You should match fabric to skin, not hair,' I said. 'Your skin is creamy. I would love to put you in coral or peach. Would you like to see some fabrics?'

She looked at me. It was the strangest moment, as though she was assessing me, deciding whether or not a mere mortal such as myself was worth taking advice from. I was a bug on a pin. Then the moment passed, she smiled again and said, 'That would be delightful, Zara.'

———

That evening, I couldn't stop talking about our film star customer to Harry. Turned out I was just as much of a starstruck fan as Elsie, but mostly because she had ordered *four* gowns, paid us in cash right away and had promised to tell everyone she knew about us. Harry was happy for me but asked me more questions about what she looked like, and if I'd seen her legs, because there had been a mad story in the press about her pouring nitric acid on her own legs so film producers would stop casting her based on her aston-ishing figure and give her more serious roles. I told him that her legs looked perfectly fine to me, and seethed a little that he'd used the words 'astonishing figure' more than once.

Nonetheless, he let me babble over our spaghetti and meatballs at Marcello's, and when I was all done, I let him talk (he never babbled) about a friendship he had struck up with a business associate named Mabel. At first I had flinched at the idea of him being friends with a woman, but soon discovered she was the president of the Queen Victoria Hospital and in her forties (though it must be said that Harry loved all women, and all women loved Harry). She apparently also wrote novels, though not the kind I liked. But for Harry, it was important that she was in the very thick of things with the United Australia Party and had promised to make him many introductions. And while we both bragged about our new networks of influence, I was convinced mine was *infinitely* more interesting.

I was proven right when Harry showed up at the salon – which he rarely did – on the exact afternoon Lotus was due in for her first fitting. Betty and I were fussing over a gown on the dressmaker's dummy – she with a mouthful of pins and me trying to perk up the bustle bow – when the door opened. Of course, we assumed it was Lotus and were immediately on high alert, Betty spitting pins into her palm, but it was only Harry.

'What are you doing here?' I said, and it probably came out a little sharper than I'd intended, because I knew *precisely* what he was doing here.

I hurried to the door to grasp his elbow as he removed his hat and looked around. 'I had a free few hours so I thought I'd come and take you to lunch. My, the place is looking different.'

I saw the salon through his eyes then. The dresses on dummies, the rolls of fabric, the cluttered counter. Signs of industry and progress from where we had started. Pride welled up, and then Harry said, 'I am so proud of you, Zara. Look what you've created.'

'*We*,' I said, indicating Betty, who was giving Harry a sharp look. 'But I can't come to lunch, and you know it. We have a very special client about to arrive.'

As I said it, I saw her approaching from the street, hugging her sable coat around her against the day's bitter southerly. Harry caught the direction of my gaze and turned, then leaped to open the door for her.

'Oh. Thank you, kind sir.' She giggled, and began to shrug out of her coat. 'Zara, I didn't know your salon came with a doorman.'

'It doesn't,' I said as Harry took her coat.

'Harry Holt,' he said, picking up her hand and grazing his lips on her knuckles. 'Such an honour to meet a real-life film star.'

She gave him a coquettish smile. There was something practised about it, and I could see she wasn't in the least interested in Harry, for all his charm and his boyish grin.

Harry didn't seem to notice. His eyes were drinking her in. 'I believe you are buying a gown from my lovely Zara.' Here he dropped her hand and slid an arm around me.

'Yes, and you'll need to leave, Harry,' I said.

Betty had joined us. 'No woman wants to be fitted for a gown while there's a gentleman lurking about,' she said sternly.

'Oh, I don't mind,' Lotus said airily, waving away Betty's warning. 'Perhaps it would be good to have a man's opinion. Shall we get started?'

The next hour was excruciating for me, as Harry sat on our couch and watched the fitting as though it were a show. Lotus was very casual about using the dressing room, pulling the curtain halfway across as she stripped down to her slip and stockings, wandering to the mirror quite unashamedly with sleeves sliding off her shoulders and, when dressed, parading in front of Harry to ask 'a gentleman's' opinion. To which Harry always replied, 'You're a vision. You should buy ten more of those!'

I don't know if Harry knew or cared that the flirting was not reciprocal. Lotus was quite clearly playing the part of the film star in front of him, while with us she was all practical questions and solemn stillness as we were pinning her.

Finally, we had everything pinned and ready for Elsie to finish. Lotus pulled her own clothes on, took her coat, and we organised a day and time for her to return to collect her gowns. She blew Harry a little kiss and creased up her nose at him, like a bunny, then headed back out into the grey street.

Harry theatrically clutched his chest. 'What a sweetheart she is. Not at all the aloof film star one might expect from somebody who's made their way in Hollywood.'

I felt so dull and ugly in that moment, and was about to shout at him to get out, when Betty surprised me by marching over to him and handing him his hat. 'Harry Holt, you are *not* welcome here. This is a woman's place, not a man's. No woman wants to change clothes while there is a man in the room.'

Harry took his hat, looking affronted. 'She said she didn't mind.'

'She was wrong to say it,' Betty retorted. 'And you were wrong to stay. I'm sorry, Zara. I know he's your boyfriend, but that was simply unacceptable.' She turned her eye on Harry again. 'Not to mention incredibly disrespectful to the gorgeous young woman you profess to love.'

Tears pricked my eyes. I loved Betty with all my heart in that moment. I clutched her hand and squeezed it tight.

Harry spread his hands. 'Oh, come on. She's a film star. There's not a man in the world who wouldn't have wanted to do what I just did. Zara understands. She knows she's no Hollywood type. I wouldn't want her to be. I love her for what she is.'

'Just go, Harry,' I said, giving him a gentle push. 'Betty's right. I don't hang about at your office charming your clients. You ought not have come.'

He shrugged, wearing a hangdog expression. 'I am sorry, my love. I will see you this evening.' He leaned in, gave me a kiss on the cheek, then left.

As the door closed, Betty turned and gave me a hug. 'Four gowns, paid for in cash,' she said. 'That's all that matters.'

'Thank you, my dear friend. I feel so low. He's right – I'll never be a Hollywood type.'

'Thank goodness! How tiresome she must be.' Betty stood back. 'Elsie and I have some sewing to do.'

'But only one sewing machine.'

She smiled. 'Shall we buy a new one? A *brand-new* one, not my aunt's hand-me-down?'

I exhaled. That would be half the money gone. But surely once word got out that Magg had dressed Lotus Thompson, more business would come. We were standing on the edge of something, Betty and I, and I didn't want to let Harry's casual callousness stop me from jumping.

'Yes. Let's be a salon with *two* sewing machines, and let's trust that they will both be running hot by the end of winter.'

CHAPTER 5

Lotus Thompson told everyone about us. She wore one of our gowns in a photograph in the social pages, and made sure the journalist wrote down Magg's name and address. The second sewing machine was put to immediate good use. We heard via our new networks of well-connected rich ladies that Lotus had returned to the United States before the winter was over, but her influence on our business endured.

Her influence on my relationship with Harry also endured. He had long forgotten about her, but I fell into a well of self-doubt that I couldn't climb out of. Every fight we had terrified me. Every passionate reunion and declaration of mad love made me want to ask, *But how much do you love me? Will you leave me for somebody more beautiful?* Because everyone seemed more beautiful to me. I made women beautiful for a living, but the image of myself that lived in my head was the one I saw in the bathroom mirror in the morning. Plain. Doughy. Nothing special. But when I begged Harry for compliments, he brushed me off.

'You're the only girl for me,' he said. 'Why else would I keep coming back?'

Which only served to make me feel undignified as well as insecure.

Something else had changed the tone of our relationship too. Desire. Sometimes, when we were kissing in his father's car and his hands began to wander, I didn't want him to stop. One thrilling night

I'd even let his fingers creep up through the leg of my knickers, and he'd touched me in a place where I had never even touched myself. Good lord, it was like liquid fire, the most intense physical sensation I had ever felt. I gasped sharply and he quickly withdrew his hand, thinking he had hurt me. I was too shy to tell him the truth.

I knew he wanted to go 'all the way' because I'd heard that all boys did; I had also heard that all girls didn't. But *I* did. And I began to see this as the way to keep him. He wouldn't lose interest if he was satisfied. His eyes wouldn't linger on other girls if I let him see me undressed. I knew it was wrong, I knew I should wait until we were married, but the matter seemed urgent. So one evening early in October, when his lips were pressed against mine while we sat in the car out near Seaford Beach, I blurted, 'I want to go all the way.'

Harry sat back. It was dark, but I could see he blinked at me, in the way he did when he was trying to figure out what I meant (which was often, during our fights).

'Zara?'

I had deliberately worn a button-up blouse, and started unfastening it. Harry reached out his hand and grasped my fingers.

'Stop,' he said.

'Stop?' My stomach went cold. He didn't want me.

He drew my hand to his mouth and kissed my fingers. 'Oh, Zara. My beautiful, beautiful Zara. Not here. Not in a car. You deserve a soft bed and a warm room with a locked door for your first time. But . . . are you sure?'

I was. I wasn't. I nodded. 'Don't you want . . . ?'

'I want.' He laughed. 'I want so very, very badly, but I would also wait. I'd wait forever for you.' He shifted in the seat, both hands on the wheel now, and his voice became practical and rational. 'Tomorrow night, if you still feel this way, come to my room. You'll have to sneak past the boarding-house superintendent, but I'll unlatch the back door. If you can manage to get the back gate open without it squeaking too much, he won't hear you.' He turned his eyes to me again. 'If you change your mind, simply don't come. I won't mind, you know.'

'You won't mind? But don't boys always mind?'

'Boys . . .' He chuckled. '*Men* have other ways of keeping themselves happy.'

I didn't know what he meant, but I didn't want to entertain the idea that he might mean having sex with other women. Women who weren't so unsure as me. Women he paid. I didn't know.

'I'll definitely be there,' I said.

'But I don't mind if you're not,' he replied.

'Definitely,' I said.

———

That Saturday was one of our busiest yet at Magg. Betty had put aside time to sew that morning, but we had so many browsers, then two early fittings, and eventually we had to take Elsie off the sewing machine to show fabrics to a woman who looked far too young to be as wealthy as she obviously was. Every now and then my mind would slip to what the evening would hold, and a thrill would course through me and make me smile, as though I had a fiery little secret.

We closed late, as fittings went over time and Elsie had to hurry home to her little boy. Betty and I waited for the tram, and I told her I'd be taking a different one in the opposite direction to go to see Harry.

'Really?' she said, raising an eyebrow. 'At his place?'

'I've been there before.'

'At night? Don't they forbid ladies after dark?'

'It's only *just* after dark.' I found it hard to meet her eyes.

She lit a cigarette as she scrutinised my face. 'Zara Dickins,' she eventually said, in the kind of voice a schoolteacher might use to talk to a naughty child.

'Oh, quiet,' I said, laughing. 'As if you and Tom haven't fool around a little.'

'We've fooled around a lot,' she said, exhaling a long stream of smoke. 'It hurts the first time and it's not really much fun for us girls. Make sure he uses a French letter.'

I had no idea what she was talking about, and was thinking about circumflexes as I had learned in French as a child, when she clarified, 'It stops you getting . . . you know . . .'

'Getting what?'

The tram rattled towards us. She laughed, hefting her bag full of bookwork onto her shoulder. 'Stops you getting married too early,' she said, rubbing her belly, and the penny dropped.

Well, good. That saved me an awkward conversation with Harry about how to go all the way without finding myself swelling in the middle in a few months' time.

'They aren't one hundred per cent safe,' she said as she stood and the tram ground to a halt. 'Be sure he's the one.'

'Oh, he's the one.'

She nodded. 'Good luck.'

My tram was right behind hers, and I climbed on board with my heart ticking hard in my throat. We rattled through the evening dark, regular beats from passing streetlights falling on my hands folded in my lap. I alighted two blocks from Harry's boarding house and made my way quickly along the street. The sky was heavy, as though it might squeeze out some drizzle any moment. But the air was still, and all the trees along the way seemed to be watching me and judging me.

'Oh, shut up,' I muttered under my breath. I was twenty. I was a fashion designer who owned my own successful business. I could do as I pleased. Then I realised I was getting grumpy with the trees and told myself to be sensible.

I walked past the front of Harry's place then around the corner and down a slip road to the back gate. The tall brick building was dark except for three lit windows. One of them, on the second floor, was Harry's. I had looked out of that window at this slip road, with its profusion of crepe myrtle trees. Carefully, I unlatched the gate and inched it open, braced against any loud squeaks. I made enough room to slip through then closed it behind me and crept up to the back door. Not quite on tiptoes but certainly with my weight far enough forward that my heels didn't click on the brick path. As promised, Harry had left the back door open, and it led directly to the stairs. The smell of cooking still hung in the air but there was no light from the kitchen, and no sign of the superintendent who kept girls like me out of this haven for men like Harry, who were respectable but not yet established.

I found his door and pushed it open. He sat on his bed reading, and looked up so casually it was almost comical, given my speeding heart.

'Oh, there you are. I thought you might have changed your mind. It's nearly eight.' He gestured for me to close the door, which I did, and latched it. He shifted aside on the bed and patted the space next to him, book in his lap. 'Come and sit.'

I slipped off my shoes and joined him, stretching out my legs next to his. He took my hand, and the first sign that he was anything but fully composed was the way he began to stroke my hand with his thumb, over and over, till he nearly wore a hole in my skin.

'You are sure then?' he said, his eyes locked on mine.

'I am so sure.'

He nodded. 'I can't say I haven't dreamed of this, a thousand times.'

I smiled. 'Really?'

He made a fist with his free hand and pressed it against his heart. 'Zara, there is a tempest in my heart with your name on it.'

'Is that a good thing? It doesn't sound good. A tempest.'

'You stir me,' he said. 'Nobody else stirs me.'

'Not even certain film stars you may have met?' I tried to say it lightly, but I knew it was silly and girlish of me.

'She was beautiful, but I meet many beautiful women, and none of them stir me the way you do.'

It had to be enough. I couldn't demand that he find only me beautiful, and besides I think I knew what he meant. There was little that was calm and comfortable about our love and that's what made it so addictive. Perhaps instead of complaining to Vieve that he drove me mad, I could simply say he 'stirred' me. The thought nearly made me giggle.

'Come here, then,' he said, and collected me in his arms. He began to kiss my cheek, my neck, and he whispered to me, 'I will be so gentle and so careful with you, and I'll protect you and make sure you like it too. I promise.'

Heat flared through me, and all doubt fled my body, and as he kissed my mouth and his fingers went to my buttons, I felt the tempest too.

———

Despite Betty's warnings, I liked it. No, I loved it. Everything about it. The slightly awkward intimacy deepening to serious desire, the casting off of inhibitions, all the physical sensations. I especially loved lying there with him afterwards, in his narrow bed, our limbs folded uncomfortably so that I could have my breasts pressed against his chest. He stroked my hair with his free hand and smiled into my eyes, and I couldn't remember the last time that we had simply looked at each other. I felt so loved.

'So, I really didn't hurt you? Not even a bit?' he asked.

'Not even a bit.' I replied. He had taken it so slowly, so carefully.

'I never want to hurt you.' His hand came down and ran along my shoulder, fingers grazing the side of my breast, then down into the scoop of my waist. 'Women's bodies are so beautiful.'

Ever primed for insecurity, a buzz of annoyance passed through me. Why couldn't he say, '*Your* body is so beautiful'? It was all I wanted to hear. But I batted the thought away. I wasn't an idiot. Of course he had done this before – his masterful lovemaking told me that – and I didn't want to ruin the moment with jealous nonsense.

Instead, I snuggled my face up under his chin and breathed the warm scent of him and closed my eyes. We both drifted to sleep some time later, and even as I slipped under I thought to myself, *just a doze*.

But when I opened my eyes, daylight glimmered under the blind and I could hear birds singing.

I sat up with a gasp. Harry stirred next to me, his hand reaching over to find me.

'Harry, it's morning.' I looked at his clock. 6 am. 'Proper morning. Oh heck. I need to get home before Mum finds out I'm not there.' I reached for my clothes, the grainy daylight making me self-conscious.

Harry sat up, the covers pooled in his lap. Lord, he looked beautiful. Ever after, I never shook that vision of him. The dark hair of his chest, the sleep-satisfied grin on his face. 'There won't be a tram running this early on a Sunday and I don't have the car. Are you going to jog?'

I sat heavily on the bed, my blouse clutched against my chest to preserve a little modesty. 'A taxi?'

'Picking up a single young woman outside a men's boarding house?' He pulled me against him, started kissing my ear. 'You'd be best to wait here until you can get a tram. I'll help you make up a plausible story. And that means we get another chance to . . .' His hand closed over my breast, and the warm flutters started again.

So, like an idiot, I stayed. If Harry had me in his spell before, now he had totally obliterated any chance of it breaking. My passionate nature found its full expression in his bed. I was his for life.

This meant though that I was creeping into church at ten o'clock – after returning home for a quick wash and change of clothes – and joining my family on the third-to-last pew. The boys seemed oblivious, but my parents gave me two very hard stares. My mother's in particular lingered. I settled next to Vieve, who leaned into me and whispered, 'Where have you been?'

I didn't answer, lowered my eyes and tried to listen to the sermon. But in my imagination, I replayed every detail of my intimate encounter, which seemed particularly shameful given I was sitting with my family in church.

It was late afternoon before Mum came to find me. I'd managed to avoid her by playing with the boys in the garden, or reading resolutely in the living room with Daddy, who would sooner die than speak to one of his daughters about sex. But around four she came in and told me I needed to come and get tea on, and once she had me alone in the kitchen, all her furious questions came out.

'Where were you all night? What were you doing? Don't answer that – I know what you were doing. Is our reputation a joke to you? Do you know how much trouble a young woman can get herself into?'

I put up my hands in a stop gesture and repeated the carefully rehearsed lie that Harry and I had concocted. 'Betty and I had customers until very late at the shop, and had so much extra bookwork to do that we went to her house to finish it. I must have fallen asleep on the couch in her bedroom, and when I woke up it was too late to get home safely.'

'Is that so? You fell asleep at Betty's? And if I were to ring up Mr and Mrs James, they would say that you were there?'

'Yes.' I was betting that my mother would *never* ring up the Jameses over this, because if they said no, the shame would cripple her.

She met my eye. I don't know if she believed me or not, but it didn't matter. I had won. She backed down. 'Well, be more careful in future.'

'I will. We've just been working so hard and –'

'And for pity's sake, find a way to make Harry propose to you. This delaying has gone on long enough.'

Neither of us had the faintest concept of just how much longer Harry could delay a wedding.

———

In many ways, that was the year I grew up. I'd left my teens behind, along with my naivety. I was a woman now. I owned a thriving business. Magazines asked my opinions about styles and trends. I was invited to fashion and textile shows and, increasingly, high-society events. Horse races, visiting dignitaries, exclusive parties – and at every one of the events I saw a Magg dress on some gorgeous, wealthy woman. Harry relished being on my arm, and we were quite the dashing couple. Well-dressed, ambitious and clearly enamoured of each other.

We didn't fight as much either. Frankly, we were both too busy to fight and our stolen moments of physical intimacy were a strong glue. When we did have a blow-up – usually always because he couldn't stop himself flirting and I couldn't stop myself flying into a jealous rage – it was terrifying to feel so murderous and so heart-broken at the same time. One of the worst was the enormous row outside the reception for Genevieve's wedding in July, where one too many well-meaning relatives asked us when it would be 'your turn to plan a wedding', which grated on Harry – who still claimed to be far too unstable and impecunious to marry – and embarrassed me. I felt certain I looked like an idiot for waiting for him. I must admit it was a terrible pang seeing my sister marry: love and pride and envy all rolled into one.

When Harry and I made up though, we made up with sweet, fierce lovemaking. I'm sure by this stage we were both addicted to the bitter rifts and breathless apologies. It couldn't have done either of us any good.

Four weeks before my birthday, in the first glimmer of 1932's autumn, I was folding my underwear away in the bedroom I now had all to myself when I realised I couldn't remember the last time I'd had a 'visit from the red devil', as Vieve and I called it. I worked long hours, was always rushing about between work and events and Harry's place – I must have simply lost track. I sat on the corner of my bed among the sketchbooks and swatches strewn about and turned my brain backwards, matching up memories with events and dates. Dread crept over me. Had it been two months? Lord, had it been three? The answer was completely beyond me; the days had all jumbled into each other. But it felt like a long time.

My hand went to my lower belly and pressed. Did it feel different? Achy? Swollen? What were the signs that I was pregnant? I genuinely had no idea. My first instinct was to ring Vieve or Betty, but I was so ashamed of myself. Only a foolish girl gets herself into trouble.

I took several deep breaths, tried to calm myself, returned to folding laundry, concentrating very hard to take my mind off it. Maybe I'd miscounted. If I waited a day or two, a week at most, surely the red devil would visit and I would be laughing at myself for worrying. Harry and I were always so careful.

It hung over me. The following day at work I was distracted, in an anxious haze. I drove a pin through my own finger during a fitting, and marred the shell-pink silk hem with a bloody fingerprint. Days passed, still no red devil. I brushed off Harry's advances and wouldn't say why; I didn't even know why myself. It wasn't as though I could get pregnant twice. I played over and over in my head the nightmare of having to tell my mother. And the dread silence that would settle over our house when she relayed it to my father.

They would make us marry, and nobody would think that was a bad thing. I will admit, a little sneaking part of me relished the idea that he would finally commit, but I was wise enough to know he would bristle against a forced marriage, and I did not want to be blamed for his unhappiness. The situation was impossible.

Somehow I struggled through another week pretending to be bright and normal, while underneath I seethed with dreadful imaginings. It became clear I had to tell Harry, visit my family doctor and find out once and for all if I was expecting a child. I rang Harry up on Wednesday night and asked him to come over the following evening after work. My plan was to take him for a walk around the neighbourhood to tell him, then have him stand with me while I spoke to my mother.

Thursday morning, a terrible pain woke me while it was still dark, before the birds had started singing. The pain was as though somebody had driven a pike into my groin and was turning it this way and that. I got up, stumbled to the bathroom and switched on the light, and when I lifted my nightdress I could see my thighs were smeared with bright red blood. I sat on the toilet seat, and great clots of it fell into the water. I sat there a while, my heart thudding. Relief, fear, pain, sadness. The cramps were like nothing I'd ever felt, and so I knew this wasn't my long-overdue period; I knew that I was losing a baby.

After twenty minutes or so, I rose and stepped into the bath, squatted down and tried to clean myself up. I scrubbed my nightdress too, then went to the box stashed at the back of the bathroom cupboard and fished out two Kotex pads. I laid them on top of each other, grabbed yesterday's knickers out of the laundry basket and pinned them in place. A gentle knock at the door made me jump.

'Who is it?' I asked, hoping it wasn't one of the boys.

'It's your mum. You've been in there for ages.'

I scrabbled up my wet nightdress and pressed it against my body, went to the door and opened it a crack. 'It's nothing. I mean . . . a very heavy period.'

She opened the door and took in the pale pink stains on my wet nightdress. 'You're lucky I don't sleep well,' she said, shrugging out of her dressing gown and handing it to me. 'Here, give me that and I'll treat the stain. How heavy?'

I winced as a cramp gripped me. 'Incredibly.'

I swapped the nightdress for her robe, which I wrapped around myself and hugged closed.

'Back to bed with you, then. I'll get you a hottie bottie.'

I gratefully returned to my room, switching on the lamp next to my bed, though the first glimmers of dawn had washed some of the dark from the sky. There were a few blood spots on my sheets but I didn't want to strip the bed. I just wanted to curl around my womb and hold very still while the savage cramps racked me. Mum came in with the hot water bottle wrapped in a towel, and I pressed it against my belly.

She sat down and smoothed my hair. 'Are you all right, sweet pea?'

'Just a period,' I said, forcing a neutral tone even as my body racked with pain.

Mum seemed about to say something, but didn't. Both Vieve and I had always managed the visits from the red devil with no fuss, mortified at the idea that one of the boys would find out. She knew something wasn't right, but I think she was as afraid to ask me as I was afraid of telling her.

'Ah well,' she said, patting my hip. 'See how you go, and if you're not feeling better tomorrow you can go and see Doctor Miles. I'd rather you saw a doctor than suffered along. Now shall I make you some tea and toast? It's nearly breakfast time.'

I shook my head. I simply wanted to lie still, braced against the pain.

'I'll check in on you once I've got the boys out of the house,' she said, and left, closing the door behind her.

By eight, it was clear I couldn't go to work, so Mum rang up Betty for me, and for the first time I missed a day of work at Magg. Mum gave me some very strong pain drops, and I slept fitfully throughout the day, rising only to change blood-soaked pads and walk them up to the incinerator at the back of the garden. It slipped my mind completely that Harry was coming by, until I heard the knock on the front door shortly after six.

I sat up, woozy from the pain drops, and listened to my mother answering the door. There were voices – Harry's deep one, Mum's light one – but I couldn't hear what they were saying. Was I mistaken, or did Mum sound . . . angry with him, as though she was telling him off? A few moments later, I heard Harry's footsteps moving off and I flung back the covers and tried to stand, then steadied myself on the bedhead as a spell of dizziness washed over me. I threw open the door and intercepted Mum coming back inside.

'Was that Harry?'

'He can wait until you're well to see you,' she said brusquely. 'Back to bed.'

For three days I bled heavily and painfully, then on the fourth day it felt like a normal period and the pain receded. I had to convince Mum to let me go back to work, but she insisted on accompanying me and helping out for the day, which we very much needed. She cut fabrics and helped pin dresses, and we slowly worked through a backlog of fittings and gave Elsie time to catch up on a few finishings. By the end of the day I was grindingly tired and seemed to ache all over. I was surprised to see Harry's face at the door just after five.

'He's been in the last two days looking for you,' Betty said.

Mum squeezed my shoulder. 'You need to go home to bed, sweet pea. Go and tell him to come back next week. Or shall I?'

I'd not seen Harry since the whole nightmare started, so I wanted to ignore her advice and run off into the night with him. But I could feel the weight of her disapproval, and the truth was that I could barely stand from exhaustion.

'I'll go speak to him,' I said, firmly but gently removing Mum's hand. 'Give me five minutes.'

I went to the door, stepped out into the chilly street and shut the door behind me.

He pulled me into an embrace. 'I have been so worried about you.'

I melted into him. It felt so good to be held. 'You needn't have worried.'

'Your mother said you were unwell, that it could be serious, and it was my fault. What did she mean by that? I haven't hurt you, have I?'

I had suspected, but now I knew for certain that Mum had guessed the true nature of my ailment. I opened my mouth to explain to Harry, but I couldn't. I simply couldn't. Because I was sad that I'd lost our baby, as much as I was relieved that my problem had gone away. If he heard that sadness, it would get under his skin. He would feel it as pressure – pressure to marry me, buy a house, have children. These things he was certain he was not ready for.

'I don't know what she meant,' I lied. 'I was just sick. Maybe she thinks you took me to a dubious restaurant for dinner.'

'She was angrier than you'd expect,' he said. 'The Scottish temper came out.'

I stood back, shrugged it off. 'You know how protective mothers can be. For instance, she's going to come out in a moment and demand I go home. I'm still not all that well and I've just worked a full day.'

'You do look pale, my love.' He kissed my forehead. 'Ring me up when you're better and I'll take you out to dinner. Somewhere that won't poison you.' He smiled, his eyes crinkling.

I watched him stride off down the street, felt the door open behind me.

'Are we heading home then?' Mum said.

Weariness washed over me, but not simply because I'd been unwell. It was weariness of waiting for Harry, waiting for that part of my life to begin. I glanced around the salon and tried to cheer myself up. 'I'll stay a little longer,' I said.

'You look plumb tired.'

'I'm happy here,' I told her, and went back to work.

CHAPTER 6

I got on with things, and probably to the outside world I seemed quite fine. Perhaps even ambitious and wildly successful. It's difficult to explain the truth though . . . it was as though a gap had opened up between my outside and my inside. Yes, I was a well-dressed, smiling woman who addressed ladies lunches with tales of her business success, who could hold conversations with Harry's powerful legal and political friends, who knew with utter conviction which textile purchases she wanted to make and how much she would pay for them. But I was also a sad, anxious little girl, never showing it but always feeling it. I might be drawing up a pattern with strong, sure lines, then I'd see myself from outside, somehow, and watch myself in terror. *What is she doing? How is she doing it when she is nothing more than a ball of unshed tears and unspoken fear?* For a time I wondered if this was what going mad felt like, as though that gap between my public self and my secret self would grow and grow and fill with dark, dangerous things until they were all I could see.

I told no-one. Not Betty, nor Vieve, nor Harry, and certainly not Mum, who was keen never to hint at the miscarriage again. The closest I came to saying anything was when I asked Harry, 'Do you ever feel as though you are two people?' and he looked at me with such an expression of incomprehension that I knew the conversation could go no further. Harry had always been coherent from skin to soul.

I tried to throw myself into my work. I had heard of people doing this before. I knew Harry did it all the time to distract himself from feeling things he didn't want to feel. But for me it simply meant I worked too hard, grew tired, and the sadness and anxiety deepened. After several months, those feelings were no longer attached to the miscarriage particularly. They had grown sticky and adhered to everything. The way the sun fell through the leaves outside my window. The way a tram bell sounded in the distance. The way a fairy wren peered at me from the fence one morning and it seemed as though my body and fast-beating heart were as fragile and light as his. And desolation would wash over me, making me feel exposed and vulnerable.

Those close to me only occasionally noticed something was different about me. Betty once called me 'serious'. Harry used the word 'moody'. My brothers exasperatedly told me I was 'no fun'. I didn't have words to say what was wrong with me so I kept pushing on. I had always been chatty and lively to the point of being annoying, so I relied on all those old tricks to get me by. But I was not well for a long time.

Meanwhile Magg kept growing. We hired another seamstress and moved her and Elsie and a young assistant out to a workroom two floors up. Betty still took care of the books and I still took care of the designs, but both of us were doing that work late at night or on Sundays. We would arrive at the salon at seven in the morning, sort through the samples and the gowns for the day's fittings, hang them or dress the dummies, then open the doors at nine and not stop. I ran up and down the stairs to the workroom so many times a day that my calves grew firm with muscles (which of course I hated because I still longed to be thin and slight). We would close the doors at seven in the evening when the last fittings were finished, sit in silence on the walnut couch together for a few minutes, then bid each other goodnight and go home to eat and keep working.

I was constantly amazed we didn't fight more given the long hours we spent in high stress together, but perhaps it was because we were too tired to disagree about anything. Apart from good morning and good night, Betty and I really only talked about business. It was a far cry from our time in the typing pool together.

In December that year, Betty and I had been invited to a party held by one of our clients, a local socialite named Gabby Powers. Her father was a rich industrialist with four sons and one daughter, whom he doted on. Gabby had bought easily a dozen gowns from us over the years and always included us on guest lists for society parties. This one promised to be the biggest of all. A Christmas-birthday party, because Gabby's birthday was Christmas Eve.

Melbourne in December was usually still mild, but that evening it was unbearably warm, as a dry hot wind from the very centre of Australia had the city in its grip. I dressed for the evening in a sleeveless, pale-pink crepe gown with a deep V-neck mirrored in a V-waist, a cluster of bracelets on my right wrist. I had enough skin bare to endure the suffocating heat, but poor Harry in his tuxedo and black tie looked as though he might expire as we found our place cards at a large round table, festooned with summer flowers and Christmas decorations. The ballroom of the Powers' mansion was enormous, but the hot air seemed to be trapped. Every window and door was propped open, but not even the shadow of a breeze came to our rescue. A band played 'If I Should Lose You'. Nobody danced.

'Are you too warm?' I asked Harry.

'I am, but I'm not complaining. This room is full of people I need to meet,' he said, running his gaze across the crowd. 'Or get to know better.' Harry was busy building a network of influential people, both to increase his client base and to advance his political aspirations. He returned his eyes to me. 'You look very pretty, Zara.'

I couldn't stop myself from smiling. 'And you look very dashing.'

He leaned in and kissed my cheek, and was about to whisper in my ear when he pulled back and said, 'Is that Duncan Haversham?'

I looked around but he was already out of his seat and on his way to meet someone.

I picked up my champagne coupe and sipped it. I was still doubtful about wines and so on, as they made me silly and gave me a headache the next day, but these society events seemed to demand the drinking of it. I'd become used to adding ice to my champagne, and adept at drinking it very slowly. My eyes followed Harry, who stopped with his back to me and engaged two very elderly gentlemen by the door. The room was lit with chandeliers, which picked out highlights and shadows on the plaster murals of Greek goddesses. I let the music and the chatter and laughter drift over me as I swirled my champagne in its glass. I caught a glimpse of Tom Ramsay and knew Betty must be nearby. I rose to go and find her, but then she accosted me suddenly from behind and said, 'Boo!'

I whirled and grasped her hands, laughing. 'Oh, you fool. You could have given me a heart attack and then where would you be? Running Magg alone.'

Her eyes grew serious. 'Ouch,' she said.

'I'm only joking.'

'Sit down,' she said, and a shiver of that constant fear washed over me.

I sat down and she moved her chair to face me and placed her hands on my knees. I saw it straight away. A diamond ring.

'Tom asked you?' I gasped, and of course my first thought was for my wretched self, still unengaged. 'Congratulations. That is wonderful. I am so very happy for you both.' I reached for the champagne coupe to raise it, but she stilled my hand.

'Thank you, Zara. But there is a sting in the tail, so to speak.'

'Go on.'

'Tom's family is . . . well, they think that . . .'

'That what?'

'That women shouldn't work once they're married. Tom said he doesn't mind, but his mother is . . . quite the opinionated lady. There is no question about it. I have to leave Magg.'

'What? No!'

'Magg is you anyway. Your designs. You keep it. Keep it all, the couch and the sewing machines and –'

'It wouldn't be right. We started the salon together, built it together. I should buy you out.'

'No, no. Tom's family has a lot of money. I won't need yours.' The Ramsays owned a boot-polish company. 'Run Magg by yourself.'

Run Magg by myself? How was that even possible? Betty and I were already doing the work of four people. No, I would have to give it up.

I did not want to give it up. Every cell in my body resisted the thought. I took a gulp of champagne. It was watery as the ice had melted so fast.

'I am sorry, darling. I've put you in a pickle, haven't I?' Betty said, rubbing my arm.

'You don't want to keep going? You're sure? Could you not just defy the mother-in-law?'

But Betty was already shaking her head. 'If I want Tom, I can't have Magg. And I do want him, so very much. And look, wonders never cease – he finally proposed. So there's hope for you too. Do you want me to get Tom to have a word with Harry?'

'Oh lord, no. Pressure makes him run in the opposite direction. We'll just end up having a row.' I forced a smile. 'I really am so very happy for you, darling. I just wish this new beginning for you wasn't also the end of something so wonderful. How much longer do I have you?'

'A month? Mama Ramsay is keen for me to be out of it. But, Zara, you will do my wedding dress for me, won't you?'

I thought of all those designs for wedding dresses I'd imagined on myself and felt a pang. 'Of course. I would love that.'

Harry sauntered over then. I turned my attention to him. 'What do you know, Harry, Betty and Tom are getting married.'

Betty wiggled her fingers in front of him.

'Very shiny,' Harry said with a grin.

'I'm a very lucky girl,' she said. 'But I had better go and find my future husband before he drinks too much of that Bordeaux. Do excuse me.'

I watched her go then asked Harry, 'How did your meeting go?'

'It wasn't Haversham at all. But I did just spend fifteen minutes in conversation with two very lovely Scottish gentlemen, one of whom is an expert on church history, the other on fly-fishing. Most fascinating.'

I couldn't tell if he was joking or not. Harry found most people fascinating, truth be told. He had a quick and curious mind, and the enthusiasm of others always rubbed off on him.

'They did tell me there's a garden out through the kitchen, and it's much cooler there,' he continued. 'Shall we take a little stroll? It's oppressive in here.'

I stood and took his arm. 'Yes, please. Because I need your advice quite urgently.'

We made our way over to where the waiters were entering and exiting the ballroom, and slipped through a huge kitchen and past a steaming scullery to an open back door. It led out to a garden overhung with birch trees. Almost as many people were out here as inside; it was not a great deal cooler, but there was far more cigarette smoke. Harry led me down towards the fence line, where it was darker but quieter. He hitched up his coat tails and sat on the fence. I leaned my hip against it and waited for my eyes to adjust to the dark.

'Urgent advice, then?' he said. 'Ask away.'

'Betty's leaving Magg.' Saying it aloud made it feel more true. A sad, heavy sensation came over me, and out of nowhere I began to cry. 'I don't know what to do.'

He very gently pulled me towards him, and I was enveloped by his smell. Soap flakes and Brylcreem. 'Don't cry,' he soothed. 'What do you *want* to do?'

'I want things to stay the same,' I sniffed. He pulled out a handkerchief and I took it gratefully, though I felt a little silly for crying. 'I'm sorry. I feel overwhelmed.'

'What do you want to do?' he asked me again. 'Do you want to keep designing dresses?'

'Yes. For my whole life if I can.'

'Then the answer is simple. Buy her out and run the business yourself. You won't have to share the profits so you can pay somebody to help.'

'Betty said I didn't have to buy her out.'

'Well, you won't listen to that nonsense. It's much cleaner if you owe her nothing.' He put his hands at my waist. 'How about tomorrow afternoon, we sit down together and draw up a document. List your assets, estimate their value and come up with a plan to pay her out. Then hire a good bookkeeper and get on with being a famous fashion designer, with a very handsome boyfriend.'

I giggled. 'You would be a dear to help me.'

'You're my girl, Zara. You always will be.'

I considered him in the dark. Behind us, I could hear the faint sound of the orchestra. 'It's going to be a lot of work, Harry.'

'Work is good for the soul, my love.' He gestured with his head back towards the house. 'Shall we return to the party?'

As the evening wore on, a huge thunderstorm blew in. We all drank and laughed and danced as the rain hammered, chilling the hot air and trapping us all inside. Harry convinced Betty that it was best for our friendship that I buy her out officially, and I was so buoyed by the company and the thrill of the storm that I truly believed running Magg solo was going to be the best thing that ever happened to me.

———

By February, within two weeks of Betty's departure, I realised just how in over my head I was. Part of the problem was simply my personality. I liked dreaming up dresses, draping them on dummies, playing around with colours and textures. But when it came to detailed work, I had relied heavily on Betty. Darts and seams and fastenings, where and how they would sit, were things I hadn't given much thought to before. I hadn't realised how much Betty's sharp reminders to me and careful instructions to the seamstresses had made Magg gowns such high quality. And then there was the book-keeper – a little bald fellow named Henry Fitzhenry, who I was immediately frightened of because of the tsk-ing noise he made whenever he looked at my system of sorting invoices (that is, all dumped on top of each other in a drawer) or how far behind we were at sending out reminder notices. I shook in my shoes every time I saw him come through the door, and foolishly nodded at whatever he said to me, even when I didn't understand it. Half the time I couldn't remember the difference between creditors and debtors – Betty had always called them 'people we owe' and 'people who owe us' – and after he tsk-ed about Betty's ledgers and drew up his own with very neat small handwriting, I lost any comprehension I'd had about what was going on with the money.

But I was far too busy to think about money. All I did was work, dawn till dark, seven days a week. Mum was horrified when I stopped coming to church, but there simply wasn't time. Some weeks I would see Harry only once, for an hour or so after he finished work and dropped in to sit on the walnut couch while I pinned paper patterns on the dummies or tried to make sense of the following day's diary. If he was upset that I wasn't creeping into his boarding house for evenings of passion, he gave no indication. If anything, he seemed puffed up with pride for me, and liked to watch me work. If I despaired at ever having free time again, he'd just kiss me and say, 'Things will settle into a rhythm soon, I'm certain.'

They did not, and once again my mood began to falter. I woke before dawn every day as if prodded by a chilly finger, and lay there for long minutes, my heart racing and a feeling of dread sitting heavy in my stomach. The first few hours of work, before the customers began to arrive, were the worst. That feeling of watching myself from outside, as I worked like a wind-up doll, didn't leave me until the first lady of the day swanned through my salon door. Then I applied a smile and made small talk or dropped vivid compliments as though there were nothing at all wrong. The dark mood would lift. I was caught in a whirl of conversation and activity, sending instructions and gowns up and down the stairs to the workroom, and playing the part of the competent, extroverted young businesswoman to perfection.

I can't remember how soon into this nightmarish period of my life I stopped eating, but I do remember the day I caught sight of myself in the long oval mirror in the salon and noticed how small my waist had become. I was highly satisfied by this, of course, and determined that being too busy for food was no bad thing.

Luckily, the first time I fainted was at home.

I had been drawing designs at the dining room table late in the evening while Daddy puffed on his pipe and listened to the wireless. I stood up to go to my room and fetch a pencil sharpener when the world around me warped and went grey. Next thing I knew, I was lying on the rug with a thudding headache and Daddy bending over me.

'Violet!' he was calling. 'Violet, come quickly. Zara isn't well.'

Then Mum was there and I was struggling to sit up, but she pushed me back down. 'What happened?' she asked.

'I fell,' I said.

'You passed out,' Daddy corrected me. 'I saw you. You stood up, your eyes rolled back and you passed out. What on earth is wrong with you?'

Mum brushed my curls off my forehead and pressed a cool hand into my skin. 'She doesn't have a temperature but she's very pale and clammy. Zara, when did you last eat? You've barely been home for your tea this month.'

I felt confused and it hurt to think. 'I can't remember,' I admitted.

'Help her up, Sydney. But slowly. I'll fetch her water and something to eat. Get her on the settee.'

Mum hurried off and Daddy put his arm around my back and encouraged me to my feet. My ears rang faintly. I eased myself onto the settee and put my feet up. Daddy stood there looking down at me. 'You're working too hard. Nobody forgets to eat unless they're working too hard.'

'I don't forget. I just don't have time.' And I liked being thin. I glanced down at my wrists and saw a pleasing lack of pudge.

Mum returned with a thick slice of bread with butter and jam. 'Here, get this inside you. I've got tea brewing as well.'

I took the bread and started eating. It was sublime.

'Things aren't right with you, Zara,' Mum said. 'The pressure of running the salon by yourself is going to make you sick.'

'I'm not going to make myself sick,' I said, though at that moment I felt distinctly awful.

'No, you're not, because I'm not going to let you,' Mum declared. 'Starting tomorrow, I'll be bringing you lunch every day and seeing that you eat it.'

'Mum, I'm terribly busy at the salon.'

'I won't hear no.'

Mum was as good as her word. At twelve o'clock every day she arrived with a lunch box, usually with a cheese scone and a cut-up piece of fruit in it. Very cleverly designed to be eaten with one hand while the other was busy. Understanding Mum was not to be refused on this, I began to clear my diary for half an hour at noon and honestly did feel better after a few days. Mum also used the visits as an excuse to help out. She was happy to run things up to the work-room for me, or tidy up, or open my mail and record the cheques in the ledger for Mr Fitzhenry. I tried to offer to pay for her help but she wouldn't hear of it, and usually left around two, taking the empty lunch box with her.

But Mum's presence didn't ease the nightmare. I was exhausted all the way to my marrow, always behind and trying to catch up, and completely without the wherewithal to organise the flow of my work to fix it. I became less reliable. I lost a few minor customers, though I was very careful not to lose the major ones. I tried so hard to please everybody, but it grew more and more difficult to hide the cold dread that had gripped me. Harder to smile. Harder to make conversation. Impossible to keep up.

It was June the day Mum came in to drop off lunch and I couldn't stop. I was dressing two ladies at once, and a third had just come in off the street to browse. Mum sat on the walnut couch, waiting for me to take the lunch box. An hour passed. Two. I dealt with all the customers but two more came in, and that's when Mum stood up and said, 'Enough!'

I froze. The two customers froze.

'Out!' she said to them. 'Come back in an hour.'

'Well, I never,' said one lady, but Mum's Scottish temper had been roused.

'Can't you see she's exhausted? Leave her be. Go on. Off you go.'

The ladies returned to the street and Mum locked the door behind them.

'Mum, they might have been paying customers.'

'I've seen the cheques coming in. You have quite enough to live on.'

'My reputation, Mum.' But I sat heavily next to her and reached for the lunch box. A sweet, fat pear and a ham roll.

She watched me eat for a few moments then said, 'You know this has to stop.'

It was the hardest, truest thing she could have said to me, and I started to cry.

'Ah, there,' she said, putting her arm around me.

'I love this work so much, Mum. I can hire more seamstresses, but I can't hire another me. The designs and patterns *are* Magg. Elsie can't do them. You can't. Nobody can.'

Mum fell silent for a little while. Then, seeming to choose her words carefully, she said, 'You are so wrapped up in Magg that you've lost sight of life. Life isn't about work. It's about love and family. You and Harry will marry soon enough, then there will be babies to look after, and this will all be behind you. Small and flat, like something you see a long way off.'

My first instinct was to rail against her words. Anyone could be a wife and a mother, but of course I had already failed at attaining both of those roles, so perhaps anyone but me could.

'I know Magg used to make you happy,' Mum said, 'but since Betty left, it's made you sad.'

'It's such a big decision,' I said, but already I was feeling the relief. I imagined waking up and having nothing to fill my day, and a lazy calm swept through me.

'Why don't you speak to Jack's Aunt Maddie, then?' Mum said. 'She's been a great supporter of yours, and Vieve will happily write to her or ring her up for you.'

I nodded. 'That's a good idea.'

'Take your time deciding. Talk to Harry of course. See if he has any plans . . . if you know what I'm saying.'

'Mum, I don't ask him about those kinds of plans,' I said through a mouthful of bread and ham.

'Perhaps you should. Don't think that you bring nothing to a marriage with him, Zara. He is very happy to meet the people you know, whether they're customers or your father's business contacts. He will lose more than you if he lets you slip away.'

'I'm not going to slip away. I love him. Madly.'

'With an emphasis on the mad, for both of you. You seem to drive each other to madness. Love ought to be a bit calmer, sweet pea. It is for your father and me.'

I stifled a laugh. I had heard Mum give Daddy the sharp edge of her tongue a few times, but she was right that they didn't fight the way Harry and I did.

A big wave of exhaustion rolled over me. 'Perhaps I'll close up early and go home to read in bed,' I said.

'Now you're talking sense. I have the new Georgette Heyer book from the library, but I'll let you read it first.' She stroked my hair away from my forehead. 'Take your time deciding,' she said. 'But listen to your instincts. They've led you well this far.'

———

The following Saturday I left the reluctant Elsie in charge at three in the afternoon, and met Aunt Maddie across the street at the Wattle.

'I've already ordered,' she said, when I joined her at the table.

'Oh, that is brilliant,' I replied, perching my handbag on the windowsill.

'Well, you did say on the telephone you hadn't much time. I do hope tea and Victoria sponge will do.'

Victoria sponge was my favourite. I nodded enthusiastically. 'Thank you so much for making time to speak with me.'

'I should be thanking you, shouldn't I? Since we first met . . . was that three years ago?'

'Nearly four,' I said.

'In that time you've become a bigger name in fashion than I ever was, my dear. I drop your name all the time.' She smiled, sending deep lines across her cheeks. 'Quite the big-time success. I like to think I played my part.'

'You did. Your encouragement meant everything to me. And your wisdom.' The waitress arrived with a tea tray, and placed a china pot and two white and blue cups between us, then served us each a slice of Victoria sponge. She was distracted and a spot of tea slopped from the spout onto the white tablecloth.

'I am sorry,' she said.

'It's fine,' Aunt Maddie told her. 'You look very busy.'

The waitress glanced behind her and grimaced. 'We've served eighty high teas today. We ran out of cucumbers.'

'A disaster!' Maddie said. 'Don't worry about the tea. You're a good girl.'

The waitress thanked her with a timid smile and scurried off.

'You see?' I said. 'You bring out the best in everyone. And today I need your advice.'

'Go on. I'll pour the tea.'

I took a deep breath. 'Since Betty left I've been running the business myself.'

'You have staff though?'

'Yes, but . . . it's all down to me. What I'm good at is designing dresses, chatting to people while they have fittings. But the rest is so difficult. I feel quite overwhelmed and I . . .' Unexpectedly, my voice cracked and I knew I was about to cry. I stopped, mortified.

Maddie placed the pot on the table and reached across for my hand. She had gold rings on every finger. 'Of course, you do, my dear. Magg is a very successful business, and you are a very young woman. Of course, you feel overwhelmed. When Betty was with you it was probably a bit of mad fun. I saw you two together – partners in crime. But now, perhaps it's not fun anymore?'

'That's exactly it,' I managed.

'It's a serious business. From here you could grow it, hire the right people, open more salons . . . How does that thought make you feel?'

'Full of dread.'

'As I said, you are very young.'

I scooped a forkful of my cake into my mouth.

'Are you thinking of closing up? Because I know somebody who would buy your business in an instant.'

'You do?' I hadn't even thought of selling. What was there to sell? Sewing machines and shop dummies?

'An Italian gentleman who is a friend of a friend. He was most impressed that I knew you. He has a salon in Sydney and would likely pay good money for Magg.'

'I'm not sure I understand. For the name, Magg?'

'No, he'd use the same name as his Sydney salon. He'd pay for your business, dear – your client list, the fixtures and machinery, whatever stock you have left. But mostly your client list. It's the envy of many in the industry.'

My lack of business savvy embarrassed me. 'I didn't realise somebody would pay for . . . I mean I supposed I would just shut down and the clients would go elsewhere.'

'You and Betty did a marvellous job of building up the business. It's worth something.' Maddie took a sip of hter tea. 'Do you want me to talk to him? Just to see? There is no obligation on you to sell. You can keep doing precisely what you're doing, but at least you'll have some options to consider. Might make you feel less trapped.'

'I . . . yes. Yes, I would like to talk to him. Would you give him my telephone number?'

'Absolutely, my dear. No promises about whether or not he'll call. His name is Alessandro and he's quite handsome, though of course far too young for me. Not for you though.'

I chuckled. 'You know I have a boyfriend, Aunt Maddie.'

'Do you though?'

'Harry. You've met him . . . at Mrs Carlinghurst's party, remember?'

'Oh, I know very well about Harry,' she said with a wry twist to her mouth. 'I think I may know more about Harry than you.'

Puzzlement fought with a prickle of fear. 'I'm not sure I follow.'

'Harry is your boyfriend, is he?'

'Well, yes.'

'Then why did I see him a week ago walking in very deep conversation with a red-haired lass in Fitzroy Gardens?'

My ears began to ring, and that all-too-familiar feeling of being outside myself came over me. Somehow I was smiling, adopting a bright tone. 'Harry has many clients and contacts. He's trying to get himself known. He wants to go into politics, you know. Perhaps she was a friend from the United Australia Party.'

Maddie sat back in her seat and sipped her tea. 'Yes, perhaps she was. I didn't mean to alarm you, my dear. But do be careful. You have a gentle heart; you need to be with a man who treats you gently.'

'I assure you Harry is very good to me.' I crumbled some more cake with my fork, but my appetite had retreated.

'Drink your tea,' Maddie said gently. 'Get your strength up for the rest of the afternoon. You looked tired, thin and pale. Not in a good way.' She reached across the table again and stroked my wrist. 'See what Alessandro says, then we can talk again if you like. I'm always here if you'd like some advice – about the fashion business, or about men.'

I feigned brightness and changed the subject, but the seed of doubt had already been sown.

———

'It's here.' Mum opened the door as I was climbing the front stairs, brandishing an envelope.

I snatched it out of her hands. 'When did it arrive? Why didn't you bring it down to the salon?' I shrugged off the large shoulder bag of work I brought home every night, and Mum helped me with my coat and closed the door behind me.

'I wanted you to be able to concentrate properly when you opened it. You have a big decision ahead of you. Come on, come on. We've eaten dinner but I kept yours warm in the oven.'

She ushered me into the dining room and I sat and turned the envelope over. The return address was Alessandro Olivetti, the man who wanted to buy Magg. He had spent three weeks making lengthy store visits, poring over the ledgers with Mr Fitzhenry and measuring up the workroom. He was a good-looking fellow in his late forties, and Harry had been pleasingly jealous about his attention.

The last I'd seen Mr Olivetti, a week ago, he had said he'd put an offer in writing 'soon'. Every day since I'd been on tenterhooks. As had Mum, who had become very invested in the idea that I stop working and start eating.

'Wait for me before you open it,' Mum called from the kitchen.

I sat there, looking at the envelope. In it was the answer. If the offer was too low, I wouldn't sell. I wouldn't let him take advantage of my youth and sex. I had poured too many hours into Magg. Harry had asked me how much it would have to be for me to say yes, and I told him I didn't know, but secretly I'd set the figure at £800. That was my estimation of the worth of the business, and enough to pay Daddy back and hold me over while I decided what to do next.

It was also enough for a deposit on a little house, if Harry could be persuaded to marry. And why wouldn't he? If his hesitation was around money problems, and the problems went away . . .

Mum appeared at my shoulder before my imagination could head too far down that path. She placed a bowl of stew at my elbow and said, 'Go on, then. Open it.'

I stilled the tremble in my hands and tore open the envelope, unfolded the letter and gasped.

Mum gasped too.

I tried to make my eyes focus on the words but all I had seen was the figure. £1500.

£1500.

I placed the letter on the table and pressed my hands into my hot cheeks. 'I can buy a house,' I said.

Mum's voice was thick with excitement. 'You can do *whatever you want.*' She turned towards the lounge room. 'Sydney!' she called. 'Sydney, come here right away.'

It was as though I was glued to my seat, and everything around me – Mum's excited voice, Dad gripping my shoulder with pride, my brothers coming to find out what the fuss was about – seemed to be happening a long way away. In my mind I was in a little house, cutting up vegetables for dinner. Harry had just come in the door and taken off his hat. We kissed. His hand smoothed over my belly, which was round and ripe. No more sneaking around the boarding-house superintendent, no more seeing each other once or twice a week because we were both so busy, no more deep conversations with redheads in Fitzroy Gardens. All of it was right here, in this incredible offer from Mr Olivetti.

Everything changes, in this moment.

David was asking me if I'd buy him a car, and he gave me a hard shake. 'Zara, I'm talking to you.'

I shook off the fantasy. 'No, I'm not buying you a car. The first thing I'm going to do is pay Daddy back.'

'Not if you're buying a house. Use every penny, and stay close by,' Daddy said.

Mum beamed at me. 'We are so proud of you, my love.'

I shot out of my seat. 'I have to go to Harry and tell him.'

'Nonsense, just ring him up. After you've eaten,' Daddy said. 'You've been working all day.'

But Mum shushed him. 'She needs to speak to him face to face,' she said.

She understood what this money meant to my relationship with Harry. She knew the stubborn hurdle to our marrying had now been removed, and she wanted that wedding as much as I did.

'I'll take you over in the car then,' Daddy said grudgingly. 'But you'll have thirty minutes, and I'm waiting outside.'

I was relieved by the offer. I was exhausted and overexcited, and did not fancy waiting for the tram in the cold dark. I snatched up the letter.

'Yes. Yes, let's go now.'

———

Daddy was mortified about parking at the back gate to the boarding house, as it became clear to him in that moment that I must have been sneaking in and out of it for months. He gruffly told me to be back by eight thirty or he would be knocking on the front door and alerting the superintendent. I promised him he wouldn't have to suffer such indignity.

I made my way through the back door and up the stairs to Harry's room, knocking twice quietly.

A few moments later the door opened. He grinned. 'There's my girl,' he said. 'What a lovely surprise.'

'I have news,' I said.

'You certainly do. Your eyes are bright and your cheeks are flushed.' He ushered me in then closed the door behind me. 'I presume the Italian has made you an offer?'

Rather than speak, I handed him the letter. In his way, he didn't even raise an eyebrow and he read it from top to bottom. It was a legal offer and Harry was no doubt interested in the details. As I waited, I glanced around his little room. Neat as a pin, the bed with its checked blanket tidy and smooth, papers in organised piles on the wooden desk under the window that looked over the street. The only light was from the lamp on the desk, shining bright and hot on the briefs he had been working on.

Once he'd finished reading the letter his eyes rose to meet mine. 'And this is enough to make you sell?'

'It's nearly twice as much.'

He took my arms and pulled me towards him. 'My clever, clever Zara.'

I let him hold me for a moment then pulled away. 'Harry, you know what this means?'

'That you're rich at twenty-three?'

I nodded. 'Yes, I can buy a house. We can get married. You can go to work and I'll keep myself busy with my designs but just here and there . . . no salon, no long hours . . . we can start a family and . . .' I became aware that the smile had faded from his face, and my body went cold. 'Harry? No. Don't say it.'

'It's not right to marry yet.'

'But we have the money now. You always said –'

'I always said when *I* was not in such an insecure position. When *I* had enough to provide for you. Not the other way around. I'm a man. I have my dignity, Zara.'

'But . . . but this is nonsense, Harry. This is pure nonsense. You earn a good living.'

'Some weeks. Some weeks I earn nothing.'

'We can budget. We can leave £100 in the bank for emergencies. Do you not see? We will have a house to ourselves.' I gestured around the room. 'You can't honestly say you'd rather be here than with me, in a house.'

'Zara, I want to be with you in a house more than anything,' he said. 'But not like this.'

My shock, my sadness, suddenly turned to fury. 'You have no intention of *ever* marrying me, do you?'

'Zara, you know that's not true. You know you're my girl and always will be.'

'Am I? Not the redhead you were seen walking with in Fitzroy Gardens?'

'Redhead? What?' Anger tightened his brow. 'What are you talking about?'

'I have friends, you know. They've seen you with other girls.' This was an exaggeration of course, but once my fuse was lit, it was impossible to stamp out. 'Do they come here too, to your nasty little room? Do you make them sneak around like whores too?'

'Why are you speaking to me this way?' he said. 'You know I have many contacts, and I can't afford to refuse a brief if it's offered by somebody you're afraid I'll take to bed. You know what you should do with that money, Zara? You should spend it on growing up. You're a petulant child half the time. You should go overseas and see the world, and understand what goes on beyond your narrow, privileged little bubble.'

'My narrow, privileged little bubble has been very useful to you, hasn't it now?' I shot back. 'How many new clients, how many of your new political friends have you greased yourself onto because of me, my business, my family? And you won't even offer me the respect of making me your wife? I'm a laughing-stock, waiting for you. You spoke of your dignity before, but you care nothing for mine.'

He put his hands up, Harry's favourite gesture for telling me he was done with an argument, which always happened at the very moment I was reaching the peak of my rage. I smacked his hands down, making my fingers sting.

'Yes, the argument is over,' I said. 'Everything is over. All of it. Maybe I will go overseas. As far from you as I can get.'

Harry turned and walked away from me, sat at his desk and picked up his reading glasses. Went back to work as though I wasn't there.

I turned on my heel and left, and this time I was determined with everything in my heart that I would not forgive him. That forgiving him was pointless. He would never marry me.

———

Mum could see on my face what had happened and she brought me a cup of tea in bed and let me cry on her shoulder. When I woke the next morning, my eyes were swollen and puffy, and dragging myself out of bed for work was next to impossible. But I did it. I instructed

Mr Fitzhenry to write to Mr Olivetti with my acceptance of his offer, and I prepared myself to hand the business over.

A strange calm settled upon me because it was finally over. Harry, of course, continued to try to ring me up, but I had instructed every member of my family to tell him I wouldn't speak to him. Daddy was so embarrassed by the idea he might have to do this that he stopped answering the telephone all together.

Harry turned up at the salon at six o'clock on Friday and stood there on the threshold, the usual sheepish smile on his face. I hardened my heart. *It's over, it's over, it's over.*

'Can I take you to dinner?' he asked.

'It's over,' I said.

'No, it isn't. It never is,' he replied.

I approached him and he opened his arms, but instead of snuggling into him, I grasped his shoulder and turned him towards the door. 'Don't come here again,' I said.

He shrugged me off, grasped my upper arm. 'Zara, what are you doing? Stop this.'

'I have stopped. I've stopped all of it. It's over, Harry.'

'You don't mean that,' he said with a smile, releasing me and spreading his palms. 'But I'll give you some time to think it through.'

He walked off down the street, whistling. *Whistling.* I loved him and hated him in equal measure, and it would always be like this as long as we lived in the same town and moved in the same circles. I began to feel the first glimmer of truth in what he had said. *Go overseas, see the world.* I remembered the feeling I'd had when I read the letter, that everything was about to change. Perhaps it was, but in a different way to how I imagined it. I closed the door to the salon and locked it, closed my eyes and wondered how far I would have to go to escape my feelings for Harry.

PART 2

PART 2

INTERLUDE

When they leave late in the evening, she drives, even though he is a terrible passenger. He flinches at stop signs and grumbles as she crunches through the gears on a steep hill. She laughs it off; they have played out these tiny dramas a million times before. 'Carguments', she calls them, and they are usually short-lived. But she has to do the driving because at any moment he might need to duck below the window line, especially leaving the Peninsula and heading out through some of the more densely populated suburbs of Melbourne. Before midnight, they are well out into countryside, the headlights on their maroon Pontiac illuminating the straight road ahead, the trees and long waving grass beside, the occasional flash of a marsupial disappearing into the woodlands. She yawns and he offers to drive a little while. She is overcome by a ridiculous but terrible suspicion that if she lets him drive, somehow he will get away from her. Reverse her plans. Foil her.

'I can drive,' she says. 'I'm not that tired. I slept well past noon.'

He reaches across and puts his hand on her knee. 'I know. I watched you for an hour. You looked so peaceful.'

Peaceful. It is not how she expected to feel after the horrors of yesterday. The rushed journey from Canberra. The relentless beating of the helicopters overhead. The feeling that the earth was collapsing beneath her feet.

'I always sleep well when you're next to me,' she replies, though it isn't strictly true. Many nights she has lain there while he sleeps; he oblivious to the hurt he caused, she glaring at him murderously in the dark. She imagines all marriages have such moments.

There is no talking for a while, just the sound of the road underneath them, when he finally asks, 'Where are we going?'

'I want to take you somewhere I know you were happy. Is that mad?'

'No, it's a lovely idea.'

'So I thought I'd take you to your grandparents' house at Nubba.'

'I haven't seen that house in years. Nobody lives there anymore.'

'It's perfect, isn't it? It's a good distance out of town so we are unlikely to be . . . disturbed by neighbours and so on.'

'Disturbed? You mean "recognised"?'

'That's right. That's what I mean.'

'Then why are we heading north-west? We should be heading north-east.'

'This road seemed quieter.'

'It adds hours to the journey.'

'I just . . . I don't want anyone to see us.'

'Fair enough.' He leans back in his seat and closes his eyes.

'Don't,' she says. 'I need to stay awake.'

He rolls his head towards her. 'Let's stop and sleep for half an hour. You take the back seat and stretch out, and I'll sleep right here.'

She nods. 'Yes, it was a silly idea leaving in the middle of the night. We should have waited until morning.' She indicates and pulls off the side of the road, down a little gully and into the long grass. 'Are you sure you're all right in the front seat?'

'Yes, of course. Go on. Get some rest. You've been driving for hours.'

She climbs over and lies down on the plump back seat, kicks off her shoes and wiggles her toes. 'I am tired.' She yawns, but she's afraid to close her eyes. 'You won't run off on me, will you?'

'What? No.'

'I don't want to wake up and find . . . you're not here.'

'I will be here. You can sleep perfectly happily.'

'Thank you, Harry,' she sighs, and closes her eyes.

———

By eight the next morning, they are driving in to Jerilderie, the town the famed Ned Kelly gang victimised nearly a hundred years ago. Zara's right knee is sore and cramping; she has never driven for this long before, and her knees are getting stiffer as she gets older. A drab motel looms on the right and she points it out.

'Can we stop? We can catch up on some sleep and head off again late at night.'

'Are we to become nocturnal, my love?'

'If that's what it takes,' she answers, but recognises this isn't realistic. She has already slowed the car and is glancing around for other traffic, other eyes. The town is small and quiet. 'Duck down and stay hidden. I'll see if they have a room.'

Harry complies. She locks the car and crosses the road. Her heel gets caught in a crack between the road and the shoulder, and she steadies herself but feels a pull in her stiff knee. Limping now, she opens the door to the musty hotel reception and rings the bell.

In time, a shuffling, plump woman in a grey dress emerges and eyes her curiously.

'Can I help? Are you lost?'

Lost. Yes, I am so very lost.

'I wonder if I might take a room for the night.'

The woman glances at the clock on the wall. 'Check-in is usually midday.'

'I'll pay for two nights. I'm in the middle of a long drive. I rather overestimated what I was capable of.'

The woman shrugs. 'You can pay for two nights.'

She reaches into her handbag and pulls out some notes, and in exchange gets a key. She returns to the car and starts the engine. 'Be very careful now,' she says to Harry.

'Come on, I'm going to do my back in hiding like this.'

She drives to the parking space directly outside the door to their motel room. Furtively, making sure nobody is looking, they hurry inside.

'Ah, bed,' Harry says, easing himself onto the quilted bedspread with a sigh.

She can't relax as quickly as him. Her mind is whirring. What now? She doesn't know what happens next.

He seems to sense what she's thinking. 'It's enough that we're here together,' he says.

'It's enough that we're here together,' she repeats, as though the repetition will make it true. Like a spell. Why shouldn't she believe in spells?

'We will wait out the day here, then head off late again. Just the same as yesterday.' He pats the bed beside him.

She can barely remember yesterday now. She's tired and confused and . . . hungry. She must be hungry by now, as must he.

'I should go and get us some food,' she says. 'I'll rest later.'

'As you wish. This is your road trip, Zara.'

'Don't go anywhere.'

'I'm not going anywhere.'

He keeps saying that, but her heart doesn't quite believe it.

——

The general store is open, and it is a wonderland of goods for sale. Sweets in jars on the counter, whips and saddles on the back wall, huge bags of grain in stacks taking up the middle of the store. She walks the aisles on creaking floorboards but can't decide what to buy. She has no appetite, for one of the first times in her life. But she can't leave Harry alone for too long in case he slips off, so she grabs a loaf of sliced bread and a jar of jam and takes them to the counter. It's here she sees a thin stack of yesterday's newspaper on the shelf below the counter. Huge letters. HOLT LOST IN SEA, PRESUMED DEAD.

Waves of heat and chill pass through her.

Well, they can presume him dead all they like; she knows differently. He is waiting for her back in their dingy motel room, and he is alive and with her and he loves her, and all is well. All is well.

She keeps her head down and sunglasses on as she pays, but the fellow behind the counter seems entirely uninterested in her. As he counts out her change, she flips over the newspaper so she can't see the headline.

———

'Harry,' she asks as they lie in bed after their long sleep and eat jam sandwiches, 'what is your favourite memory of our life together?'

'There are too many,' he says. 'Don't make me choose. We have done so many exciting things.'

'I mean ordinary things, not exciting things. You know, I am perfectly happy lying here in bed next to you eating jam sandwiches. That to me is more wonderful than attending Queen Elizabeth's coronation.'

'Ordinary things? Then all of it, Zara. Why do you push me to isolate moments? Time and love don't work like that. When you are with me, I'm content.'

She snuggles her cheek against his shoulder and strokes his hairy chest, realising too late her fingers are sticky with jam. 'Sorry,' she says. About the jam, about asking for reassurance, about everything.

'You don't need to be sorry.'

———

They resume their journey at night and arrive at the old farmhouse before dawn. Harry takes the torch out of the glove box and they mount the front stairs to the veranda. She hasn't thought about how they will get in, but Harry is already standing on tiptoes, reaching for one of the wooden beams under the veranda roof. On top of it he finds a key.

'Grandma always hid one up here,' he says, holding out the key for her to see.

All right, then, she thinks.

He unlocks the door and a musty smell greets them.

'How long has the house been sitting here with nobody living in it?' she asks.

He doesn't answer. Perhaps he doesn't know either. He tries the light switch, but there's no electricity. 'Going back in time.' He laughs, sweeping the torch beam around. Furniture under dust covers, rat droppings on the floor. 'Home, sweet home,' he says.

'For now,' she answers.

———

The first few days are easy. They clean and scrub the house down, bring the furniture back to life, wash the linen in the cupboard and hang it on the back veranda in the sunshine. When evening comes, they sit on the veranda and watch the rolling land change colour. Right on the edge of twilight, she sometimes sees traces of sparkling light. Fairies, perhaps. She has always loved them, and now it seems they might be real. As though anything might be real.

But at the end of the first week, she is struggling to think what they might do with their time. Harry, in particular, who has spent his life rising early, working for two hours before breakfast, then steadily making his way through briefs and paperwork until dinner-time, must surely be struggling.

'Don't be bored,' she says to him.

He nods agreeably. 'All right.'

'I think we will be here a long time.'

'I can occupy myself painting the railings and fixing the house and taming the garden. You'll need to go into town to get everything I need, though.'

'That will work.'

She visits a different place every time she goes shopping. A network of tiny towns exists out here, and she doesn't want to draw attention to herself. Sometimes she even goes all the way to Yass, and finds that in some ways it's easier to go unrecognised here. People in larger towns don't notice strangers as much. Hiding in plain sight.

———

She is not so afraid of leaving Harry anymore. Months pass and he stays put reliably. The days fall into a rhythm, entirely predictable. No surprises. She is mostly content.

But then she starts to think about the children, because of course they must be missing her. Harry had said nobody could know, but surely it would be cruel not to contact them.

A telephone booth stands outside the post office in Wallendbeen, and next time she's in town she drops a coin in the slot and dials her daughter-in-law Caroline's number. It's the only one she knows by heart because Caroline has been working in Zara's business the last few years.

'Hello?'

'It's me.'

A short silence, then a gush of emotion. 'We were all so worried about you. The boys are frantic.'

'I've been taking some time to . . . think things through.'

'Everybody's looking for you.'

'For me? Don't you mean for Harry?'

Caroline's voice is puzzled. 'Why would they look for him? They know he's dead. But you took the car and disappeared the next day.'

They're looking for her. Of course, they are. Once she has reassured Caroline that she's fine and will be home when she feels better, she hangs up the phone and berates herself.

This is not going to work. An old man with a white beard leaves the post office and looks at her curiously, and she fears he has recognised her. If he tells the newspaper then they will come to ask her questions and they will find Harry. She needs to come out of hiding, but keep Harry in hiding somehow.

She needs to hide him in plain sight.

CHAPTER 7

The concourse at Grand Central Station seethed with people. Sunbeams shot through the huge arched windows far above, and I was momentarily awestruck by the size and noise of the place. A cathedral full of steam and the smell of coal and the chatter of crowds surging against each other. On the one hand, I was relieved the journey from San Francisco was over. What a long, hungry, embarrassing journey that had been . . .

But on the other hand, this was New York, and I didn't know which way to go. My bags pulled my arms out of their sockets but I didn't dare give them to a porter in case I had to tip – I hadn't a penny on me.

Luckily a guest at Betty's wedding had advised me before I left to book the Biltmore Hotel, as it was joined to the station. It seemed a lifetime ago that I had rung up the operator to make that long-distance call from Australia, the very day after the sale of the shop had been finalised. I had barely known where I wanted to go, just 'away'. America had seemed a good choice.

I dragged my bags to an information desk under a globe-shaped clock, and asked which way to the Biltmore. The gruff man behind the counter barked directions from under his huge moustache, and I made my way to a lift in the distance. The doors closed out the station, and when they opened again I was in the lobby of the Biltmore.

I stacked my cases beside a tall potted plant and took a deep breath, before walking sheepishly up to the reception desk. A tall man with thinning auburn hair smiled at me. I adored his uniform: his white shirtsleeves and satin-trimmed vest. 'May I help you, madam?'

'I'm Zara Dickins and I . . . I have a reservation, but . . .'

He flipped through the large crisp pages of a reservation book. 'Yes, Miss Dickins. Welcome to New York.'

'I'm sorry,' I said. 'But I haven't any money and I'm not sure what to do.'

He cocked his head slightly, and I rather suspected he was wondering if this young woman in front of him, dishevelled from five days on a train and speaking in a broad accent, knew what kind of establishment the Biltmore was.

'I didn't realise . . . I've just come from San Francisco, you see, and I had all my money in a bank there and forgot to withdraw it before I got on the train.'

Off in a daze, wandering to the station, getting sidetracked by fashion boutiques and shoe stores. Fifteen minutes out of the station it had hit me. I had five dollars. And contrary to what I'd believed, none of the meals on the journey were included. I had relied on the generosity of two other young women in my carriage, and my own ability to pretend I wasn't hungry even when I could have eaten the hind leg off a horse.

'Oh,' he said. 'Well, you can use the hotel phone if you'd like to call and get them to wire it to you here in New York.'

'But you see,' I said, 'I haven't anything to give you now, and I'm quite hungry and . . .' I pulled up before I started crying.

He smiled at me kindly. 'You don't pay for anything until you leave, and you can charge all your meals to your room. With a bit of luck, it will only take a few days for the bank to get you your money and I see you are staying for two weeks.' He winked. 'I trust you, Miss Dickins.'

The relief. He gave me some papers to fill in, then handed me the hotel phone to call the local branch of the bank, and in ten minutes it was all sorted.

I turned to fetch my luggage, only to see a porter hauling the bag onto a trolley. 'No, no!' I said. 'I'll take them.'

'Madam, we insist,' he said, pushing ahead of me to the lift.

I followed him, my heels echoing on the stone floor, mortified that I wouldn't be able to tip him. Up on the ninth floor, the porter led me down a wallpapered corridor to my room, which I opened with a key tied to a small metal disc. The porter went ahead and placed my bags inside, then stood looking at me expectantly.

I reached for his hand and shook it soundly. 'Jolly good. Thank you.' Then I quickly turned away so I couldn't see if he was angry at me for not tipping. I heard the door close behind him.

With a huge sigh I collapsed onto the bed and kicked my shoes off. The room was carpeted in velvety brown, and the bedspread and upholstery were a dark gold colour. The mahogany wardrobe and drawer had shining brass handles, and the room smelled sweet, like some kind of floral oil mixed with lemons. The ceiling was moulded with trims shaped like flowers and a chandelier hung from the centre of it. The heavy crimson curtains were pulled away from the tall windows and secured with gold ropes. I took this all in within a few seconds, before I closed my eyes.

I could still feel the train moving under me.

'It's all right,' I said to myself, under my breath. 'It's all right, you've come to rest now.'

That wasn't entirely true. In two weeks I would be moving again, just as I had been moving for months. In the end, I'd stayed in Melbourne long enough to attend Betty's wedding. Given Tom was Harry's friend, I'd agreed to attend with Harry, but only as friends. That hadn't worked particularly well and another huge row had ensued, followed by an early morning visit the next day (tapping on my window and scaring the life out of me), when he asked me to promise I would always be his girl no matter what. I had promised nothing, of course. I wanted him to think I was done with him; for the first time in our relationship it felt as though I had some power over him. Of course, I wasn't really done with him. I still missed him every day. He would never have let me leave San Francisco without money. He would have said, *Zara, focus. You are on your way to the bank. Stop looking at shoes.*

I opened my eyes, brushed away the familiar pang of having broken my own heart, and hoisted myself up to look out the window. Below was a busy avenue. I could see shops. How I longed to go shopping in New York, but until my money came I couldn't so much as buy a cup of tea outside the hotel. I hadn't imagined arriving in New York would make me feel so defeated and lost.

Somebody rapped sharply at the door. Puzzled, I went to answer it.

The receptionist from downstairs stood there with an envelope in his hand. My first thought was that the bank had wired my money already, but then I recognised the handwriting.

'I'm sorry, Miss Dickins, I should have given this to you when you checked in. It's been sitting here for nearly two weeks.'

I took Harry's letter from him and said thank you, and he left with a cheerful smile.

I returned to the window, pulling up the armchair so I could sit in it with my feet on the sill. I wasn't sure how to feel. It had been months since I'd seen Harry and this was the first he had written to me. I gently tore open the envelope and pulled his letter out.

Dear Zara, I wanted you to have something waiting for you when you got to New York, as I knew it was the first time you'd be on your own.

He'd remembered not only which hotel I'd booked, but that the chaperone for the first leg of my journey, an elderly friend of Mum's named Miss Gough, had stayed on in San Francisco. I missed him so fiercely then. It was such a very *Harry* thing to do – remember an important detail, plan to send a letter, time it perfectly. All charm and to-do lists.

The letter was not a love letter. It skimmed over the top of any feelings he may have been having about me. It was mostly news of people we knew, of things he was doing. He was readying himself to stand for election in my family's suburb, but his chances of success were apparently slim. Nonetheless he seemed in good spirits about it. The tone was positive, upbeat, and I would have thought he didn't miss me at all except that it was signed off, *Always yours, Harry.*

Could people belong to each other? I couldn't shake the feeling that Harry and I did, even though it made no earthly sense as he'd proven himself quite incapable of making me happy. I leaned forward on my knees and stared out the window at the traffic below. Behind me on the desk I had spotted a sheaf of letter paper with the hotel's name across the top. I imagined taking the hotel fountain pen and writing a letter in return, telling him about the wonders I had seen, the storm we'd endured at sea and how everybody in my cabin had thrown up except me (*You always were a strong lass,* he would think), the friendships I'd made aboard and how difficult it was to leave the ship, the street markets in Honolulu and the steep roads in San Francisco, where I couldn't believe any car had sufficient brakes to drive them safely. And of course, my stupid forgetful boarding of the train to New York with no money (*Away with the fairies,* he would think and smile). But I didn't get up and I didn't write the letter. I stayed by the window until dusk crept into the room.

Maybe he would always be mine, but he would never be good for me.

———

I had intended to indulge in window-shopping until my money arrived, but I woke the next morning to the sound of heavy rain.

Opening the curtains barely made the room any lighter, and I knew I'd have to stay in for the day. I dressed and made my way down to the Palm Court, a tearoom on the ground floor where I could order a light breakfast. It was eight o'clock and already very busy, but I found a free table in the middle of the room and gave the waitress my order of tea and toast with jam – my lifelong favourite breakfast – and pretended interest in the newspaper that had been left on the table by the last guest.

I don't know why, but I had the feeling I was being looked at. I've never been sure where that feeling comes from. Harry used to say I was simply more self-conscious than the ordinary person, but I was rarely wrong when I had the feeling, so I lifted my head and ran my gaze around the room. Sure enough, a gentleman with a silvery beard and little round eyeglasses was looking my way. As our eyes met, he quickly darted his eyes toward something else and so did I. The room had a huge high ceiling with a skylight, and directly above me hung the most enormous chandelier. If it fell, I'd be crushed to dust. When I sneaked another look, the gentleman was gone. Breakfast arrived, and I thought no more of it for a few hours.

There was plenty to do inside. The train station itself hosted an art gallery, home to an astonishing array of paintings, tapestries and sculptures. The hotel had a garden on its roof – though it was rather too windy to stay up there for long – and also an enormous wood-panelled library that, at two thirty that afternoon, I had entirely to myself. It smelled of old paper and wood polish, and the dark colours seemed to suck up the sunlight. Unfortunately, the books weren't the kind I preferred to read, but I studiously pulled down a leather-bound edition of *Pride and Prejudice* and curled up in an armchair by the window. At some point I slipped my shoes off and twisted so my back was against one arm of the chair while my knees hooked over the other to dangle my feet. That is to say, I wasn't in the most ladylike of poses when I realised I was not alone.

The squeak of a chair told me that somebody had just sat down at the long table in the middle of the room. I leaned out past the bookshelf to look, and it was the same gentleman with the long beard. He sat down, opening a large book of photographs on the table, and switched on the lamp. Then he began to turn the pages, humming to himself.

I shrank back into my nook by the window and tried to concentrate on the story, but his humming turned into a mumbled, grumbling commentary about what he was viewing. Quite clearly he thought he was alone, and I became terrified he would say or do something mortifying and then realise I was here. So I rearranged myself noisily, both assuming a more dignified position in the chair and deliberately dropping my book.

His humming stopped immediately, and I thought that was that until he appeared at the end of the bookshelf, peering down at me.

'Oh,' he said. 'I thought I was alone.' A precise, British accent.

'It's very quiet in here,' I said.

He waited a few moments . . . too long for comfort. The sun caught the last shreds of a red sheen in his beard. I cleared my throat.

'I saw you in the Palm Court this morning,' he said. 'I think I know you.'

'I'm sure you don't.'

'You're Australian? I can tell from your accent. Let me think where we've met.'

I waited, hoping this wasn't some strange ruse so that he could ask me out for dinner. He was easily twice my age.

He clicked his fingers as he remembered. 'You owned a dress shop. In Melbourne. I took my wife there when we were staying with friends, about two years ago. I remember paying you.' He chuckled. 'You added up the bill wrong three times. Nearly did yourself out of five pounds.'

I relaxed. 'That does sound like me. Though I'm afraid I don't remember you . . . perhaps if you told me your wife's name?'

'Aileen,' he said, a shadow crossing his face. 'She . . . uh . . . she passed. Very recently.' He spread his hands. 'That's why I came to America. Our house in London felt . . .'

'I am very sorry,' I said, not sure what to do with his visible grief.

'Empty,' he finished. 'But then I got here and realised I'd brought the emptiness with me.'

'It must be very difficult to lose somebody you love.'

'It is, my dear.' He smiled a little. 'But I shouldn't be burdening a bright young lass like you with it. In any case, I'll be heading back to London soon enough. Running out of money to stay in hotels! I say, have you any plans for dinner? There's a gaggle of us Londoners staying here for Lord Gallagher's daughter's birthday. Quite a few young ones among the party, including my children. Would you like to come and meet them?'

A party. I hadn't been to a party since I left Australia. Miss Gough was not at all interested in parties. What passed for evening entertainment with her was card games and embroidery. More than that, I was heading to London next and it would pay to have friends and connections already.

'I would love to come,' I said, nearly dropping my book again, but for real this time as I flung my hands out for emphasis. 'Thank you so very much for inviting me.'

'It's in the Cascade Ballroom on the mezzanine floor. Arrive from seven?'

'I shall.'

'In the meantime, I'll let you go back to your book. And I'll go back to mine.'

I had to ask. 'What are you reading that has you muttering so furiously?'

'Old newspapers,' he said. 'Come and I'll show you.'

I followed him to the table. The leather-bound book held yellowing newspapers, what looked like a year's worth.

'Here,' he said, pointing at a headline. '"Steel Baron Returns to England with Tail between His Legs". Can you imagine such rudeness?'

I had no idea what he was talking about so quickly skimmed the first few lines of the piece. It was about a wealthy steelworks owner who set up a business in New Jersey only to have it fail very quickly, causing over a hundred men to lose their jobs.

'Tail between his legs. Not so. Papa walked away with his head held high when the Americans made it impossible for him to continue. Tied up in regulations.'

I gathered from this explanation that the news article referred to his father, and realised I hadn't asked the gentleman his name. 'So your father is in the steel business?'

'Was, my dear. It's all mine now.'

'We haven't introduced ourselves,' I said. 'I'm Zara Dickins.'

'Porter Pepperwell,' he replied, and as soon as I heard the name I remembered his wife, who had been awful. That was why I'd miscalculated her bill; she'd been rude to Betty, demanded an endless series of fittings and had generally been impossible to please. By the time it came to calculating what she owed, I'd become frightened of her. I didn't mention any of this to Mr Pepperwell, given his recent bereavement.

'And I shan't keep you from your book a moment longer. I insist.' He gestured towards my armchair under the window. 'I will see you this evening.'

I returned to my book, but couldn't keep my mind on it. I was busy in my head choosing a gown and a lipstick and gloves, and after I heard Mr Pepperwell leave, I left too. I stopped forlornly at the front desk to ask if the bank had sent me a note, but there was nothing. So I returned to my room to lay out all my clothes and turn my mind to parties for the first time in months.

It took no small amount of courage to set foot inside the Cascade Ballroom alone that evening, not knowing a single person except for Mr Pepperwell, who was nowhere in sight. The ballroom was extravagant, with a square wooden dance floor surrounded by long dinner tables, huge wrought-iron lamps hanging from the ceiling, and a balcony above the dance floor where the older gentlemen had gathered to smoke cigars, drink whisky and watch the young people below. My eyes swept the room, taking in the general shape and colour of the gowns, and I was impressed but not intimidated. I wore a silvery-blue Magg design: an embroidered crepe slip with an organza overlay, loose draping sleeves and a train. My dark hair was smoothed flat to my ears then pinned in curls, which had taken forever. I hadn't spotted Mr Pepperwell yet, so I walked up the stairs to the balcony to see if he was among the cigar-smoking set. Sure enough, I found him tucked away in a corner deep in conversation with two men in their twenties, one with dark auburn hair and the other blond.

'Ah, Miss Dickins,' he said, leaping to his feet. The young men did the same. 'How pleased I am to introduce you to my sons, Peter and Percy.'

I stifled a laugh. Porter, Peter and Percy Pepperwell. It sounded like the name of a children's book. Instead I extended my gloved hand to be taken gently by the young men in turn. Peter, the blond, barely seemed interested to meet me, while Percy lingered rather too long before releasing my hand

'Go on, you young folk,' Mr Pepperwell said. 'Take Zara downstairs and introduce her around.'

Percy offered me his elbow and I took it out of politeness. On our way down to the ballroom, he asked me a few banal questions about whether or not I liked New York, and then we were subsumed by a table full of people my age and Percy let me go. There were four other girls and two other boys, and all were very welcoming and seemed a lot of fun. Annabel, who was Peter's fiancée, was particularly friendly to me. None of them knew the girl whose birthday the ball was in honour of, but Annabel pointed her out to me and giggled, 'What *is* she wearing?' in my ear, and I chuckled in spite of myself.

'It's not her fault nobody has ever dressed her properly,' I said sincerely. The young woman was tall and gangly with quite masculine shoulders, and was dressed in too many flounces and ruffles.

Annabel turned to the other girls and repeated my comment, but made it sound as though I'd intended it as a withering put-down. They all laughed, and I let it pass, but I did feel bad. As somebody who struggled with a body that didn't always suit the fashion, I tried to make it my business not to judge others. The conversation went elsewhere, and I took turns dancing with all the boys. Percy had taken an obvious shine to me, which was a little embarrassing as he wasn't at all the type of boy I was interested in, but I smiled and went along nonetheless.

When dinner was served, the music died down and I sat with Peter, Percy and Annabel around me, while they asked me questions about myself. When I told them I was a fashion designer, Annabel lit up. She told the other girls who leaned in and asked me eager questions about famous people I had dressed. I tried to brag about Lotus Thompson but all they wanted to know was if the stories about her having burned her legs with acid were true. They soon lost interest when I admitted I hadn't seen anything unusual while dressing her.

Percy pulled his chair a little closer to me. His thick auburn hair was full of too much scented wax and the smell made me queasy.

'I think it's marvellous that you are so creative,' he said with moony eyes. 'I am creative too, you know. I write poetry.'

For some reason, the words *Poet Percy Pepperwell* leapt into my head and I had to stifle a roar of laughter. Unfortunately, Percy saw my smile and took it as encouragement.

'I would love to read you some if you are ever in London. All my notebooks are in the family library.'

'That's a lovely offer.'

'Do you intend to come to London?' Annabel chimed in. 'It would be so brilliant to show you around.'

'I am actually boarding my ship for England in about two weeks.'

'Ooh,' Annabel said, 'what date? Is it the twenty-fifth? With Cunard?'

'The twenty-second,' I said. 'And yes. The Cunard Line ship to Southampton.'

'Oh, but you must come on the twenty-fifth because that's when *we* go back to London, and we would have such a good time on the ship together. You're going alone, aren't you?'

'Yes,' I answered, and honestly I had been dreading it since my terrible train journey across America. I did much better with people around me. 'But I have already booked so . . .'

'I can help you change your ticket,' Percy said eagerly. 'Daddy's bound to know somebody at Cunard. Will you let me try for you? Then you don't have to run around or worry about it.'

'Let him try, Zara,' Annabel said. 'The four of us would have such a terrific time together, and I don't want to be the only girl with these two.' She pulled an exaggerated pout that made me laugh.

I glanced at Peter to see if he would offer any encouragement, but he remained profoundly uninterested in me. I turned their offer over in my head. Presuming I could convince the hotel to let me stay a few more days, and presuming my money arrived at some point, there was no reason I couldn't travel later. I intended to stay with Betty and Tom, who had moved to London after the wedding, so I could easily wire them and change the dates. So why was I holding back? Peter, Percy and Annabel all seemed very nice, as did Mr Pepperwell, who would be travelling with them. It would certainly be more exciting than travelling with Miss Gough.

Yet still I hesitated. I couldn't quite put my finger on it, but I sensed that they weren't my kind of people. Annabel took too much joy making fun of others; Percy was so attentive it was almost aggressive; Peter didn't bother to hide that he thought little of me.

But they were company. Dinners and dances on the ship. A chance to dress up. Somebody to laugh with. It was only a week . . . perhaps I was being stupidly cautious.

'All right then, yes,' I said. 'Thank you, Percy. If you can find out if there's room for me on your ship, I would love to cross the Atlantic with all of you.'

'Hurrah,' said Annabel, lifting her champagne to her lips. 'You won't regret it.'

———

I regretted it as soon as the next morning, when I opened my eyes to a champagne headache and a memory of Percy trying to kiss my neck while we were on the dance floor. I'd warned him sternly away from kissing me, but he didn't strike me as the sort to give up easily. He had already promised to call by that afternoon and tell me how he'd got on with the people at Cunard. I wished fervently that there were no spare first-class cabins and I would be able to sail off on the twenty-second as planned.

After breakfast, I paused hopefully at the reception desk to see if I'd had word from the bank.

The gentleman who had been assisting me gave me a brilliant smile and said, 'Ah, Miss Dickins. Good news! If you make your way across to Liberty Union Bank in Yonkers, they can organise your money for you.'

'I'm so relieved. Is it easy to find? It's a beautiful morning for a walk.'

He was shaking his head, a startled expression in his eyes. 'Oh, you can't walk. It's more than ten miles. I'll get you a taxicab.'

'I haven't any money to pay a taxicab,' I said. 'Unless I get him to wait outside . . .'

The receptionist glanced around him. Another well-dressed man was busy signing a guest into the guest log, and the lobby was empty apart from that. He dropped his voice. 'I can loan you the money out of our till, as long as you pay it back this afternoon.'

I sighed. 'Thank you, thank you. I don't know what I've done to deserve your kindness.'

He opened a drawer and pulled out a key and a silver tin. 'You turned up looking lost and sad,' he said. 'You are a long way from home.'

He handed me a two-dollar note and had me sign an IOU, and before long I was speeding through New York streets in the back of a bright yellow taxicab. I drank in the scenery, trying to commit everything to memory. I imagined the letter I might write to Harry, then reminded myself I wouldn't be writing to him. Instead, I focused on how wonderful it would be when I had my money and could go shopping in all the fabulous boutiques and department stores. I had thought Melbourne quite a large and sophisticated city, but it was nothing compared to New York. Shop after shop flashed by, signs over entries for subways, traffic so thick that we sometimes had to slow down and sit for two or three changes of lights, buildings taller than I'd ever seen, and crowds of people on sidewalks or trying their luck scurrying across the road. I experienced it all from the quiet interior of the taxicab, but I longed to get out among it.

Twenty minutes later I paid my driver, took my change, and headed inside the Liberty Union bank. It was a small, musty building, and I waited on a seat with a tear in the leather while somebody fetched the right person for me.

In time, a thin, grandfatherly fellow and a young blonde woman approached and sat across from me.

'Here we are,' said the man, handing me a yellow envelope. 'We've charged a twenty-five-cent transaction fee, but the rest is all there. We'll just need to see some identification. Your passport will do.'

My heart stopped. My passport was back at the hotel. 'I . . . ah . . .' I opened my handbag and started searching through it, hoping to find anything at all that would prove who I was. I didn't have enough for a return fare to the hotel, and I couldn't borrow any more money from them.

The young woman started to chuckle. 'I believe she's Zara Dickins,' she said. 'It says so right there on the inside of her purse.'

Before I left Australia, my mother had sewn labels into all my luggage and my handbag, which I found mortifyingly babyish. The blonde woman was pointing to one of the labels now.

'We really ought to see her passport,' the older man harrumphed.

The blonde woman gave Zara a smile. 'She looks trustworthy.'

'I promise you, I am very trustworthy. Just a bit forgetful.'

The older gentleman shrugged his shoulders. 'Well, then, Miss Dickins, off you go and good luck in your travels.'

I almost squealed my gratitude, stashed the money deep in my handbag and clipped it up firmly, and went outside to hail a cab. In no time, an Italian driver had picked me up and I slid into the back seat feeling light and happy.

'Where to, ma'am?' he asked.

'Bloomingdale's,' I said firmly.

———

By the end of my first week in New York, I had to make the choice between buying another suitcase or shipping some clothes home, so I did the latter, dropping in a note to Mum that I had made lovely new friends who I would travel to London with. I had dinner with the Pepperwell family including Annabel every night, and Annabel came shopping with me most days and we rubbed along well enough together. I grew used to her declaring things were either 'hideous!' or 'exquisite!' and tossing her blonde curls in every shop window reflection. Percy remained persistent, which was a shame as he was a terrible dancer and I spent a lot of the time on the dance floor with him. At least I had more opportunities to wear my fabulous new dresses, out with the Pepperwells and their wealthy New York friends, who treated me as a charming oddity because of my accent.

Every night when I came back to my hotel room, I would ease my shoes off my dance-swollen feet and write all their names down in my diary, in case I ever went into business again. Some nights I went to sleep fantasising about a Magg department at Macy's, or even a little Magg salon in the Garment District, among other women like me with big ideas and creative spirits.

The truth was, I doubted such dreams would ever come true and, while I was obviously happier without all the stress, I missed Magg a great deal. My life opened up ahead of me, but it seemed a vast uncertain space where I couldn't grasp a foothold.

CHAPTER 8

The day I boarded the RMS *Cameronia* to England, the sun was bright but the air was cold, so I wore the new fur-trimmed coat I had purchased the day before on my last hurrah in midtown Manhattan. Even though I didn't know anyone on the dock, I waved energetically at the crowds as the ship pulled out and then stood wistfully on the deck watching the Statue of Liberty grow smaller and smaller behind me, before going to find my cabin.

Life on board the *Cameronia* differed vastly from my journey to America. For one thing, there were no stops along the way to buy cheerful junk on little islands. We moved relentlessly forward. Also, the weather remained excellent throughout so all the young people on the ship spent their days out on the deck, playing games and smoking and larking about. One day, I won a tin ship in a deck race, which for some baffling reason made Annabel resent me and shut me out of the Pepperwell clique for the remainder of the journey. By then, I was relieved. I had lots of young and energetic company at dinners and I danced every night.

I met a lovely man named Alexander once I was free of Annabel, and he kept me company for the rest of the trip to London. He made it clear on our first evening walk around the deck that he wasn't interested in women, but that he needed to seem as though he was so his parents would stop foisting marriageable ladies upon him. I was also keen to avoid the Pepperwells, so we happily pretended we were having a shipboard romance then parted ways at Southampton. Alexander gave me directions to Betty's on Guildford Street, and I set off via a series of trains, the phantom swell of the sea still beneath my feet.

I very quickly found myself lost, my hands raw from holding my suitcases, and was debating whether to hail a taxicab when a group of men walking in the other direction bumped into me as though I was invisible, flinging one of my suitcases to the ground. They kept walking, but the lock on my case broke, and there were my books and clothes – even my underwear! – all over the street.

I began to cry. It was heading towards late afternoon and the sun was sinking. It had taken so long to disembark, waiting in lines and having papers stamped, and I so very much wanted to come to rest with a cup of tea and my dear friend Betty. And now I was crawling abjectly on a London footpath, gathering my smalls.

A shadow fell over me and a deep voice said kindly, 'Can I help you?'

I looked up to see a man in his late twenties, with a strong jaw and thick dark hair, smiling down at me.

'I'm fine,' I said.

'You're crying.' He crouched and began gathering my things, wisely not touching my clothes. 'Here, a problem shared is a problem halved.'

Between us we got the case packed and closed, but the clasp was broken so he removed a shoelace and tied it for me. I could barely meet his eyes from embarrassment. He seemed to sense I was uncomfortable and didn't engage me in questions until I was once again standing with a case in each hand.

'Thank you so very much,' I said. 'I owe you a debt, Mr . . . ?'

'Colonel Fell,' he said. 'And you are?'

'Zara Dickins.' I managed a smile. 'I'm meant to be staying with a friend. She lives on Guildford Street near Russell Square and I'm quite lost.'

He nodded. 'Yes you are. It's nearly a half-hour walk, and I don't recommend it with a broken suitcase. Let me take you to Piccadilly

Circus and put you on the underground train. It's four stops. Will you be all right?'

I nodded. I was relieved he wasn't insisting on taking me all the way to Betty's door. But at the same time, I'd never caught the underground train and I understood it could be quite confusing.

Colonel Fell walked me all the way down to the platform and helped me onto the train with my suitcases when it arrived.

'Thank you, Colonel Fell,' I said to him, and felt a prickle of regret that I wouldn't see him again.

'My pleasure, Miss Dickins.' Then he stepped back onto the platform and was gone.

———

A few hours later, I recounted all this in a much happier and more relaxed mood while sitting in the living room of Betty and Tom's cosy flat on Guildford Street. My shoes were off, I had a scalding cup of sweet, strong tea in my hands, and Betty and Tom found the whole story so amusing that it dissolved all my guilt.

'Oh heck, Zara,' Betty said. 'Underwear all over the street? What a greeting you gave London!'

Tom stood and stretched. 'I have some papers to look over before tea. Do you mind if I leave you girls to it?'

'Not at all,' Betty said, smiling up at him. He kissed her forehead and left, closing the door behind him. Evening deepened outside the windows.

'How is married life?' I asked.

'Wonderful,' she said.

I smiled over the pang in my heart, thinking of how the four of us – Betty, Tom, Harry and me – had spent so much time together. Two couples. Now one couple, and one spinster. 'I'm very happy for you.'

'There's something else,' she said.

'What?'

'Come here.'

Curious, I placed my teacup on the table in front of me and approached her. She lifted the hem of her blouse, and I could see that her normally flat stomach had started to swell.

'No!' I said, falling to my knees with delight. 'Really?' I reached out and put my hand on her tummy.

'It's not kicking yet. At least I don't think so. Sometimes I get a feeling like bubbles breaking, but I don't know if it's the baby or just gas.' She laughed. 'Can you believe it? I'm going to be a mummy.'

It was almost too much for me, that firelit scene. Betty was married, living in a cosy flat, expecting a baby. I suddenly and violently wanted all of it for myself.

Betty touched my hair. 'You look sad.'

I climbed to my feet and returned to my chair. 'Not at all, I'm delighted for you. Do you have names chosen?'

'Zara, I know you too well. Tell the truth.'

I sighed, curling my feet under me on the settee. 'I suppose it's a kind of envy, but not the kind that would make me love you any less.'

Betty laughed. 'That goes without saying. I know how kind-hearted you are. But is it the baby, or something else?'

'All of it,' I said. 'I had enough money to buy us a house. But Harry was such a slippery eel and I had to let him go. I was exhausted from trying to hold on.'

'And here you are with a broken heart, and there he is back home with a broken heart.'

I scoffed. 'I doubt it. He will have found himself somebody else by now.'

'He writes to Tom. He has a broken heart, trust me. He never stops telling Tom about how he let you get away.'

I tried not to let my heart leap at the thought. 'I would have been easy to keep,' I said.

'Zara,' Betty said, rising and coming to sit next to me, slipping her arm around my shoulders. 'You know it's for the best. He didn't make you happy. Well, he did sometimes, but it seems just as often he made you wild with anger or limp with sorrow.'

'It doesn't feel "for the best". But yes, I know. We were bad for each other.'

We sat for a moment, listening to the fire. Then Betty said, 'You ought to have asked for that young colonel's telephone number.'

'Scandalous,' I said, chuckling. 'He was quite handsome though.'

'Can you even imagine falling in love with somebody other than Harry?'

I shook my head. 'Not yet. It's as though . . . oh, I know it sounds like some of the dreamy nonsense Harry was always complaining about.'

'Go on, say it to me. I won't judge you.'

'It's as though we are two parts of the same puzzle. When I'm with him there's a sense of things finally falling into place. And no matter who else he or I may eventually find ourselves with, there will never be that feeling. That . . .' I brought my hands together, fingers interwoven. 'We fit, as though we were made to fit.'

'By whom?'

'God. The powers that be. Don't ask me to explain because then it all sounds ridiculous. But it doesn't *feel* ridiculous, it feels right. So I don't just miss him, something in me is missing too.'

She gave me a squeeze. 'One must always be careful not to let the stories in our heads influence our choices.'

'You said you wouldn't judge.' I laughed, giving her a hard tap on the thigh.

'I'm not. If you weren't a dreamer there would have been no Magg. But at some point we did have to learn how to make the books add up.' She looked around. 'Is it me, or is it warm in here?'

'It's warm,' I said.

'It isn't really cold enough to have the fire, but I so wanted to show off my cosy living room.'

She went to the window and lifted the sash, and I joined her. It had started to drizzle, and the air smelled of damp earth and coal smoke. A bus rattled past, its tyres hissing on the wet road.

Eventually I asked her, 'And so your marriage to Tom, is it a dream come true or are you just making the books add up?'

I immediately regretted the question, as I didn't want to cause offence, but she answered very directly. 'More like making the books add up, I think,' she said. 'Because at some point, we become adults and must do adult things.'

'Yes,' I said. 'I suppose we must.' I gazed out at the London skyline against the churning clouds, and tried not to calculate how many miles lay between me and Harry.

———

My weeks with Betty were easily the best time I had spent on this entire trip around the world to exotic places. It made me realise the value of home and loved ones, and in my last days in London I began to grow increasingly homesick. The smell of Tom's pipe tobacco reminded me of Daddy, the endless traffic outside Betty's windows made me long for my quiet Melbourne street, the peeps and twitters of the little English sparrows and robins could not compare to the otherworldly warbling of the Australian magpie.

I found London exciting but exhausting. Betty took me to all her favourite boutiques and department stores, but she had become much more interested in collecting baby clothes than ladies clothes. One Saturday, Tom declared that there was more to England than London, and borrowed a friend's car to drive us into the deep green countryside, which looked so much like a painting on a biscuit box that I couldn't quite believe it was real.

Tom worked relentlessly and over long hours, so we barely saw him. I had a glimpse of Betty's life, which seemed lonely to me. She had friends, of course, and we had several lunches and high teas with them, but they were mostly women in their fifties who seemed old-fashioned and obsessed with manners. Betty was very well-bred and knew how to hold her own in these situations (I often felt awkward and unsure), but the very fact that she had an Australian accent seemed reason enough for them to patronise her.

Because Tom was so busy, we only got to one party the whole time I stayed with them. Betty and I both wore Magg gowns, and spent the evening talking about how wonderful it had been to run the salon together, though we didn't talk about how she left me in the lurch to sink under the work.

'One day,' she said, sipping fruit punch, 'we shall do it again.'

I agreed, but couldn't see how that would fit into our lives now she was living in a different country and about to have a baby.

I had never stopped sketching fashions, of course. My trip had inspired me to design wild things, gowns that would be impossible to make or ridiculous to wear. But I enjoyed it. Nobody pressured me to actually make the clothes, so if I wanted to design a dress inspired by a hula skirt, why not? The important thing was to not let go of my creativity and imagination, in case they never came back.

Eventually it was time for me to leave Betty and Tom and take the train up to Edinburgh to meet my mother's family and stay for a month. I was running out of money. From Scotland, I would be sailing home, and whatever happened next would happen. I had no idea what that might be.

CHAPTER 9

My cabin aboard the last ship home was dark and drab, with one round window, a tiny dresser with an even tinier mirror and a saggy armchair so close to the bed that my knees wouldn't fit in the gap. I had been on land so long by the time we steamed away from Paisley Harbour that I had to get my 'sea legs' again. I was lucky not to get seasick, but the restless movement of the ocean made me very tired, and I spent the first two days aboard dozing in my bed, ignoring the call to meals and surviving on the box of biscuits my Aunt Daisy baked for the journey. The third afternoon, I grew alert and restless, and so I dressed and took a long stroll around the decks, making friends with a group of women about my age – all Australian and heading home like me – and they made me promise to come to dinner that night and sit with them.

I wore a grey silk-crepe dinner suit with a crimson chiffon scarf to match my lipstick, and pinned a crystal-flower hairclip in my curls. The vast dining room was carpeted and hung with chandeliers, and dozens of round tables with floral centrepieces were arranged around it. It was bright and airy, and filled with the chatter of people. Waiters moved on deft feet among the tables, always smiling, bringing wine and bread ahead of the main course. I scanned the room looking for the faces of my new friends. One of them, a long-limbed freckled lass named Stella, was standing and waving at me. I made my way over between tables and patrons and waiters. They had saved me a seat.

I was in high spirits that night. I had new friends, I had proper food, and I was heading home. I drank a little too much champagne and I laughed a little too loudly, but so did the other girls in my warm cloud of happiness.

After the main course, but before dessert, I heard a crisp English voice behind me say, 'Miss Dickins?'

I turned, expecting a steward or some other staff member. Then I gasped. 'Colonel Fell?'

He grinned at me, placed his hand on the back of my chair and squatted down so he was face to face with me. He was in uniform – dark blue with gold buttons, embroidery and epaulettes – and looked very striking.

'I thought I saw you when you came in, but have spent the last hour watching you from across the room, making sure it was you. Is this not an astonishing coincidence? I didn't see you when we embarked at Southampton.'

'I got on at Glasgow. You're going to Australia?'

He shook his head. 'India. I'm off at Bombay, then a long train ride to Poona. You're returning home, are you?'

'Yes. Melbourne.' I took in his dark hair, dark eyes, open smile. 'I don't think I said thank you enough for helping me that day.'

'Oh, you did,' he said with a smile. 'I was in no doubt about how grateful you were.'

'I felt a bit of a fool, a graceless Antipodean with her things strewn over the street.'

'Nonsense. You were and are the soul of grace.' Then he blushed, and it was the most gorgeous thing I had ever seen.

The waiter leaned over then with my dessert, and Colonel Fell stood and said, 'I shall leave you in peace.'

I didn't want to let him go just yet. 'Perhaps we could dance later?'

'I'd like that.'

'Find me in the ballroom.'

He nodded. 'I will. I will. Thank you, Miss Dickins.'

'Oh, you should call me Zara, and I should call you . . . ?'

'James. Agreed,' he said, lightly touching my shoulder. 'Agreed, Zara.'

I watched him return to a table across the room where a half-dozen other men in uniforms sat, and they mobbed him with back slaps and laughs when he sat down.

At my own table, the girls had a million questions for me, and I told them about how we had met. All of them were astonished and delighted, and Stella said, 'It's like a story. Maybe fate has thrown you together.'

'Yes,' said Iris, a curvy blonde from Sydney. 'If this were a novel, you'd end up marrying him.'

'Hardly,' I said, glancing over at my shoulder at James again, to see that he was also looking at me. I smiled and turned back to my new friends. 'He's leaving the ship at Bombay. That's rather a long way from Melbourne.'

'Love will find a way,' Stella said. 'You'll see.'

We went on laughing and joking, and their nonsense about me marrying James delighted me but I didn't believe for a moment anything like that would transpire. However, I was entirely ready for a shipboard romance, and I hoped James was too.

The ballroom was small and the dance floor crowded. The band was right next to where James and I danced, so we could barely hear each other speak. But after a foxtrot and a rumba, they played a slow waltz and James pulled me close against him. I felt the warmth of his body under the stiffness of his uniform.

'Your hair smells beautiful,' he said.

I sighed and leaned into him a little, but my hairclip must have been sitting slightly askew (I'd had rather a lot of champagne) and James called out, 'Ow!' I pulled away suddenly, and then he said 'Ow!' again even louder and I realised the sharp edge of the hair clip had caught him up one nostril and now he stood in front of me patting blood from his nose with his fingertips.

'Oh my goodness!' I exclaimed.

He reached into his pocket for a handkerchief and pressed it against his nose. 'You could have warned me you had a deadly weapon in your hair.' He laughed.

'I'm so sorry,' I said, but then I began giggling. I knew I oughtn't giggle after I'd just injured James in a romantic moment, but trying to suppress the giggles only made me want to laugh harder. James saw my expression, and he too began to roar with laughter. I laughed so hard I couldn't breathe. Two of his friends joined us and asked what was going on, but we were both laughing too hard to explain that I had stabbed his left nostril with a hairclip.

By now I was completely enamoured of him.

One of his friends suggested we should both go outside for some fresh air to calm ourselves down, and he did this with a knowing wink at the other lads. James grabbed my hand and I willingly left the crowded, noisy ballroom, up the stairs and out under the iron threshold to the deck.

The sea breeze was brisk and salty, instantly cooling my flushed face. Clouds covered the stars and the distinct cold humidity of approaching rain hung in the air. The music was faint behind us and I could hear the sound of water rushing along the hull. We weren't the only ones on deck. A few couples leaned against the rails here and there, and a trio of middle-aged men smoked aromatic cigars. Lanterns were hung around, and I pulled James under one and moved his handkerchief out of the way to look at his nostril.

'It doesn't look too bad,' I said. 'It's not bleeding anymore.'

'Are you inspecting up my nose?'

I giggled. 'Yes, I am.'

'Not quite the romantic scene I had hoped for this evening.'

I handed back the bloodied handkerchief and he folded it away in his pocket.

'What had you hoped for?' I asked, blinking coquettishly.

He took my hand. 'How about we sit out here in the fresh air and get to know each other better.'

A row of carved wooden seats dotted the deck, but most were under lights. He took me to the last one in the row, which was more secluded, and we sat down.

'You go first,' I said.

I learned that James was twenty-nine, from Warwickshire, and a cavalry officer who had been in the British Indian Army for four years. I suppose I found his posh accent and the fact that he rode horses into battle (hypothetically – he hadn't been in any battles yet) quite thrilling. But it was something else that I liked about him. He had an innocent quality. He was sincere and earnest and . . . *good*, somehow. Of course I compared him to Harry, who never missed an opportunity for a quick, wicked witticism, or a dry put-down of somebody out of earshot. It wasn't that Harry was bad, because he could be kind and he wanted to do good in the world, but he was definitely irreverent and naughty.

The thing I liked best about James though was that he seemed entirely besotted by me. In that hour we sat on the deck, the compliments never stopped falling from his lips. I had such a pretty face, like a doll. He loved my laugh. I seemed so full of life to him. Every time he told me how much I sparkled, I felt myself sparkle more and more brightly until I was sure I lit up the dark.

Then the rain came. A light mist at first, then suddenly thundering down. We hurried along the deck, him trying to keep me dry by hugging me against his tall frame, but we were drenched through in seconds.

We stood dripping at the top of the stairs, laughing again.

'I'd better go dry myself off,' I said, self-conscious about my bedraggled curls.

He seemed to sense this and touched my cheek. 'You are beautiful even when you're soaked.'

'Come find me tomorrow,' I said.

'I most certainly will, Zara.'

I had hoped for a kiss goodnight, but James was too much of a boy scout to ask for one, let alone just plant one on me without permission. I didn't mind, but I certainly went to sleep that night imagining him kissing me.

———

I didn't see James over breakfast, but that was likely because I slept well into the gloomy morning in my dark little room, and I assumed all military men rose early. I spent the time before lunch in the games room with the girls, playing gin rummy and winning the most matchsticks by far. The rain from the previous night had set in, and nobody was out on deck so the inside spaces felt warm and cramped. Then the announcement came that, as a special treat, we were going to watch a movie after lunch. In the dining room, I sat with the girls and James sat with his army companions, but we exchanged smiles and waves across the room. As soon as lunch was over we found each other and returned together to the games room, which had been set up with a projector and a screen at the front.

Only it wasn't a real movie. On board, we had a gentleman named Professor Delaware, and the promised movie was actually made on his own Swiss movie camera when he'd been on a trip to East Africa. He stood at the front and announced what we were seeing as jumpy images appeared on the screen. Those in the front rows, realising they were trapped by politeness, sat very still. But the people on the edges of the audience began to grow as restless as the lions in his movie after the first ten minutes.

I leaned into James and said, very close to his ear, 'This is boring. Shall we run off?'

He darted a look of shock at me. 'Can we?'

I looked around, saw a couple of young women escaping through a side door, stifling giggles. 'Absolutely. Come on.' I grasped his hand and leaned out of my seat, shifting my weight to my feet so I didn't have to stand up directly. We had to walk in front of the rest of the row, but we kept our heads low and moved fast. We ran up the stairs and stopped at the threshold. Rain came down in sheets.

'I didn't think this through,' I said.

'I hope nobody thinks we were rude,' James said with a glance over his shoulder.

'I'm sure they won't. Well, perhaps Professor Delaware will but I'm almost certain he was watching the elephants when we left.'

He squeezed my hand. 'I know a place. We might get wet getting there.'

'All right.'

We slipped along the deck, backs close to the wall, until we were almost at the bow of the ship. James indicated a narrow set of spiral stairs made of iron, and then we were out of the rain heading down. My hair and shoes were damp but I'd avoided most of the downpour. The stairs led to an anteroom, beyond which a corridor ran off towards what looked like officers' quarters. On either side were more stairs, and we took the ones on the left down further until we arrived at an iron deck stacked with old furniture. It was dark and smelled musty. Only a little light from a single porthole illuminated the upturned tables and chairs. The rain drove against the side of the ship and it felt cosy somehow. James pulled down one of the tables and turned it the right way, then helped me up to sit on it. He sat next to me, and we were up against the wall behind the stacked chairs, so nobody could see us.

'How do you know about this place?' I asked.

'Our boys moved all this furniture in here when we got aboard in Southampton. It's spare furniture from the dining room. There were supposed to be a hundred of us from the regiment on board, but only forty came.'

'Goodness, the dining room would have been crowded with a hundred of you.'

'Yes, perhaps too crowded for me to have spotted you. It's a sad tale when you think of it like that.'

I smiled up at him. 'My friends think it was meant to be that we met again.'

'Do you think they're right?'

'I'm not sure if presuming anything is "meant to be" is such a good idea,' I said, thinking about Harry.

He leaned back, tilting his head against the wall. 'It's nice to imagine though, isn't it? That God or fate or whoever intended for us to cross paths again. I had so wanted to ask to spend more time with you that day we met in London, but you were so tired and distressed.'

'I told my friend Betty about you. I kept calling you my knight in shining armour.'

'Something tells me you're not quite the damsel-in-distress type.'

'Oh, I'm often in distress.' I laughed. 'But usually because I'm off in a dream and miss important information. It's not fatal.'

He smiled at me. 'I think you are a delight.'

We gazed at each other for a long moment.

'You should kiss me,' I said.

'Are you sure?'

'It's meant to be.'

He leaned in. I felt his breath, warm on my cheek. And then his lips were on mine and I closed my eyes and pressed up against him, and he caught my hair with his big hands and murmured between kisses how beautiful I was.

From that moment on, we were inseparable on board. The others from his regiment egged him on to sit 'with the girls' at dinner, and we held hands and only had eyes for each other. We must have been tiresome company, and my new friends soon stopped asking me to join them for games or walks. I spent every moment I could with James.

And every day we drew closer and closer to India.

To say I was confused about my feelings was understating the matter. I told myself it was nothing but a shipboard romance, and I would forget his lips and his hands the moment he was gone. But at other times, the thought of him leaving my life forever made me ache with sorrow. There was something so earnest and simple about him that I felt was missing from my life. He smelled like sunshine and soap, and he grinned like a boy, and he kissed me with an artful restraint that made all my senses flutter. I woke up thinking about him and I went to sleep thinking about him. We delighted in each other, but neither of us could bring ourselves to talk about what would happen next.

We were three days out of Bombay and I was certain I was in love with him, when he came to the door of my cabin one evening while I was getting ready for dinner. He knocked, and I opened the door and let him in, shutting it quickly behind him. The stewards frowned on men being near the women's quarters.

'What are you doing here?' I asked, wrapping my robe tightly around me. 'I'm not dressed.'

He grinned. 'And what a treat you are in your robe, Zara. You're lucky I'm a decent sort of fellow.'

I waved him away. 'It must be urgent. Is everything all right?'

'I think so.' He shifted from foot to foot. 'I've been speaking with my commanding officer.'

'The short fellow with the big moustache?'

'Yes, the brigadier. He, his wife and their children have a second home in Poona where I'm meant to stay for a few weeks. He told his wife about us and . . . well, she's invited you to come and stay with them.'

'In India?'

He nodded, smiling. 'In India.'

I had never thought of myself going to India. I was a little scared, honestly, as they spoke a different language and I wouldn't know how I would get on. But then presumably the brigadier's wife was English.

And it would mean that I could spend more time with James.

Mum and Dad would kill me. My new friends would find it exciting but scandalous nonetheless.

'You haven't spoken for a whole minute,' James said nervously.

'I'm surprised, that's all,' I said. 'I hadn't thought to go somewhere so . . . exotic. What if I don't like it?'

He shrugged. 'Then you go home. But Zara . . .' He came forward and took my hands in his. 'I'm not ready for this to end. I think I'm falling in love with you, but we need to know each other off this ship. On land.'

'Yes,' I said, and a sensation like falling came over me, but it wasn't unpleasant. It was thrilling. 'Yes, I will come with you.'

The next morning I wired my parents and explained the situation – in the least amount of words so it didn't cost me a fortune – and gave them the address in Poona where I'd be staying. By the evening they had wired back, one simple line.

COME HOME DIRECTLY.

I looked at it for a long time, before scrunching it into a ball and throwing it in the bin in the corner of my cabin.

CHAPTER 10

I loved India from the moment I stepped off the ship. The light fell bright and warm, and there was an intoxicating, slightly swampy, slightly spicy smell about the place that I couldn't inhale enough of. James, the brigadier and I took the electric train to Poona in the second-class carriage. James held my hand as I gazed out the window, enchanted with the wide fields and big sky. Along the way, a woman with three little children came to sit in our carriage, and I tried not to gape at her beautiful sari. Magenta and gold and blue. Sandals peeped out from under it, and her hair was thick and long. She smiled at me and said something in Hindi, which the brigadier translated for me. 'She said she likes your dress too.'

I laughed then looked away self-consciously. I had to make sure I didn't stare at everybody I saw.

Poona station was a long modern brick building. A man in a turban with white clothes and black vest came for our luggage and wheeled it on a trolley out to the kerb. We walked behind him, past a vendor with a three-wheeled cart. The cabinet was full of nuts, biscuits and sweets. The station was busy with both Indian and British people, and the mixing of their clothing styles intrigued me. Some of the Indian women looked quite Western, and some of the British women wore woven silk scarves and rows of golden necklaces. I was already designing dresses in my head when the driver picked us up, and continued as we sped past cyclists and horse-drawn carts and street vendors. We turned away from the main streets and found ourselves on roads less well-kept with woodland between houses. James and the brigadier chatted about work, but they seemed a long way away from me. I was so engrossed in my surroundings, my imagination whirring like a busy machine. Finally, we drew up outside a grassy bank that sloped upwards to a vast stone house with a long colonnade. The driver insisted on taking all the bags, though one of mine looked precariously positioned under his arm. I followed James and the brigadier up the stone steps as an army of servants in collarless shirts and loose trousers descended on us and carried the bags away, leaving the driver to return to the car. Waiting under one of the keel arches of the colonnade was a tall slender woman in a midnight-blue sari, but with blonde movie-star curls.

'Welcome!' she said, coming forward and giving me a hug. Her hands were very cool and I was huffing and flushed from the walk up the stairs. I felt quite the dishevelled little lump next to her pale elegance.

'So pleased to meet you,' I said as she stood back and gave the brigadier a kiss on the cheek.

'This is my wife, Penelope,' the brigadier said.

'I have heard so much about you,' she said, in a cut-glass British accent. 'And you can call me Penny. Only Gordon and my mother call me Penelope.'

It was odd to hear the brigadier referred to as Gordon; I had only known him as 'the brigadier', which suited him much better. He was a nuggety little man with a bristling golden moustache, at least four inches shorter than Penny.

'Come in, come in,' she said. 'Leave the bags for the servants, Zara. They will take them to your room. I've got Surabhi making us tea.'

She hooked her elbow through mine and led me through an enormous entrance hall into a sitting room. Folding doors all along one wall of the room had been opened to admit a view of rolling hills, the town in the distance. Fans turned slowly from the high ceiling, rustling the leaves of palms in ornate ceramic pots. A vast, elaborately framed mirror hung from one wall, reflecting me back at myself, dusty and hot from travel. Penny gestured to a cane settee and I sat among the brightly coloured cushions. She sat next to me while the men went outside, chatting about a new motorcycle the brigadier had bought. A plump woman in her forties in a checked blue sari brought us a tray of tea and teacakes.

'Thank you, Surabhi,' Penny said. 'Would you get the children up, please? I'd like Zara to meet them.'

'Yes, Mrs Fitzherbert,' she said.

'I don't know what I'd do without Surabhi,' Penny said to me as the servant left the room. 'If you end up living here in India, remember to always treat your staff like family. One good servant is worth six ordinary ones. Tea?'

'Yes, please. I don't know that I'll ever live in India.'

'Oh, won't you?' she said with a smile. 'Gordon thinks quite the opposite. In his telephone calls he said you and James are very close. That James thinks you might be the one.'

'I've only known him a few weeks.'

'How long do you need?' she said with a light laugh, handing me a cup of tea. 'Milk?'

How long *did* I need? Harry hadn't married me after seven years. 'Yes, please, but no sugar.'

'Oh, I am so *glad* you are here, Zara. I ache for female company. And Gordon says you are a fashion designer! I long to hear about dresses and shoes and lipsticks. I get about in a sari most days because it's so frightfully hot here, but look at you in a wool travelling suit. Oh, my heart.'

'I hope you'll teach me how to wear a sari,' I said, 'because this wool travelling suit was not the most practical choice.'

'I will, I will. Oh, look, here are my babies!'

Surabhi entered the room leading a sleepy-faced toddler with wild blond curls by the hand, and holding a bonny round-headed baby wrapped in Indian silks. I was instantly enamoured. The toddler sat in a chair and looked at his feet.

'Reggie has just woken up,' Surabhi said. 'He's not usually this quiet.'

'Oh, isn't that the truth,' Penny said, taking the baby and handing her directly to me. 'This is my little girl, Isabel. Isn't she divine? Surabhi, will she be hungry?'

'She'll cry when she's hungry,' Surabhi said, leaning over and stroking the infant's head. She clearly adored the children.

I had only held one other baby, and he had been a wriggly, noisy baby who cried instantly and had to be handed back to his mother. But this child, Isabel, gazed up at me with serene blue eyes, smiling a gummy smile at me.

'Good lord,' I said. 'I'm quite in love with her already.'

'She is such a *good* baby,' Penny said. 'No trouble. Not like Reggie. He was and continues to be a terror.'

Reggie seemed to take this as his cue to prove the point, and jumped to the floor to begin crawling about while meowing like a cat. He bumped the tea table, setting all the cups and saucers jingling, then howled with pain.

'Reggie, you aren't hurt. That's nonsense,' Penny said.

Surabhi seized him, placed him back in the chair and handed him a teacake, which he began to eat messily.

I was entranced. Not of the children, but of the life Penny was leading. A vast house in an exotic place, a loving husband, beautiful children, servants to help with everything . . . And if Penny was right, if James thought I was 'the one', I could have it, or something very close to it.

Perhaps James wasn't just a shipboard romance, perhaps he was my 'one' too.

———

After dinner and an evening playing canasta with James, Penny and the brigadier (who proved to be alarmingly competitive), James was relegated to an outdoor guesthouse while I was shown to a large bedroom where my suitcases awaited me. The tall windows were framed by broad shutters, and all of them were pushed open to let in the night breeze. A neat bathroom with no windows led off the guestroom. I gladly peeled off my travelling suit and stepped into the bath under the shower to wash the day's sweat and grime off me. In my nightdress, I switched off the lamp and blindly found my way under the mosquito net and into bed.

I had been lying there only a few minutes, my sleepy thoughts starting to blur together, when I heard a 'Psst.'

I sat up, eyes adjusting to the dark. Outside the open blinds, on the grass, stood James. I fought my way out of the mosquito net and switched on the light.

'James?'

'I know I should be in the guesthouse,' he said in a whisper. 'But I had to see you.'

I rose and pulled on my robe, wrapping it tight around me. I grasped his hand and pulled him over the sill and into the room, throwing my arms around him. We kissed, then he stepped away. 'I've been longing for a chance to sit and talk, just you and me.'

I gestured to the chaise against the opposite wall and we settled there for more kissing and not a lot of talking. Something about the thick night air, the exotic location, the fact that he was in a uniform and I just in a thin nightdress and robe, made me passionate and bold. James had been nothing but gentlemanly in all the time we'd been together, his hands never wandering, but now I took his hand, which was pressed into my back, and led it around to my breast. His fingers lingered there a moment, making my belly tighten with desire. Then he moved them away.

'Please,' I said.

'No, Zara,' he whispered against my ear. 'Not yet.'

Awkward dejection came over me. 'I'm sorry,' I said, not sure why I was saying it. I felt ashamed.

He sat back, took my hands in his and looked at me very directly with those dark sincere eyes. 'I need to be very clear with you so that you never need to feel sorry again.'

I squirmed under his gaze.

'I love these private moments with you,' he said. 'I love to see you in your nightdress and gown, seeing the private you. It's thrilling and such a privilege. But the secret you, underneath your nightdress . . . the secret moments we might have as a couple? They must wait until we're married. Only when we trust each other enough to say, "Yes, you are mine until we die," do we reveal all the secrets of ourselves.'

My cheeks flushed, and I swore to never let him know I'd had those secret moments with Harry. But why had I done that? Why hadn't I waited until Harry said, 'Yes, you are mine until we die'?

I nodded. 'You're right, James.'

He leaned in and kissed me again, but I felt chastened and confused, and when he pulled back, I said, 'I really should sleep. Penny said she would take me to the markets in the morning.'

'Of course, my love. But just one last question.'

'Go on.'

'Do you like India?'

'I love it.'

'Then you wouldn't mind living here?'

I couldn't quite meet his eye. He had already talked openly about marriage, Penny had raised it, and I was afraid he was about to propose.

'Under the right circumstances,' I said.

'Good,' he replied. And that was all. I kissed him goodbye at the window then went back to bed, both disappointed and relieved that he hadn't asked me to marry him.

———

Time in Poona ran slowly and deliciously. It was something about the heat, the beautiful house, the good company. Penny and I became firm friends, and little Reggie began to call me Aunty Zara, which made my heart melt. I became incredibly fond of Surabhi, who was a cross between a nanny, a lady's maid and a friend to Penny. The three of us and the children spent our time at the markets, where I bought some incredible Indian silks to play with when I got home, or had tea together at the tearooms in town, or took late afternoon walks to the pond at the bottom of their property so Reggie could see the ducks and goats. It jarred me a little when we'd return from our outings and Penny would turn to Surabhi and give her orders – always politely and gently – but I supposed that life was like that in India, and didn't question it.

Through the long hot afternoons I lay on my bed under the fan and drew. Indian style and colours now inflected everything I designed, and I very much missed having a dress salon to design for. James was working most days, but I saw him every evening, both in the parlour and then later in my bedroom. Sometimes we spent the time kissing, other times he would lay his head in my lap and gaze up at me while I stroked his hair, and tell me all his opinions about the world. He wasn't as intellectual as Harry, but he was wonderfully earnest and committed to doing things the right way.

As to whether I loved him. Some days I did, with burning heat. Some days I still loved Harry. I can't begin to describe how confusing this was, and I would spend long hours in bed at night trying to think it through, as though I could make my feelings change by talking to them rationally. I no longer wanted to be in love with Harry. I wanted to be in love with James.

Two weeks into my visit, a telegram arrived from my mother, telling me I was needed at home. I was prepared to ignore her again, but James saw it and became quite exercised about the idea that my parents would blame him for my truancy. He was very keen that they like him or, in the absence of meeting him, not actively dislike him. So I packed my things again, booked my passage home and said a tearful goodbye to Penny, Surabhi and the little ones.

James and I were silent with each other on the way to the train station in the car. I could feel the wrench of leaving him coming. He probably felt the same.

We pulled up, and James instructed the driver to take my bags to the porter. We stayed in the back seat, and James took my hand and said what I'd been expecting him to say for weeks. 'I want to marry you.'

I nodded. 'I know,' I said. 'I have known you nine weeks. Give me a little time apart from you to see if I still feel the same.'

He grimaced, and I realised that it caused him pain that I hadn't instantly said yes.

'I can do that,' he said. 'And I will write to you and . . . I won't let you go.'

I kissed him hard, then pushed him away and climbed out of the car.

'I love you,' he called after me.

'I love you too,' I called back. Then made my way to the platform.

———

I was sick of trains. I was sick of ships. I would wake up in my cabin and forget which ship I was on, which leg of my journey. I was weary of being in transit, of living out of my now-battered suitcases. I was well and truly ready to be home.

I spent a good deal of the journey from India to Australia in my cabin. I didn't try to make friends or join in games this time. I was a little heartbroken, missing James terribly. But I was also apprehensive. Betty had been sure Harry was missing me. Did that mean he would be back in my life? I had no idea what I was to do next. So I avoided all thought of it and lay on my bed all day drawing endless designs for dresses and suits. I ran out of paper and started drawing them on the ship's letterhead. Bad weather set in and it all went on without me, in a world beyond my creative bubble, where I did some of my best work so far.

When we finally docked at Princes Pier in Melbourne, it was like waking from a dream. I kept saying to myself, *I am home, I am home*, letting the feeling sink in. I had been away for months and months, and I had seen and done so many new things. I was a different woman from the one who had left. Suitcases in hand, I followed the crowd down towards the station. That was when I heard my name being called.

'Zara!' It was Harry. He had climbed onto the base of an iron pole to see over the crowd and had luckily spotted me.

My heart leaped, and I realised the firm talking-to I had given it had not worked. I turned back and made my way against the traffic towards him. I put my suitcases down and he jumped off the pole and drew me into an embrace. 'I missed you.'

I lay my head against his shoulder, intoxicated with the familiar smell of him. 'Oh god,' I said.

'You don't sound pleased to see me,' he replied, his voice rumbling in his chest.

'We ended on such a bad note. I thought all this was over.'

'We always fight. It's nothing.'

I didn't know how to answer; I just squeezed him hard against me and wondered what on earth I should do next.

CHAPTER 11

Harry wanted to immediately resume our life as it had been, as though we hadn't been apart for eons. He'd organised for us to attend a party the very night I came home, but I refused, and told him to give me a week or so to rest after my travels and to make amends to my parents who were incredibly cross with me. To Mum especially, it was scandalous that I should jump ship with a cavalry officer in India. When I told her that he'd asked me to marry him, she softened a little.

'But what about Harry?' she asked.

Yes, what about Harry?

I spent as much time as I could at Genevieve's house as she had a new baby, who I was utterly smitten with. I had learned a thing or two about looking after babies from Surabhi, including a beautiful Hindi lullaby that I sang to little April. Despite my inability to hold a tune, it seemed to settle her. Being around so many babies and little children in recent weeks had made me clucky, and I can't say it didn't play on my mind as I tried to decide between my two suitors.

Mum was the only one who knew about my tortured heart. Every evening I would join her in the kitchen to help prepare tea – the kitchen being the only place the boys would never dare to set foot – and pour out my feelings to her. I went round in circles. I loved both, but had my doubts about both.

Mum got fed up one night and exclaimed, 'Perhaps you should marry neither of them!'

But it wasn't an option. I was in my mid-twenties and I didn't want to be left on the shelf. I wanted a husband, a house and babies.

At the end of that first week, Harry begged me to come to a dinner with him. He had spectacularly lost his election in September, but needed to thank some business supporters who had donated money to his campaign.

'It will be boring,' he warned me over the telephone, 'but I need you there. Please?'

I agreed. I had always loved to be needed by Harry.

The dinner was in the Grand Dining Room of the Windsor Hotel where Harry and I had attended many dinners before, as it stood across the road from Parliament House on Spring Street. It was one of Melbourne's finest hotels and I loved the rich carpet and brass chandeliers of the dining room. Harry was right that the evening was dull, but I had become adept at smiling and nodding while my brain whirred away thinking about something else. On this occasion, I was watching myself from the outside as I sank easily back into my old life, the old way of doing things. As though my trip had never happened (though I wore one of my New York gowns). As though James had never happened. The feeling of being away and out in the world hadn't left me. It was a buried ache. I didn't *want* to keep doing things the old way and I forgot I had ever been homesick. I thought I had become bigger than this biddable puppet at the table, smiling at old men who talked endlessly about what the electorate wanted but never bothered to ask the woman sitting right beside them.

Somehow I managed to get through dinner and dessert, then stayed at the table with the other wives while Harry went off to smoke cigars with the men. On one side of me sat a woman in her sixties with tight grey curls and a fox fur, on the other, a woman of around forty who was so thin that I could see her wrist bones peeping out from under her scalloped cuffs. They knew each other and leaned across me to talk, not excluding me, but not inviting me in either.

I let my mind drift and was once again back in Poona with James, one of those long, warm nights when he'd come to see me and had fallen asleep lying in my lap. I'd watched his sleeping face and marvelled at what a privilege it was to watch somebody sleeping.

'A penny for your thoughts,' said the younger woman.

I snapped out of my reverie. 'Pardon?'

'You were smiling. Obviously having some delicious thought. Tell me, was it about young Harry? He seems quite enamoured of you.'

Was I doomed to think about James when I was with Harry, and about Harry when I was with James? Rather than answering her question, I asked one of my own.

'Do you mind when the men all go off together and leave us here?'

The younger woman blinked as though she didn't understand the question, but the older woman nodded emphatically. 'You grow used to it, dear. Being a politician's wife means learning to be an independent dependant. You must be the good woman who follows him about wherever he goes, but also able to hold your own when he's not around.'

'It gets easier once you have children,' the younger woman said. 'You have your own little world then.' She glanced at my hands folded in front of me. 'But you're not engaged yet? So there's no wedding on the horizon?'

I was suddenly so weary of people asking me when Harry was going to marry me. I couldn't sit a moment longer, so I pushed back my chair, grabbed my evening bag and said, 'Excuse me.' I was halfway to the exit when Harry suddenly returned, dangling a hotel key in front of him.

'Where are you off to?' he said, and an expression crossed his face I had not seen before. A kind of fearful puzzlement. I had never tried to walk out of one of these events before.

'I'm tired,' I said.

'Not so tired that you don't want to see the most expensive suite in the hotel?'

'Where did you get that key?'

'Lord Hansom is staying there tonight. He said we could go and take a look. Come on.'

My curiosity was piqued. He grasped my hand and I smiled. 'All right then, but after that I'm going home. Don't make me sit with the ladies any longer.'

'I shall do no such thing. I shall accompany you all the way to your front door.' He was dragging me towards the lift, which arrived with a subtle ding.

'Third floor, please,' he said to the lift operator, who nodded obediently.

Once the door was closed, Harry pushed me up against the wall and kissed me. Passionately kissed me like he hadn't since I returned. I melted against him, scandalously careless of whether or not the lift operator saw us. When the door opened again, Harry dragged me out and I hurried after him, catching his excitement. He unlocked the door to the suite and I found myself standing in an immense apartment with thick red carpet, gleaming polished wood, brilliant chandeliers and deep leather couches.

'Oh my,' I said, stopping at the windows to take in the view across to Parliament House. The gardens were lit by lamps, which illuminated light rain as it fell.

'Come here, Zara,' Harry said, and I turned and followed the sound of his voice to another room. A four-poster bed sat in the middle of it, with Harry lying on it, on his side. He patted the brocade bedcovers.

My feet hesitated.

'I said, come here,' he repeated gently.

I sat on the bed, feet chastely on the floor. He tackled me playfully so I was lying on my back and kissed me fervently. My body responded as it always had to him, the spark that could always set me on fire. His hands began to wander, down my front, across my thighs, to the hem of my dress, which he slowly began to inch up.

I took a deep breath. 'Stop,' I said.

He stopped, propped himself on his elbow. 'Zara?'

I sat up and pushed my hem back down. 'No, Harry,' I said. 'I won't do that.'

'Why not? We've done it a hundred times.'

'That was before. Do you forget what happened? I broke it off with you.'

'Well, we've done that a hundred times too.' He stroked my thigh through my dress. 'I've missed you.'

'I am very confused, Harry. And until I know what I want, these . . . secret moments must wait.' I remembered what James had said. 'It's only when we trust each other enough to say, "Yes, you are mine until we die," that we should do such things.'

He nodded slowly, then said. 'Did you meet someone else?'

No point in hiding it. 'I did. A cavalry officer from the British Indian Army. His name is James and he fancies himself in love with me.'

Harry smiled, but that fearful puzzlement had returned to his face. 'Well, I fancy myself in love with you too, Zara, and have for a lot longer than this Indian fellow.'

'He's English. From Stratford-upon-Avon. He studied at Sandhurst.'

'Oh, I see,' he said sarcastically. 'Sounds quite the fellow. I wonder that you don't fancy yourself in love with him, just as you say he's in love with you.'

His snipy anger was too much for me to bear. I climbed to my feet. 'I don't want to play out this nonsense with you tonight. I'm too tired and too . . . unsettled. Have a heart and take me home.'

He softened, and rose to come and take my hand. 'Certainly, my dear. I'll drop this key back to Lord Hansom, and perhaps tonight we'll take a taxicab instead of a tram. My treat.'

I waited in the foyer while Harry returned the key, trying to understand what it meant that I had told Harry about James, but I had never told James about Harry.

———

I knew I had a decision to make, but I had no idea how to make it. My feelings pitched as wildly as a ship in a storm, and because I couldn't make sense of them, I ignored them. I had no job to go to, so I spent the day in my room drawing. At night, I returned to parties, dinners and dances, and behaved just like the old Zara, but inside I felt profoundly different. Profoundly ready for something to change forever.

The first letter that arrived from James made my heart leap. It was pages and pages in his tidy handwriting, telling me every detail of what he'd done since I left. Only the final paragraph was dedicated to his feelings for me.

> *Zara, meeting you was the most wonderful thing that has ever happened to me. I miss your shining eyes and your mischievous laugh. I miss that dreamy expression that comes over your face when you slip into deep thought. I want more than anything for you to join me over here as my wife. I know you need time to decide, but I will wait for you forever.*
>
> *With boundless love, James*

I folded it and pressed it against my heart, feeling the swell of the sea inside me again.

James wrote to me once a week, though sometimes the post delivered them days apart or all together. Every letter both thrilled me and racked me with guilt because I spent most evenings with Harry. Mum saw all the letters arrive and saw Harry every time he collected me, and while she said nothing, I knew she was judging me. In fact, she mentioned it to Genevieve, who took me to task over it.

We were sitting in her sunny front room while little April fussed on her lap. We had been talking about something else completely when Vieve suddenly said, 'So what are you going to do about this cavalry officer?'

'What do you mean?' Guilt thudded in my throat.

'Mum says he writes you letters and you write letters back, and I know he's in love with you. Are you going to put him out of his misery?'

'I told him I need time to decide.'

'Did you tell him you were going back to your old boyfriend too?'

'Well, no . . .'

'Is that fair? Leaving him pining over you back in India while you run around to parties with Harry?'

I fell silent. April continued to squeak grumpily. Vieve continued jiggling her.

Finally I asked, 'What do you think I should do?'

Vieve sighed and stood up, began rocking April from side to side. 'I don't know, Zara,' she said at last. 'I'm tired and cranky and finding this life' – she took her hand away from April's downy head and gestured around – 'really hard to manage.'

'You seem as though you're doing it perfectly well.'

'*Seem.*' She repeated. 'It's all in the seeming and not in the being. I longed to marry Jack, and I thought it a dream come true. But now I spend my days as a servant to him and a slave to this little being.' Her hand came to rest on April's head again. 'I love them both dearly, but I had no idea that love would be so entrapping. So my advice would be: marry neither of them. Stay a spinster.'

I stifled a laugh.

'Seriously, Zara. You need to choose one. You and Harry have been an item for years, why would you change course now?'

'Because Harry gives no indication of wanting to marry.'

April roused and started full-throatedly crying. Genevieve excused herself and took the little one off to the nursery to feed her, leaving me sitting alone in a sunbeam. The hedges outside the window were unruly, uneven growth sticking up at odd angles. A butterfly rested on one of the disorderly shoots, its wings moving gently and slowly. I concentrated hard on it, as April's cries faded and eventually stopped in the room behind me. I didn't want to be a spinster. As much as Genevieve was finding life with a new baby difficult, I wanted what she had, and sometimes I wondered what was wrong with me that I hadn't managed to make it happen yet.

———

Perhaps, in some unacknowledged part of me, I had wanted Harry to find the letters.

Daddy had bought me a set of watercolours. I usually used coloured pencils for my drawings, but I liked the way the watercolours blended, and I had been creating a children's story about fairies for April, and illustrating it lavishly. When Harry came by for lunch one Friday, and I was the only one home, I invited him to my bedroom to show him my art. But the letters were sitting right next to us on top of the bookcase, so after he admired my paintings, of course he picked one up.

He turned it over and inspected the back. 'India, eh?'

'Give it back, Harry.'

'I didn't know you were still stringing this fellow along. There's quite a lot of letters here.' He lifted the flap of the envelope.

'Harry, don't.' I reached for the letter, but he was much taller than me and held it out of my reach as he pulled out the handwritten pages. Anger began to boil in my stomach. 'That's private.'

He turned away from me, glancing through the pages. 'Does he tell you what he does every minute of every day? It's a wonder he has time to ride his horse around persecuting the natives.'

'Harry!'

'Oh, oh, what's this? "I know you need time to decide but I will wait for you forever." What a fine specimen of a man, he is.

A veritable kicked puppy. Where is his dignity? Well, make him wait forever, Zara, because you're my girl, not his.'

I snatched the letter out of his hands and slid it back into the envelope. I couldn't speak for fury. Harry had made *me* wait forever ... did he think I was a kicked puppy too? Did he wonder at my dignity? I imagined how I must look through his eyes: a pathetic little lump, always gazing at him hopefully.

'Oh, I've upset you,' he said, and tried to pull me into his arms. 'I've insulted your Indian.'

'Harry, don't. Honestly, how can somebody as clever as you be so oblivious about how people might feel.'

He grabbed my hands and brought them up to his lips, kissing them. 'You're my girl, Zara. Not his,' he repeated.

'Why, Harry?' I asked. 'Why do you love me?' I was already pathetic, I may as well ask outright for some kind of compliment, some kind of confirmation that he *saw* me.

'Because you're my girl. I've always known it and so have you,' he said lightly. He kissed the top of my head. 'You're always going to get the same answer, Zara. Until the day I die.'

'Then why are we not married?'

'You know the reasons. I've told you many times.'

'Money.'

'And it's temporary. I'm on the up, my love. Not much further to go, and then we'll get married, have a little house, some babies ...' He smiled at me, that heart-melting grin, those wretchedly long lashes. 'To do that, we'll have to resume our "secret moments", as you called them.'

A warm thrill passed through me despite myself. As always, madly in love with and madly infuriated by Harry.

———

On the weekend, Mum often took herself out to weed the flowerbeds. On Saturday afternoon I found her in a patch of shade in the front garden, head down among the foxgloves, pulling weeds. It was a mild day, the last gasp of summer.

'Mum?'

'Hmm-mm?'

I stood by uncomfortably. I hoped she had seen me moping all week and would understand I needed to talk. 'Do you need any help with the weeding?'

She leaned back on her haunches and looked up at me. 'You've never offered to help before so I can only assume you want me for something else.'

I sank to the grass beside her. 'Yes,' I said miserably. 'I'm so confused.'

'What's new? You've been confused since you got back from your trip. I think you've got too much time on your hands. You spend all your days thinking and not doing.'

'I want to *do*. I want a life like Genevieve or Betty, or the brigadier's wife. I'm too old to be living here doing nothing. I'm going to be left on the shelf.'

Mum pulled off her gardening gloves and grasped my hand. 'No, you're not. In fact, you have not one but *two* suitors. You simply need to choose one.'

'How do I choose? I love them both.'

She shook her head. 'You're asking yourself the wrong question. It's not about which one you love the most, but about which one loves you the most. That's the one that will make you happy. I hate to say it, Zara, because you know we adore Harry, but he makes you sad on as many days as he makes you happy.'

'He doesn't make me sad, he makes me angry.'

'The anger is from sadness, because your heart knows he's not being gentle with it. And you're half-Scottish,' she added with a smirk. 'We're angry people.'

I laughed. 'I do have a temper.'

'It only proves you're alive. You've a shining spirit, my darling. You'll make one of them a wonderful wife. But choose the one who will appreciate it most.'

And in a moment, I made my decision. A little *clunk* of truth fell into place, and it was so satisfying and so right.

'Thank you, Mum,' I said, kissing her cheek and scrambling to my feet.

I grabbed my handbag and went directly to the post office to telegraph James, inviting him to Melbourne to meet my family.

————

The truth was there wasn't a good time to tell Harry. James had wired me back within hours, telling me he had requested special leave to come to Australia and been granted it. He would be with me in three weeks, and it happened that the three weeks coincided with Harry taking on a complex brief that kept him late at work and too exhausted for more than the occasional telephone call.

Every time I got off the telephone, Mum would ask me, 'Did you tell him yet?'

But what was I to tell him? I hadn't actually said yes to James's proposal, though no doubt my invitation had elevated his hopes. I had heard the expression 'cold feet' before, and now I understood it. Every time I thought about marrying James, I'd get a cold shiver all over and the arches of my feet felt hollow, as though I was about to step off a great height. So my answer to my mother was always 'not yet', and my answer remained the same for three weeks until the afternoon James was to arrive.

Half an hour before I was due to catch the train to Princes Pier, I was in a lather at home, finding the right clothes and shoes, pinning curls and choosing lipstick. Mum buzzed about me, telling me not to say yes to James before he'd met the family, and especially Daddy, who was traditional enough to expect him to ask for my hand.

The sound of the doorbell barely registered, but then David knocked at my bedroom door and said Harry was here to see me.

My heart quickened. Mum and I exchanged glances.

'Did you invite him over?' she asked.

'Are you mad? Today of all days? Of course I didn't.'

'I'm sorry to say it, Zara, but this is what you get by not being completely honest.'

'There's nothing to tell him yet, Mum.'

'Well go and put him off somehow. We can't have you missing your train.'

Barefoot, I hurried out to the living room where Harry leaned on the back of a chair chatting to Daddy.

'Ah, there you are, Zara,' Harry said. 'Have you got a minute?'

'Just a minute,' I said.

Harry looked around. 'Somewhere private?'

'Come out to the patio.' I figured he'd be easier to send on his way if he was already out the front door.

'Lovely,' he said, and followed me out.

Long shadows in the garden moved with the afternoon breeze. My feet were instantly cold. He sat down, then indicated I should as well.

'You seem tense,' he said.

'I really only have a minute.'

'Sit down.'

I perched on the edge of the bench. 'What is it, Harry?'

'I rather thought you were keeping me at arm's length the last fortnight or so.'

'Nonsense. You've been busy. I haven't wanted to get in your way.'

'Oh, Zara. You are a shocking liar. In any case, I ran into your brother-in-law Jack in the city and he told me everything.'

A hot white light seemed to creep up around my field of vision. Guilt made me mute.

'I'd like to hear it from you though. What's going on?'

'James is coming to meet my family,' I managed to say.

'And you're going to marry him?'

'I don't know,' I said honestly.

'Mm,' he grunted softly, his gaze turning towards the garden. Then he sighed, and fished around in his pocket, withdrawing something held in his fist. 'Close your eyes and open your hand.'

'What?' I couldn't think straight.

'Come on,' he said. 'I promise you'll like it.'

I closed my eyes and held out my hand, and felt something small and hard pressed into my palm. I didn't need to look at it to know what it was. My stomach dropped.

'Harry,' I breathed.

'You don't want me to get down on one knee, do you? You have never struck me as the old-fashioned type.'

The ring was gold, with a swirling design over its shoulders and a square-cut diamond sitting flush in the head. 'When did you get this?'

'I've been saving up for a while. But know this, if you take this ring, you are not to go to Princes Pier and meet that Indian fellow.'

The pressure inside me surged. I was trapped in a nightmare.

He leaned away, his arm along the back of the bench. So assured of himself. Almost smug. 'Zara, you look sick. This isn't how I imagined my proposal going.'

My body woke into a rage. I stood up and handed the ring back. 'This isn't how I imagined it either,' I said. 'For a start, I imagined it happening several years ago. I imagined it happening because you loved me, not because you were afraid of losing me.'

'I do love you.'

'But you don't want to marry me, not really. You just want to stop me from marrying James. This is not love – it's territorial pissing.'

A flutter of alarm crossed his face. I rarely used such language, and had never used it with him, despite how infuriated he made me over the years.

'I do want to marry you,' he protested. 'I've spent a fortune on this damned ring. The least you can do is say yes.'

'Listen to yourself. Is this any way to ask me to be your wife? What am I supposed to think? You've strung me along for more than seven years, Harry. I would have said yes in any of those years if you'd asked me willingly and lovingly. But I won't say yes now. This is too little and too late.'

A cloud moved over his eyes. He stood and pocketed the ring. 'You're a child. I thought going overseas would make you grow up.'

'Don't condescend to me, you infuriating man,' I said. 'You are not better than me.'

'I'm not the dreamy fool you are though,' he shot back. 'Go off and have your fairytale with your cavalry officer and your mansion run by unhappy servants. You will regret this.'

'As will you,' I said icily. 'You threw away my love with both hands.'

He seemed to be about to say something, then decided on silence. He nodded once then walked away briskly. I sat heavily on the bench and dropped my head in my hands. I thought I might cry, but tears wouldn't come. I felt sick and awful.

Mum was there a moment later, her arm around me. 'You did the right thing,' she said. 'A marriage made under duress is bound to be unhappy.'

I lifted my head and took a deep breath. 'I'm done with that man.'

She nodded. 'I would wish for something calmer and more peaceful for you, my dear.'

I thought of James, with his soft eyes and his boy-scout earnestness, and I knew that he could provide me with calm and peace. 'I had better get my shoes on,' I said. 'I don't want to miss the train.'

Down at Princes Pier, the ship had already docked and let its passengers off, and most had caught the earlier train or been picked up by loved ones. A dozen or so passengers still waited, dotted around on benches or stairs. I saw James straight away, in full uniform, his back to me and his gaze out over the harbour. My heart hitched and my knees seemed to go loose at their hinges. I paused, watching him.

Then he turned and saw me and smiled, and all the rough turbulence of my relationship with Harry fell away. With James, I believed I could have smooth sailing. I smiled and ran towards him.

He caught me and kissed me, and I leaned against him. Then he pulled away and said, 'Zara, I –'

But I put my finger up against his lips and said just one word. 'Yes.'

His eyes lit up.

Within a month, I was married and on my way to India.

PART 3

CHAPTER 12

JUBBULPORE, 1935

The first time I saw what was to be my marital home, it was in the sweep of headlights, late in the evening. We had already driven past the regiment barracks and through the front of the officers compound. Here, two-storey bungalows separated by gardened spaces sat in a row. Ours was the second-to-last in the row. Like the others, it was whitewashed stone with a hipped roof and a veranda whose columns were overgrown with flowering vines. The car stopped directly in front and the driver fetched our luggage while James came to open my door.

I took his hand and stepped out as two servants in collarless shirts came to help from opposite directions. Lights came on inside the bungalow.

'What do you think?' James said.

I couldn't find words to articulate the stirring sense of destiny that had just gripped me. Instead, I smiled up at him and said, 'I think I shall be very happy here if I ever grow used to the heat.'

He slid his arm around my side and it came to rest on my waist. It was early enough in our physical relationship for me to find this small intimacy thrilling, and I couldn't wait to get him inside.

The servants hovered around though, offering us food and tea. I asked all their names but couldn't remember any, and promised I would write them down tomorrow and memorise them.

James sent the servants on their way. 'We can manage fine this evening. It's late. We'll see you tomorrow morning at seven for breakfast.'

One by one they withdrew, and James and I found ourselves standing in our hallway alone. I wound my arms around his neck and pulled him down to kiss me. He responded with depth and heat and passion, then when I moved my body against him, he pulled back.

'I'll show you your new house first. Then straight to bed for us.'

'All right.'

The bungalow was set out simply. The veranda functioned as reception, then beyond the front door was a hallway with rooms off either side. The first two were a dining room and sitting room, the second a library-cum-parlour and an office. We had reached the back door, which he opened onto an external breezeway, which we crossed to get to a small outbuilding.

'And here's the kitchen, not that you'll need to use it,' James said, opening the door and flicking on the light.

I took a sudden step backwards when I saw that standing in the middle of the little room was a horse. The floor had hay spread over it and balls of horse dung sat on the floor by the ice chest. 'Good lord!' I said.

'I'm so sorry,' James said, opening the back door and shepherding the horse out. It was a beautiful golden creature, with no bridle or saddle. 'Somebody will be here in the morning to clean that up.'

'Why was there a horse in the kitchen?'

'As I said, we don't tend to use our kitchens much. Servants do all the cooking in the central mess. And when it gets really hot, some of the horses do better inside. Pilot is one of those horses.'

'Pilot?'

'He's my horse. Only been here from England a few months.' A smile of pride and affection came over his face. 'Think of him as being like one of my friends.'

'I don't know that I'd stand for you letting one of your friends relieve himself in the kitchen either,' I joked.

He closed the kitchen door and we returned to the bungalow to make our way up the stairs to the second storey. Here, there were two bedrooms, both in darkness. James gestured to the first. 'Ours,' he said, then gestured to the other and added, 'and the nursery.'

A fluttering, delicious falling sensation washed over me. 'Ah, the nursery. Well, we'd best get busy.'

He scooped me up – not the first time he'd done it, and despite how strong and tall he was, I feared he would hurt his back – and carried me across the threshold to the bedroom. Faint light from the waning moon illuminated the room through the open shutters. He found the opening in the mosquito net and laid me down on soft cool sheets. I asked him to switch on the lamp but he said no. I wanted to see my new bedroom, I wanted to see him and have him see me. On our wedding night on the ship, he'd refused to have the light on too. It seemed he was always going to say no, so I decided to stop asking.

Our clothes and shoes still jumbled down the end of the bed, we fell asleep naked and entwined in the balmy night air.

―――

The heat and light woke me early, but James was already up. I heard him in the adjoining washroom, humming to himself while he shaved. Our bungalow, he had warned me, had electricity but no running water. Instead, the servants would keep our washroom supplied with barrels of water and a jug, and collect the porcelain bowl that fit inside our thunderbox: a smoothly carved wooden toilet under the washroom window. My nightdress was somewhere in my luggage, which James had brought up and left at the foot of the bed, so for now I pulled on yesterday's petticoat and joined him in the bathroom. I slid my arms around his waist. He wore breeches and a white singlet. 'Good morning, handsome.'

'Good morning, my lovely wife. Breakfast is in half an hour. I'll meet you in the dining room. Just have to go and check on Pilot.'

He flicked soap off his razor and rinsed it in the sink. I touched his face. 'Very smooth,' I said. 'Give my love to Pilot.'

I listened to his footsteps descend the stairs, then washed up and readied myself for the day. I slid into a sleeveless silk shift, and put on a dash of red lipstick for good measure.

It felt as though I was awash with perspiration before I had even hit the bottom stair. The humidity was soupy. I followed the sound of plates and cutlery being laid out in the dining room and peeked around the threshold.

'Come in, come in,' said a man in a thick accent. He was little and wizened like a nut, but his hair was still black and shiny. He wore the collarless shirt and loose pants I had seen on all the male servants, but his clothes were a rich, stiff blue, unlike the muted greys and browns of the others. 'Sit here,' he said, indicating the setting at one end of the table. I could see another setting for James, who wasn't here yet. It was several feet away at the other end of the table.

'Thank you,' I said.

'No trouble at all, Mrs Fell. I am Mr Parakh and I am head of your household staff. Here we have Daljeet and Girish . . .' he gestured with his hand towards two much younger men, one who looked no older than fifteen. He had that thin, gangly body that was all knees and elbows.

'Yes, I believe I met you last night,' I said, and committed their names to memory. Daljeet was the one who looked very young. Girish was the one with the melancholy eyes and the flare to his nostrils. They both nodded at me submissively.

'Ah, and here is Urvashi, your house girl,' Mr Parakh continued, as a slight woman about my age entered the room with a tea tray.

'My pleasure, Mrs Fell,' she said, placing the tray on the table. 'Welcome. Would you like tea?'

'Ah, yes. Thank you.'

'My pleasure,' she said again. I liked her lilting accent. She wore a soft grey sari over a white short-sleeved shirt. All of them had bare feet, and I longed to kick off my shoes and feel the cool stone floor under them.

I drank my tea and waited for James. Everything looked different in daylight. Bright sunshine flooded in through the shutters and made rainbows on my eyelashes. A fan turned overhead, stirring the thick air and gently moving the fronds on the tall palm in the corner of the room. A bustle in the hallway told me my husband was nearby, and soon he was kissing my cheek and telling me I looked beautiful, and sitting down for his tea. We chatted for a few minutes while servants refilled our tea, and Urvashi brought in a full cooked breakfast the way the English have it. Bacon, sausage, eggs. It was far too much for a person like me, who had little appetite in the mornings. I picked around the edges while James told me his plans for the day. I knew he'd be working, but I hadn't realised he'd go back to it the minute we arrived.

'But don't worry, I shan't abandon you completely,' he said at last. 'Have you ever ridden a horse?'

'Once. I wasn't very good at it.'

'I'm going to teach you to ride. Starting tomorrow morning. We'll get up an hour earlier so it's nice and cool. What do you think?'

'I think that sounds thrilling,' I said.

I had left the rest of the food untouched for a few minutes, so Urvashi approached and gently said to me, 'Mrs Fell, are you finished with your meal?'

'Yes, Urvashi,' I said, sitting back so she could take the plate. As she did, we bumped each other, and the next thing I knew there was a fried egg in my lap.

'Oh, I'm so sorry. So sorry,' she said.

'It's fine. Not your fault, dear,' I replied, picking the egg up and plopping it back on the plate.

Mr Parakh approached, roaring at her in Hindi. She drew her head down and braced, as though she had experienced such a tongue-lashing before.

'Mr Parakh, there's no need,' I said. 'The accident was my fault.'

He gave me an obviously false smile. 'Urvashi is clumsy,' he said. 'She has been warned before.'

Urvashi scampered out of the room with her head down, Mr Parakh behind her. I was horrified by what had just happened, but it seemed James had barely noticed. He was buttering a roll.

'That Mr Parakh is a fierce little fellow. Does he talk to all the servants like that?'

'Don't know. I don't understand enough Hindi.' He reached for his teacup. 'What do you have planned for the day?'

'Is Penny here?'

'She's still back in Poona. She spends most of her time there. I'm sure she'll come up with the children once she hears you're here.' He gave me a boyish grin. 'You should come and watch the parade. It happens every morning, but I think you'll like it. And some of the other ladies will be there.'

'I should change my dress first,' I said, looking at the oily print on the silk.

He finished his roll and drained the last of his tea, then beckoned Girish to clear the table. 'Parade is at nine,' he said, climbing to his feet. 'I have to get away now, but you go ahead and take your time to change, then have a wander about the compound. Come down through the gates just before nine and there will be somebody around to show you down to the field.'

He leaned down and kissed my cheek again, then whispered in my ear, 'I can't wait to show off my new wife. Your cheeks are rosy with happiness.'

Even though my cheeks were rosy from the heat, it was true that I was stupidly happy. I quickly changed into a cotton belted dress in a cheerful floral print with butterfly sleeves, and grabbed a hat and gloves to ward off the sunshine.

Our front veranda was made of stone, and blossoms in the vines smelled sweet and strong. Two cane chairs with huge round backs sat in the shade. Out on the steps, the sun hit me. I felt it on my back as I headed down the dirt road, past identical bungalows with only a few differences here and there. Different types of cornices, rails and trims. Different furniture. Potted plants and vines. At about the fourth house down I saw a woman emerge from her front door and waited to introduce myself.

'Hello,' she said, in a clipped, slightly nasal but terribly British accent. 'You're new.'

'Zara Fell,' I said, offering her my gloved hand.

She looked at my hand and then looked at me, as if puzzled. 'Only men shake hands, darling. I'm Larissa Honeybird, Major Honeybird's wife.' She grasped my upper arms and kissed both of my cheeks in turn. 'There you are. That's how we greet each other. Are you coming down to the parade?'

'Yes, I am,' I replied. 'I was going to have a quick look around the compound first.'

'I'll take you. Come along.' She strode off quickly. She was about my height, but straight up and down in shape and buzzing with energy. Her hair was light brown, worn in a long plait around her head. Quite old-fashioned. I had to hurry my steps to keep up with her as she took me through the grassy spaces between the bungalows and down towards the servant quarters, pointing out the well, the fountain, the huge cooking pit under a timber and thatch gazebo, and the path into the jungly woods that I was 'never ever to go to' on my own. I could see the gardens of all the bungalows from here, and some of them had arches and beautiful flowerbeds.

Ours didn't, and I made that first on my list of things to do. Though perhaps if James was leading Pilot in and out through the garden it wouldn't be such a good idea. She also took me past the stables, and I mentioned that James was going to teach me to ride.

'Oh, how divine,' she said. 'I've asked Frank a hundred times and a hundred times he's said he's too busy. I even have a riding outfit, which I'll give to you on our way home today as I've no use for it, and now you do.'

I was about to refuse when I realised I had nothing to ride a horse in. I had one pair of high-waisted twill pants, but they didn't fit well at my waist if I sat down. So I accepted, or at least I didn't refuse because Larissa was onto another topic now as she unlatched the gate to the regimental grounds and pointed out the barracks, a series of single-storey, lime-washed stone buildings with arched verandas and square roofs. Further down the hill, I could see horses and troops gathering in a field. The heat was really blazing now and I longed for a drink of water.

'Oof, we'd better hurry, they've started,' she said.

I tried to cling to shade on the way down the hill, but there wasn't much. Sweat gathered underneath my breasts, and I vowed I would stop wearing petticoats as of tomorrow. I'd stop wearing clothes all together if I could, as they were sticking to me everywhere. I had felt summery and cool when I slipped the dress on, now I felt flushed and sticky.

Finally we were behind a stone building in a delicious strip of shade as the regimental horns blew and the parade started. Larissa waved to another two women a little further down, and they waved back at her and mouthed 'hello' at me. A surprisingly warm welcome. I could see James, mounted on Pilot, in his flared riding coat and gold and blue turban. He carried a tall lance. Everything seemed to glimmer and gleam: the burnished lances, the jingling metal parts of the bridles, even the horses shone. I was enchanted.

Larissa elbowed me gently and leaned into my ear. 'Look, it's the Pathan.'

'The what?'

'The *who*,' she said with a mischievous grin. 'See?'

The first line of foot soldiers after the cavalry were not as impressively dressed, but still looked crisp and sharp in paler blue uniforms. Most of these men were white like the cavalry, but there was one man – the one Larissa was breathlessly pointing out to me – who was quite the most spectacular human of either sex I had ever seen. He was tall and beautifully formed, with amber skin and long black hair and striking blue eyes. A strong nose and heavy eyebrows made him look almost like a bird of prey.

Larissa hooked her arm through mine and sighed, 'Most of us wives come down every morning just to get a look at him.'

'What's his name?'

'I don't know. We just call him the Pathan, because that's what the boys call him. I think it might be something to do with where he's from.' She shrugged, then glanced at the other two women, one of whom was miming a swoon. Larissa laughed. 'That's Franny. She's a hoot. And the other is Cleo. I'll introduce you to them afterwards, and we should all get together for a ladies afternoon tea, don't you think?'

'I'd like that,' I said.

———

It turned out that a 'ladies afternoon tea' in the officers compound meant sitting around Larissa's dining table, drinking gin cocktails out of teacups, smoking and playing Scrabble. I found myself staring at my letters in an unexpected fog – Cleo had made the cocktails very strong.

'Come on, Zara, it's your turn,' Franny said in mock impatience.

'I know, I know,' I said. 'Somebody got me drunk.'

Cleo giggled softly. She was a round woman with a round face and round curls, and a round pregnant belly. Everything about her was softness and calm. Franny, by contrast, was pointy-nosed, thin and tall, with a booming laugh.

My eyes darted back and forth to the Scrabble board, then I had a flash of inspiration and put down my A and two Gs next to the M at the bottom of a word.

'Magg? What's a Magg?'

'That was the name of my dress shop,' I said. 'We got it from a Scrabble word. Only now . . . I'm not so sure if it was a *real* word.'

'You had a dress shop?' Larissa gasped. 'Your own business?'

'Yes,' I said nodding. 'I was a fashion designer.'

A round of oohs. We were all three sheets to the wind.

'Why on earth did you stop?' Franny barked, slamming her hand on the table. 'Why are you here?'

'Australia is probably worse than here,' Larissa said.

'Australia's perfectly nice,' Cleo interjected. 'I've been there twice.'

'Yes, Australia's . . . here is perfectly nice too,' I said.

'Ugh, the colonies,' Larissa said, on a long exhale of smoke. She pointed to a framed painting of London Bridge that hung on the wall. '*That* is the finest view in Asia, and you won't convince me otherwise. Zara, you can't play a word if it's not a word.'

'I'd accept mag with one G,' Cleo said.

'I want to hear more about you having a perfectly wonderful life as an independent businesswoman designing dresses and giving it all up for love,' Franny said.

'No, no, I didn't give it up for love.' And just like that, for the first time in weeks, Harry came into my mind. A shudder of pain moved through my soul. I had lost him.

'Then why did you give it up?'

'It was too hard. I was too young. Let's play Scrabble.'

I removed the second G, and then it wasn't my turn anymore and nobody was asking me questions about those lovely days, but the pain left footprints. What was wrong with me? I was perfectly happy this morning. Happily married. In a new home, with new friends.

And then Harry came along and ruined it. Even the thought of him drove me mad. I was so much better off out of that relationship.

I sighed and closed my eyes.

'Are you all right, Zara? Cleo, look what you've done to her. We should have gone easy on the gin. It's only her first day.'

'No, no,' I said, opening my eyes. 'I'm still shaking off the long trip. Will you excuse me?'

'Of course, darling. Don't forget this.' She tapped her knuckles on a linen bag hanging off her chair containing her never-used riding outfit.

'Thank you, Larissa. Thank you, all of you, for making me feel so welcome.'

They all rose to double-kiss me, just as Larissa had that morning, in clouds of perfume and cigarette smoke. I made my way home to wash my face and sober up before James returned.

Warm breath on my cheek woke me the next morning. My eyes flickered open and I found myself looking up at the mosquito net above me while James gently kissed my ear.

'Good morning,' I said sleepily.

'You are luscious,' he replied.

I reached for him and pulled him down to kiss me. 'Did you wake me for some wifely duties?' I asked coquettishly.

He laughed softly but pulled away. 'The morning is cool. It's time to go riding.'

I sat up as he rose and strode naked to the washroom.

'Riding a horse, I presume you mean?' I said, admiring his buttocks.

'Honestly, Zara, are all Australian girls so full of wicked humour?'

I laughed and swung my legs out of the bed, and went to the linen bag for the riding outfit. The breaches fit fine, if a little snugly, but I could barely get the buttons on the shirt done up.

James reappeared. 'Oh dear,' he said. 'I can see your bosom.'

I looked down at my shirt. He was right. The shirt gaped wide enough to see clean through to my bra.

He hooked his fingers inside my shirt, and slid them under my bra. 'Perhaps we will ride horses later.'

We tumbled back into bed, and I had my dream of finally making love in the light, but he kept his eyes closed the whole time.

We did eventually get out for our horse ride. He put me on a lovely gentle pony named Freya and we went slowly once around the compound and then onto the path in the woods that Larissa had warned me about. When I asked James why, he shrugged and said he'd never had any problems. We couldn't go very far though because we'd already used up part of the morning, and breakfast would be served soon enough.

'And I mustn't be late for parade,' he said. 'Will you come down again?'

'I think I will, and see what my new friends are up to.' I suddenly had a thought. 'James, what's a Pathan?'

He glanced across at me, a little frown on his brow. 'Where did you hear that?'

'Larissa pointed out one of your regiment. She called him "the Pathan" but didn't know why.'

'Pathans are people of Afghanistan who have settled in India. They make fine soldiers. We only have the one.'

I expected him to tell me the fellow's name but he didn't. Perhaps he didn't know it.

'Why was Larissa pointing him out to you?' he asked.

I blinked rapidly. 'No reason. She thought him of interest, with his long hair.'

'He's of no interest to ladies. None of the soldiers ought to be. That Larissa can be quite the fool. Do be careful, dear.'

Had I imagined the chastening tone in his voice? Heat suffused my cheeks. I felt embarrassed, a silly teenager making eyes over a handsome boy. But it wasn't like that at all. Yes, I thought the fellow magnificent, but I didn't *want* him. I wasn't going to fall in love with him. I was a new bride and madly in love with my husband. I wanted to tell James all this, but he was already instructing me how to guide my horse's head around so we could point back towards the compound.

———

I was buoyant on our return, determined not only to learn to ride but to be good at it. I gabbled on and James patiently smiled at me, then I said, 'James, dear, I'll need riding clothes.' I pointed to the gaping blouse.

'Ask Mr Parakh to organise you a car and go into town. Get whatever you need, my love.'

After breakfast, when I was dressed for town, I found Mr Parakh in the kitchen, hurrying young Daljeet through washing the breakfast dishes while he sat at the table drinking tea.

'Hello, Mr Parakh,' I said pleasantly, smiling.

The smile was not returned. He looked up at me from the table, his fierce dark eyes fixed on my face.

'Colonel Fell says I can ask you for a car to town,' I continued, though I felt awkward, as though I was putting him out.

'When?' he snapped.

'As soon as possible.'

He rose from the table with a deep sigh. 'If you wait out front, I'll send somebody around.'

'Oh, finish your tea first,' I said. 'I didn't mean to interrupt.'

A dish slipped out of Daljeet's hands and clattered back into the sink. Mr Parakh snapped at him in Hindi.

'So noisy,' Mr Parakh muttered for my benefit. He thrust his half-full teacup onto the edge of the sink. 'Wait around the front please, madam.'

'Yes, thank you.' Still smiling hopefully.

I walked straight down the corridor and to the front veranda, where I sat in one of the high-backed cane chairs and waited for my car. I realised my heart was ticking faster than usual because the encounter with Mr Parakh had been so awkward. I'd never had servants before so I didn't know how to deal with them. I vowed to ask Larissa how to speak to them. A few minutes later, a car pulled up and Mr Parakh strode past to open the back door for me.

'Madam, in future please allow an hour to arrange a car,' he said unsmilingly.

'Oh. Sorry. I didn't know. Thank you.'

He said nothing, simply waited for me to get in then closed the door behind me. Barked something at the driver and then we were away.

The driver dropped me at the end of the main street of town and agreed in broken English to meet me there again in two hours. Then I was free. My heart was light as I gazed down the street to the pointed domes of the temple on the river, the Bara Mandir. Most of the buildings along the way were made of stone, with wide archways and cool porches, and off these porches market stalls had been set up. Mostly rudimentary: branches and thin cloth. But they sold all kinds of things: pottery, woodcraft, slaughtered geese, sweetmeats, tea in barrels. Turbaned police walked by on tall horses. Local men who had given up on the heat and dressed only from the waist down. Running children with jingling bracelets around their ankles. Women in bright saris and scarves. I loved it. I felt myself sinking into its unfamiliarity, its richness and colour. I happened across a stall selling saris and lengths of brightly dyed fabric, and paid for an armful with the coins James had given me.

I ducked under one of the archways and through a tea house, and popped out the other side to another shopping street. This one had English shops in tall wooden buildings, and trees were planted along the way so that it felt shadier and quieter. James had told me that here I could buy whatever I wanted, and simply leave his name for them to mail the bill. At the first store I bought a beautiful bone china tea set with bright yellow sunflowers on it. Sunflowers always made me cheery. The gentleman behind the counter, a tall middle-aged fellow with impeccable English, offered to package it up for me and deliver it to the compound, along with my armful of purchases from the markets. I continued on my way, buying cushions and lamps, riding boots and gloves and a sun helmet, and charging it all to my husband, all of it to be delivered that afternoon. Finally, I found a dress shop run by a plump woman in a bright pink sari, who also sold English fabrics and patterns. I bought some white cotton for shirts and some dark grey twill for trousers, and then I was ready to head home. I only kept my driver waiting for ten minutes.

That afternoon I sat on the veranda drinking tea and receiving my deliveries. I had my sketchbook open and designed a riding blouse with a ruffle trim while eating the most incredible sweets that tasted of condensed milk and rosewater, and drinking an endless series of cups of tea that Urvashi insisted on bringing me. I was afraid I would slosh when I walked. By the time James came home, the new cushions and lamps were installed, and he commented merrily on how I was already making his house a home.

'Are you happy, my darling?' he said, pulling me under his wing and kissing the top of my head.

'So happy,' I answered, and it was true for a time.

———

Between watching the parade a few mornings a week and attending the polo matches on weekends, I grew interested for the first time in men's clothing. I was inspired both by military costume and by local costume, and filled a few pages of my sketchbook with designs. Long shirts, shirts with band collars, coats with swirling hems, jodhpurs with braided piping, colourful vests. Some I drew on a figure who looked a little like James, as he was tall and long-legged and could wear a coat well. Some I drew on a figure who looked a little like Harry, and chuckled to myself imagining him wearing a shot-silk vest to one of his political functions. Some I drew on the magnificent, long-haired Pathan, imagining his exotic looks contrasting with a very British tuxedo. It was all just nonsense, a way to entertain myself on the long afternoons when the ladies weren't playing Scrabble or gin rummy. I lay on my belly on the settee under the fan, and drew until my sweaty palm smudged the pencil.

———

After two weeks, James lost interest in teaching me to ride. Well, that is what I assumed as he pleaded being tired from work when I tried to wake him early to get going. I was disappointed, not least because of how proud I was of my riding costumes, which I had cut and pinned and which Urvashi had stitched for me with tiny neat stitches, indistinguishable from a sewing machine's. When I asked, in a possibly fed-up voice, if we would ever go riding again, he muttered that I would be perfectly fine on my own, or to take one of the ladies with me. Neither Larissa nor Franny were interested, and Cleo suggested she *could* be interested if I taught her how to ride, but I had no confidence in my ability to do that.

For several mornings I tried to accept my fate, but then decided that I would just be bold and go myself. I missed the early morning smells, damp and pungent, of the bright green woods. After breakfast, when James headed off to work, I dressed in my riding clothes and sun helmet and strode to the stables. The stablehand helped me saddle up Freya, and I led her out into the sunshine.

As I did, a gentleman I recognised from the evening polo matches was leading his horse towards the stable. I smiled and nodded, and he said, 'Good morning. Colonel Fell's wife, correct?'

'Yes,' I said. 'And I've seen you playing polo with James. You're Doctor Namboothiri? Is that right?'

'Very good. Not an easy name for the English to remember.'

'I'm Australian.'

'I can tell,' he said with a grin. He was perhaps in his late forties, tall and with grey hair at his temples. Impeccably dressed in the British style, he sounded almost wholly English, with only the faintest trace of that percussive, musical accent. 'Are you heading out for a ride?'

'Yes, I miss the smell of the woods,' I said, gesturing towards the woodland path.

'Ah, the woods.' He chuckled. 'I think you mean the jungle.'

I glanced towards the thick green bushes, the palm trees bent over with the weight of vines, the dark hollows. 'I suppose it is. I always thought jungle would be more impenetrable.'

'It is in places, but not here. However, it's not a place I'd recommend a woman go alone. Would you like company?'

'Yes!' I said, too eagerly. 'Only, I'm not a good rider yet. I'll be slow and potentially clumsy.'

'All the more reason that somebody experienced come with you. Here, let me help you mount your horse.'

In a few minutes, after he'd helped me inelegantly into my saddle and checked that my tack was all secure, we were off. The sun was searing already, but once we were in the shade of the trees the heat was not too unbearable. 'So, you're a doctor. Is that your role here in the officers compound?'

'No, I'm not that kind of doctor.'

'What do you mean?'

'I have a PhD in history from Cambridge. Peterhouse College.' He laughed. 'I'm not some common physician. That's a joke, by the way.'

I smiled. 'Then what is your role here?'

'Administration. I run the place.' He wagged a finger at me. 'I pay all your shopping bills.'

'Lord, that's embarrassing. You must think me a spendthrift.'

'Quite the contrary. I also pay the brigadier's wife's when she is here. Spends money like water.'

'You definitely shouldn't tell me that,' I replied, thinking of all the lovely clutter in Penny's holiday house.

'Too late now,' he replied. 'I trust you.'

There was something warm and funny about Doctor Namboothiri. He didn't seem to take things too seriously, and I liked that, after spending so much time with earnest English James. He was also terribly good at explaining how to ride a horse. I hadn't realised that Freya would feel any nervous twitch on her bridle and become confused. He described how to communicate calmly with her, and within ten minutes I already felt more comfortable in the saddle. He was also willing, unlike James, to tell me exactly why it was dangerous to take the jungle path alone.

'Wild animals, for a start,' he said. 'Though they tend to stay away from us because we are noisy and smelly. But you might encounter a snake, and a lot of them are dangerous. Biting insects. Don't rub up against anything. But the real problem is beggars. They haunt these jungle-fringed paths and if you give them nothing, they grow angry.'

'Oh dear. But surely if I encountered one, I could just give them a coin.'

'And then there will be twenty of them the next day, waiting for you.'

'So I should never give a beggar money?' That didn't feel right.

He sighed. 'The way to end begging is to have a better government, a better system.'

We ducked under a low-hanging vine. I swear I saw an ant on it over an inch long.

'I'm afraid I don't understand much about the political system here. For example, why so many of our servants are Indians and why . . .' I stopped myself, realising there was no way I could ask the question without sounding rude.

'Why I'm in charge of the administration of a regiment?' he asked with a comically arched eyebrow.

'Well, I don't mean to be . . .'

'I'm Brahmin, Mrs Fell. The highest caste. Your servants are probably Shudras. That's why *I* oversee a regimental budget and *they* empty your thunderbox, through nothing more than an accident of birth. And a little help from the British, who it must be said are also obsessed with class. Surely you've noticed.' His sharp observations were delivered with the kind of half-smile Harry would give me when pointing out what was wrong with the world, inviting me to share his cynicism.

'Ah, yes. I suppose I have. But clearly I have a lot to learn about India.'

'I should be most happy to teach you. I often take a short ride after breakfast. You'll join me?'

'I will.'

———

And so within a short time, I was well furnished with company. Breakfast with James, riding with Doctor Namboothiri, attending parade with the other wives and then often piling into a car together to go shopping. I'd have a break from them around midday, when Urvashi made me a quiet lunch and I would sit on the veranda and read and write letters home or sketch things I had seen, then it would be afternoon tea with gin and games over at Larissa's, before we'd all stroll over for the early evening polo game. James was always delighted to see me, waving his mallet at me from atop Pilot and showing off adorably. We made love every night, still in the warm blush of our honeymoon feelings. I was perfectly content.

The first fat drops of the monsoon came while I sat on the veranda drinking tea with Penny, the brigadier's wife, who had just arrived the day before. She turned her eyes up at the sky, which had been stifling and grey for nearly a week, and said, 'Well, that's it, then.'

'That's what?'

'It will rain now until October. I arrived just in time. Some of the roads around the holiday house are impassable during the monsoon.' She lifted her teacup to her lips. 'Glad I made it.'

'I'm glad too,' I said, reaching out to squeeze her hand and turning my eyes up to watch the rain.

CHAPTER 13

I missed my horse and I missed my morning rides with Doctor Namboothiri. Day after day it rained, until ten days had gone by and I hadn't stepped outside the house. On the eleventh day, the clouds parted and sun shone down hard and steamy. I trudged over marshy ground down to the stable to check on Freya.

Doctor Namboothiri was there too, saddling up his horse.

'Mrs Fell,' he said, with a little nod. 'Hadn't expected to see you here.'

'You're going riding?'

'The jungle comes alive after the rain.' He glanced at the stablehand and indicated he should saddle up Freya. 'Come and I'll show you.'

'Is it not too marshy?'

'There's a beautiful secret, about two hundred yards into the trees. You don't want to miss it.'

I nodded at the stablehand and said to Doctor Namboothiri, 'Give me five minutes to get changed.'

I ran back over the grass, flicking up muddy water behind me. Ten minutes later, still smoothing my blouse, I was mounting Freya and heading off.

The feeling of freedom from being out again was heady. I talked and laughed too much, but Doctor Namboothiri didn't seem to mind. He warned me there wouldn't be many days between now and the end of the monsoon when we could ride, but that he would find me when he could. I chattered all the way into the jungle along the usual wide path we took, among sagging trees so laden with raindrops that some of the branches looked to be cracking. As we came into a clearing – a clearing I remembered as being overgrown with ferns and creepers – I saw it was now a shining lake, dotted with lotus blossoms. Pale pink with dark-tipped petals and bright yellow pistils. I squeaked with surprise and delight.

'Can I collect some?' I asked Doctor Namboothiri.

'I wouldn't if I were you,' he said. 'They have a sharp spike. Also, I wouldn't dismount. I know you have your riding boots on, but the leeches are very persistent here. Shall we continue on?'

'No. Let me stay a moment. They are so beautiful.'

'Very well.'

Doctor Namboothiri waited patiently as I gazed at the flowers. Their symmetry and colour were so sublime that I wanted to commit them to memory. I imagined a pale pink gown graduating to a dark pink hem, bright gold piping, soft tulip-like layers . . . Eventually my eyes had had their fill and we rode on, but the lotuses stayed with me.

The rain set in again that afternoon and stayed. It was like nothing I had ever seen. The drops were fat and hard, slamming into the ground and creating tiny explosions of mud. The volume of it was astonishing as it sheeted off the eaves and flowed down the stairs like a river. I was enchanted by it, as I was enchanted by everything in India. I asked James if I could, for a rainy-season project, paint flowers on one of the blank white walls of the sitting room. He agreed, then was perplexed when I painted pale pink lotuses.

'What's this?' he asked, standing in his damp socks after stomping mud off his boots in the entryway.

'They are lotuses. You must have seen them.'

'Damn Indian flowers. I thought you were going to paint roses.'

The heat was relieved slightly because the sun was blocked by persistent cloud, but the rainy season was not as cool as it was back home. The air remained sticky – damp enough to drink, it seemed – and none of my clothes ever became truly dry after washing them. Even if they had, within seconds of donning them I'd make them clammy with perspiration. I bought a typewriter to write letters home because I was sick of aerogramme paper disintegrating under my hand. James came home every night sodden and muddy and in a foul mood. He never took it out on me, but nonetheless I walked on eggshells around him. I felt terribly sorry for him having to continue with his duties in the wild weather. The wives, including Penny, met every afternoon for games, but the mornings were long and I was mostly stuck inside. The rain made it unpleasant to go to town more than once a week.

About two months after the rain started, we were playing poker for matchsticks while we listened to an old Savoy Orpheans record on Penny's gramophone. Cleo had baked the most incredible cake: moist and lemony and infused with gin. I tried very hard not to have a second slice, but somehow it made its way onto my plate. I overhead Larissa saying something to Franny about going to watch the parade this morning as the rain had eased for a few hours, as it did most days, leaving us all gasping in a pall of suffocating humidity.

'I haven't been to parade in over a month,' I said guiltily.

'Nothing's changed. Still the same,' she said. 'Oh, except the Pathan is gone.'

'Gone?' Franny asked, pouting theatrically. 'My poor heart shall miss him.'

'You should know about it, Zara,' Larissa continued. 'I asked Reggie and he said it was James that organised his transfer.'

'James doesn't talk to me about such things,' I said, but my voice sounded hollow and a long way away. James had been so angry about me asking about the Pathan, and now he was gone. Was it my fault?

Of course, I didn't ask James. If it had nothing to do with me, he would ridicule me for thinking myself so important. I came to wonder for the first time, though, whether James might have a jealous nature. If I thought back over our relationship, I could see it in small ways. A tightening of the jaw if I spent too long talking to another man, a sense of unease if we were too long in male company, the casual way he always asked if there were any husbands around at our ladies afternoon teas. I had found all these things flattering; they accompanied James's endless compliments and declarations of love for me. It did make me wonder why he tolerated me spending so much time with Doctor Namboothiri, but then I realised I'd never told him. I had of course said that I went riding some mornings, and I'd also mentioned having this or that conversation with Doctor Namboothiri, but I had never put the two together. Precisely because, somewhere down deep, I knew he wouldn't like it. A sin of omission. But that was ludicrous. I was married, as was the doctor – though his wife was back in Bombay with their two teenage sons. I was significantly younger than him, and we didn't call each other by our first names. In fact, I didn't even know his first name. I vowed that on the next occasion I spent time with Doctor Namboothiri, I would speak openly to James about it.

———

One damp day in early September, I hosted a special ladies afternoon tea for Cleo, who was about to head off to London to have her baby. Apparently, none of the English women had their babies in India. When I asked why not, they said they didn't trust the Indian midwives, but then Cleo let slip that she wanted her child to be English, not Indian.

'What about you, Zara?' Franny asked. 'Would you go to London to have a baby?'

'I . . . hadn't thought of it. All my family are in Melbourne, so perhaps I would go there.' If I ever fell pregnant.

'You are *trying*, aren't you?' Penny asked, lighting a cigarette.

My face grew warm. 'Yes, of course.'

'Some bodies are slow,' Larissa said in my defence.

I knew it wasn't my body that was the problem. I'd managed to fall pregnant to Harry even though we were using a French letter. But I didn't say any of that, of course.

'Some bodies can't do it at all,' Franny said miserably. Larissa had told me privately that Franny had been married ten years and no babies.

Penny rubbed her shoulder. 'You can borrow my children any time,' she said. 'They love you.'

Fierce little Mr Parakh entered the room to set the table for tea, and we chatted on about babies and what names Cleo had chosen for a boy or a girl. Larissa declared she knew for a fact Cleo was going to have a boy because she'd craved oranges during her pregnancy and citrus always meant a boy, when suddenly Urvashi skidded into the room and said something fast and breathless in Hindi to Mr Parakh.

Mr Parakh snapped his head around and then hurried off.

'What . . . ?' I rose to my feet.

'Oh, just leave them, Zara,' Penny said, opening a pack of cards. 'Your head of house will sort it out.'

'Let me just check,' I said, and followed Mr Parakh down towards the kitchen.

Lying on the floor was Daljeet, the very young servant. He was out cold. Mr Parakh knelt over him.

'What's happened?' I asked.

'He was just standing there and he fell,' Urvashi said. 'I can't wake him.'

'Is he alive?'

'Yes, yes,' Mr Parakh said, not-so-gently tapping Daljeet on each cheek with an open palm. 'Come on, stupid boy. Get up.'

'Oh, do be gentle with him, Mr Parakh,' I said. 'He isn't well.'

Daljeet's eyes flickered and relief flooded me. At least he wasn't dead.

'Get up, boy,' Mr Parakh said again, trying to drag Daljeet into a sitting position, even though the boy's eyes were rolling in his head.

I saw red. 'Out of my way, Mr Parakh,' I said, kneeling next to Daljeet. 'Urvashi, pass me a glass of water.'

I became aware we had an audience of officers' wives standing at the entrance to the kitchen. I helped Daljeet to sit and held the glass to his lips. He drank it, but he was still woozy and pale.

'Mr Parakh, get a car. You're taking him to the hospital.'

'Mrs Fell, there is no need. He's just a lazy boy.'

'Mr Parakh,' I repeated, with heat in my voice. 'I said get a car.'

He scuttled off silently. I had my arm around Daljeet's ribs. He was painfully thin, cold, and his heart seemed to be racing.

'What's wrong with him?' Larissa asked.

'He collapsed.'

'You really ought to let the head of house sort it out,' Cleo said. 'It doesn't pay to get too involved.'

'I don't trust the head of house with this. This young man is unwell and I want a doctor to see him in case it's serious.'

Within a few minutes Mr Parakh was back and I helped him to the car with Daljeet. I stood in the drizzle, leaning in through the driver's side window and fixed Mr Parakh with my most fierce gaze. 'To the hospital. Make sure a doctor sees him. Do you understand?' It was the first time I had ever commanded one of the servants without sweetness in my voice. Mr Parakh was quite clearly irritated but knew better than to ignore a direct command.

'Yes, Mrs Fell,' he said. 'I am sure a doctor will be able to tell if he's just a lazy boy.'

Daljeet sat in the back looking weak and sheepish. I gave him a smile. 'You be honest with the doctor,' I said. 'Tell him all your symptoms and how long they have been coming on, no matter how small the detail. I don't want you to be sick.'

'Yes, ma'am.'

I hurried back under the cover of the veranda to watch them drive off. Penny waited for me, and slipped her arm around my middle.

'You are such a kind person,' she said with a smile.

'He's so young,' I replied. 'And he's a human, just like you or me.'

'I know. We all get desensitised to it, living here. They are like invisible machinery. I love that you still see their humanity. What a beautiful soul you are, Zara.'

'I don't trust Mr Parakh,' I said. 'Perhaps I shall follow them to the hospital in an hour or so.'

'Do what you have to,' she said. 'But first, come inside and let's play a couple of hands of gin rummy. A cocktail and a cigarette will make you feel better.'

———

When Mr Parakh returned home, I pressed him for details.

'What is wrong with him?' I asked.

He shrugged. 'Probably nothing.'

I didn't believe him. I arrived at the hospital just before four o'clock. It was a squat brick building down near the train station, with dim corridors and a strong smell of ammonia.

The ward was rudimentary, cramped with narrow cots, nurses bustling between them. Everything clattered and clanged. The walls were brightly limewashed but there were grimy marks around cupboard handles. Several of the overhead lights were flickering or out altogether. I saw Daljeet immediately, in the very last cot. I walked over and stood next to his bed. He looked up at me, fearful.

'Daljeet? How are you?'

'I am very well, ma'am,' he said.

'Daljeet, you're in hospital. I know you are not "very well". What does the doctor say?'

'The doctor says this young man is malnourished,' a voice said from behind me.

I turned to see a tall man with a big belly straining at his white doctor's coat. He had the same accent as Doctor Namboothiri – both English and Indian. Musical and crisp.

I offered him my hand. 'I'm Mrs Fell, Daljeet's employer.'

He looked at my hand for a second before he took it, clearly perturbed that I had offered to shake first.

'I am Doctor Tiwari,' he said, then dropped my hand. 'Young Daljeet has not been eating properly for a very long time.'

'Is that right, Daljeet? But don't we feed all the servants?' I was embarrassed to realise that I had no idea how servants got fed. I assumed they all ate over at the cooking pit in the evenings.

Daljeet nodded his head reluctantly. 'You do, ma'am. But I was taking most home for my family.'

'Your family?'

Doctor Tiwari interjected again. 'Young Daljeet tells me he has fifteen at home.'

'Fifteen?' I turned to Daljeet astonished. 'You mean, fifteen *people*? And you've been feeding them all?'

'When I can, yes. My brothers, sisters, cousins and my uncle. Some of them work too. We all bring home what we can.'

'I see. Well, then, Colonel Fell and I will have to give you a raise.'

Daljeet gulped, his eyes huge and uncertain in his skinny face.

Doctor Tiwari said to him, 'You'd best explain the situation to Mrs Fell.'

'If you give me more money, it won't go to my family,' he said.

'I have no idea what you mean.'

'The head of house has been taking a cut of the lad's wages,' Doctor Tiwari explained.

'But why?' I sat on the cane chair next to the bed and took Daljeet's hand. He seemed shocked that I would touch him.

Before Daljeet could answer, Doctor Tiwari said, 'I will say, Mrs Fell, that Daljeet's plight is fairly common among the servant class, though this instance is particularly unfair.'

Daljeet licked his lips and began to speak hesitantly. He explained that all the servants who had been hired by Mr Parakh paid a portion of their wages to him, sometimes as much as half. Any extra money they made – through raises or tips – he took entirely.

If they complained, Mr Parakh would threaten to tell James that they had stolen from us, thus ensuring they would never work again.

Back when the servants were preparing for my arrival, Daljeet had been charged with adding feminine touches to the bungalow. Vases and cushions and so on. He had accidentally broken a decorative pot, and since then Mr Parakh had been taking sixty per cent of his wage to pay for the breakage, though Daljeet was certain he was keeping it for himself. The more details he told me, the more my ribs burned with rage. I hated any kind of unfairness, but this was perhaps the most unfair thing I had ever heard of.

'Daljeet,' I said when he had finished, 'I am going to put this right.'

'Please, ma'am, please don't tell Mr Parakh I have said this to you. He will say it is a lie, and then I will lose my job.'

'You absolutely will *not* lose your job. I will ensure it. You must trust me. Doctor, how long will he remain in hospital?'

'No more than a week,' Doctor Tiwari said. 'We'll get some nourishment into him and let him have a proper rest.'

'But my family needs my wage,' Daljeet blurted to him. 'I can't stay in here a week.'

'I will send your family some money, directly,' I said. 'All I need is the address.'

Daljeet reluctantly gave it to me. I said farewell, reassuring him again that I would protect him, and hurried home. I dashed up the stairs in the rain, then went banging through the house calling for Mr Parakh.

Urvashi looked up frightened when I arrived in the breezeway between the bungalow and the kitchen. She was sitting on a three-legged wooden stool peeling potatoes, sweat beading her brow.

'Have you seen Mr Parakh?' I asked her.

'He's in town,' she said. 'Is everything well with you, ma'am?'

I crouched down next to her. Her long black hair was tied in a knot on the back of her head, but a strand had escaped and clung to her cheek. 'Urvashi, does Mr Parakh take your money?'

She blinked rapidly. Nervously.

'I take it that's yes?'

'He . . . it is a commission, he says. He hired me when I could not find another job. I am very grateful to him.'

'How much commission?'

She shook her head. 'I don't know, ma'am. I just take what is given to me each month and I am thankful for the work.'

'Are you frightened of him?'

Urvashi averted her eyes. 'I couldn't say, ma'am.'

'Are you frightened of me?'

She met my gaze and shook her head. 'No, ma'am.'

'You understand *I* am your employer, not him.' I patted her knee. 'Let me sort this out.'

'Sort what out?' That was James, who was striding up the breezeway, soaked through, eating an apple. He stood at the back door and stomped out his boots, then slid them off and slung them towards Urvashi. 'Can you get Girish to dry these out for me?'

'Yes, sir.' Urvashi plopped the potato she was holding back in the bucket of water and hurried off with the boots. Gratefully, I would say. My line of questioning had made her uncomfortable.

'James, the most awful thing has happened. Poor Daljeet is in the hospital suffering malnutrition.'

'He always was a skinny thing,' James said, shrugging out of his jacket. 'He'll be fine in a day or so.'

'It's more than that, James, it's . . . Come inside and get dry and let me tell you.'

I sat on the edge of our bed while James stripped and towelled himself off, dropping his damp clothes in the tub for Girish to launder later. I told him the whole story, while he hmm-hmed and nodded through it. He pulled on a robe and sat next to me, his hand on my knee.

'You are very kind to care so much about the servants,' he said.

'Don't you?'

'Not as much as you do, obviously. I did know Mr Parakh took a cut of the servants' wages. It's common practice.'

'It's not fair.'

'Without him, they wouldn't have any wages. They wouldn't be working, at least not for us. They'd be working for somebody else who also skimmed their wages.'

'Can we not do something about it?'

'Perhaps we should speak to Mr Parakh and hear his side of the story.'

But I was already shaking my head. 'No, no, no, James. Poor Daljeet collapsed from starvation. It isn't right.'

James gazed at me, smiling gently. 'My god, I love you. "Though she be but little, she is fierce." That's a compliment, by the way. I don't know if Shakespeare intended it that way.'

'Can we do something, James?'

'I'll talk very discreetly to Mr Parakh at my earliest convenience.' He kissed the top of my head. 'You make me want to be a better person. In the meantime, you can check over Mr Parakh's accounts ledger. It should tell you how much he is stiffing the lad.'

He got up and stretched, then headed down the stairs calling for Girish. My stomach was uneasy. What would talking to Mr Parakh achieve? He would lie or diminish his culpability, and then he might take out his anger on Daljeet when he came home from hospital.

That evening at dinner, I noticed Mr Parakh darting his glance at me repeatedly, a chilly expression on his brow and sometimes – or did I imagine it? – a smirk on his lips. I remembered I'd told Daljeet he could trust me to fix his problem, and I knew I couldn't leave this issue for James to deal with. He seemed blithely uninterested in anything to do with the servants – like most of the English I'd met – and once Mr Parakh knew Daljeet had complained about him, I doubted James could stop him from persecuting the boy even more.

This led me to knock on Doctor Namboothiri's office door with a sense of urgency the following morning, directly after James left for work. His office was a detached timber building on the western end of the barracks, with a veranda densely shaded by overgrown vines. They heaved under the weight of last night's rain. One of the regimental cars was parked directly in front of the building, close to the bottom of the stairs. Doctor Namboothiri came to the door and considered me curiously as I shook out my umbrella.

'Mrs Fell?'

'I need to talk to you.'

'I am due for a meeting at the bank very shortly.' He indicated the car. 'You can travel with me to town if you like, and talk on the way?'

'Yes, please.' I wasn't exactly dressed for town – no hat, no gloves – but I doubted anybody would notice or care. In this weather, most people scurried about with their heads down.

'Come along then.'

I followed him down the stairs and he opened the passenger door for me, then started the car. We bumped out over the rutted, muddy drive and then were on our way.

'Can you explain to me how the servants get paid?' I asked him.

'There is a budget that's distributed to the heads of household. They handle the rest.'

'One of my boys, Daljeet . . . he's just a young fellow. He's being forced to give sixty per cent of his wage to Mr Parakh. Not only that, but he's sharing his food with his rather large family. Now he's in hospital with malnutrition.'

'Sixty per cent!'

'It's criminal, isn't it? It must be stopped. Can it be stopped?'

The rain began to intensify and the windscreen wipers could barely keep up. Doctor Namboothiri slowed the car to a crawl.

'All heads of household charge a commission. We don't usually interfere.'

'I want to interfere.'

'Have you spoken to Colonel Fell?'

I chose my words carefully. 'Yes, and he's sympathetic of course. But I am worried nothing will change or that things will get worse for poor Daljeet.'

'And what would be your ideal outcome?'

'For James to do something about it.'

'Yes, yes. But you clearly worry he won't, so what would *you* do, if you had the power?'

I thought for a moment, listening to the rain popping off the roof of the car and the windscreen wipers heaving to keep up. Then I said, 'I'd fire Mr Parakh, promote Girish to head of household, and make everybody promise to be fair to each other.' Then I had a moment of doubt. 'Would it be very bad for Mr Parakh to be fired? Would he starve?'

Doctor Namboothiri chuckled. 'No. I imagine he would return to his family in Jaipur and find another job. You could offer to let him go with very good references if you are worried.'

'But I don't have the power to make that decision. It must come from James.'

'Well . . .' Doctor Namboothiri hedged a few moments, thinking it through. 'Even though the servants work for the families, they are paid for out of the regimental budget. So the lines of reporting are not that clear cut.'

'You could fire him?'

'*We* could. If we decided it was best for your household.'

'Without James's consent?'

'He's a busy man. Perhaps we'd be doing him a favour taking it off his plate.'

'He might be cross with me for making the decision without him.'

'Would he be cross for long, do you think? And would the good that came from the decision outweigh his crossness?'

'Hm,' I said, and turned to stare out the window. I very much did not want to fight with James. The turbulent years with Harry had taught me that conflict in a relationship was miserable and tiring.

But I didn't want Mr Parakh in my house anymore, roaring at the other servants. They weren't invisible machinery to me. I wanted a calm and peaceful household.

We were turning into the main street of town now, the rain easing as we pulled up in front of the bank.

'I won't be long,' Doctor Namboothiri said as he opened his car door.

'I want to do it,' I blurted. 'Will you help me?'

'I will,' he said. 'Now wait here where it's dry and we will sort out the details when I'm back.'

He closed the car door and the rain kept beating on the roof. I watched the rivulets on the windows, and then the clouds parted and sunshine lit up the droplets. It cheered me a little. I have always loved sun showers. When Doctor Namboothiri returned I was almost buoyant, certain I had made the right decision.

'We should go for tea over at the Victoria,' I said, pointing to the hotel across the road with its cusped arches and openwork balustrades. 'The ladies and I have been a few times. They have the most delicious scones.'

Doctor Namboothiri placed his bank books on the back seat of the car then fixed me in his gaze. 'You and I, tea together at the Victoria?' His brow was furrowed. I couldn't read his expression. Was it puzzlement? Cynicism?

'Yes. Why not?'

'They won't let us in.'

'I assure you, I have been there many times.'

'No, they won't let *us* in. Together. A white woman and an Indian man? Never.'

I tried to picture the inside of the Victoria's tearoom and remember if I'd ever seen anybody in there who wasn't white. Surely . . . 'I'm certain I've seen locals in there,' I said, sounding anything but certain.

'It's a place for the British,' he said, starting the car. 'Besides, I have rather a lot of work today. Shall we head back to the regiment to fire Mr Parakh?'

I nodded.

We drove in silence a little while, then I said, 'Perhaps I don't understand India very well. You are happy that the British have developed India, aren't you? Medicine, railways, trade? James always says that the British are managing three hundred million Indians with only twenty thousand troops. No large-scale rebellions. That must mean you're happy?'

'Me personally? I do all right. But if by "you", you mean all Indians, I should think that Colonel Fell has a . . . slightly biased view.' He shot me a smile. 'Respectfully.'

'You've never been anything but respectful,' I said.

'The benefits of the Raj have not flowed equally to all in India. Let us say . . . there are Mr Parakhs at every level, among the British, among the Indians . . . India is not a fair country.'

I turned this over in my head while we drove home, and for the first time in several weeks I thought about Harry. It wasn't that I'd forgotten him, far from it, but usually if he crossed my mind I'd push the thought away. But now I found myself wanting to talk to him about all this, about fairness, about how a nation can treat its people justly while also allowing some to thrive if they work harder or take risks. These were his favourite things to discuss. The English seemed already to have made up their minds and were not open to debate, as I discovered that afternoon when I broached the topic at ladies afternoon tea. We were at Franny's. Cleo was back in London and we waited every day for a telegram about the baby. The rain had not come back all afternoon, and a swampy heat engulfed us all under the big, slow-turning fan.

'Could you explain something to me?' I asked as Penny dealt us our cards. 'I was in town with Doctor Namboothiri today and I suggested we go to Victoria's for tea. He was utterly convinced they wouldn't let us in together.'

'Good lord, Zara,' Larissa said, throwing her hands up. 'You can't go about town with an Indian.'

'But it's Doctor Namboothiri. He has a PhD. From Cambridge. He runs the regiment.'

'My husband runs the regiment,' Penny said, her cigarette gripped between her lips as she dealt. 'Namboothiri is an administrator.'

'Yes, and highly competent and well respected.'

Franny picked up her cards and looked at them. 'It's just not done, Zara. English woman, Indian man – it's not a good look.'

'I'm Australian, not English,' I said, grating against the constant assumption that I must share all their values. 'We are a very egalitarian society.'

'He did the right thing not going in with you,' Penny said. 'Tongues wag and it's a small town.'

'Oh, and imagine if music had come on and he'd asked you to dance,' Larissa said with a shudder. 'How awkward that would have been.'

'Dance? What? He has no interest in dancing with me. He's old enough to be my father.'

'No, he's not and you know it,' Franny scoffed. 'When I married at twenty, Alfie was already forty. I'd be careful. And he's probably right – the Victoria would never have let you in together.'

I brimmed with other questions but could feel myself growing irritated so instead I concentrated on the card game, trying to ignore the way perspiration made my clothes cling. I told myself I'd get used to it in time, all of it, but for the first time since I arrived, I felt a long way from home.

CHAPTER 14

When I told James before dinner that I had called Mr Parakh over to the regimental office and had him fired, his only grumble was that we were now short-handed with Daljeet still in the hospital. I was astonished. I had spent the whole afternoon choosing my words, certain my confession would bring his anger down on my head. But he admitted he found household matters tiresome and part of the joy of having a wife was that she could take care of them.

'Besides,' he said, 'you once ran a successful business. I think I can trust you to run a successful household.'

I loved him so dearly in that moment. We sat on the veranda together that night to enjoy the warm evening. There were stars between clouds from time to time as the rain had eased. The whole world smelled damp and fragrant, and the air was filled with the sound of crickets and strange soft hoots from the jungle, which could have been night birds or monkeys for all I knew. We talked about how much we both wanted a baby and I couldn't believe I'd felt so sorry for myself earlier that afternoon.

It was a few days later when things between us took a turn for the worse. I was sitting on the settee drawing in my sketchbook when James came home unexpectedly for lunch. I leaped up, excited to see him and to tell him we'd finally had word from Cleo, who had given birth to a little girl. But before a word came out of my mouth, I noticed the thunderous look on his brow and drew a quick breath.

'What's wrong?' I asked.

'The brig says you invited Namboothiri for tea at the Victoria.' He spat it as though the thought tasted bad.

My heart thudded in my throat. 'Yes, I . . . we were in town together and I didn't realise that –'

'You were in town together? Why?'

'I had been to see him to ask his advice about Mr Parakh, and he was just on his way to the bank so I asked if we could talk on the way.'

He shook his head in bafflement. 'Why?' he said again.

'Doctor Namboothiri and I had become friends. Before the monsoon, we rode together some mornings.'

'And who knew about this?'

'I don't know, I . . . I didn't think it mattered. The stablehands, I suppose. The servants.'

'The officers' wives?'

'Perhaps. I didn't think it controversial, James, or else I would have mentioned it to you.'

He drew his lips into a thin line.

'James,' I said. 'Really, it's nothing.'

'It's not nothing!' he roared. 'It's an embarrassment. It's undignified. What must they all think of me?'

'Everyone who meets you thinks you a tremendous man, my love. I'm not sure why you would worry it was otherwise.'

He fixed his eyes on me. 'Sit down.'

I sat down, presuming he would sit next to me. Instead, he stood in front of me, the fan stirring his dark hair, and launched into a lecture. 'I taught you to ride, and then the moment I was off at work you went riding with another man. You asked my advice about the household staff, then ignored me and asked the advice of another man. And while you were out in town with this other man, you invited him to eat with you at a hotel. Not just any other man, I might add, but a bloody snake-charming native. I must be a laughing-stock.'

'Nobody is laughing. Nobody. It's all entirely innocent.'

'Is it? Then how come it's only coming out now. Your secret horse rides and trips to town and advice sessions. Never mentioned a word of it until you were caught out, did you?'

The moment had grown so dark, as though shadows were crowding my vision. I realised I was frightened of him. No matter how angry Harry had been with me during our fights, I had never been frightened of him. James's fury was volcanic. I actually wondered if he might strike me, and pulled my sketchbook against my chest as if it could protect me.

'I swear, James, I swear. There is nothing between me and Doctor Namboothiri.'

His eyes lit suspiciously on the sketchbook and he reached for it. I tried to snatch it away, fearful he would tear it up. This only enraged him further.

'What are you hiding in here?'

'I'm not hiding anything . . . Be gentle with it, please.'

He leafed roughly through the pages, and I remembered the drawings of men's clothes. I prayed for him not to make it all the way back to those designs, but he was certain I was hiding something and wasn't going to give up until he found it.

'Ha!' he said.

'James, please . . .'

He turned the page around and stabbed at one of the models. 'That is me, yes?'

'Yes,' I said.

'And is this Mandokhel?'

'Mando . . . ?'

'The Pathan all you ladies lost your minds over.'

'Yes, well it was based on him but I –'

'Good lord. What a blind fool I've been.' He kept leafing, then stopped and turned it to me again. 'And who is this?' He was pointing at my sketch of Harry in a waistcoat and collarless shirt with gathered sleeves.

I couldn't answer.

'If these other two fashion models are real, then this one must be too.'

My instinct was to lie and say he was imagined, but the chances were that James would meet Harry one day if we visited Melbourne. I did not want to risk another nightmarish fight like this one. 'It's an old friend back home. Harry.'

'Harry who?'

'Holt. Harry Holt.'

'What kind of friend? An old flame?'

'There is no flame there anymore,' I said decisively.

'Then why draw him?'

'To model clothes. All of these drawings . . . look through the book. There are people who look like Larissa and Cleo and skinny Franny. When I think of designs, I think of them on people.'

'Is Namboothiri in here too?'

'No, I've never drawn him. But none of them mean –'

He roughly tore out the pages with the men's designs on them and flung my sketchbook back at me. The hard corner of the binding caught the side of my nose and made my eyes water. James balled up the pages and threw them at me too. 'Get rid of these. I never want to see them again.'

Then he stormed out, leaving me clutching the ball of paper, fighting back tears.

———

James simmered for over a week, barely saying a word to me, turning his back pointedly when we climbed into bed together at night. In that time, I had a letter from Mum telling me that Harry had won election for a seat in parliament and was now genuinely a politician as he had always dreamed. I longed to write him a letter to congratulate him, but the idea of James finding out I had contacted him deterred me. I didn't even dare reply to Mum asking her to pass on my best wishes – apparently he still visited Mum and Daddy every few weeks – because I could imagine all too easily James reading my letters before I posted them, and I wanted very badly for him to act as though he loved me again.

I ran into Doctor Namboothiri one morning coming back from parade with Penny and her children. I hesitated, not sure whether to say hello. But he looked right past me as though he didn't know me at all, and I understood in that moment that James had already warned him not to speak to me again.

I began hiding my sketchbook from James. Not because it had drawings of other men in it: I had learned my lesson there. But simply because him seeing it made him cold and tight-lipped. I only drew when he wasn't around, and hid it in my bedside table at other times.

Eventually, just as the monsoon passed, so did James's anger. He softened, we started making love again, and we didn't speak of his violent outburst. Girish did a wonderful job as head of household, Daljeet fattened up and things became settled for a time.

———

Before I knew it, Christmas was approaching. Both Penny and Larissa were heading home to England for Christmas with their husbands, but James had used up his leave coming to Melbourne to marry me, so we stayed in Jubbulpore. Cleo had returned with a chubby-faced cherub named Daphne, but she and Franny were very close and I often felt on the outside of our afternoon teas.

I was delighted, then, to receive a fat envelope from Betty the week before Christmas. Inside was a Christmas card that I added to the cards pegged on string in our living room. Then I curled up in the wicker chair on the veranda to read her letter. The air was heavy with the smell of manure and cut grass. December was the mildest month so far, with even a little chill in the morning air.

If I stayed in the shade I could avoid the heat until the middle of the day at least, when I would take refuge once again under the fan.

The first three pages of Betty's letter were as expected. Apologies for not having written as much this year as she'd promised; stories about little Hamish and how much she adored him; gossip about our old crowd including a sordid tale about my Harry, who had been running about on dates with our mutual friend Lola, only for her to turn around and start running on dates with his father. *Can you imagine, Z?* she wrote, *Not only may he end up with a stepmother three years younger than him, but he's probably kissed her! If not more!*

I didn't feel sorry for Harry – in fact, I took a bit of joy at the idea that he might be experiencing the kind of jealousy I often had.

On the letter went, and then on the second-last page the tone changed acutely.

Well, here I am this far in and I haven't told you the most important thing. Mainly because I didn't want it on any of the early pages in case somebody else picked the letter up and I am so full of guilt and shame, but I must tell you, Z. I must tell somebody. Since we have moved back to Australia, I have been so unhappy and confused. We hired an architect who is remodelling the back of our house so we have a bigger room for Hamish and any other babies that may be on the way. The architect's name is Roy.

So now I must confess the thing that I haven't dared speak. I think I am in love with him. He says he is in love with me and it makes me so unhappy because I wonder if I have married the wrong man. Tom has no time for me or Hamish, and Roy is here every day, and he is lively and funny and terribly terribly attractive. What on earth should I do? I feel as though life is so very long, stretching ahead of me and forever constrained by the choice I've already made to marry Tom. This can't be right, can it? I might live another fifty years. Am I to yearn for something else for fifty long years? It would be no better than prison in a foreign country, where the words people say to me make no sense.

Z, what on earth shall I do?

This last sentence was underlined so hard that the ink had bled through the paper.

I folded the letter quickly and shoved it back in the envelope, pulse thudding guiltily. James could *never* see this. If he thought that I had even the barest tolerance for Betty conducting an affair, his terrible jealousy would be roused. I wanted very badly to write back to Betty and tell her I would love her no matter what choice she made, that she was right that fifty years was far too long to yearn for something else. But if James should idly pick up my notebook, as he so often did if I was writing to Mum or Vieve . . . he would infer from it an imagined unfaithfulness on my part.

So I took Betty's letter down to the cooking pit where a group of women in saris were stirring over the coals ready for the day's roast. Without saying a word to any of them, I slipped the letter among the coals and bright orange flames licked over it. In a few moments, it was curling ash.

I didn't write back to Betty, and while the guilt over that omission was intense, it was the lesser evil while I was still trying to make things right with my husband. And so I turned my back on my closest friend.

———

A new year dawned and my relationship with James settled, largely because of the tremendous effort I made not to engage other men. Even when Penny and the brigadier had us over for dinner, I would make sure not to get caught in a conversation with him. I was polite, of course, but didn't offer my opinions as readily. It worked very well and my marriage was smooth as we approached our first anniversary, still not pregnant. By the time the monsoons came again, I knew exactly what to expect from life in India. I had a loving husband, fun friends, time to draw and write letters . . . everything but a baby. And not for want of trying. I wasn't sure who wanted the child more – James or me – but we tried every single night, until all passion had left our lovemaking and it became the last chore we had to complete every evening. Lights off, his hand on my hip and away we went. Five minutes later, we lay flat on our backs, holding hands in the dark. He always fell asleep first.

In July, I decided to try my hand at gardening. Mid-monsoon was a terrible time to plant anything, as seeds would get swamped and there wasn't sufficient sun, so I decided to start modestly. Behind the house, there was a sheltered alcove recessed into the blank stone wall. I often sat there on hot days if the wind was coming from the north. I had some small pots delivered, which I filled with soil and left in the alcove. My intention was to wait for good weather and dig up a few ferns from the edge of the jungle to plant in them, and have my own little fernery. However, the next morning when I came out, I found all the pots had been moved and were sitting in the rain. I moved them all back, only to find them gone again the next day. I asked James if he knew whether they were readying the house for limewashing, perhaps. I couldn't understand why somebody would continue to move my pots. He knew nothing, so I put them back again and left a note saying, *Please do not move.*

At ten the next morning, there was a knock at my door. I opened it to see a thin, wrinkly man, not much taller than me, wearing a grimy turban and no shoes. He was holding my note.

'Hello?' I said.

'Mrs Fell?'

'Yes.'

'I am Purab,' he said, and his accent was very thick. 'I am one of the groundsmen here.'

I couldn't remember seeing him before and wondered if the servants were becoming invisible to me too. 'It's a pleasure to meet you,' I said with a nod. 'You're the one who moves my pots?'

'Yes, my lady.'

'Is there a reason?'

'Yes, my lady. I have come to tell you the reason.'

'Go on, then.'

His voice was soft and thin, his sentences rising at the end like questions. 'The place you put them is a holy spot. The holy man comes at midnight. The area must be left free.'

'The holy man?'

'Yes, my lady. He comes at midnight.'

I was curious. 'Every night?'

'Yes. Every night.'

I had lived here a year and never heard of a person who came to the back of the bungalow at night, let alone for holy purposes. But then the penny dropped. 'Is . . . is it a real person? Or a spirit?'

He averted his eyes. 'It is a holy man.'

'If I was there at midnight, would I see him?'

'You might, yes, and if you did he would bless you with great good luck.'

'And he doesn't like my pots?'

'The space is holy, my lady.'

'Why?'

'Because that is where the holy man appears.'

Unluckily, right where I wanted to place my fernery. I smiled at Purab. 'Thank you very much for telling me. I will put my pots somewhere else.'

'Yes, my lady. If you require assistance from me or the other groundsmen with your garden, please do come to see us.'

I brought all my pots onto the front veranda, deciding I'd plant them with flowers instead, but perhaps at a drier time of the year. I remained curious about this holy man, and asked Urvashi about it. She said that yes, she did know about the stories. All the servants did. Our bungalow was where the holy man appeared at midnight, and it was good luck for the household and the regiment.

She was bustling about my bedroom, putting away our folded clothes. I sat on the edge of the bed and questioned her further. 'So everyone but the English knows about the holy man?'

'The English wouldn't believe us, ma'am.'

'Do you believe it? Do you believe we are blessed by a holy man?'

'I don't know, but we have never had bad luck in this house. Colonel Fell is very kind, and he brought you to us.' Here she gave me a shy smile. 'And then you looked after Daljeet and now Mr Parakh is gone so . . . all good luck from my view.'

'Do you know anyone who has seen the holy man?'

'Yes, ma'am. At least they say they have. Devika sat out there all night when she was hoping her father would recover from an illness, and she said she saw a strange light and then the next morning her father woke up breathing easily again.'

'Really?' I said, more to myself than to Urvashi. I found it fascinating and beautiful, this myth of a holy man who granted wishes. Especially so because he had decided to ply his trade behind our house. I asked James about it that evening, but he dismissed it as superstitious nonsense and reminded me we are English and Christian. I nearly reminded him that I was Australian and largely agnostic, but it didn't seem wise given he looked tired from his day's work.

I might have forgotten about it. Life in India was full of colour and the story of the holy man might have become part of that rich background to my life, but over my second monsoon in India, James began to grow agitated that I hadn't yet fallen pregnant. It became a low hum of discord in our lives. I strongly suspected that somehow his jealousy had attached itself to our infertility, which made no logical sense. He began to question me on everything I did in my day, criticised my female friends for 'filling my head with silly ideas', and forbade me from going to town without him. I felt rather like the hen we'd had when I was a child, who would wander around the garden and leave her eggs where the foxes could eat them. We'd had to lock her in her coop twenty-four hours a day until she started laying in there again.

One night, we began to make love as usual, but James could not finish. He kept trying, grabbing my breasts roughly, screwing his eyes shut, but nothing seemed to work. Eventually he rolled off me with a frustrated sigh and, for some reason, I said, 'Sorry.'

He propped himself on his side and stroked my hair. 'No, my darling. I'm sorry. You have nothing to be sorry for. You are beautiful.' He kissed my shoulder. 'It's in my head. Why aren't you pregnant? Is it me? Am I not . . . ?'

He couldn't finish. I pulled him against me. 'It will work out. Perhaps it's simply not the right time yet.'

'I think we need to speak to a doctor.'

'Do we?'

'Would you? Would you go to London and see somebody? A specialist? He could tell us if the problem was you or . . . if not you, then me.'

'I . . . London? I could go home to Melbourne.'

'We have better doctors in England.'

I didn't correct him. The main thing on my mind was whether or not a specialist, in examining me, could tell that I had already been pregnant once. And how likely that information was to make its way back to James.

'You haven't answered, Zara,' he said, and I could hear the frown in his voice.

'Yes, darling. Yes. Whatever would put your mind at rest. But let's wait until October when the weather is more likely to be fair for sailing.'

He agreed, and soon after he fell asleep, still curled against me. I stroked his hard, bare shoulder and lay awake in the dark. Eventually he murmured and turned in his sleep, and yet still I was awake, scenarios playing themselves out in my mind.

I was still awake when I heard the grandfather clock downstairs *bong* gently to let me know it was midnight.

I sat up suddenly, a wild thought occurring to me. The holy man. Perhaps if I saw him . . .

I threw back the covers and pulled on my nightgown, then hurried down the stairs and out the back door. The rain fell steadily, but the winds had died down. It was very dark and I stumbled over an uneven tile then righted myself. I made my way to the alcove, but saw no holy man.

I sat in the alcove watching the rain, my heart thudding then slowing. The sound of the rain on a dozen different surfaces. Stone. Tin. Mud. Leaves. A calm feeling crept over me and I closed my eyes.

I became aware that there was light beyond my eyelids. I opened them, but could see nothing. I closed them again . . . but the light was still there, making my field of vision dark red instead of black. I took a deep breath. 'I wish for a baby,' I said softly.

A slow warmth moved over me, from my toes to my crown. I pushed away all doubt and fear and let the sensation wash through. Then the sensation passed and I went back to bed, feeling mildly foolish.

By September, I was pregnant.

———

James and I travelled to Poona with the brigadier's family for Christmas. James was his old self now he had some time off, boyish and fun, sleeping easily and waking happily. The weather was mild, rather more like an Australian summer, and it was a delight to have Penny's children around us all the time, toddling about, growing excited over Christmas presents and lovingly calling us Aunty Zara and Uncle Jim. As my belly started to push out against my dresses, James and I were the very picture of a loving young couple.

Except . . . James no longer wanted to make love. At first I'd thought it because he was so exhausted from us trying nightly for so long, but soon enough he revealed it 'just didn't feel right' now I was growing a baby. He shrugged me off, but gently, and after a few weeks I gave up. I missed it, but it was hard to be sad when we were so close and so happy.

One bright morning, Penny and I took the little ones for a picnic in the Empress Garden. They had their shoes off and were wading in a stream with Surabhi teaching them to skim stones, while Penny and I sat twenty feet away on the picnic blanket under the branches of a huge, vine-covered tree. My appetite knew no bounds at the moment. James had laughingly called it 'eating for three or four'. I picked at the raisin teacakes we had brought with us, while Penny wrapped her arms around her knees and smiled indulgently at her children's squeals of delight. She wore a pale pink sari that left her right shoulder bare, and her skin was pink too from the sun. I wore a tent. Well, I wore a dress I had run up quickly that would be cool and loose and cover me from the sun, but at just over five feet tall, anything of that design looked a little tent-ish.

Penny turned back to me. 'You'll know this joy soon,' she said, indicating the children with a tilt of her head.

'I already take so much joy in yours.'

'Your own are completely different. It's deep. Almost painful.' She smiled at me. 'Oh, don't pick raisins out of the cakes, Zara. Just eat it. You're making a baby. Keep your energy up.'

I did as she said, trying not to feel guilty. Three cakes was a lot for a small woman.

'What are you looking forward to the most about it?' Penny asked.

'I'm dying to know if it's a girl or a boy,' I said.

'Do you have a preference?'

I glanced over at her little ones. 'Isabel is such a poppet. It's hard not to imagine having a girl. The dresses.'

'Yes, she is divine. But Reggie is so fiercely in love with me. There's nothing quite like the love between a little boy and his mama.' She patted my knee. 'You'll be smitten either way. Is James happy?'

'Yes! So, so happy. We have never been so close.'

'Ah, lovely.'

'Except . . .' I hesitated. It was one thing to make risqué jokes over gin cocktails, but the officers' wives and I rarely talked about anything very personal.

Penny lit a cigarette and passed it to me, but I refused it. The taste had made me feel ill since I'd been pregnant.

'Go on. What were you going to say?' Penny prompted. 'We are women of the world, are we not?'

I chuckled. 'I don't know about that. Rather a small sample to draw conclusions from.'

Now Penny was laughing, blowing two streams of smoke out her nose like a dragon. 'Oh heavens. What is it?'

'James doesn't want to' – I pushed my palms together – 'anymore.'

Penny jammed her cigarette between her lips and imitated my gesture. 'This? This is how you two do it?'

'Penny, that's scandalous.' I laughed.

She began to make other shapes with her hands. Back-to-back, fingers interlaced, fast clapping. I couldn't breathe for laughter.

Finally, we stopped laughing and she answered me. 'Is that a bad thing though? I always think it's nice to have a break from it.'

'I worry that maybe he doesn't find me attractive anymore.'

'Oh, darling, you're beautiful and always will be.' She leaned in and gave me a hug. 'Don't worry about James. He'll be back at it once you've had the little one, then you might long for more time without it! Nothing made me so tired as having a tiny baby reliant on me. I don't know what I would have done without Surabhi.' She turned her eyes to Surabhi and her children and smiled, then looked back to me. 'And you're heading home for the delivery directly from Poona?'

'Yes, in three weeks. I'll miss James, but I'm dying to see my mum.'

'You're lucky she's still alive. My mum died when I was little and I had to endure my stepmother directly after I gave birth. She thought she knew everything about babies and drove me utterly mad.' Penny puffed at her cigarette then pointed it at me. 'That's my best advice. Trust your instincts. Don't let anyone tell you what to do. You're the mama.'

'Thank you, Penny. I shall miss you too.'

'But you'll be back.'

'Yes, James will come and fetch me in June. I'll return just in time for another monsoon.'

'Glorious,' she said with a cynically raised eyebrow. 'We'll keep him company while you're gone.'

After Christmas and New Year, when I was so tired I could barely keep my eyes open during the parties, I boarded the train that would take me to Bombay and my ship home. James enclosed me in a rib-cracking hug, then bent and kissed my belly. 'I can't wait to meet you, little one,' he said.

'James, you're causing a scene,' I said, glancing around and seeing an elderly woman judging us with her eyes.

'Don't care,' he said, and kissed me full and hard on the mouth. 'I will see you on the other side, darling.'

'I'll miss you so much.'

'Not as much as I'll miss you.' He took my face between his hands and looked hard into my eyes. 'Zara,' he said in a firm voice, 'remember our marriage vows.'

I was surprised but tried not to show it. What a thing to say to me as I was about to head on a long journey, hugely pregnant. 'Of course,' I answered lightly.

He gave me a single nod, then let me go and jumped back onto the platform to wave until I couldn't see him anymore.

CHAPTER 15

The light fell differently in Melbourne, as though the air was not so thick and heavy. In the car journey from the docks, exhausted from travel and feeling swollen and huge, I drank in the pale sky and the familiar trees and felt something inside me loosen and relax. Daddy drove with intense concentration, as he always did, which I believed was a way to avoid small talk. I was happy to spend the journey looking out the window.

When we pulled up outside the house – their new house on St Georges Road – Mum was there on the patio and the sunshine hit her face in a way that I saw she had aged in that little while I had been away. It was strange to me. She had always been strikingly beautiful, so to see the sag in her jowls filled me with a sense of sad inevitability. But then she moved and smiled and she was her gorgeous self again.

'Zara! My darling girl!' She embraced me as I left the car then stood back to look at my belly. 'Jingo, you're enormous, you poor thing.'

'I'm short. I'm not carrying it well.' Her words had been meant kindly, but they cut me because I was embarrassed about being so round.

'Come inside and take the weight off your feet. I'll make us tea.'

The new house was roomier, with higher ceilings and new light fittings. It still smelled the same though – lemon polish and tobacco smoke. My youngest brother David, seventeen now, asked

223

me a million questions about India. Both he and Daddy found it impossible to look at my swollen belly. John was off with his new girlfriend and Genevieve was at home busy with little April. I drank disappointing tea – India had ruined me for good tea – and Mum sat next to me with her hand on my belly, oohing with excitement whenever the baby kicked.

Finally, when David and Daddy had gone off to run errands, Mum asked me if I'd heard from Harry.

I shook my head. 'I haven't spoken a word to him since that day.' The memory of it came back to me . . . the ring, the half-hearted proposal, my anger.

'He's done so well for himself. Your dad and he are in touch a lot. He helps with contracts and the like. We've had him over for dinner a few times . . . You don't mind, do you?'

'No. I've known Harry for years. I'm married now and no doubt he will be before long too. I'd say we will always be friends.'

'He's more than your friend, he's your local member of parliament.' Mum laughed. 'George Maxwell finally died. Oh, I know it sounds cruel but he'd been in that job far too long. Anyway, your dad and I were so proud to vote for Harry. He's living in a friend's house down on Hill Street at the moment. Not far away. He'll probably pop by. I said that would be all right.' She paused, examining my face. 'Is it all right?'

'Yes, yes,' I said. 'It will be fine. I'm not angry with him anymore.' That part was true. 'In fact, I've barely thought of him in nearly two years.'

Not entirely true.

———

Now I was in Melbourne, I could resolve something that had been weighing very heavily on my mind. I went to see Betty the very next afternoon.

A cab dropped me off outside a tidy brick house with a low front fence. The front garden was small but perfectly laid out and maintained. A little dog greeted me with happy barking while I unlatched the gate, and sniffed my heels as I walked up the path. I rang the bell and a moment later Betty was there.

Her expression was unreadable for a moment, but then turned into a happy smile. 'Zara! Darling! Oh, you look so ripe and beautiful! What a delightful surprise. Come in, come in.'

She ushered me in over a polished parquetry entranceway and into a bright sitting room with a long settee and two huge white armchairs. Quiet music was playing on the wireless. Dark wooden furniture gleamed in the light coming through the large windows. Betty gestured I should sit in one of the armchairs and bent to turn the wireless off.

She sat opposite me, barefoot with her knees folded to the side. Her green dress was immaculate. I was certain her smile was forced.

'I'm sorry,' I blurted.

'What do you mean?'

I glanced around. 'Is there anyone else home?'

'Just Hamish. He's sleeping.'

'Your letter,' I said, and dropped my voice even though there was nobody home to hear us.

She shook her head. 'A silly passing phase.'

'I need to explain.'

'No, no. You don't.'

'I wanted to write back, to tell you I would love you and support you no matter what. But James is terribly jealous, and I was afraid he might read my letter or yours and . . . I'm sorry.'

She glanced away, swallowed hard. I thought she might be about to cry, but then the smile came back.

'Thank you,' she said. 'But it's over. There's no need to apologise. Something about having babies can make women quite mad.'

I felt there was more to be said, but she clearly didn't want to say it.

'Tea?' she asked.

'In India, we have gin cocktails in teacups for afternoon tea,' I said.

This time the smile was genuine. 'Let's do that then.'

We drank gin rickeys and she showed me around her house, tiptoeing and whispering when we approached the new nursery wing, only to find little Hamish lying awake in his crib, thumb firmly in his mouth. We got him up. He was an adorable, quiet little boy who toddled about after us and played with a wooden car while we sat and chatted. I was smitten and started for the first time to long for a boy. It was late afternoon when he started getting whiny and Betty said she best feed him and get dinner started for Tom.

As we waited in the front garden for my cab, Hamish lying on the grass looking at a dandelion, I tried one last time with Betty. 'So are you happy?'

'Yes, perfectly. Really. It was nothing.'

'I didn't sound like nothing.'

'Marriage is a very long journey,' she said. 'And every relationship has its problems. You said yourself, you have a jealous husband.'

'I do.'

'I wouldn't mind that,' she joked lightly. 'At least it would mean he noticed me, thought me capable of attracting somebody else.' Her voice shaded from light to bitter.

I took her hand. 'Betty, you can tell me anything.' I heard the cab pull up.

The bright smile was back. 'I know, dear. Now you go home and rest, for there will be no rest when this little baby comes along, trust me.'

I kissed her cheek and headed home.

———

An unfamiliar car was parked outside our house, a gleaming aqua-marine Hudson. As I let myself in the front door, I heard a familiar voice from the lounge room, in conversation with my father. My heart did a little flip – it knew that voice was Harry's before my brain had reckoned it. I felt suddenly shy, uncomfortable in my own skin. I was doing my best to have a stylish pregnancy but there was little that was flattering about my waistless polka-dot dress. I applied a smile and peered around the threshold.

There he was. My ribs seemed to light up with electricity. Harry. It was Harry.

He leapt from his chair and boomed a jolly, 'Hello, my dear,' before pulling me towards him for a chaste peck on the cheek. He kept my hand in his and his face shone. 'You look wonderful.'

I couldn't hide my smile. 'Thank you. I feel quite the elephant.'

'Oh, no no no. You're a Madonna, sweet face and all. How *good* to see you.'

'And how good to see you. You look so sharp. Being an MP agrees with you.'

I became aware that Mum and Daddy were looking at us curiously, and wondered how much of the shining wonder we took in each other was visible to them.

'Let's sit down,' I said.

He returned to his seat, and I sat next to Mum on the couch. Music from the wireless, friendly chatter and Daddy's pipe smoke filled the air until evening came in and Mum turned on the lamps and asked Harry to stay for dinner. He sat across from me at the table, and every time I looked up he was giving me twinkling eyes. I bathed in his glances as though they were champagne – a delicious, fizzy treat that made my head spin but I knew wasn't good for me in too much measure.

After dessert, I offered to see him out. We stood on the patio, the warmth of the day just cooling towards an overnight chill. I indicated the aquamarine Hudson. 'You bought a car?'

'Yes. I needed it to get around the electorate. I drive to Canberra for sittings too.'

'How long does that take?'

'A whole day, but I love the countryside. I could fly if I needed to.'

'I've never been on an aeroplane.'

'I know. Zara, I know more about you than anybody. Though you are rather well travelled now, aren't you?'

I smiled up at him. 'You were the one who told me I needed to see the world. It was one of your favourite ways to upset me.'

He cringed. 'I hate myself for things I've said to you, Zara. And done to you. The way it all ended . . . it was madness. You were right. Territorial pissing.' Here he chuckled. 'I expect to be sworn at in public office, but I never expected it to come from you.'

'It's all in the past,' I said, and a melancholy tide swept over me. 'I bet you're seeing somebody else now.'

'I am always seeing somebody,' he said vaguely. 'None of them are . . . none of them the girl for me. But you know I love women.' He spread his hands and stood back. 'Especially when they look this womanly.'

'Oh, stop,' I said, glad it was dark so he couldn't see me blush. 'I'm a whale.'

'You really must stop comparing yourself to elephants and whales, Zara. You look to me as you always have – sweet-faced and well turned-out. A pregnant body is a beautiful body.'

'Daddy can barely look at me,' I said.

'It must be hard for a father to see his daughter . . . you know.'

'Despoiled?'

We laughed.

'Want to go for a drive? We could go and visit some old friends. Everyone still talks about you. Why, I had a middle-aged widow bail me up at a horseracing event just last week asking when you would be opening Magg again.'

I looked down at my belly. 'I hope you told her that the next ten years at least are spoken for by this little person.'

'I did. I very proudly told her you were off in India, married to a cavalry officer and expecting your first child. She told me I was an idiot for letting you get away.'

I shook my head at him. 'You were.'

'I was.'

'I don't want to go for a drive, Harry. I get very tired, and my feet start to swell and I just want to put them up. But another night I would love to see some old friends.'

'Very well. Goodnight.'

'Goodnight.'

He hadn't moved.

'Goodnight?' I said again.

He leaned in to kiss my cheek. I was overwhelmed by the familiar, wonderful smell of him. As if both operating out of instinct, Harry and I turned our faces so our lips met. Softly at first, then hungrily. He parted my lips with his tongue, and only then did I leap back, hand to my mouth.

'Sorry,' I said.

'No, I'm sorry,' he replied. 'I'm so so sorry.'

I nodded, not meeting his eye. 'Goodnight.'

He patted my shoulder once, then strolled off to his car whistling. I stayed outside after he drove off, waiting for my thundering heart to slow. Mum came out eventually.

'Everything well with you, daughter?' she asked.

'Just enjoying Melbourne smells,' I said.

'Nice to see Harry?'

'He's a dear friend.'

'Hm,' Mum said, and nothing else, then left me standing in the evening air, still feeling the heat of Harry's lips on mine.

———

The next day, a delivery arrived for me, wrapped in brown paper, no return address. Curious, I took it inside and tore off the paper. Inside was a framed print of Botticelli's *Primavera*, Venus and the goddess of spring, surrounded by nymphs, all of them pregnant and beautiful. I smiled to myself. Harry didn't need to put his address on the package for me to know it came from him.

I propped it up on my dressing table in the spacious guestroom where I was sleeping. It couldn't come back to India with me; James would lose his mind if I told him another man had given me this. But I would enjoy it while I could.

———

Harry was very sweet to me and we did not mention the kiss again. He was a perfect gentleman, taking me for country drives with friends, to parties, to dinners with my sister and her husband, or with Betty and Tom, and always quick to see the signs I was growing tired. He took exceptional care of me, never touched me more than a guiding hand on my elbow or a peck on the cheek in company.

But it was there. The desire that had always brewed between us. For my part, I thought of Harry as I went to sleep at night far more than I thought of James. I felt so embarrassed and ashamed by this. My belly full of another man's child, and me replaying past passionate trysts in my imagination. But then I remembered what Betty said, that something about having babies can make women quite mad, and I didn't feel as bad. I was in a mad phase, and it would pass.

I enjoyed the last month before the birth, being a whole person and not two people, as I would be soon. But I got more and more enormous until I couldn't go out at all, because the baby sat upon my bladder and I couldn't risk being out at a picnic so far from a toilet. I told nobody this, instead begging off for tiredness, which was not untrue. My ankles swelled up so badly that they looked like tree trunks and I spent the last two weeks on the couch, feet up and reading. Harry popped by every few days to see if I needed anything, but eventually I was too tired even for him.

So very, very tired.

When the first labour pain hit me, it woke me in the dark. A dagger in my back. I waited for it to pass, almost dozing, then there was another. I sat up and turned on my lamp. The clock on the dresser, in front of *Primavera*, said it was midnight. Was I to go through labour with only two hours of sleep?

I waited, and for a few minutes there was no more pain. False labour, then? But then a huge contraction gripped me and I actually called out in pain. I waited for it to pass and went to wake up Mum.

Within an hour we were at the hospital, and I was finding the pain increasingly difficult to bear. A nurse gave me an injection and then I started to feel fuzzy and a little less in pain. Time turned to molasses, and my dread ebbed away. I remembered so little later. I remembered telling them I was going home and I was not going to do this. I remembered a bald doctor coming in to the bright white room and his hands being very cold on my thighs. I remember shouting as the baby crowned and heaving all my strength into pushing him into the world. And then he was crying in my arms, a perfect bundle. Nicholas. My little Nicky.

———

How quickly the world shifted on its axis. Before I was Zara, and after I was Nicky's mama, and that was the only thing that mattered to me. I breastfed him for three weeks in a happy fog, until Mum advised me to switch to bottled milk so I could get my strength back. I wrapped my breasts up tight and they ached and ached, as if they missed his sweet little lips upon them, but within a fortnight they had settled and resumed something approaching their previous size.

The first two months, time crawled. I relied on my mother heavily, and she was kind and patient with me and of course smitten with Nicky. There was a constant stream of visitors, bringing flowers and cards and tiny blue clothes. Telegrams arrived from everywhere. James was over the moon to have a little boy and demanded I get some photographs taken to send him as he wasn't able to make it over to collect me for three more months.

I found the visitors tiresome, to be honest. At the start, especially, I seemed to be leaking from everywhere, and having to pretend I was as whole and dry as I used to be took such an effort. Poor little Nicky was passed around like a church collection plate, and everybody wanted to be the one to feed him or rock him, when I wanted those things for myself. I loved it when he woke crying in the deep of night because the two of us were together alone at last.

One of Harry's friends had a friend with a photographic studio out at Brighton, and Harry arranged to take us out there for pictures to send to James. It was nine weeks to the day since Nicky's birth, and I felt both as though no time at all had passed, and that my old life was a hundred years ago.

It was a grey cold day in June, but Harry's car was warm and Nicky slept happily bundled up in my arms. We chatted idly, but I couldn't stop thinking about how James would interpret this scene. I wondered if I was being faithful enough to our wedding vows.

We arrived at a rambling brick building two streets from the sea. Harry greeted the owner, an elderly man who looked like he wouldn't know which end of a camera was up. In fact, it was his daughter who was the photographer, and she had a little studio in the garden that the older gentleman led us to and let us in. We sat and waited on a long wooden bench. In every corner of the room, a different background was painted. Mountains. Floral fields. A window in a garden wall. A Victorian wallpaper pattern. Round the place were dotted various props – a fake palm, a large urn, books on a round table. Nicky had woken up and was fussing, so I handed him to Harry while I felt around in my tote bag for his bottle.

'Lively little chap, aren't you?' Harry said to Nicky, who wriggled violently.

Harry's strong hands around Nicky's little body made something stir inside me. 'Would you like to feed him?' I asked.

'Would he allow me to?'

'Let's see.' I handed him the bottle and helped him tilt it at just the right angle, and in a moment Nicky was suckling happily, little fists curled gently up by his ears.

'Bring him in a little closer to you,' I said.

Harry snuggled Nicky against his chest, smiling down at him. 'Ah, there,' he said. 'That's better, isn't it?'

I reached across and stroked Nicky's downy, warm head. What bliss it was, leaning in together like that.

Harry met my eyes, and his were full of tender wonder. 'He is beautiful.'

'I know.' A moment passed between us. I saw the life that might have been for us, and I know he saw it too because there was a dull pain in his expression.

We were interrupted when a middle-aged woman with grey-streaked red hair piled on top of her head bustled in. 'I am so very sorry to be late. Daddy let you in all right?'

'Yes, yes,' I said. 'And it's fine to be late. The little one is just having some lunch.'

'He's a sweet little fellow. I'm Lillian. You must be Mr and Mrs Fell?'

Harry and I both began to make awkward noises and explain that he was *not* Mr Fell and, yes, it might have looked that way but really he was Mr Holt and only a long-time friend of the family. Lillian was uninterested in our explanations, brushing them off with an airy wave. She had me choose a background, and I chose the garden because it looked most like the lush wonderland of India. I was dressed in a dark wool suit, pulled in very tight at my waist to show James that my figure was back (it wasn't; I was sucking all my breath in for every photo). Nicky fussed a little at first, but then happily snuggled against me in his long crocheted shawl, which his delicate fingers kept getting tangled in. He even managed a crooked smile, something he had only been doing for a week. Finally, Lillian declared we were done and said she would send some prints to my address in a week.

Harry insisted we drive down to the beach for a walk on the sand, but when we arrived it was drizzling and windswept, and Nicky had fallen asleep in his basket on the back seat. Instead, we sat in the car looking across the grey water through the rain-smudged windscreen, listening to Nicky's soft breathing.

We sat without speaking for a long time. I stole a glance at his profile, admiring the noble line of his nose, when he turned his eyes to mine and the space between us became charged. He held my gaze and I held his, and it was like sinking my toes into warm sand. I realised with some alarm that I was still in love with him. But I was in love with my husband too. Everything I had been taught about love had been wrong. It was entirely possible to be in love with two people; it was just hideously confusing. I imagined how blissful life would be if I could live six months of the year with Harry in Melbourne and six months of the year with James in India, then berated myself for such scandalous thoughts. What kind of woman was I to think such a thing with an infant in the back seat?

'You'd best take me home, Harry,' I said, breaking the moment.

He nodded. 'As you wish,' he said and started the car.

———

Harry had to go off to parliament for a few months, and I was relieved. It meant he wouldn't return until after I had gone home to James, unless he made a special trip for the weekend. I hoped the eight-hour drive each way would discourage him.

James called me every Friday around morning-tea time, which was first thing in the morning for him. We would chat for a strict half-hour, and I would put the phone up to Nicky's ear for James to say hello and Nicky would gurgle something back. This delighted James no end. He received the photograph I sent – I had chosen one where I was smooching Nicky's cheek and he was smiling directly at the camera – and told me he had it framed and hanging in our bedroom so he could see us both when he opened his eyes in the morning.

I spent all my time on family things. Mum, Vieve and Nicky became almost my whole world. I saw Betty from time to time, but she was stand-offish, probably still feeling ashamed of what she'd told me. I decided to stop pressuring her to see me, and missed her very badly.

Slowly the little one started sleeping better, the days were distinguishable from each other, my figure began to return, and it was time to start preparing to head back to India. I organised shipping for some new clothes for both Nicky and me, plus toys and spare baby items. James was due to arrive on the seventh of September, and I made a reservation for a welcome dinner, just the two of us, at L'Albero Rosso on Bourke Street. I was about to start sorting through which clothes to pack when a telegram arrived.

DELAYED IN BOMBAY ON URGENT BUSINESS STOP NOW
SAILING 1 OCT
COL JAMES FELL

If James wasn't leaving Bombay until the first of October, that would mean he would be more than a month late. I found myself growing restless and impatient. My mindset had already switched over to India and James. Now I found myself in Melbourne.

With Harry.

He returned from parliament in mid-September as the daffodils and hellebores were starting to bloom in Mum's garden. I had been out walking Nicky in the white wicker pram when I rounded the corner and saw his car out front. I stopped, my breath caught in my throat. Then I turned the pram around and walked back in the other direction.

A moment later I heard him calling me. I paused again, listening as his footsteps caught up with me.

'Out walking, eh?' He leaned in to tickle Nicky's chin. Nicky giggled madly. 'He is a big bonny boy now. Aren't you, little man? Can I join you on your walk, Nicky?'

'Perhaps that's not . . .' I trailed off.

Harry straightened up, tilted his head. 'I thought you'd be glad to see me. Wait . . . were you running away from me?'

I couldn't meet his eye. 'Let's walk. Nicky loves being out.'

The weather was divine. Pale blue skies, a brisk breeze in the treetops and sweet floral smells in the air. We made small talk. My new date for leaving Australia would be after the election, so he tried to convince me to help him on polling day. I turned him down and he made a joke about what a disappointing friend I was. I wasn't in the mood to laugh at such a joke, and when I had walked on in sullen silence, he finally asked, 'Zara, what on earth is wrong?'

'Harry, I'm married, with a child.'

'I know that.' He gave me that twinkling grin.

'I find this very difficult. If James knew we had spent so much time together, he would be . . .' I couldn't finish.

'He would be what?' Harry asked, serious all of a sudden.

'Furious,' I answered.

'Nothing you have ever said about your husband indicates him capable of being anything but sweet and wholesome.'

'Well, I don't tell you everything. The point remains, I'm married.'

'And I am one of your oldest friends, regardless of my sex. I come to see your family as much as you.'

I stopped the pram and dropped my voice. 'We haven't always been simply friends and you know it. James thinks I came to him untouched on our wedding night. It isn't right to keep behaving in a way that he would despise, simply because he's so far away.'

'What do you want then, Zara? You want me to leave you alone?'

I wanted entirely the opposite. I wanted to be near him all the time. 'Yes. You'll have to. If you can just wait a month or so until I'm gone that would be so much easier on me. You can visit Daddy after that, if you want to. But just . . . I need to be free of you.'

'I see.'

'And for the love of god, don't contact me when I'm in India. I think we need to put this' – I gestured at the space between him and me – 'well and truly behind us. Harry, you'll want to marry one day too and you don't want your wife to be haunted by me.'

He gazed at me for a few moments, the shadow of the tree above us moving across his face. Sun, shadow, sun, shadow. 'I won't marry, Zara.'

'Yes, you will. A young man in parliament needs a wife, especially if he wants to be a minister one day.'

'I lost the only girl I would have married.'

I couldn't speak for long seconds. Then I said, 'You have to leave me be. It's making me miserable.'

'I wouldn't want to make you miserable. I care too deeply for you.' He gave me a little salute. 'Your wish is my command, Mrs Fell. I'll leave you and young Master Fell here in peace. Give me a head start and I'll go back to your house to fetch my car. Then I'll disappear.'

I should have thanked him, but the words wouldn't come. I didn't watch him go. I pushed Nicky in the other direction, swallowing down hard on the pain.

———

It wasn't right for a married woman to be pining over a man who wasn't her husband so I simply refused – *refused* – to do it. I woke, I tended to Nicky, I had tea with friends and family, I read magazines, I window-shopped fashion stores. I was determined I would not feel those feelings. And when James phoned me weekly from Bombay, I was the sweetest, best wife to him, telling him how wonderful he was, how much I missed him, how I was counting down the days. That was true. I couldn't wait to get out of Melbourne and back to India, because then Harry would fade into the background again, as he had the last two years.

I expected James's arrival two days after election day. Harry organised an election night party at his house and invited everyone I knew. *Everyone*, including my parents who insisted on going. I couldn't say no without making them all speculate on why, so I submitted to my fate. I dressed more soberly than I had ever dressed for a party: in a belted gingham dress, with only a pale cherry-blossom lipstick, and low-heeled brown shoes with monk straps. I also had with me the most effective fashion accessory for warding off a man's attention, my six-month-old son.

Harry was staying in a two-storey white brick house with painted shutters and an open courtyard to cross to the wide entranceway. It belonged to a wealthy benefactor of his who was currently in Spain, so I didn't have to endure the pain of imagining myself the mistress of the place by Harry's side. Nicky and I had taken a lift with Mum and Daddy, and Mum rang the bell twice. I could hear noise and music inside so I suggested we just go in. Daddy opened the door and we found our way into a large living room, where all the chairs and tables had been pushed against the wall to create space. The room was crowded with very well-dressed people in tuxedos and evening gowns, chattering and lifting drinks off the silver trays being bustled about by a trio of young waiters. Harry saw us and waved, hurrying over to shake Daddy's hand.

'Sydney, Violet. And Mrs and Master Fell. I do hope the noise won't be too much for the little chap.'

'Oh, nought seems to unsettle this one,' Mum said, and if she thought it strange that Harry had called me Mrs Fell, she gave nothing away.

'Please, go ahead and mingle. We won't have final results until late in the evening, but so far I'm ahead.'

'Well done, Harry,' Daddy said, seizing a whisky from a passing waiter. 'Look, Zara, is that your friend Betty?'

I waved to Betty, who beckoned me over. She was with Tom, who was deep in conversation with another man who had the same Clark Gable hair and moustache as him. Betty released Tom's arm and came to greet me. 'Thank god you're here. And little Nicky too. May I hold him?'

'By all means,' I said. 'You didn't bring Hamish?'

'Trust me, they are easier at this age. Once they can start walking, all the peace and quiet is over. Oh, dear little fellow. Let Aunty Betty kiss you.'

Nicky, who had been unsettled by the noise up until now, began smiling and giggling as Betty smooched his cheeks in turn.

'How I love the little ones, Zara.' She leaned in, her voice dropping. 'I think I might be expecting again.'

'Really?'

'I haven't said anything to anyone else yet, so keep it under your hat.'

I wanted to ask a hundred questions about how she felt, if she was happy that she was tying herself tighter to Tom, if she still thought of her paramour Roy . . . but she had proven in the past that she simply wouldn't be drawn on the issue, so I had to assume she was telling the truth that all of those feelings were behind her. Which gave me heart that I would get over my feelings for Harry too.

'I won't say a word,' I said. 'And congratulations.'

'What about you? Going to have another?'

'I haven't yet seen my husband since this one was born,' I said, stroking Nicky's head. 'Give me a chance.'

'We should aim to have all our babies done and the worst of these years over in a decade. Then we can go back into business.'

'You want to go back into business?'

'I think about it all the time. Don't you?'

'Well, I think about dresses all the time, if that counts.'

She shot me a dubious expression. 'Not tonight, you didn't.'

I laughed. She was in an emerald chiffon gown, and most of the other ladies were similarly turned out. 'I dressed modestly on purpose.'

'Is this some kind of new-mother thing?'

I turned my eyes towards Harry, who was laughing with an older gentleman, then back to Betty. 'I'm trying not to attract attention to myself. Things between Harry and me have been . . . confusing.'

'Ah, I see.' A waiter scooted past and she lifted two champagne coupes off his tray. 'Here,' she said. 'Champagne helps.'

Just then, Genevieve popped up at my shoulder with an excited 'hello' and we fell into talking. She too had left her little charge at home, and both Vieve and Betty were keen to enjoy the party. Nicky was very patient with me as we larked about, found a smoking room to play cards in, even danced a little in the parquetry entrance hall. Yes, we were all a little drunk. Throughout the evening, Harry would answer the phone every half hour to get the vote count. By eight he had won his seat and by ten his party had won the whole election. A great cheer went up, and singing of 'For Harry's a jolly good fellow'. Then the older people began to leave, including my parents.

I was midway through a game of canasta when they came to find me.

'Let me take Nicky home,' Mum said to me. 'You haven't had a night out since before he was born.'

'Yes, stay,' said Betty, who was my pair. 'I can't lose you now.'

I hesitated. A few hours ago I had been dreading coming out. Was I now really considering staying longer?

'Oh, do stay, Zara.' That was Vieve. 'We're going to lose you to India again shortly. Have some more champagne and let's keep celebrating.'

Betty nudged me and whispered in my ear, 'Don't worry. I'll be here to look after you.'

'I'll stay then,' I said to Mum, relinquishing a sleeping Nicky. 'If you really don't mind taking him.'

Mum was already cuddling Nicky against her. 'I adore him, Zara. I'm very happy to take him. Enjoy yourself.'

The night wore on. Betty became very, very drunk: far too drunk to 'look after' herself, let alone me. I nearly left when Vieve and Jack did, but Tom was busy smoking cigars with a bunch of fellows by the fireplace and I didn't want to leave Betty alone. Harry and I had managed to stay separated for most of the evening, but as the numbers dwindled, that became impossible. I sat on a red velvet chaise with Betty, who appeared to have dozed off with a cigarette between her lips, when Harry finally slid onto the seat next to me.

'How is she?'

'Well-lubricated,' I said.

He nodded, peering over at Betty. 'She's been like this a few times the last year or so.'

'Really?' I turned to my friend and gently slipped the cigarette out of her mouth before it fell in her lap. She sighed a little and snuggled against my shoulder. A woman didn't drink herself into a stupor unless she was desperately unhappy.

'I was surprised to see you,' Harry said.

I returned my attention to him, passing him the cigarette so he could rest it in the ashtray beside the chaise. 'It would have looked odd if I didn't come. Suspicious even. Congratulations, by the way. Not that I ever doubted you'd win.'

'Did you vote for me?'

'I did,' I said. 'The first time I have ever voted for somebody I actually know. It felt quite satisfying.'

Betty stirred then sat up. She had gone a pale greenish colour around the lips.

'Oh dear,' I said, helping her up. 'Which way to the bathroom?'

Harry pointed and I hurried Betty along a hallway lined with dark wallpaper, and found a large tiled bathroom. I helped Betty to kneel next to the toilet and she said, 'I'm fine.'

'You'll feel better if you vomit up some of that champagne,' I said. 'But I'm fine.'

The next moment she was heaving up her stomach's contents. I rubbed her back gently, then helped her wash her face. The vomiting had sobered her a little, and we sat on the edge of the bath, which was recessed into the wall and taffy pink.

'Do you want me to get Tom?' I asked her. 'He's probably worried.'

'He hasn't noticed I'm gone,' she said bitterly. 'And he'll be cross about me making a fool of myself.'

'You haven't made a fool of yourself. It's a party. Everybody was drinking.'

She nodded miserably, then hitched and began to cry. I slipped my arm around her and she buried her face on my shoulder and wept. I could feel my dress grow damp.

'There,' I said. 'Let it all out.'

'I loved him, Zara,' she said, and I knew she wasn't talking about Tom.

'I know,' I said. 'You loved him and he loved you, but it didn't work out.'

'It didn't, it didn't,' she sobbed. 'I think about him all the time. Every spare moment, my thoughts wander back to him. I know I should just stop myself but I can't. I can't. I'm living two lives at once – the real one with Tom, and the fantasy with . . . him.'

I stroked her hair and let her cry. Finally, she sat up and palmed her face. It was pink and blotchy. 'I'm sorry. I'm sorry. Please don't tell anyone.'

'Never. Betty . . . is there any way you can be with him?' I asked.

'He's married. So am I.'

I saw how insurmountable this problem was. The scandal it would create would tear Betty's life to pieces. I wished for something more peaceful for her than that. 'Then you must try to put him out of your mind. The first arrow was falling in love with him. You couldn't help that. But the second arrow is driving yourself mad, and you are in charge of that.'

She nodded, sniffing, gathering herself. 'Yes, yes. You're right. And look, you are doing it. You and Harry clearly still carry a torch for each other, but you're heading back to India happily and calmly and with that darling baby.' She put her hand over her belly. 'And I'll have a new darling baby soon, and by then all of these feelings will be gone.'

'Yes. That's the spirit. Here, let me help you up.' I put my hand under her elbow and got her to her feet, and we emerged from the bathroom to an almost empty house.

'Ah, there she is, my drunken wife,' Tom said in a jolly tone. 'Have a few too many again, my darling? Shall I get you home?'

Betty nodded dumbly, and I could tell from the tension in her shoulders, the slight tuck of her chin, that she expected an argument as soon as they were alone. I nearly volunteered to go with them, then came to understand that one of the other gentlemen was driving them home with his wife and daughter, so there was no room for me. I saw them off, then called out 'goodnight' to Harry and headed out the door. It was a ten-minute walk home and I didn't mind the cold evening air.

Harry called after me just as I was crossing the courtyard.

I turned to see him standing in the doorway under the patio light, holding up one of Nicky's shawls. 'Is this yours? I think your mother might have left it.'

I turned back and came to take the shawl from him. 'Thank you,' I said.

A trio of well-dressed and very drunk men pushed past us, shouting their congratulations to Harry and singing a song they had made up. I could hear the waiters inside cleaning up.

'That's the last of my guests,' he said. 'Are you walking?'

'Yes.'

'I can drive you.'

'There's no need.'

'Then let me walk with you.'

'Really, there's no need.' At that instant, the sky shivered and soft drizzle began to fall.

'I'll drive you. Come inside where it's dry while I get the keys.'

I came inside, waited in the entranceway with a knot in my stomach. I folded Nicky's shawl over and over in my hands. A few moments later I heard him whistling as he approached, keys jingling.

'Come on, then,' he said, placing his palm gently under my forearm.

The moment his skin touched mine, I couldn't move. I couldn't speak. Nor could he. It was as though a spell had been cast. His hand tightened on my arm and he pulled me against him and swooped in to kiss me. This time I didn't turn him away, I wrapped my arms around his neck and all I could think was, *I am going back to India.* So far away. A different world. A different life.

'I don't want to go,' I murmured against his lips.

'Then stay.'

I realised we were talking about two different things, but the deep surge of desire in his voice in the word 'stay' lit me on fire. 'Yes,' I said. 'Yes.'

He seized my hand and hurried me up the stairs and into his bedroom. Everything smelled like him. He sat on the edge of the bed and pulled me between his knees, buried his face in my belly and sighed my name. My hand was in his hair as his fingers crept up my thighs, over the tops of my stockings to find the soft flesh there. A few moments later, my girdle and silk knickers were on the floor around my ankles and his face was under my gingham skirt. An image of James came to me, eyes screwed close when we made love. I pushed the image away and sank into the pleasure.

Harry then grasped me firmly by the hips and pulled me down onto the bed next to him, hurrying out of his clothes, hurrying me out of mine. I grew suddenly self-conscious. My body had changed since he'd last seen it, and I had no idea if I would feel different too.

'Harry, slow,' I said. 'I don't know . . . this is the first time since the baby.' My ears rang faintly, as thoughts of Nicky stirred up full knowledge of how wrong this was. But I couldn't stop. Neither of us could.

———

Harry did eventually drive me home, though both of us were silent. Guilt had seized our voices. He stopped outside my parents' house and we sat a moment, the car idling.

'We must never ever speak of this,' I said.

'I know. I don't regret it. Please say you don't regret it.'

'I don't know what I feel.'

'Do you love me?'

I took a deep shuddering breath and repeated more softly, 'I don't know what I feel.'

He took my hand and raised it to his lips. 'You'll always be my girl. No matter where you are in the world. I don't know how I will let you go, but I'll try.'

I nodded, lips pressed together against tears. 'Thank you,' I said.

I climbed out of the car. He waited until I'd opened the door of the house, then sped off, his tyres hissing on the damp road.

PART 4

CHAPTER 16

JUBBULPORE, 1937

I attended parade my first morning back in India, after a listless sleep where I was up and down with Nicky, worried about mosquitoes. Larissa and Franny were there – Penny being back in Poona and Cleo off in London with family – and they embraced me warmly and cooed over Nicky. But that was nothing compared to the fuss the servants made of him when we'd brought him in the night before. Daljeet had salaamed before him, and Urvashi nearly wept when I asked her if she would help me with the baby care, as another house girl was easy to hire but a good nanny was harder to find. All the way down to the regimental field we had been stopped repeatedly by Indians who exclaimed, 'A son! A son!' and wanted to give me wildflowers they picked or, in one case, a feather.

I watched the whole parade, keeping my eyes steady on James. My guilt was sickening. He had been so kind, so decent and so enamoured of the baby. The perfect husband. I hated myself for breaking my wedding vows when he had specifically asked me to keep them in mind, and for breaking them in the way he feared the most. In his uniform, atop his gleaming horse, he seemed to me a shining example of a man. I felt very dirty and tarnished by comparison.

After parade, Larissa, Franny and I walked back to the bungalows and ended up on my front veranda, drinking tea while Nicky kicked his chubby legs on a blanket laid out on the boards. Urvashi sat on the blanket next to him, tapping his little heels while he giggled madly. It had been difficult to hand over primary care of him to somebody else. Those giggles should have been for me. He wore nothing but his nappy, an attempt to keep him from overheating in the oppressive weather. The sky was grey and the air thick with moisture. Cicadas sang their hoarse song from every inch of the regimental grounds, a constant harsh background noise. I had almost forgotten how humid India was.

'Tell us what you did in Melbourne,' Franny said, swatting at a fly that was trying to land on the rim of her teacup.

'It was all such a fog. I was either exhausted and pregnant or exhausted and looking after Nicky. The nappies he went through in the early days! I was constantly in the laundry washing and wringing them through the mangle. And when he was waking up three and four times a night and I couldn't settle him . . . that was hard. I'm lucky my mum was so helpful.'

'Helpful mothers are one thing, but nothing beats a servant,' Larissa said, crossing her legs at the ankles.

'Don't you think there's something sacred about it though, something you miss when somebody else is looking after your little ones.' It felt awkward to have this conversation while Urvashi was right there in front of us.

'I don't think it's possible to miss washing nappies,' Larissa said.

'I have never felt my life the poorer for it,' Franny added.

'Did you go to any parties? Dances?'

I hesitated. I couldn't really speak about what I'd done without mentioning Harry, and I didn't want his name to get back to James. Also, I didn't want to say his name aloud because the guilt was still making me ill. 'One or two. It took quite a while for any of my party clothes to fit again.'

'Well, it must be nice to be home with us, dear,' Larissa said with a light pat on my hand. 'And with James. You were away a long time. You must have missed him.'

'Yes, of course,' I said, sounding rather more defensive than I'd intended.

The familiar hoofbeats and bells of the mail-delivery camel distracted us as it appeared on the path and stopped in front of the bungalow. The cameleer climbed down and handed me a bunch of letters tied with string. Nicky had rolled over onto his stomach and was staring at the camel agog.

'Little boy?' the cameleer said to me, pointing at Nicky.

'Yes. His name is Nicky.'

'Nicky Sahib ride camel?'

'Oh, I don't think so. He's too young.'

But the cameleer was already picking him up, chatting to him in Hindi. Urvashi stood and said something to the cameleer, then turned to me and said, 'He just wants to take him once around the bungalows. I can follow behind.'

'I don't know . . .'

But now the cameleer was handing Nicky to Urvashi so he could climb back on his beast, and then demanding Urvashi hand him back up. She looked at me nervously.

'Oh, go on, Zara,' Larissa said. 'You don't want the boy to be soft.'

All I could see was his softness – his pale little bent arms and plump knees.

Franny laughed. 'Look, he loves it.'

Nicky was laughing and reaching for the cameleer, who took it as a sign to grab him away from Urvashi and sit him on the saddle. The cameleer secured him with one arm and picked up the reins with the other, and they set off.

Urvashi gave me an apologetic smile and took off after them on swift feet.

'Be careful!' I called, gripped by a sudden fear that I would be punished for my unfaithfulness by something awful befalling my son.

'Come and sit down, Zara,' Franny said. 'Try to relax. They love little boys here. He'll be well taken care of.'

'Yes, and tonight you can tell James he's had his first camel ride. He'll be such a proud daddy.'

'Why are they so mad on little boys?' I asked.

'Some silly belief that having a son will get you into paradise with dancing girls,' Larissa said. 'I haven't listened closely to the stories.'

'I get dancing girls?' I said, amused.

'No, I think only the father does,' Franny laughed. 'Typical.'

'That's good as I wouldn't know what to do with dancing girls,' I replied. 'Perhaps design them some costumes.' It had been a very long time since I had even opened my sketchbook. Perhaps I would have more time now I had Urvashi to watch Nicky.

Soon enough, I heard the camel bells again and walked down the stairs to reclaim my child. I only exhaled fully when he was back in my arms, though he was bright-eyed and clutching the air to signal a desire to return to the camel.

I kissed his cheek and turned him away. 'Stay here with Mummy,' I whispered, and the camel bells jingled off towards the regimental offices.

'Shall I take him inside for his morning nap, ma'am?' Urvashi said.

I reluctantly relinquished him a second time, and returned to my chair.

'You're love-struck by that boy, aren't you?' Franny asked.

'Who wouldn't be?' I replied.

'Planning a second?' Larissa asked. 'It's nice when they're close together.'

'I would love a second,' I said, and for exactly that reason. Vieve and I were close in age and had been such great companions for each other all through our childhoods. 'Though it did take us quite a while to make the first, remember.'

More than that, James and I had not yet successfully returned to any kind of baby-making duties. Ever since we'd reunited, he had been unable to perform. He would start out fine, but the moment he entered me he was simply unable to keep going. It made him grumpy, and when I asked what was wrong, at first he said he didn't feel right about it yet as I'd only just had a baby. When I pointed out that was months in the past, he was more specific and said, 'You don't feel right.'

I was mortified, already worried about what bearing a child had done to me. Even thinking about it now made me squirm.

Franny was saying something to me and it snapped me out of the memory.

'Sorry, I missed that,' I said.

'Away with the fairies again,' Larissa joked affectionately. 'You look tired, so we'll let you be. Come on, Franny.'

I saw them off, realising I actually was very tired. I lay down on my bed with my sketchbook and drew a line of dancing girls. I began sketching costumes, but soon fell into a doze under the fan, only to wake up with a start when I heard James come in for lunch. I rose and smoothed my hair and dress, and went downstairs to play the perfect wife, even though I knew how enormously far from perfect I actually was.

Within a month, a large portion of the regiment had to travel to the north-west for special duties. It was the first time I'd worried about James, as it was active service, helping another regiment with bandits coming down from the Pakistani border making life difficult for the Raj. The night before he left, I clung to him in bed even though it was too warm to be so close together, while he reassured me. But again, I was convinced I would be punished for my sin of unfaithfulness.

'I'll be back in four weeks, and everything will be normal again,' he said, pulling my hands to his mouth and kissing my knuckles. 'Just in time for Christmas.'

How I wanted everything to be normal again. But I had ruined that for myself with my moral weakness and my sick regret, and my inability to stop thinking around in circles. The worst part was, even the guilt didn't stop me reimagining that time with Harry, over and over again.

———

So, for a few weeks at least, I was to be by myself. Not entirely true, because I had Nicky and all the servants, but Larissa and Franny took the opportunity to return home to England to see their families. I had hoped to receive an invitation from Penny to come and stay with her in Poona, but nothing had yet arrived and it didn't feel right to ask her directly. She was pregnant again, according to Larissa, and suffered terrible morning sickness.

The morning they all left, a lovely quiet settled over the place. A standing guard was left behind but there wasn't the constant sound of rifles, horses, men yelling at each other distant on the wind. The monsoon was behind me and the slightly cooler fresher months ahead. Urvashi was settling Nicky for his morning nap, so I stole him from her and went back to bed, drifting off beside him to the sound of the beating fan. I woke when he cried about forty-five minutes later, and told Urvashi to have the rest of the day off. I wanted to be with my boy.

We sat in the garden. I took him for a walk around the compound, stopping to look at any flowers he pumped his little hand at. I took him down to the stables to show him the horses, and the stablehands went wild for him and wanted to put him up on a horse, which I wouldn't allow. I imagined him in several years, learning to ride. Taking him off into the jungle. Showing him the lotuses in the lakes that only fill in monsoon . . .

Being with Nicky was bliss. All my churning feelings were soothed by his presence.

We spent our days like that. Urvashi became plainly anxious that I kept sending her away, so I let her take him every afternoon while I did some drawing. I had been inspired by some of the romantic gowns I'd seen in Melbourne and doodled endless bishop sleeves, shirred busts, ruched waists, and cascading flowers and bows on skirts. It was as though the quiet in the compound was allowing me to grow quiet in the mind. If I did think about my unfaithfulness, it was when I woke in the middle of the night, hot with fear. Sometime in that first fortnight that James was away, I managed to convince myself that the past could not be undone, and the best I could do now was to be a good wife from this second on.

It was never to be that easy.

I was in one of the Indian shops in town, buying a length of blue silk. I had decided to make one of my designs with Urvashi, who would help with the hand-sewing, as she was a woman who needed to be needed and I preferred to look after Nicky myself. I overheard an Englishwoman talking to another about a bolt of silk they were inspecting.

'It's a devilish red,' she said. 'It looks like sin. I'd never get away with it.'

Devilish red. My mind tripped over itself and my ears started ringing. The red devil. My period. My period hadn't come. I was three weeks late.

I stood in the store, frozen to the spot, unable to talk or think or run or scream. Trapped in the bright, searing moment of realisation. I was pregnant.

To Harry.

———

The darkness seized me and held me under for the next two weeks, as time slipped by and slipped by and I knew I had to tell James. I considered lying to him, suggesting that many a good Christian lass had found herself pregnant after 'fooling around' without real intercourse, and that in one of our failed attempts at lovemaking his arrow had hit the mark. I decided to tell the truth though – not because I didn't think he'd believe me, but because he deserved the truth. He was my husband. He was my son's father. He deserved my honesty.

And what happened next would happen. I didn't let myself imagine it because whatever it was, it would be painful and difficult and *all my fault*.

I rehearsed my revelation so many times. Imagined the perfect conditions. The tea and cakes I would serve. The soft hand upon his knee I would use to show him I was vulnerable. The exact words that would elicit his forgiveness.

But then he walked through the door unexpectedly at noon, having ridden ahead of his colleagues and arrived home a half-day early, and the sight of him made me burst into tears.

'Zara? Whatever is wrong?'

And I blurted it in one sick bubble of sobs. 'I'm pregnant and you are not the father.'

I would never forget the pale shock, turning to pale fury. The words he said to me – words I had not imagined a gentleman would know, let alone unleash on his wife. I would never forget sitting there waiting for a blow to land. It never came. He could swear at me, but it appeared he drew the line at striking me.

I wasn't grateful. If he had hit me, I could feel justified in some way – his sin in exchange for mine. But James won the moral high ground easily, and within seventy-two hours I was on my way home to Melbourne with Nicky.

CHAPTER 17

Down, down, down I went. My mother took one look at me as I climbed out of the taxi at the front of their house, and rushed down to take Nicky from me. 'Bed,' she said. 'You can tell me everything later.'

I did not tell her everything. How could I? To do so would mean admitting my shame. I confessed only that James and I had split, there was no hope for us to reconcile, and any further questions I greeted with a teary silence. Her instinct was to assume I had been wronged, and she railed against James, cursing him for abandoning me and making Nicky spend his first Christmas on a ship from India. I let her vent her spleen, carefully not mentioning that I was pregnant. Not yet.

The next few weeks were nightmarish and the New Year dawned ghastly. I knew from what James had said that he would pursue divorce on grounds of infidelity, which meant court and public humiliation. I had begged him to let us separate quietly for five years and then divorce just as quietly, but he was determined to punish me. He'd promised me a letter with all the details, and every day when I heard the postman's bell, my guts would clench until I'd sorted through the post and seen his letter wasn't there.

Harry was away with his father, but I knew the moment he got back he would be around. He had bought into Daddy's new food-packaging business while I was in India and was now forever linked to my family. I had no idea why he did it. I know he and Daddy were terribly fond of each other, but I wondered too if it was a way for him to keep a connection to me. Part of me longed to see him, but another part could foresee that this pregnancy would finish us forever. Harry was barely ready to be a husband; he'd never be ready to be a father. And he could hardly be seen to be hanging about with me, freshly separated, and risk his reputation being named in a divorce court. For the sake of him, for me, for Nicky and for my unborn child, I had to break cleanly from him. So I asked Vieve if I could move in with her, Jack and April.

At first it was such a relief to be away from Mum's questions and Daddy's brooding expression. Vieve gave me their sunny front room and we moved in a cot for Nicky, but he mostly slept curled up next to me in my bed. He was the only purely good thing in my world. But I had never been so tired. My first pregnancy hadn't been this bad as I didn't have a one-year-old and a looming divorce suit to trouble me.

Vieve was gentle with me, and April was a darling for helping entertain Nicky. I spent a lot of time in the first two weeks lying on the couch feeling sorry for myself, and Vieve said nothing. But one warm January morning, while Nicky was napping and I could hear April in the garden talking to her dolls, she sat down next to me, tapped my hip with a warm, flat palm and asked, 'Zara, you are terribly tired all the time. Is there any chance you're pregnant?'

I closed my eyes.

'Oh dear,' Vieve said.

'I haven't told anybody.'

'Did James know?'

I opened my eyes again, struggled into a sitting position and grasped her hands in mine. 'If I tell you something, will you promise you won't love me any less? You will judge me, and I don't mind being judged. But just . . . don't stop loving me.'

'What have you done?' she asked softly.

'This baby is not James's.'

'Harry?'

I nodded bleakly.

'Does Harry know?'

'No, and I shan't tell him. This is my mess to solve.'

She pushed her lips together as though she were trying to hold back from saying something.

'Do you hate me?' I asked.

'Zara, I love you so very much. This is a mess and, yes, it's a mess of your own making. But I promise that I don't think any less of you.' She squeezed my hands. 'You must feel awful.'

'I do. I'm tired, and heartbroken, and worried. James said he would take me to court for infidelity. Daddy will die of embarrassment. It will drag you all through the mud.'

'Well, it's lucky you know somebody with good legal knowledge who might be able to help,' she said.

'I won't ask Harry for help. Not for anything.'

She surprised me by laughing. 'Honestly, your stubbornness, Zara! Even in these circumstances. This was how you drove me crazy when we were young.'

I chuckled despite myself. 'We did rather drive each other crazy. What do you think?' I placed a hand over my belly. 'Nicky and this baby will be so close in age. Like you and me. They will be good company for each other, won't they?'

'Life without a sibling is too sad,' she said. 'Poor April. A lonely only, and not for want of trying.'

'She won't be lonely if I don't find somewhere else to live,' I joked grimly. 'Ah, the future continues to come rushing in on me, Vieve, and I can't stop it. I feel it will crush me.'

'One thing at a time,' she said. 'Let's go and see Doctor Miles. I'll get Mum to come over and watch the children – we'll say you're feeling weak and tired. If you like, when we come back you can reveal your news then as though you just found out. And we don't need to mention Harry.'

I had been so used to living in a swamp of indecision and uncertainty that Vieve knowing about the baby and her simple next steps appealed to me greatly. Here was a way forward, at least a little distance.

The day after Doctor Miles had declared me healthy and most definitely pregnant, the letter from James finally arrived. In fact, it was from James's solicitor, a Mr Whitelock with rooms here in Melbourne, as this was where we were married. The *Matrimonial Causes Act* meant that he could not divorce me until we'd been married three years, and we were a few months short of that date. James's intention was now to wait until our third anniversary, then the solicitor would begin compiling evidence and court could be as long as a year away. On the one hand, this was a relief. A stay of execution. On the other, it meant a legal case hanging over me for another year and landing when I would be a single mother of two little children. The letter also informed me that, because of Nicky, I was entitled to a small pension from the army. The first cheque was enclosed, and I tried to give it directly to Genevieve and Jack, but Jack refused it.

'You're our family,' he said. 'You'd do the same for us if our situations were reversed.'

The tiredness never really left me, and I spent the summer on the couch or sitting on the porch in the shade while Nicky played at my feet. I saw Harry three times, but he didn't see me. Twice, it was his picture in the local paper, smiling at a school fete and looking serious at a memorial service. Once, it was at Toorak Village. I was passing in a tram and he was walking, head down, talking to a tall, well-dressed man. His hat obscured almost his entire face, but I would have recognised him anywhere – his gait, the way he held his shoulders. I ached for his comfort fiercely. If I hadn't been in a tram I might have run after him, calling his name . . . The reunion played out in my imagination the entire tram ride home.

Mum wanted to make a fuss for Nicky's first birthday and have a party, which I felt was ridiculous as he'd never remember it. As she had missed his first Christmas, I yielded, but it did mean I had to have a serious conversation with her about how Harry absolutely could not be invited.

'But he's part of the family,' she said. 'Are you sure? You haven't even spoken to him since you got back.'

She was helping me fold laundry in Genevieve's sunny kitchen. I had never seen anyone who could fold as neatly as my mother. Every towel and pillowslip was reduced to a flat, smooth package, then lined up on the kitchen table like soldiers. I was quite ashamed of my slapdash piles of little singlets and playsuits. I couldn't see the point of smoothing them, as Nicky crushed or dirtied them the second he put them on.

'He's a member of parliament and I'm a recently separated woman,' I said. 'It wouldn't be good for either of us.'

Mum huffed. 'I can see you're right, but I'm not happy about it. He's been your friend for years.'

'You know he's been more than my friend, Mum. And there are plenty of newspaper pictures over those years of us together as a couple.'

'Still. It must be hard.'

Hard didn't begin to describe it. I was mourning the loss of James from my life. Being angry with him for punishing me helped a little, but sometimes Nicky would smile and I'd see his father in his face and a sort of blunt pang would make its way into my chest and lodge there for hours. I also longed for the comfort of Harry. I wanted to cry on his shoulder and have him hold me and tell me I was his girl, and have everything go back to how it used to be when we were younger. But now responsibility and obligation and reputation weighed us down. I mourned the loss of Harry too, or at least the idea of Harry and me being young and unencumbered.

Mum kept folding in silence. I lifted up a playsuit I'd made for Nicky, picking at a loose stitch. There seemed little need for me to do my best sewing on clothes that he outgrew in a couple of months. I was drifting into a daydream about a daughter, about tiny rose-pink dresses and bloomers, when Mum said, 'Zara, is there any chance that . . .'

She stopped. A dark feeling crossed my heart. I held my breath.

'Is there any chance that James had good reason to want a divorce?'

I swallowed hard, not meeting her eye. 'Do you want to know?'

She placed a pillowslip on the table and smoothed it with her pale knotted hands. 'Perhaps I don't,' she said. 'But would you come to Daddy and me for help if you needed it?'

'Of course.'

She finished folding the pillowcase then said brightly, 'Right then. I'm off. Give my love to Nicky when he wakes up, and make sure to pass on a kiss to Vieve and April.'

'I will.' I saw her out the front door just as Nicky started calling, 'Ma-ma-ma-ma,' from his cot.

———

By March, I was huge. Much larger than I had been at the same time with Nicky. My ankles swelled, my whole undercarriage felt unstable and I experienced pains in my back and my pelvis. I began to develop an unfounded fear that there was something wrong with the baby. I suppose I was still expecting to be punished by God, even though I hadn't really believed in him for a long time. I took myself off to Doctor Miles, and lay on the soft white mattress in his surgery as he applied his stethoscope to my impressive girth.

All was silent while he listened, moving his stethoscope from one place on my belly to the next. It was so quiet I could hear the soft tick of his watch. On the wall in front of me was a tuberculosis poster with a picture of a child wearing a bib that read, *Don't kiss me.*

The copy beneath listed statistics about childhood deaths. It felt like some sort of omen as the doctor continued searching for a heartbeat. I closed my eyes. I knew what he was going to say and I braced myself for the worst.

When he straightened and pulled down my blouse to cover my belly, I still didn't open my eyes. 'Is my baby all right?' I managed in a desperate whisper.

'Yes,' he said. '*Both* of them are perfectly fine.'

Doctor Miles – on account of the babies' size, my tiny frame and my ongoing pains – ordered bed rest for the remainder of my pregnancy. He was concerned they would come too early to survive otherwise. So I had plenty of time to contemplate my situation. The notion that I was soon to be a mother of three children, all under the age of two, while living in my sister's guest bedroom, would have been funny if it didn't frighten me so much.

Vieve proved her credentials as the best sister in the world by looking after Nicky and me as well as her own daughter and long-suffering husband. Mum came to help most days, and neither of them would so much as let me stand up except to go to the toilet. I had a little bell, which I had to ring if I needed anything. On the first day I was so determined not to ring the bell too much that Vieve came and told me off. 'If I can't trust you to ring it, I will be in here every half hour asking if you need anything, and that is more inconvenient.' So I embraced the bed rest and spent the days dozing, reading, drawing and being quite bored.

Friends came to visit, and Vieve would set me up on the couch with my feet up and a quilt to cover my tree-trunk ankles. Of course everybody assumed the twins were James's and shook their heads and tsk-ed about the divorce at a time like this. I didn't correct them, but I did temper their blame by saying the divorce was mutually agreed, that the marriage hadn't worked out and that I was happy to be back in Melbourne. Word got back to Harry that I was pregnant and ordered to rest for my health, and he rang Genevieve and Jack several times asking for me.

'Are you sure you don't want him to visit?' Vieve asked after one such phone call while I was propped on the couch waiting for Betty to visit with her new baby. 'With me here as chaperone it would hardly be scandalous. He is a friend of the family, after all.'

I shook my head. 'My life is already complex enough.'

'Perhaps he could make it easier.'

'The words *Harry* and *easy* have never belonged in the same sentence for me, Vieve. You know that.'

A little frown formed between her eyebrows, but she held back whatever thought she was thinking. The doorbell went then and Vieve rose to answer it. I smoothed the quilt over my legs, hearing Betty's voice in the entranceway and the soft hiccough of a small baby fussing.

Next minute, Betty bustled in, wearing an immaculate silk afternoon dress in pale coral with butterfly sleeves and a bow around the waist. I believed I could have circled that waist with my two hands. How Betty had become so thin only a few months after giving birth was astonishing and something I knew would never happen to me. After these two babies, the chances of me having a tiny waist again were practically nothing. Then I noticed how etched her face had become, and realised: Betty was deeply unhappy.

Still, she smiled and sat down and presented little Robin for my inspection. 'Another boy.' She grimaced. 'I hope those two inside you are girls so we can make some adorable frocks for them.'

'I don't know,' I joked. 'I made Nicky a few playsuits with butterflies and flowers on them. James told me more than once I'd make the boy soft.'

Betty rolled her eyes. 'James. The one who abandoned you with a belly full of babies?'

My eyes flicked to Vieve, who was pouring us tea. She shook her head almost imperceptibly, a warning to keep the secret. But this was Betty, my oldest and dearest friend.

'What is it?' Betty asked, as ever sharply aware of the unspoken currents in any interaction.

'The babies aren't James's,' I confessed.

Betty's eyes widened. A moment passed, then she held up one elegant white hand. 'Say no more, for the whole story is apparent to me now.' She rose and came to perch on the edge of the couch next to me, bent down and hugged me. I had a sensation of her perfume, her bird-like bones, and then she had returned to her chair. 'Isn't life complex?' she said with a brittle smile.

Genevieve, amused by the understatement, started laughing, and in a minute we were all chuckling away, three women sitting around a tea tray looking like perfect ladies of good society but dealing with messy, messy lives.

Little Robin was, as Betty said, 'a good baby' and slept through our entire afternoon tea. At one point Nicky started fussing and my instinct was to get up and walk him around, but of course I couldn't. Vieve rose and took him in her arms, grabbed April's hand and said she'd take them out to the garden for ten minutes to see if the fresh air would settle him.

The moment she left, Betty came back to the edge of the couch and grasped my hand urgently.

'What is it?' I asked, expecting perhaps a tongue-lashing about getting myself into so much trouble.

'I'm leaving,' she said.

'Oh. Did we say something to offend you?'

'No, no. Not leaving Genevieve's house. I'm leaving Melbourne. I'm running away.' She smiled, but it resembled a baring of teeth. 'I haven't told anyone but you.'

'Where are you going to go?'

'London. To meet up with Roy. He's leaving his wife and I'm leaving Tom and we're going to be together because life is so short, Zara, and I am so so unhappy.'

'What are you going to do with the baby?'

'I'll leave him here for now. We have a wonderful nanny whom both he and Hamish adore. And as soon as I'm settled I'll come back for them. But if I wait until they're old enough, I'll never go.' She put her hands over her eyes. 'The anxiety I feel is monstrous. Like blackbirds in my skull.'

I struggled to sit up a little so I could take her hands in mine, look into her eyes. 'I love you, Betty. You must do what is right for you.'

'It's going to be a terrible scandal.'

'Think of all the women who avoided scandals and let their hearts shrink and their souls be crushed,' I replied. 'It won't be easy, Betty, but I will always be your friend. No matter what.'

Vieve returned, Nicky fully in tears now with two scraped knees. He had only just started walking, and seemed to fall more than he toddled. 'I'm sorry!' Vieve said, handing him to me for comfort while Betty leaped out of the way. 'You give him a cuddle and I'll get the mercurochrome and a couple of plasters.'

She bustled off and I cuddled Nicky while he sobbed loudly, though my eyes were still fixed on Betty's.

'And you?' Betty said finally. 'Is your heart shrinking? Is your soul being crushed?'

I shook my head. 'I don't know what I'm going to do,' I confessed. 'I'm frightened all the time.'

'There is someone who can fix that.'

'Or make it worse.'

'You won't know until you talk to him.'

I distracted myself tending to Nicky, telling myself not to take advice from a woman about to run away from her husband and family. But I couldn't bring myself to think she was in the wrong on any count.

I rang the bell.

I had been contemplating for two days, curled on my side between chapters of the book I was reading. Three people now knew that Harry was about to be a father: me, Vieve and now Betty. Was it not unfair that Harry himself didn't know?

So I rang the bell and I asked Vieve to invite Harry over. Her eyes rounded, but she didn't say a word. Merely nodded, and went off to ring him.

While my brain called upon me to regret my decision, my heart felt light as though sunshine had just been let into a dark room. After months of nightmarish guilt and shame, I was going to see him. My Harry. My imagination took me down so many paths that afternoon. Tearful reunions, terrible declarations of denial and every shade in between. When Vieve said he had moved something in his diary so he could pop by tomorrow for morning tea, I wondered how I would sleep that night. It turns out I slept very well. Growing two babies was a recipe for constant tiredness.

The next morning Genevieve helped me into my prettiest polka-dot house dress, and I dug out my mascara and lipstick for the first time since I had been on bed rest. Vieve combed my hair for me and organised my curls with a couple of well-placed faux-pearl pins. I was quite pleased with how I looked in the mirror; pregnancy made my skin glow and my cheeks pink. As long as I kept the quilt over the lower half of my body, I was sure Harry would be happy with what he saw, if not with what he heard.

He arrived on the dot of eleven. The sound of the doorbell made my heart jolt. Vieve patted my knee and mouthed 'bon courage' before heading to the door to let him in.

Moments later he stood in front of me, dressed in a dark suit, holding out a bouquet of pale pink camellias. 'Zara,' he said simply, his eyes crinkled in a smile.

My heart flipped over. I took the flowers. 'Thank you,' I said. 'It's good to see you.'

He leaned over and kissed my cheek; I felt his warm breath on my skin. Then Vieve interrupted and he stepped away.

'There are rules, Harry,' she said. 'Zara absolutely must not get up, so don't take her anywhere, even to the garden. You are not to upset or excite her, and you are not to stay above an hour as she must be kept very quiet.'

I suppressed a laugh. Vieve had never given anyone this lecture before. She was clearly worried that I would become so exercised by Harry's presence that I would go into early labour.

Harry mimed a salute. 'Absolutely, captain. You have my word that I will be as bland as a boiled egg without salt.'

I saw the corner of a smile touch Vieve's lips. She took the bouquet from me. 'I'll put these in water and make us some tea. It should take me about ten minutes.' She looked at me pointedly. 'Then I'll be back, and Nicky will be up and we can all sit down to morning tea together.'

We had ten minutes. I took a deep breath. Harry sat down on the edge of the coffee table, which was closer than the wing-backed chairs across from me. He smiled down at me. 'You look too pretty to be considered unwell.'

'I'm not unwell, really. The doctor is worried about the babies coming early, so I live a very quiet life.'

He nodded and his face grew serious. 'I was very sorry to hear about your separation from Colonel Fell. I wouldn't wish unhappiness upon you, even in the smallest measure.'

'Thank you, Harry. It means a lot.'

'How is the little fellow coping without his papa?'

'He's too young to understand, I think. Certainly too young to express anything in words. He's had some unsettled days but –' I had ten minutes. I couldn't waste it in small talk. 'Harry, there's something I need to tell you.'

'Ah,' he said, and I don't know what he expected, but he clearly expected something. I wondered if Vieve had hinted, or if he had just guessed that somehow he had been implicated in my marriage breakdown.

'It's difficult,' I said, realising tears were about to brim over. 'I'm so frightened.'

He leaned forward, grasped my hands and bent his head all the way down so it rested on them. 'I still love you, Zara,' he said. 'I will always love you. Whatever you have to say, I will continue to love you, whether that be from afar or from up close. Just please say it and put me out of my misery.'

For the first time I realised Harry was also experiencing his own hopes and fears about the two of us. It emboldened me to say what I needed to say through sobs. 'These babies are yours,' I managed.

His head snapped up. Genuine shock on his face. 'What? Are you sure?'

'I'm sure. There was no way they could be James's. He couldn't . . . we didn't . . .' I wiped my face on my shoulder, sniffing back tears.

He squeezed my hands and I could see he was trying not to smile. 'It's all right, it's all right,' he said. 'Zara, is this real? It feels like a dream.'

'You're happy about this?'

'The timing is terrible, I'll grant you that,' he said with a chuckle. 'Oh, my darling girl, you don't need to be afraid. I will take care of you, and the babies, and Nicky too.'

'But aren't you worried? People will talk. James is determined to take me to court and –'

'Sh, sh. They will only talk if there is something to talk about. This is nothing we can't solve without some patience and a decent plan. Explain to me what James is up to.'

I quickly told him what James's letter had said and that I expected to go to court within a year.

'Does he know who I am?' Harry asked.

'He knows who you are, yes, but I never told him you were the father. I wanted to keep you out of a court case.' It had driven James mad that I wouldn't disclose his name. He hadn't stopped asking me, even on the awful final morning when he was kissing his son goodbye.

'If a man is very determined to find such a thing out, he'll hire a private detective,' Harry said. 'We're not safe as long as he's single-minded about taking you to court. I will have a colleague draft a letter for us. Give him a few options.'

'Like what?'

'Don't worry. Just give me the solicitor's correspondence before I go and I'll take care of it all. And as for us, well, if James lets you go without a court case, that's a five-year wait, and you're right that I put my political career in jeopardy if we are seen to be a couple. But nobody pays all that much attention to me, Zara, and if we are discreet and have a few people on board to help keep our secret, there's nothing stopping me being some kind of a father figure to these children, even if I don't live under the same roof.'

It was like waking up from a nightmare, all the shadows and monsters shredding apart and exposed for what they really were – the phantoms of my own imagination. Harry heard my problems and found their edges, pinned them down and systematically thought his way through them. Waves of relief washed through me and I started to cry.

'Oh dear,' he said, fishing his handkerchief out of his pocket to hand to me. 'I'd hoped to stop you crying, not to make you cry harder.'

I took the handkerchief. My face was absolutely streaming and I imagined that the mascara I had so carefully brushed on was surely now smeared everywhere. 'I was trying to look so pretty for you,' I joked, dabbing under my eyes. 'I must look a fright.'

'Zara, you always look beautiful to me, and at no time more than now, pregnant with my children and showing me your heart.' He bent and kissed my enormous belly, then straightened and said, 'Do you mind if I don't stay for tea? I need that letter, and I need to start figuring this out. I'm afraid my brain will continue to revolve around that until I have, which won't make me good company for a pair of ladies.'

'Just stay one more minute and say hello to Nicky,' I said, indicating the bell on the coffee table. 'Ring that and Vieve will come back.'

He rang the bell, and a moment later Vieve was there. She took in the scene, with me snivelling and Harry sitting with me. 'Are you all right?' she asked me.

I nodded. 'Vieve, would you be a darling and fetch Nicky to meet Harry? And there's a letter from a solicitor named Mr Whitelock on the table beside my bed. Would you bring that here for Harry?'

She looked at Harry and nodded at him with a smile. 'Yes, I will.'

Soon, a sleepy-faced Nicky emerged in Vieve's arms. At first he shrank away from Harry despite Harry reminding him they had met before, when he was a tiny baby. But then he indicated with a clutching hand that he wanted to go 'down', and when he did he toddled up to Harry and put his hand on his knee.

Harry made a face and Nicky smiled a gummy smile. Then Nicky turned his attention to me and put his thumb in his mouth and curled his fingers in my hair.

'What a fine young man you've become, Nicky,' Harry said, standing up. 'But I'm going to leave you with your mother and aunt as I have important business to take care of.'

Vieve handed him the letter, which he tucked into his pocket. 'I'll call again soon,' he said to me. 'In the meantime, you're not to worry. I'm going to take care of everything.'

CHAPTER 18

Sam and Andrew were born on a freezing rainy day but I remember none of it. The doctor gave me the twilight sleep medicine and it was as though I wasn't there. I woke up and the nurses tried to hand me the twins, but I didn't recognise them and was confused about where I was. I woke up again some time later, looking for my babies.

'You have two healthy boys,' the nurse said, and wheeled them over for me to look at.

How strange. They had been inside my body and somehow now they were out of my body, without me having any recollection of the effort. I was sore in both expected and unexpected places – my wrists and ankles were red and tender where I had been strapped down – but it didn't feel as though I had given birth twice. When she handed me the babies, one then the other, I didn't know how to hold them. Surely I needed four arms for this. The nurses said I would never be able to keep up with breastfeeding two hungry boys, so my breasts were bound and my sons were brought to me to feed with a bottle on a strict schedule. I didn't name them straight away because they were identical and I wanted to be able to tell them apart first. But slowly I began to see the nuance in their little scrunched-up faces. Andy's head was slightly narrower; Sam's chest was slightly wider.

My first visitors were Vieve and Nicky, but I don't really remember them arriving. They returned the next day with Mum when I was more alert. She was instantly in love, and Nicky found this impossible to bear and threw an enormous tantrum. I had no idea how I was to handle him crying as well as the twins.

I was one week in the hospital and then they sent me home, swimming in babies.

The boys were two weeks old when Harry came to see them. We had spoken on the telephone but were being careful about who saw us where. Vieve let him in and took Nicky for a walk, and Harry and I lay down on my bed together with the babies between us.

He stroked Andy's soft head, a look of wonder on his face. 'They are so . . .'

'Beautiful?' I suggested.

'It doesn't seem to mean enough,' he said.

'I know.'

He scooped Sam against his chest, where the baby sighed and closed his eyes to sleep. Harry reached for my hand. 'How are you?'

'Tired,' I said. 'Sore, still. I have stitches . . .' I pointed to my nethers. 'But having the weight off my joints is very freeing.'

'You look wonderful,' he said.

I laughed. 'Well, that isn't true. What, between the eyebags, my inability to wash my hair and a stomach that still looks six months pregnant. I'm hardly a movie star.'

'A movie star didn't just give me two perfect sons whom I love madly,' he said.

I smiled up at him, and then he said, 'I have news. Do you want it now or later?'

'Is it good news or bad news?' I asked, a little fearful.

'I'm not sure how to characterise it, but I've known it for nearly a week and have been holding off in case you weren't up to dealing with it.'

I braced myself. 'Go on, then.'

'My colleague has heard back from Whitelock, your husband's solicitor.'

Everything tensed. 'And?'

'He has decided not to take you to court.'

I exhaled. 'Harry, how did you not know that was good news?'

'Because I know the separation is hard on you, that you loved him. No, you don't need to avert your eyes. I could tell you loved him. Also because this means you have to wait five years to be divorced. These boys will be at school by then, before we can be . . . a proper family.'

I gazed down at the twins. 'I wasn't going to get away with what I did without some kind of punishment.'

'You did nothing wrong,' Harry said.

'We both know that's not true.'

'Then I'm sorry for not stopping you that night.'

I met his eyes. 'I wasn't able to be stopped.'

He smiled, kissed his palm and pressed it against my cheek.

'And besides,' I added, stroking Andy's head. 'Look what we got from it.'

We lay there for ages in companionable silence, until the twins started crying. I left them with him and went to the kitchen for bottles, and we fed them and changed them and cuddled them back to sleep. The afternoon passed in bliss.

'I'll come again tomorrow,' he said, and so he did most afternoons for two hours, which were always the happiest two hours of my day. Nicky got used to him and sometimes joined us, fidgeting and rolling about and being told off about not crushing the babies. To which he answered with his most frequent phrase after 'Mama, up!', which was 'I a baby'.

It's true that Nicky was still a baby, but next to the tiny twins he looked gigantic. Harry was far more patient with him than I could be, but then he was only there for two hours and there were twenty-four in a day. I experienced every single one of them tending to babies.

Around the fourth week, Sam and Andy started to cry constantly, sometimes one a time and sometimes in unison, and they wouldn't be consoled for anything. I walked them up and down the hallway in turns, rocking them and humming, and utterly losing my mind.

Vieve helped where she could, and Harry took them when he came, but that blissful peace was shattered beyond repair. Guiltily, I started to understand I couldn't continue to impose on Genevieve and Jack. Nobody was getting any sleep, least of all me. If I wasn't up with crying babies, or with Nicky having a nightmare, I was lying in bed wondering where I would live and how I would support myself and my three little boys for the next five years.

I worked out that with my pension I could rent somewhere small a long way out of town, but on a train or tram line so I could get to my family readily enough. I left the babies with Vieve one Monday afternoon and headed off to inspect a one-bedroom flat under an elderly man's house in Box Hill. It was close to the train station, which was convenient, but was marred by the sound of the goods trains rattling in and out of it, not to mention the choking diesel smell and coal steam. I imagined me and the little ones all crowded in there, panes rattling and unable to open the windows on a warm day, and I cried all the way back to Vieve's for dinner. She told me they were happy for me to stay with them as long as I needed, but I saw a flicker of an expression on Jack's face that told me quite the opposite story.

The next day I phoned the elderly gentleman and told him we would move in the following week.

In the cracks of the day, while the boys slept or Nicky was busy playing with the tin cars Jack had bought him, I folded my dresses between tissue paper and laid them in a suitcase, wondering if I would ever fit into any of them again. It seemed unlikely. Apart from clothes, I had pathetically little to pack up. I tried not to think about all of the money I had burned through on my long trip around the world. I tried not to think about the luxury of servants and beautiful furnishings back in India, and the valuable knick-knacks I had left behind.

One afternoon, four days before my brothers were due to borrow a friend's milk truck to help me move, I heard the telephone ring deep in the house. I lay on the bed, exhausted, next to a sleeping Nicky, who had passed out with florid cheeks after fighting me about napping for forty-five minutes. I estimated I had around half an hour before Sam and Andy woke, and was trying very hard not to fall asleep myself. The shock of waking after only a few minutes was somehow worse than remaining tired. I fought bravely, but the tide of sleep rubbed my thoughts together and I was half in a dream when Vieve knocked gently at my door and peeked her head around. 'Telephone call, darling. It's Betty Ramsay.'

Vieve was not smiling. Betty fleeing her husband and small children had been a terrible scandal in our circles, though I had been protected from hearing most of it due to the fact I hadn't attended a party or dinner in months. According to Vieve and Mum, people gossiped about child abandonment, adultery, even theft, as Betty had withdrawn a chunk of money to pay for her passage and live on while she and Roy established themselves. But I had turned my back on Betty once and I wouldn't do it again.

I rose and made my way swiftly to the lounge room, where April played quietly on the floor with a little wooden dollhouse. I picked up the phone and ducked around the corner into the kitchen, stretching the phone cord almost straight. 'Hello?'

'I just got your letter! Congratulations! Two more little boys!' Her voice was thin and hollow, coming as it was from thousands of miles away.

'Gosh, that took its time. They're six weeks old.'

'Roy and I were up in Scotland.' At least I think that's what she said. The line crackled and cut in the middle of her sentence, but came back strong. 'You must be tired, my love.'

'I am. And how are you?'

'I have another one on the way,' she said. 'Roy's baby. A girl this time, I just know it. I've been *so* sick, and with the boys I had no sickness at all.' Then she sighed. The line cracked again.

'Are you still there?' I asked.

Her next sentence was unintelligible for all the cracks and gaps on the line.

'Say it again, Betty? I'm having trouble hearing you.'

'Tom won't let me have my boys.'

'What do you mean?'

'He says he hasn't time to bring them, and we haven't the money to come and get them. I asked if his mother could bring them but she has refused. They all hate me so much. They . . .' Again, the line cut out but her meaning was clear enough. Then her voice came back again. 'I imagined them living with us, Zara, but Tom won't have it. He says they're better off cared for with him and his vile mother. I can't bear for them to grow up thinking I didn't love them. I miss them so much.'

I tried to imagine myself separated from Nicky if James had insisted he stay in India. The thought made me wince. 'Oh, Betty, that sounds terrible.'

'I had hoped you might ask Harry . . .' The line crackled over the rest of her sentence.

'Ask Harry what?'

'If he can help. We've hardly any money and another baby on the way. We can't afford a lawyer and . . .'

'I will ask,' I said, not sure if she could hear me through the noisy line. 'The very next time I see him, I will ask.'

The operator's voice came on the line then, crisp and officious. 'Would you like to extend your call a further three minutes?'

'I'll have to go,' Betty said. 'Write me a letter. Tell me about your little ones. I've been cut off by everyone.'

'I will,' I said over the pips that told us the call was about to end. Then the line went silent.

I replaced the phone in the cradle and saw April sitting still, looking at me. 'Who were you talking to?'

'My friend. She's all the way over in England.'

'Are you worried about her?'

'Yes, I am. She doesn't have many friends right now.'

April returned to her dollhouse. 'Tell her I'll be her friend.'

I bent to kiss her. 'You are the very best niece in the world. I will definitely tell her that.'

Vieve brought Nicky in. He was grumpy-faced and sucking hard on this thumb. 'Sorry,' she said. 'He was wandering about your room and about to wake the twins.'

'Do you want some juice, Nicky?' I asked, leading him into the kitchen. I had squeezed oranges this morning, and he happily sat and drank his juice while I stroked his hair and gave thanks over and over that I had been able to bring him to Melbourne with me.

'How is Betty?' Vieve asked in a tight tone.

'Whatever people are saying about her, she's miserable and missing her children. Tom won't let her see them.'

'She might have foreseen that when she ran off and left them with the nanny,' Vieve replied.

'Was what I did any better?'

Vieve softened. 'Well, you made sure your children had a mother. And you were honest with James. Everyone says Betty left Tom a note. He had no idea what was coming. Apparently he was distraught.'

I remembered James the day he'd come home from the Punjab, finding out that I was pregnant to somebody else. The pain in his eyes had been too much to bear, was still too much to bear when I thought about it now.

'Ah, now I see I've hurt your feelings. I'm sorry, sister.' Vieve gave me a hug. 'I will try not to judge her. And I have something to cheer you up. Mum and Daddy are coming over to take you and Nicky for a surprise.'

'A surprise? What is it?'

'That's not how surprises work, Zara. They'll be here at three. Go and put on a nice dress and some lipstick.'

I was curious, but feared my parents intended to take us to a fete or some such thing, where I'd have to drag my tired body around while wrangling Nicky. Still, I did as she asked, and unpleasantly noted that I had to fasten the belt on my favourite blue day dress at the furthest hole. I chose a sensible pair of flat shoes for chasing Nicky, combed and pinned my hair and dabbed on some bright pink lipstick.

Shortly after three, Mum and Daddy arrived. The twins had just been fed and were lying on a blanket on the lounge room floor while April showed them her dolls.

'Thank you for looking after them,' I said to Vieve.

She waved me away, a merry glint in her eye. 'It's my pleasure, but also, this surprise will be good for both of us. Trust me.'

'Now I am very intrigued,' I said.

'In the car then, my love,' Daddy said.

Nicky was already in Mum's arms. He adored his grandma and was twirling her hair with one hand, the other thumb in his mouth, as though he had never been anything but a sweet, amenable boy.

We hopped into Daddy's old blue car and headed off back towards my parents' house. But a block before the turn-off, Daddy veered right instead of left, and then brought the car to a stop outside a neat white weatherboard cottage with latticework along a front colonnade and a red iron roof.

'Who lives here?' I asked.

'You do,' Daddy said.

'What?'

The door of the house opened, and I could see Harry standing there just inside the threshold, beckoning me.

I opened the car door with a shaking hand and walked up the front path with Mum, Daddy and Nicky behind me.

'Come on in,' Harry said. 'Come see your new home.'

'What is this?' I asked, heart beating so hard I could feel it in my throat. I stood in a hallway with timber floors and pressed-metal ceilings.

Harry grabbed my hand and dragged me past two bedrooms and into a tiny lounge with big windows looking into an overgrown back garden. 'Vieve told me you wanted to move out on your own. It's only right that the father of your children should provide for you.'

'You're renting this for me?'

'Actually, I bought it. Much less messy than me paying your rent and the papers finding out. It's an investment. You are my tenant.'

My pride told me to say no, but I thought of the one-bedroom flat on the train line and I started to cry with relief. 'Oh, thank you. Thank you.'

Mum and Daddy were there then. 'So she'll accept your generosity?' Mum asked.

'Yes, it looks like it.' Harry laughed. 'I brought your parents in on it so they could talk you out of any proud nonsense.'

'The boys have to be looked after,' Daddy said. 'Their father isn't likely to help out, so you're lucky to have a friend like Harry.'

I hid a smile. Did Daddy really think we were just friends? If we could fool him, we could fool the rest of the world surely.

'Don't worry, Daddy,' I said, scooping Nicky up into my arms. 'Pride won't get in the way here. Harry, I gratefully accept your offer.'

———

That evening, Harry and I sat alone on the bare floor of my new home – the boys were asleep at Vieve's place – a bottle of wine between us.

'I'll need furniture,' I told him. 'I can't pay you any rent until I've bought some.'

'You won't be paying me any rent,' he said. 'And I'll help with the furniture.'

I was too tired and stupidly grateful to argue. 'Thank you,' I said.

'They're my boys,' he replied.

'Nicky isn't.'

'He can be my boy too. I wouldn't treat him differently from Sam and Andy. That would be too unfair.'

I reached out and stroked his hand. 'You are a good person.'

'I love you. And them.'

I shifted so I could see him in the dark. 'Betty needs your help, Harry. Tom won't let her little ones go to her.'

He was already shaking his head. 'I'm not involving myself in the Ramsay scandal.'

'But her children will grow up not knowing her.'

'She must have known that her choice was dangerous and she made it anyway.' He said this gently, but I wore it roughly.

'You helped me,' I said. 'I'm no better than her.'

He relented. 'I can't help her. Not with my reputation on the line. But I can give you the name of somebody who might.'

'She has no money.'

'Then she'd better find some if she wants her children back. The young fellow she ran off with can't be completely without means, or he won't be forever.'

'I suppose not.'

He pulled me against him. 'I'll give you the name of somebody good and kind who will give her advice for free as a favour to me. How about that?'

'Thank you.' I smiled up at him in the dark. 'For everything.'

He kissed my forehead and we both turned to the windows, the shadows of the trees flickering in the wind.

———

We played house as fervently as children did, though Harry did not live with us. He remained in the house he had undertaken to look after for his Spanish friend, who had no imminent plans for return. It was walking distance from where I lived with the children, so he was over every day, unless he was away in Canberra for parliament. Nobody knew that we were a couple, or that Sam and Andrew were his. If he stayed over, he left before dawn so as not to be spotted. I didn't go to parties and dinners with him, and I had to endure the sting of him being called parliament's most eligible bachelor and the ladies pages speculating on which gorgeous young socialite might be his future bride.

When he was with us though, all was contentment. Raising three small boys consumed me and I didn't feel I was missing much at all. Christmas and New Year flew past as I dealt with nappies and bottles and teaching Nicky to kick a ball in the garden. Summer was over in a blink. First Sam and then Andrew started crawling and that's when I finally got my figure back, running from one end of the hallway to the other continually, stopping them from pulling furniture down on their soft heads. When they began to walk, I had to hire a nanny an afternoon a week just to give myself a break.

But as exhausted as I was, my days were filled with love. Love as pure and soft as the white butter I'd eaten in India. For once, Harry and I never fought. I was blissfully unaware of any flirtations at parties that might arouse my fiery jealousy, and we simply weren't together enough for that ordinary contempt of couples to grow. We were always genuinely delighted to see each other, had always missed each other, always desired each other. I began to wonder if this wasn't the secret to a good long-term relationship: living in different houses.

———

It was around this time that my dear, disgraced friend Betty wrote to me from London, where she lived with her handsome, rakish lover Roy. The letter included a photograph of a baby – her much longed-for daughter, named Katy. I set aside time every evening after the boys had gone to bed and ran up a pink smocked baby dress. Sitting by the fireplace, I embroidered the bodice and collar with tiny red wattle flowers to remind her of home. I sent it off with a letter telling her to come home soon, that I missed her, that I wanted to kiss that little girl's toes and fingers. But something huge was about to keep Betty and me apart for a long time.

———

As the twins grew and began to sleep better, I started to pay a little more attention to the world around me, and soon realised that all was not as sweet in the wider world as it was in my cosy bubble. The front page of *The Argus* mentioned Mr Hitler's ructions in Europe nearly every day, and our Prime Minister Mr Menzies (who had become a great friend of Harry's) grew warier and warier of events taking place closer by in the Pacific. By August, all anyone could talk about was war. It upset me so much that I wouldn't look at the newspapers if I went to the shops. I wanted my bubble to stay impermeable and for my boys never to know hard times.

Harry was recalled to Canberra urgently on the last day of August. He kissed me goodbye early that morning and told me not to worry about anything.

Less than forty-eight hours later, late on Saturday evening, the phone rang. I had just got all the boys to sleep so I ran to answer it so the ringing wouldn't rouse them again. I was breathless when I said, 'Hello?'

Harry was breathless too. 'Hitler has invaded Poland,' he said. 'The British are going to declare war, and the PM is going in with him. It will be all across the news tomorrow. I wanted you to hear it from me.'

My bubble burst. 'What do you mean?' I asked, clutching the collar of my blouse.

'Zara,' Harry said, 'Australia is at war.'

CHAPTER 19

Every newspaper, every radio broadcast, every conversation between neighbours at the shops was about the war. It was inescapable, but at the same time everything seemed strangely normal and calm. We didn't wake up to bombs and gunfire, and Europe seemed a very long way away. Daddy became obsessed with listening to the evening broadcast, shushing the boys impatiently if we were over there for dinner. Mum said he was very consumed with war news, as were many others. I began to suffer an ongoing sense of unease that never left me, as though I had forgotten something important. It made me jumpy and distracted. As consumed as I was with the boys, some days I forgot for hours at a time that we were at war. Then I would remember with a jolt and think, *can this be real?*

So I reasoned with myself that to be both a good mother and a sane woman, I had to stop thinking about the war. Just stop. And if that meant I was a bad person, then I was a bad person. I had little children, so many of them, and I didn't want to waste these precious early years consumed with worry. By the time the twins had their first birthday, and Australia still hadn't sent any troops anywhere, I had settled into my new way of thinking. When Daddy shushed us all to listen to war news on the wireless, I would simply pack up the children and take them home. I didn't follow any news, and if somebody wanted to talk to me about Churchill or Hitler I would change the subject. I had enough little boys on hand to distract me from any conversation so it wasn't difficult. Harry was happy not to talk about matters of the world, as his working life was never matters of the hearth and home. In my mind's eye, I put a heart-shaped bubble around us all, and it stayed there for years. I was privileged enough to experience the war quite differently from most, I suppose, but I had no regrets.

The only time my bubble threatened to pop was when Harry started making noises about enlisting. When he mentioned it to me, gently and calmly, I responded with equal calm, saying it would be a shame to lose his seat in parliament and reminding him how much good he could do in the country while *in* the country, rather than out on some foreign field. He went off to Canberra to talk to Mr Menzies about it, and I wondered if I should put aside a lifetime of agnosticism and pray for him not to go. God, however, if He was real, would be unlikely to grant favours to an apostate.

That evening, after the boys were asleep, I opened the back door to the garden and sat on the stoop under the stars. My feet were bare and cold on the chilly grass, but I took a deep sigh and thought about the stories Mum used to tell Vieve and me about fairies at the back of the garden. I peered into the back of my garden, but all was in shadow. I could hear the soft rattle of wind in the trees and discern the azalea bushes, their pink flowers made grey by evening light. I closed my eyes and instead of praying to God, I said aloud, 'If there are fairies in the garden, and if they are the kind that grant wishes, I wish that Harry would not go to this stupid war.'

Then I opened my eyes, feeling a little silly. A noise behind me alerted me I wasn't alone. It was Nicky, standing in the kitchen in the dark.

'What is it, sweetie?'

'Who were you talking to?'

No point in lying. 'The fairies. Asking them to grant me a wish.'

'It was about Haddy.'

'Yes, that's right.'

'Haddy' was what he called Harry. It came about because he couldn't pronounce his r's very well; he often called him 'Hanny' as well, but 'Haddy' stuck the most. I liked it because it rhymed with Daddy, and sometimes when Nicky used the name, I could imagine we were already that happy, entire family that I longed for us to be.

He toddled over and climbed into my lap. 'Is Haddy going away?'

'I don't know. Maybe.'

He sucked his thumb and looked at the stars, then seemed to remember why he had left his bed. 'Bad dream,' he said.

'What was it?'

'A bear.'

'No bears in Australia.'

'Koalas are bears.'

'No, they are not. Common misconception.'

He looked puzzled.

'They're marsupials. Not bears.'

'Mar-soop-als,' he tried.

'Exactly. How about we have some warm milk and then I'll sing you another lullaby?'

He nodded, and I rose with one last glance at the azaleas.

Now, while I don't mean to suggest it was the fairies, the Prime Minister *did* stop Harry from going to war. My bubble remained intact. And I became a little more inclined to believe in magic.

———

The first year of wartime was most strange. Endless speculation swirled around when it would end. Some said it would all blow over in a few months, some said it might last until the following year, some said it would go on for years and years like the Great War. Something about the way we all expected it to finish soon or not at all meant time became a thing that couldn't be measured anymore. I would try to remember an event, and could not calculate if a day had passed or a week or a month. This strange effect of time telescoping out and in was heightened for me because my children were so small. I began to measure time in other things – the arrival and disappearance of tiny teeth, the size of little shoes I bought, the complexity of new vocabulary.

As the boys grew and became more and more difficult to manage, Harry hired me a nanny and housekeeper. We called her Red because she'd come from Alice Springs, where the ground was very red, and she was dark-skinned and raven-haired and beautiful, but very straight-talking. The boys quickly fell in love with her. Admittedly, so did I. I had no husband, and Harry's relationship with us – constrained by work and what people would think of him visiting me – was loving but not sustained enough to be helpful on a daily basis. Red got us all organised and one day I realised that I was free enough to think. I felt like an individual person again and not part of a chaotic eight-armed creature. While my mind turned very quickly to drawing dresses and following fashion – the ladies pages were all I ever read in the newspaper – this wretched war *still* continued and Daddy was having a hard time with his business. Because Harry was so close to our family and had invested a small amount in the business, we couldn't pick up any government contracts without it seeming to be favouritism. I knew Daddy needed hands on deck, and so I volunteered to go and work at Trading and Agency, his food-packaging factory. Many women were working in factories and the like while the men were away. I made myself three wraparound dresses in plain blue poplin and got to work.

I would kiss the boys goodbye at seven when Red arrived, then spend the day pulling boxes off the cutting line and stacking and tying them. My arms and wrists grew firm, and I did rather worry I'd look too muscular for Harry's liking, but he didn't seem to notice. As for most of my life, I was well-supplied with a soft layer of womanly flesh.

It soon became apparent though that my creative brain was being wasted on the shop floor. I happened to overhear Daddy talking about a redesign of packaging that had to be done to comply with wartime regulations, and while he was puzzling through it, I could see immediately what needed to be done, sketched it up for him, and from the following day those new boxes were in production.

So Daddy brought me into the office to work with him on sourcing materials and advertising our products. It was as though my brain lit up when finally given a path to run along. I could not stop thinking about the business, about ideas for new things and how to grow. Granted, packaging was not as interesting as fashion, but I felt something stir inside me that was very similar to those early days with Betty, where possibilities seemed to appear all around me like dandelion clocks, just there to be grasped and wished upon. We would walk home from South Melbourne along the river in the late afternoons, and I would ask him questions and try out ideas – most that he batted away from him as nonsense – and we grew closer than we'd ever been. I think Daddy came to understand then what value I had. He was an old-fashioned type, and me loving dresses and running off to India and having babies had only affirmed to him what he had always thought – that girls were silly and unreliable. But during the war, he learned that I had an entrepreneurial spirit and I could work as hard as anyone else. And in seeing myself reflected that way in his eyes, I grew in confidence. I knew it was only a matter of time before I would open another dress shop. Not just one – a series of them. An empire, maybe.

I excitedly told Harry about all this on the weekends, and he was kind and smiley as always, but really very distracted by drama in parliament at this time. He'd had a lovely year up until then, and to great acclaim had sponsored the *Child Endowment Act* through parliament, an achievement of which I was immensely proud, being a single mother. But Mr Menzies had lost support in his party, and there were even people trying to convince Harry to topple him and take the top job. He never would. Harry was ambitious, but he was also loyal and he loved Mr Menzies. Nonetheless, the fellow who did topple him led the party to the next election, which they lost. Harry kept his seat, but he lost a ministry and his place on the war council, and he was hard to console for several months.

One afternoon a few months after all this transpired – I suspect it was late 1941, though my grip on dates was always loose during the war – I was on one of my regular visits to Mr McTavish, an old friend of Daddy's and the owner of a small printing and plastics company a few blocks from us. We often relied on them for advertising signs and to print directions on our boxes. Mr McTavish's office was a comfortingly stuffy room above the shop floor, with one very high, grimy window letting in a little light. His desk was a huge oak slab, always covered in papers that seemed to have been filed horizontally. I didn't judge as my own filing and paperwork left much to be desired, but on this particular day he was looking for a folder by the light of his lamp and not finding it. As I waited, I strolled to the door of the office and looked down at the men and women sweeping up long narrow strips of some kind of plastic material. I watched for a while, curious, and when Mr McTavish, smelling strongly of tobacco, appeared at my shoulder to say he'd found the folder, I asked him, 'What are they sweeping up?'

'Cellulose offcuts,' he said. 'From gun wrappings.'

A tremor of an idea was forming in my mind. You must remember, my whole life I had been able to see the three-dimensional potential of two-dimensional materials, and I'd spent months and months thinking about packaging. 'May I take some home? I have an idea.'

Arrival at home was the busiest time of the day. The boys were desperate to see me and tell me about school or kindergarten; Red would have all the vegetables chopped and be out the door, lighting a cigarette and on the way to a well-earned evening break. Then it was dinner, baths, stories and settling them all to sleep. I was not one of those mothers who wielded military precision to get my children to close their eyes; I was terribly lax, letting them get up over and over for drinks of water or extra cuddles. I missed them so much during the day that it would have made no sense to deny them a thing in the night-time, and more mornings a week than not I would wake up with at least one of them in my bed from a midnight incursion.

Once they were all settled and quiet, I set up my ironing board, switched on the iron and, working with the long offcuts, melted them carefully into little packets. They held together beautifully, but there was no way to close them. So I tried again, folding them lower and leaving a little flap at the top that could fold under and tuck in and . . . I'd done it. I'd found the cheapest material imaginable – shop-floor offcuts – and turned them into a product. I made eight with all of the cellulose I had, and couldn't wait to show them to Daddy the next day. He loved them, and had the very bright idea of turning our cardboard offcuts from box-making into little display boxes that the transparent packets fit in. The deal was struck with McTavish, and by the end of the year we were making thousands upon thousands of these little packets and selling them to stores all over Victoria, who would fill them with sugar or flour or rice or anything that needed to be weighed and labelled, and line them up in our display boxes on their counters.

Oh, we probably would have been fine if I hadn't come up with the idea, but Daddy would, at any opportunity, tell his friends that his daughter Zara was a born businesswoman and had saved the company. I cherished the warmth from that compliment a little more than humility dictated.

———

Christmas came and went, and still there was no end in sight to the war. We all made a guilty peace with the horror that was the news from the front, missing our boys who were in Europe and feeling very happy that such things weren't happening to us. That all changed in February when the Japanese bombed Darwin. That evening, as the news broke and everybody began talking about it, I did not sleep one wink. I lay all night, flinching against any noise, making plans for how I would get my boys out if the Japanese flew their planes to Melbourne to drop bombs on my little house. Like everyone else, I dug an air-raid trench in my garden, which the boys loved to play in (to my dismay). While the Japanese never came to Melbourne, hearing the constant news over the next few months of them hitting ports in the far north and Western Australia left me in a constant state of unease.

Added to this, I was worried about money. Everyone was doing it tough, and I was so lucky that Harry paid for Red to look after the boys, but things were really terribly tight. It depressed me. Once, I'd had so much. Now I found myself needing to choose between firewood and food when winter came. Food always won, of course. There were two fireplaces in the house: one in the boys' room and one in the lounge room. I would stoke up the one in the boys' room and sit there to read after they'd slept, before getting into bed to keep myself warm until morning.

The exception was when Harry arrived home from Canberra or came for the weekend. Then I'd light the lounge fire, I'd cut flowers from Mum's garden and fill the vases, and the boys and I would tidy the house and ourselves up so he would only ever see a shiny, happy version of our life. I knew Harry had money now, but I did not want to appear desperate. My divorce was still two years away at least, and of course I wanted Harry to marry me after that. I dreamed of it fervently. But I wouldn't have him thinking I depended on that outcome. I wanted him to marry me for love, not because I was needy.

One Saturday in midwinter, Harry came by for dinner with two friends – a couple about our age named Eric and Glenda Simmons – whom he had met at a charity function. He tended to go to such things without me these days, though I had been to a few society parties with him as his 'friend' Mrs Zara Fell (I couldn't bear to be introduced by my ex-husband's name, but in the eyes of the law, that was still who I was). I was keen to impress Eric and Glenda – or at least to impress Harry with my hostessing – but with rationing and a lack of money, I had to be highly inventive in preparing a dinner for four. I rolled potato parings in cheese and breadcrumbs and deep-fried them to make little savouries. My vegetable garden gave me carrots, cauliflower and radishes, and I bought a scrawny chicken from the butcher and hoped the Simmonses did not have big appetites. For a dessert, I soaked peaches in sherry overnight and served them up in glasses rimmed with sugar.

Afterwards, we sat by the fireplace while Red took charge of putting the boys to bed for me. Harry always brought something to drink, and this evening it was brandy.

Glenda was one of those languid women who always made me feel insecure, with long limbs and a polished leanness about her. Eric, by contrast, was round in the middle and red in the face, and at least ten years older than her. Given he owned a large property business leasing out factory space all over Australia, it would have been easy to say she married him for the money. But it simply wasn't the case. They appeared to adore each other, deferring to each other as they told stories, ending every sentence to each other with 'my love' and each constantly searching the other out with their eyes. While I smiled to see them, I also found myself wondering whether I was faulty somehow. They seemed so happy to be married and in love. So far such happiness had eluded me.

At one point, Eric leaned back, brandy glass in hand, and gestured to Harry and me with a free finger. 'So . . . what is happening here?'

I glanced at Harry. As with all of our social engagements, we presented ourselves as old and good friends. We went out for dinner every Saturday and kept our hands chastely to ourselves. It was only when the doors were closed behind us that the kisses and hot gazes of our mad love would flare into life. But surely anyone who saw Harry with the twins, now they were growing into little boys rather than formless babies, could see the similarities around their eyes and brows.

Harry smiled and smoothed his hands over his trouser legs. 'Zara and I have been close since we were in our teens,' he said. 'She is currently awaiting a divorce from Colonel Fell.'

Glenda raised her eyebrows, catching the inference. '*She* is awaiting it? Or are both of you counting down the days?'

Harry met my eyes, and the familiar jolt of desire brought a blushing smile to my lips. I imagined it must be visible to the Simmonses, so I looked down at my brandy glass.

'We are just good friends,' Harry demurred.

He said it so convincingly that it made me feel deflated, as though something good was always beyond my grasp.

———

For Sam and Andy's fifth birthday, Harry took us all for a drive into the country for a picnic. The weather was glorious – a big blue sky and the sun shining but not hot. We found a grassy place by a creek under some enormous red gum trees. We had fish paste sandwiches and boiled eggs, and Red had baked a syrup cake that was so sweet it made my teeth ache. After we had eaten, the boys insisted on splashing about in the creek, so I let them strip to their shorts and go in. I sat in the shade with Harry and watched them. We both had our shoes off. The breeze picked up in the trees.

'They are such beautiful boys,' Harry said wistfully.

I smiled, not taking my eyes off them. Nicky was getting long and skinny, but Sam and Andy still had round sticky-out bellies. The sun was in their hair, on their shoulders. They laughed and shouted at each other. 'They certainly are.'

He touched my cheek gently. 'Well, they have a beautiful mother.'

I turned my eyes to him, our gazes locked, and that familiar spike of desire passed between us.

'Oh, how I'd love to push you back on this picnic blanket and get my hands under your skirt,' he said.

'I would love that too,' I joked. 'Though the boys may find it a little alarming.'

Harry roared with laughter, twined his fingers in mine and pulled me gently backwards so I was lying down, and he curled next to me. He stroked my face. 'I had some news from Whitelock this week.'

'Whitelock? James's lawyer?'

'Yes. I am sorry, my love. All is being held up by the war and the fact he lives in a different country. We'll have to be patient.'

I sighed. 'If a war teaches us anything, it's patience I suppose.'

'We're all right though, aren't we? We still have dinners and picnics, and time together with our three boys?'

One thing I adored about Harry was he never made a distinction between Nicky and the twins. They were all 'our boys' to him.

'Yes, we're all right.'

'Are you in a hurry?'

Yes! I was! But I didn't say so. I knew Harry well enough to know he'd experience any overenthusiasm for marriage as pressure. 'I'm happy for now,' I said instead.

He kissed me, and it was such a deep passionate kiss that I did worry for a few moments that he actually was going to slide his hands under my skirt. But then he pulled back and away, laughing, and sat up. 'We'd better watch those boys in case they get themselves into trouble.'

The afternoon ended poorly, with the boys cold and damp and whining in Harry's car on the way home, and Sam vomiting from carsickness or too much cake or both. But there was something about that balance between idyllic and ordinary messiness that made me feel closer to Harry.

———

In all the old fairytales, promises and curses and journeys often only lasted a year and a day. I had always loved the poetry of that idea – not a year, but a year and a day. Then the reward would arrive, or the spell would be broken, or the brother would return home, and life could resume. The war lasted six years and one day, far too long for anyone's liking, and certainly it meant that my children's early lives were hemmed on all sides by this terrible fact. Rationing and going without, frightening images and – later when they could read – headlines in the newspapers, and the endless dismal reckonings of the people around them. The whole world talked of war over and over and over for six years and one day.

And then it stopped. Four months after Mr Hitler gave up, so did the Japanese.

We were all wrong-footed for a while, didn't know what to say to each other in shops or at the hairdressers. But optimism seemed to have dawned sunnily in the world again, and I was so grateful.

Six years and a day. Such a very long time.

CHAPTER 20

One Saturday shortly after Christmas, Harry came by as he usually did. He knocked and pushed open the door, calling out, 'Hello, hello!' and the boys ran to him and threw their arms around him for cuddles and a bit of roughhousing.

'Now, now, don't overwhelm him,' I said to the boys, but faintly. I was really a terrible mother in that regard. I let them do what they wanted as long as it didn't hurt anybody, and from the way Harry was laughing and joking about, he didn't look as though he was being hurt. While Andrew plucked at his jacket, looking for treats in his pocket, Harry held out his left hand and in it was a letter, opened.

'Go on, take it,' he said, as the boys dragged him to the settee to test his pockets further. He often buried boiled lollies very deep in them.

I pulled the letter from the envelope and unfolded it, my eyes jumping over the lines, heart racing. Not only was I divorced – and had been for four months without knowing it – James had remarried. Somebody else was Mrs Fell now. I was simply me again.

It felt as though I had been dumped by a big wave. One minute I was swimming along in my depth, the next I was turned upside down in deep, deep water. I burst into tears, from relief, from sadness, from shame . . . I don't know. All I know is I simply couldn't stop sobbing. Harry settled the boys with handfuls of sweets and summoned Red to take them into the garden, and he held me close against him. I took a deep breath of the familiar, intoxicating scent of him – the soap flakes he washed his clothes in, his hair cream – and let the feelings course through me.

'Well, Zara, you are a free woman,' he said, gently easing me away so he could look in my eyes. 'Does this mean I can take you out for dinner tonight?'

'Yes,' I said, delighting with anticipation. Why else would he want to take me out for dinner, but to finally, *finally* propose?

I wore a wine-red, draped jersey column gown, which I had made in the early years of the war and never got to wear. I loved its butterfly sleeves and its sequinned collar, and it still fit – marvellous! I brushed my curls out and pinned a satin rose behind my ear, being careful to match it exactly with red lipstick. Harry was chatty when he picked me up, telling me I looked gorgeous and then launching straight into a funny story about one of his constituents who came into his office every day to complain about something, and that day had complained about the weather as though it was somehow Harry's fault.

He parked the car on Bourke Street and we walked up to Florentino, where he had upstairs reservations for us. I ascended the stairs lightly, happily, but was surprised to see Eric and Glenda Simmons up there, and they greeted us as though they expected us.

'Darlings! Oh, look at you, Zara. So pretty!' That was Glenda, waving a champagne glass. 'And such a happy occasion. Come let's sit down so we can all have a drink to celebrate.'

It quickly became apparent that the intimate dinner for two, where Harry would no doubt ask me to marry him, was not going to transpire. Instead, it was a rowdy dinner for eight, in the end, as four of our other friends showed up. Champagne flowed and everyone toasted me for being free of my marriage. The women complimented my gown, and Harry bragged that I had no doubt designed and made it, and he was proud that I had run a business as a lass and travelled the world on my own. It was strange to hear him

talk about me like that, as though he adored me, but to find myself
in such a radically different situation from what I had expected.
I felt like two people – one was smiling and drinking champagne
and laughing at jokes, the other was brooding and sad and wanted
to shout at everyone that it wasn't a joke or a celebration to have
so thoroughly ruined a marriage, tipped my young sons' life into
turmoil and wound up struggling for money at age thirty-six.

I said none of these things, ever careful of Harry's reputation as a
member of parliament and quite a famous person in our community.

As the night wore on and people began to leave, Harry noted
that he had a community picnic to attend in the morning and had
best go home to write his speech. I was engulfed in the hugs and air
kisses of our friends, and then back in the cool quiet car.

'Did you enjoy yourself?' Harry asked, starting the car.

'I . . . yes.'

'You looked so pretty. I was proud of you.'

I didn't know how to answer, and he seemed to have slipped into a
reverie himself. My heart – my stupid heart – started to hope again.

But then we were idling outside my house and he gave me a peck
on the check and yawned. 'Sorry not to come in, love. You understand. The picnic's at ten and I haven't even started writing. It's for
a commemorative statue for the boys we lost, and I want to read up
some good quotations about war and hope.'

'Oh, I understand. It's fine.'

'Wasn't expecting your divorce to come through today, or the
letter at least. Looks as though it's been held up in India a while.' He
tilted his head slightly. 'You seem down. The thought of somebody
else being Mrs Fell bothering you?'

I smiled tightly. 'It's not the happiest occasion I can imagine, is
it?' I said. 'Having failed at marriage.'

'Good night's sleep will fix you,' he replied, rubbing my thigh.
'I'll pop by in the afternoon and take you and the boys to the beach
if it stays fine.'

Somehow I climbed out of the car, slightly drunk and still a single mother to three little boys, and made my way to the house. Red greeted me from the couch where she was reading a magazine. An old one, because I couldn't, afford new ones these days.

'Good timing,' she said with her usual open smile. 'I've just boiled the kettle. After a cuppa?'

'I think I'll just go to bed,' I said. 'But thank you. Boys went down all right?'

'Sam did. Nicky and Andy had a competition to see who could ask for the most extra stories.'

'I'll go check on them,' I said.

The boys all slept in one room. Sam under the window, Nicky in the middle, and Andy so close to the wardrobe there was barely room to open the door. I bent over each of them and kissed their foreheads. When I got to Sam, he roused, said, 'Mummy,' then went back to sleep. I lay down next to him, stroking his hair. He smelled of soap. I closed my eyes and hot tears squeezed out from under my lids.

———

By the next day, I was furious. Furious. The depths of sadness I'd plumbed the night before burned away before an indignation that could have lit the world on fire. Sam and Andy were *his children*. Not James's. He couldn't simply leave me to raise them alone like this. There he was, bouncing around between here and Canberra, living his happy life where people fawned over him, while I spent my days at Daddy's factory and my nights fetching glasses of water and tending to bad dreams. It was so unfair, and it made me feel like an idiot. Twenty years I had known him. Twenty years. I gave him access to my adoration and my kisses and my body, and he took it all for granted.

Good as his word, he came by at two and I greeted him coldly. He didn't seem to notice, chatting with Red while I triple-checked that all the boys had swimmers, buckets, spades and towels. On the car ride he was chipper, playing I Spy with the children and leading them in a rousing chorus of 'Riding in My Car'. When Harry asked why I wasn't singing along, I turned my head to the window diffidently. He took his hand off the wheel and squeezed mine briefly, but gave no other sign that he'd noticed I wanted to roast him with the rage in my eyes.

We set up at the beach and the boys ran straight for the water's edge, their little limbs and chests pale in the sunshine. Harry fiddled with the beach umbrella, trying to get it stable against the stiff sea breeze. When he was satisfied, he sat down next to me and smiled.

I did not smile back.

This didn't deter him, and he got a sparkle in his eyes. 'Zara,' he said.

'What?'

'I have been your devoted slave for twenty years,' he said. 'So are you going to marry me or not?'

My breath was pulled out of me on a hook. I made a noise so loud that the boys looked over to see if I was all right.

'You . . . bastard, Harry!' I managed, through tears and laughter.

'Is that a yes or a no, because I can't tell from the language you're using.'

'Yes, you bastard. Yes. I'll marry you.'

Harry leaned forward, knuckles in the sand on either side of me, and while everyone in the world looked on, he kissed me as though he intended to keep me.

PART 5

INTERLUDE

She has never driven this far in her life. Most of her car trips have been local – running to shops or visits with her grandchildren. Harry always drove or, if she was travelling Melbourne to Sydney, she flew. Her back and legs are tired, but as she takes the turn-off into the city, she remembers the first time she ever flew in an aeroplane – her honeymoon. Harry had organised a trip to Sydney, but the flight was delayed and delayed, and they hadn't arrived until nearly five in the morning. Completely sobered up from the wedding breakfast by then and just dying to sleep. And yet, on final arrival at Hotel Australia, the receptionist had recognised Harry but not her, and decided they were having an affair and would *not* let them stay together in the honeymoon suite.

Zara hadn't minded. She booked a different room and just slept for hours and hours. Which is what she wants to do right now.

They own a tiny eighth-floor apartment in a Macleay Street art deco building at Potts Point. Zara bought it in 1963 after a particularly good year in the business so she had a place to stay when she visited her Double Bay boutique. It is here that she now pulls up the car, wakes Harry – he has been quiet for many hours – and says softly, 'We're here.'

It's midmorning, and getting him out of the car without being seen is impossible. He lies in his car seat looking at her wordlessly, waiting to be told how to exit the vehicle and enter the building unseen.

'Would you wear a disguise?' she asks him.

'Do we have a disguise?'

She hasn't thought this through. She knows once she has him upstairs, he never needs to leave the apartment and they will be safe.

'I have a scarf . . .' She wants to cry. She cannot make this work, and she needs it to work so badly. If it doesn't work, well . . . this whole dream shatters and they are back in the world again, and having to deal with consequences. Consequences so great and weighty that she cannot imagine her body supporting them.

'I think if I were to put on a ladies scarf, it might draw attention rather than deflect it,' he says. 'Let's count on the fact that I haven't shaved in two days to help, and I'll pull my collar up and my hat all the way down.'

She nods. 'Let's try it.'

She gets out of the car first, looks around. A postman is across the street and she gestures at Harry to wait until he is gone around the corner into Hughes Street. When the way is clear, she wrenches the door open and Harry hurries out, sunk deeply into his coat and hat, and they make for the stairs rather than risk meeting someone at the lift. Her thighs are aching and when she gets to the top she's puffed, but then she has the apartment door open and they are in.

They are inside and safe, and nobody knows.

'It's against my gentlemanly nature to let you fetch the suitcases on your own,' he says.

'Then be ungentlemanly. If this is to work, nobody can see you. Ever.' Then a wave of doubt washes over her. 'Though this place is rather small. No garden to keep you busy.'

He opens the door to the balcony and takes in the view. The Harbour Bridge. The Heads. He gestures to cranes on a site to the north. 'I'll watch them build that opera theatre,' he says. 'I'm still not sure how its roof will stay up, so that should entertain me.'

She joins him, gratefully feels the breeze on her face. She has always loved this apartment, but they have never stayed here together. By the time she owned it, he had been rocketing towards the top of his profession and so had she. But her life, her wishes, her will had always come second to his. The thought makes her uncomfortable, and she pushes it away and remembers the breeze, and the view, and the feel of his hand in hers.

'Will this do for a while?' she asks him.

He turns to her and smiles, a little puzzled. 'I don't know. Will it?'

'I think it will. I can be seen and you can be hidden . . . and life can sort of move on a bit. I think it needs to?'

Her last sentence comes out as a question, but he neither agrees nor disagrees with her. He turns his eyes to the horizon and seems lost in thought a while.

—

'We've been worried about you.'

She hears this a lot in the weeks that follow. Family, friends, business associates. Worried about her. *What happened was such a shock; of course you feel terrible. But you should be with the people you love.* Nicky had pulled no punches. 'We are grieving him too,' he said, flint in his voice.

She came so close to telling him, but she held off. She reasons with herself – *wait a month and tell the boys then.* She can change her mind any time she likes. Nothing is set in stone. She and Harry are seeing what happens today, what happens tomorrow, in this new and strange life they have chosen.

Betty sits across from her at a coffee lounge in Kings Cross, idly stirring a sugar into her espresso.

'I don't think one is meant to drink espresso with sugar,' Zara says.

'I don't care. It's barely drinkable otherwise.'

'Then drink tea.' She gestures to the teacup in front of her. 'Like me.'

'I'm determined,' Betty says. 'All these lovely new coffee lounges, authentic Italian . . . I'm determined.' She taps her spoon on her cup and places it on the table. 'So,' she says. 'Everyone has been worried about you.'

Zara sips her tea, glancing around the room. The square tables and round stools. The scales and the green cash register. It's noisy, but cheerfully so. Every now and again a curious glance turns her way. Betty had lost a child. Betty should understand. 'When Katy died . . .' she ventures.

Betty flinches, but Zara pushes on.

'When Katy died, was everyone worried about you?'

'Oh god, yes. I grew so tired of it. All I wanted to do was hide and sob.' She smiles tightly. 'All right, I see your point.'

'Let me hide and sob a little longer,' Zara says softly. 'It's only been six months.'

Betty reaches across the table, grasps Zara's knuckles. 'I have lived . . . quite a life,' she says. 'I have known pain so excruciating that I thought I would die from it. I didn't die. I kept going. I was even happy again.' She withdraws her hand. 'But you hide and sob if you need to, darling. Just . . . stay in touch. Don't fall off the edge of the earth.'

'I won't. I'm just at Potts Point,' I joked. 'Nowhere near the edge.'

'I'm always here for you,' Betty says.

And Zara almost tells her, but then stops. It's too much, even for her oldest and dearest friend.

'Thank you,' she says instead, and returns her attention to her tea.

———

Some days, she just walks. She leaves the apartment and walks along the waterfront for miles and miles. Or sometimes she walks into the city and browses in the dress shops and dreams about dresses, or remembers happier times in her business before it all became too much. And when she comes home to the apartment, Harry is sitting on the balcony watching the Opera House being built, and he reminds her of nothing so much as a cat, trapped indoors, tail twitching as it dreams of the world beyond.

———

She is in demand. People want to talk to her. Solicitors. The press. People in high places. Most she bats away, but her family begin to pressure her to speak. Her brothers, Vieve, the boys and their wives. 'People want to know how you are.'

She concedes to an interview with *The Age*. The journalist, a salt-and-pepper-haired fellow named Paul, asks repeatedly if he can come to her apartment to take photos of her 'in her home environment'. Clearly this won't do, so she finally convinces him to meet her in Centennial Park. The photographer arrives with him, and takes photos of her sitting on a bench under a spreading fig tree. Her smile feels frozen. Her heart races. She wants to get back to Harry.

Hide and sob.

Once the photographer is done, he gives Paul the journalist a thumbs up and heads off. Paul settles next to her with his notepad and pencil.

'So, thank you for meeting with me,' he says. 'While last year ended in tragedy for you, this year has been quite something.'

'It has,' she answers slowly, bringing details to mind.

'Let's start with the Queen's birthday honours,' he says. 'You are now Dame Zara Holt. How does that feel?'

Is she? A dame? She feels like a girl, not a grand woman with a title. But somehow, even as she thinks these thoughts, she answers the journalist with genuine feeling. Of course it's an honour to be recognised for her public service and, yes, a small consolation during a terrible year. Then he asks her about the uniforms she designed for the Australian Olympic team this year, then about the memoir she is writing about her life with Harry. All of these things she had forgotten. Being on the run with Harry had taken up so much of her attention.

The interview continues, Paul scribbling down her answers in shorthand as though she is a perfectly sane, perfectly successful woman who is getting on with her life after a tragedy. Well, that's all right, isn't it? It will throw them off the scent.

Finally, his questions slow down. He flips over his pages then looks at her. His eyes are very blue, and the sun is lowering and a beam has caught his cheek. 'One last question, then,' he says. 'I know you must miss Harry terribly. Would you tell us your fondest memory of your time together?'

A panicky feeling washes over her. How she hates to look back over a whole life like that. It reminds her of mortality. Hers. His.

'I'm sorry,' Paul says, sensing she has faltered. 'If it's too difficult.'

'Bingil Bay,' she says mock-confidently. 'We have a house there. Our little paradise in Far North Queensland.' She feels both a smile and a sob pull at the corners of her mouth at the same time. 'That's where we were always happy.'

'Do you think you'll ever go back there?' he asks. 'Now he's gone?'

And Zara thinks what a grand idea. Why hasn't she thought of it before? Yes, the drive will be hellish and long, but happiness surely waited at the end of it, and the world always went away when they were up north.

'I think I will,' she says vaguely, pulling her handbag onto her lap and making motions to leave. 'Now, if you will excuse me . . . ?'

'Of course, Dame Zara,' he says with a broad smile. 'Thank you for your time.'

She rises and heads towards Oxford Street, wondering what Harry will say when she tells him it's time to get moving again.

CHAPTER 21

My hands were full of fabric, one of my favourite feelings. On this occasion it was silvery-grey satin, and I was pinning the waist so that it would fall in flattering drapes over its wearer's wide hips. I had pins in my mouth and was weighing the fabric, considering the light and the line, when Nancy, one of my seamstresses, arrived at the workroom door, breathless from the run upstairs.

'Mrs Holt! Your husband is here.'

Harry was here? He never set foot in Magg. I rose and handed Nancy the pins. 'Finish this will you, Nancy?' I smiled at the woman wearing the dress. 'I'm so sorry, Mrs Parker, but –'

'Your husband is an important man,' she said, nodding with understanding. 'I wouldn't want you to keep him waiting.'

I hurried down the stairs to the shop floor and found Harry in conversation with Betty under the bronze and glass chandelier. This version of Magg, which Betty and I had opened barely a year ago, was spacious and opulent with polished wood and thick rugs and racks of beautiful gowns. It was all ours, the thing we did to keep ourselves happy and make our own money. But neither of our husbands had shown the slightest interest in it, so busy were they with the world of men.

'Ah, there she is,' Harry said, and I could tell from his voice that he was exasperated with me though trying to cover it up in front of Betty. 'It's Wednesday,' he said.

'And?' I asked, puzzled.

'You are, at this moment, meant to be at the Girl Guides meeting giving the Christmas address.'

'Oh, hell!' I exclaimed, even though I rarely swore.

Harry rolled his eyes and let out a brief laugh, then held the front door of the shop open for me. I threw a desperate glance at Betty, who shooed me. 'Go on,' she said. 'We'll survive.'

Harry had his car – a brand-new black FX Holden – parked at a jaunty angle just outside the shop on Toorak Road. 'Hop in, I'll drive you,' he said.

'My notes are at home.'

'We haven't time to stop. Do it from memory.'

My head was whirling from switching between my two personas: the dressmaker focused on what I looked at and the politician's wife focused on who was looking at me. I really didn't think it was a good idea to give my address without notes, which one of Harry's secretaries always prepared for me (no doubt the one who rang Harry to alert him I hadn't shown up), but we were already pulling up at a brightly painted community hall in South Yarra.

'Off you go, then,' he said. 'I have to get to a committee meeting.'

'Thank you, thank you,' I said, checking my hair and lipstick in my compact mirror. 'I'm sorry.'

'Off you go,' he said again, more curtly.

I hurried out of the car and pushed the door to the hall open, closing the warm summer sunlight out behind me.

'Oh, here she is!' a young woman in a gorgeous pink cardigan said as she spotted me. 'Come in! We are *so* glad you could make it, Mrs Holt. It is *such* an honour.'

I still wasn't accustomed – and perhaps never would be – to people being 'honoured' to meet me. I understood my husband had honour from being an elected representative, and certainly in the last week – since his party had finally returned to government with Mr Menzies back at the helm – from having an important ministerial portfolio.

The hall was decorated with crepe-paper chains and tinsel. The event was for Girl Guides and their mothers; there wasn't a man in sight. Some of the party dresses the younger mothers were wearing made me feel terribly underdressed. I always looked my best when I was attending fittings at the store, but I might have chosen a different outfit had I remembered that I was to be speaking today.

I chatted with women and their daughters over tea, circulating around the room as I had been taught by Harry's press secretary Tony, and mindful not to eat too much lest it repeat on me while I was speaking (again, a tip from Tony, who really was marvellous at helping me not embarrass myself at these events).

Finally, the time came for me to get up and speak. They had a podium set up for me, which was wrapped in tinsel that fluttered in the breeze from the open windows. I remembered so little of the speech I'd prepared, but I had spoken at women's events before . . . in fact, that's all I spoke at. Any community group or business in Harry's electorate that wanted somebody to come and talk to women always got me. It seemed a pity that Harry wouldn't stand in front of a room full of women at least once in a while and let them know he cared about their votes as much as the men's.

So I talked a little bit about girls and education and helping them be independent, the usual thing, but then I ran out of steam for a moment, and took a breath to observe the room. The girls in their blue uniforms were so still and quiet.

'I must say,' I continued, 'as the mother of boys, it's very interesting to me how well-behaved girls can be.'

A warm laugh ran across the room. I continued, improvising. 'My boys are always running about or fidgeting and fiddling with their things.' I had meant to say 'fiddling with things' but something about the accidental addition of the word 'their' made the comment sound vulgar and I stifled a laugh. I caught the eye of one of the Guide Leaders in the front row, a florid woman with a merry twinkle in her eye, and she too had heard it and was trying not to laugh.

'You know, their toys and so on,' I said to clarify, which drew more attention to the comment and a ripple of laughter broke out in one corner of the room. I pressed my toe hard against the inside of the podium so I didn't burst into giggles. There would no doubt be at least one society journalist in the room, and with Harry so high up in government now, I didn't want to be seen as disrespectful. I took a deep breath and continued, turning the observation about the girls' ability to listen and consider into a call for more listening and consideration in public life, so I was pleased with myself that I saved the day.

I caught a taxi from the event back to the store and finished up a few small chores before walking home. Our beloved Red had left us to get married, but we had recently hired a new housekeeper-cum-nanny with the fabulous name Mary Lawless. She was in her late forties, widowed and the most petite little thing you could imagine. Elfin, really. The boys took to calling her Tiny, so that is what we called her too. She seemed to relish this familiarity and we had come to rely on her very heavily. She was the linchpin that made our household function without falling over. Not only could she cook, organise and wrangle children, but she could drive. I was still in the long process of learning (Harry despaired of the way I went off in a dream while behind the wheel) so having a person in the house who could ferry the boys to their various sporting matches was a godsend. We were living on St Georges Road now, a red-brick house just a few doors down from my childhood home. It was a modest place but it had an upstairs room for Tiny right across from the boys' bedroom. Harry was often away in Canberra so it never felt too crowded, and it had a large front yard for the children to play in and room in the back garden for a vegetable patch that I tended to carelessly.

When parliament wasn't sitting, like this week, Harry was home with us and I must say it was the deepest happiness to have us all in one place. I let myself into the front room, which we'd decorated for Christmas by taping coloured cellophane to the windows and hanging lights all around. Harry and the boys had driven out to the countryside to dig up a pine sapling. It now sat propped in a bucket, drooping under the weight of the glass baubles attached to it. Every now and again our cat Wally would run about like a mad thing and knock one of the baubles to the floor, where it shattered and became a hazard until Tiny or I swept it up.

My moment of arrival was always a sharp intake of breath before the busy chaos of the evening. Boys requiring help with homework, dinners to be prepared, ironing to be done ahead of the next day. I never complained; I had Tiny to help me with all of it, but after an afternoon spent with quiet little girls, my boys seemed particularly rambunctious that night. It was nearly dinnertime before I realised I hadn't even taken off my hat.

Harry escaped it all, sitting in his study. I didn't begrudge him. The man never stopped working. He woke at dawn and read papers in bed while I was still snoozing. When I woke, he would sit and have tea with me, then take his breakfast into his study and only emerge for meals or to ask me for opinions (rare, but it did happen). Even on weekends he carved out a few hours for work.

On this evening, we were just finishing our meal when the telephone rang and Tiny, who hardly ever finished what was on her plate, volunteered to answer it. Harry nodded, and began rushing the last of his potatoes.

'That will be the Chamber of Commerce people,' he said. 'I'm expecting them.'

But it wasn't. Tiny re-emerged and said, 'Mrs Holt, it's a journalist from *The Argus* for you.'

'Oh,' I said. 'Right, then. Excuse me.'

I rose, and Harry called after me, 'Don't take too long. I'm expecting a call.'

I hurried to the hallway where the telephone was kept and scooped up the receiver. 'Hello?'

'Hello, Mrs Holt. Jennifer Carmen from *The Argus* ladies pages. I wondered if you'd like to talk to me about what fashions we can expect to see coming to Australia in 1950. New Year's is just over the horizon, and you and Betty Grounds always seem to know about international fashion.'

'Oh, yes. Yes, I'd love to talk to you about fashion,' I said, settling into the chair next to the phone. 'And 1950 is going to be such a special year. We're all finally shaking off the austerity of war and embracing glamour again . . .'

I rattled on, talking about colours and fabrics and styles. Betty and I subscribed to a number of American and UK fashion magazines and we budgeted to have them air-mailed to us so we weren't a sea-journey behind in trends. Some of the things we saw we laughed about – unflattering clothes, no matter how popular, would always raise our disdain. I told Jennifer the journalist this, and we had a little laugh about some of the mad ideas people had when I became aware that Harry was standing in the hallway staring at me, mouth in a hard line.

His call. I had forgotten, enjoying myself so much talking about fashion.

'Jennifer,' I said, 'can I ring you back tomorrow? It's just my husband is waiting for a phone call and –'

'It's going to press in the morning, but don't worry. You have given me so much, and I can always call Robyn Foy for more comments if I need them.'

I felt a pang. Robyn Foy was a recent blow-in from Sydney who had set up a shop a little too similar to ours for my comfort. I wanted

Magg's to be the only opinion in this article, but Harry was definitely displeased with me.

The uncomfortable fact was that when I asked Harry if he minded me having a fashion business again, he had said absolutely not, so long as it never interfered with his public life. I'd already let him down today by forgetting the Girl Guides event.

'Ah well,' I said. 'I think I told you my main opinions.'

'You've been so helpful, Mrs Holt. Good evening.'

I hung up then raised my palms. 'Sorry. I got carried away.'

'I'll be in my study,' he said.

I watched him walk away, then made my way to the kitchen to help Tiny with the cleaning up.

I noticed his telephone call never came.

———

In that strange timeless week between Christmas and New Year, when I could never remember what day it was and the heat became unbearable, Harry found a gossipy write-up in the local paper about my 'boys fiddling with their things' comment at the Girl Guides address. He found it utterly hilarious, though I was embarrassed and annoyed – I had said so many other clever things that day. This newspaper article he cut out and kept, while my long interview with *The Argus* about fashion barely raised his interest at all. I shrugged it off.

Harry was due to go on his first overseas trip in his new role with a large Commonwealth association: first to London, then home via Kenya. His berth had been booked, but even the fastest route by sea took nearly four weeks, so altogether he would be gone for nearly three months. On the third of January, the night before he was to leave, we met with Betty and Roy at a Russian restaurant at South Yarra. They weren't licensed, so Roy had sneaked in a flask of whisky, which we passed around surreptitiously when the waiters weren't looking. Roy, from his start as Betty's scandalous bohemian lover, had become one of our dearest-loved friends. He was the darling of the architectural world and they forged enough wealthy alliances to overcome their sordid history. It was impossible not to smile when Roy was around. He was funny and warm and so full of life and love, and with his thick hair and handsome brow it was easy for me to see how Betty had fallen for him. And he was hardly bohemian anymore – his architectural designs were winning prizes and acclaim all over Australia. I sometimes envied Betty that she had a husband who was creative and understood the language of light, lines and fitness for purpose.

I tucked into a meal of delicious chicken morsels stuffed with butter and herbs. We got drunk and rowdy, and Harry swore if he drank anymore he'd be seasick tomorrow, but it didn't stop him.

Later in bed, Harry and I snuggled against each other naked. We rarely wore pyjamas. I knew my body had changed over the years – I now allowed myself to love food and I always knew how to style an outfit to skim my lumps and bumps – but his had hardly changed at all. The other thing that had hardly changed was his desire to touch and hold my bare flesh. So while I would hide behind a long flannel nightie if I could, Harry simply wouldn't allow it.

'I will miss you so so *so* much,' I said. The window was open to let in a breeze, and I could hear crickets and a soft rustle in the leaves. I pressed my lips against his shoulder. 'How will I bear it?'

'Surely you must be looking forward to it a little,' he rumbled, stroking my hair. 'You can spend your day thinking about dresses, and you won't have to put up with me snoring.'

'You don't snore. Well . . . not often.'

He laughed.

'But, yes, I will throw myself into work. It's as though I never get tired of fashion, Harry.'

'Well, you are a woman.'

I didn't want to be dismissed, even jokingly. 'It's not that,' I said. 'It's the *art* of it. It's the imagination. I see a colour or a weave, and

I imagine who it would look good on. Pale skin? Tanned skin? Blonde, brunette? And then I imagine her standing on a patio at a party on a hot night, or stepping out of a car and onto a red carpet, or walking down the aisle towards the man she wants to spend the rest of her life with . . .' I paused, wondering if he was still listening. 'It's art that you wear. I feel like a painter, but my medium is fabric.'

'I'm glad you love it, my darling,' he said. 'I am proud of you, I hope you know. The other politicians' wives are . . . just politicians' wives.'

On the one hand I didn't like him being dismissive about other women, especially as some of those politicians' wives were my friends and clients. But on the other hand, I loved that he had singled me out as special and different. I sighed into him. 'Write to me every morning?'

'How about every second morning? I imagine I'll be busy.'

'Send me telegrams, then? Once a week at least. The boys will love that.'

'All right. Easily done.' He gathered me against him, and I began to drift off to sleep.

'You're a rose of a woman, Zara,' he said. 'I do love you.'

I let the compliment sink all the way into my soul.

———

For some reason, the boys got it into their heads that what Harry would want most of all on his return from Africa was a welcome-home party. The idea took root about a month before his return and grew from there. Tiny suggested we just let them organise it because Harry would be delighted with whatever they did; he was so good and patient and kind with those children. Given they were nearly eleven (the twins) and thirteen (Nicky), what harm could come from letting them throw him a little family party?

On the morning Harry was due to arrive home, Tiny took them to the shops while I was at work. I came home to find my house covered in coloured paper chains. They had glued together loops of paper but the glue had gone everywhere. It was in Nicky's hair, and in the carpet, and on the couch, and the paper chains were uneven and messy. The house decorations were a testament to enthusiasm, but not to care. Sam and Andy had made a sign that said, *Welcome Home*, which hung in the entranceway, slightly askew.

'Wait until you see the garden, Mummy,' Andy said, grasping my hand and dragging me through the house. I stood on the back step and saw more paper chains, and on the ground, eight Chinese paper lanterns.

'We have candles in all of those,' he explained. 'When Harry is on his way, we'll light them and climb up the trees to hang them.'

'Candles? In paper lanterns?'

Tiny appeared next to us. 'It's a still night,' she said. 'I'm sure it will be safe. And Mr Holt is due around dusk, so it will be very pretty.' She dropped her voice. 'Prettier than the house.'

They'd also dragged their art table outside and covered it with a tablecloth, and in the kitchen Nicky was busy decorating a cake. I went to my bedroom and removed my hat, tidied my hair and touched up my lipstick. I felt oddly jittery. I knew it was excitement but I also recognised it as fear – since we'd been married, we hadn't been apart for this long. His trips to Canberra lasted only a few weeks, though they would be longer now he was back in a ministry. But still, he tried to get home for a weekend in the middle of any long periods away.

I suppose I worried that he would walk in – after time in exotic places with terribly clever people, no doubt including glamorous women – and a house decorated with sagging paper chains, three noisy boys, a messy cake and my 41-year-old body would be deflating for him. And that he would want to run straight back to the ship.

The taxi arrived shortly before six and the boys ran down to the street to 'help' Harry out, but in fact they seemed to get in the way. Harry had brought me back a real zebra-skin rug and this created enormous excitement among the children, who wanted to unroll it right there on the front lawn. I held back and waited for Harry to come to me, and he squeezed me so tight my ribs hurt, then gave me a kiss – I can only describe it as improper for a public street – in front of the children. Dear god, that kiss made my knees tremble, and for a few moments everything disappeared except his body and his mouth and I was sixteen again.

Then he stepped away and we all headed back up to the house, a noisy entourage of excitement and children's prattle. While Sam and Andy showed Harry the ugly paper chains, which my darling husband praised as 'very creative', Nicky disappeared into the garden to light the candles and hang the paper lanterns.

Harry barely had time to drop his suitcase in the living room before Nicky came haring back in, telling him to come and see the garden. We all emerged out through the back door and onto the patio, where the table was set up with cake and cordial, with a bottle of whisky hidden behind a pot plant for the grown-ups. I must admit, the garden looked magical. We had a big cottonwood tree that the boys loved to climb, and it swung with four lanterns. Apart from that, he had spread them around on low branches on the lilly pilly and ash trees. Inside, Tiny put on the gramophone and soft jazz music drifted out to the patio.

'Sit down, sit down.' That was Sam, tugging Harry towards one of the folding chairs. 'We made a cake!'

'Sam, darling,' I said, 'poor Harry has just this moment walked in from a long trip. Let's let him –'

'It's fine,' Harry said. 'I'm happy to sit down, though the ground is still rolling underneath me. And the cake looks delicious. Let's all have some.'

We sat down, and Andy was determined that he was going to carve up the cake, and so one by one we all received a plop of messy cake on a plate.

Oh god, it was delicious. Suddenly all my petty worries melted away, and we were a family enjoying homecoming cake with shining faces and a glowing garden. I realised I'd spent too much time in this marriage anxious that the boys and I were bothering Harry. It started the moment he moved in with us after the wedding, dissipated for a little while when we moved house and weren't so much on top of each other, but had built steadily over the months. Having released the house to chaos again while he was away, I had experienced a growing dread of how he would see us, if he regretted it.

I was about to find out I couldn't have been more wrong.

Harry polished off his cake and helped himself to another slice (though 'slice' is the wrong word; the way Andy cut, it there were sort of blobs of it) then said, 'I've had a lot of time to think while I was away, especially on the long sea journey.' He smiled that gorgeous smile that still looked boyish on him despite his approaching middle age. 'And I can't have you three boys going around calling me Harry anymore. I've married your mother, so that makes you my children. I'm going to start the process of adopting you officially tomorrow.'

I gasped, and hot tears began to leak from the corners of my eyes. 'Harry, are you . . . ?'

'What does that mean?' Sam asked.

'It means, my son, that you will call me Dad from now on. Is that all right?'

'Sure thing, *Dad*,' Andy said with a cakey grin.

I looked at Nicky – the only one who was not biologically Harry's, though he didn't know that; they all thought James was their father. Nicky's eyes were locked on Harry's face. The expression was something akin to awe, but mixed with love. Tenderness. I let out one involuntary sob.

Harry turned his face to me. 'Zara?'

'I'm so happy,' I managed, though my face started to crumple and tears ran down my cheeks.

'You don't look happy, Mummy,' Andy said, hopping up and giving me a sticky hug.

'Oh no! The tree!' Tiny leapt to her feet.

I spun around to see one of the Chinese lanterns had gone up in flames, and now those flames had set a clutch of leaves on fire.

'The hose!' Harry shouted, skidding back his chair and running for where the hose was coiled up in an empty plant pot. While he fumbled to attach it to the tap, the flames leaped higher.

My pulse thundered in my ears. 'Hurry, Harry!' I shouted.

Harry got the hose attached and ran to the tree, spraying it madly. The water didn't quite reach the top flames, but the night air was still and, without anywhere further to go above, they began to dim and flicker. A few moments later, they were out.

We all looked at each other and began to laugh with relief. Harry pulled me against him, shirt damp from where the hose leaked on him.

'Welcome to the family,' I said.

'Nowhere I'd rather be,' he replied.

CHAPTER 22

Betty and I had finally found our strengths and had the staff to cover our weaknesses. I designed clothes. It was all I'd ever wanted to do – I was rubbish at sewing and there wasn't time anyway. Alongside the dozens of commissions that 1950 brought, we launched a summer collection of evening gowns and accessories. That year I was mad about embroidery, and would draw elaborate designs that I'm sure my seamstresses rolled their eyes at behind my back. Betty discovered a drive and temperament for business and planning. I was ambitious, but too dreamy and caught up in drawing. She listened to my ambitions and made them into realities. By the end of that year we had small but respectable Magg collections in the Grace Bros store on Broadway in Sydney and Betty was already looking at plans to open our own boutique up there. Betty was savvy too about how we built our market. She knew that the two of us, as the faces of Magg, had resources beyond simply designing and manufacturing clothes. Betty and Roy were socialites – they knew many wealthy people. She once confided to me that for every rich male client Roy acquired, she would ask to meet his wife or daughters and persuade them to come visit us at Magg. I had my own, overlapping but different social circles. She did not let a single opportunity pass to remind people that my husband was a minister in the Australian government and she encouraged me to do what I had found so difficult – bring my two personas together and make them work for Magg. Fashion designer and parliamentary wife. Whenever I was asked to speak as Mrs Holt, I mentioned fashion and how important it was to me and to women. To feel and look beautiful, to accept our flaws, to present our best faces to the world. And whenever I was asked to speak as Magg's head of design, I talked about the joys of public life, of being married to a man who was committed to making a difference in the world. Because I loved speaking about women, especially women in business, I was invited to speak on more occasions than I could say yes to.

When Magg was invited to contribute to the 1951 spring fashion parade at David Jones, we were thrilled. When we discovered Dior were also sending garments for the same parade – original designs that would not have even been shown yet in Paris – we drank champagne from teacups in the kitchen of our workroom.

I couldn't remember a time when I was happier than when I designed that wardrobe. I was invited to contribute seven pieces, so I decided three would be ball gowns, three would be elevated day wear and one would be a bridal gown. All of them fashioned from miles of silks and satins and wool and taffeta . . . all of the fabrics that had been rationed until so recently but were now available. It would be a riot of folds and pleats and utterly *decadent* yardage.

In the morning, while Harry and I drank our tea or coffee in the thin dawn light, I sketched. All day at work, outside fittings and meetings, I sketched. While waiting for Nicky to finish cricket practice or outside the twins' piano lessons, I sketched. I sketched ball gowns with pleated trains in plains and patterns, sometimes both at once. I sketched high-waisted trousers and blouses with wide embroidered collars. I sketched jackets with fur, with satin, with ribbons and bows. And I drew sketch after sketch after sketch of immense and complicated bridal gowns, with layers of satin and lace billowing from tiny embroidered waistlines. So many of my sketches I gave up on before they were complete. I don't know what I was following a sense of, I just knew that when it was right, it was *right*.

I felt a clunk in my chest as though something heavy and smooth had fallen into place, and then I would show it to Betty. She sometimes vetoed them as being ridiculously lavish, but more often than not she would respond with an enthusiastic 'Yes!' and we'd start the process of sourcing the material, breaking down the design into patterns for the seamstresses, and finding the right shoes and other accessories for the final looks.

The show was in March and we started nine months ahead of time. We worked on ten items for the collection (we would have to make the painful decision about which three not to include) around our other work, which was significant. Women were beginning to think about outfits ahead of the racing season and then the party season. Betty and I had days when we barely spoke to each other beyond a nod and a 'good morning', before she started work on the telephone and I started work in the workroom. I returned home exhausted but so happy.

Really, having a member of parliament for a husband suited me. He couldn't accuse me of ignoring him because he was so rarely there, either away travelling, sitting in Canberra, or up late at night in his study. When he was home, he always took an interest in what I was drawing, though sometimes it felt like the same amount of interest he might take in one of Sam or Andy's science experiments for school. *Oh, look at that. Aren't you clever?* I understood he was busy and distracted and didn't take it to heart.

One Saturday afternoon he came to find me at the kitchen table with my sketchbooks and sat down beside me.

It took me a moment to notice, I was so lost in my work. An afternoon sunbeam fell across the table and I could hear the boys in the garden playing tag. Tiny had gone away for the weekend with her sister so I was pleased they were entertaining themselves. I glanced up, saw Harry's serious face and my heart quickened. 'What is it?' I asked.

'Nothing bad,' he said with a slight smile. 'But I have to go away again.'

'You're always away.'

'Overseas – Holland, among other places on the way.'

My heart dropped. 'Oh. Will you be gone long?'

He shifted in his seat and didn't answer immediately.

'Harry? What is it?'

'After the last trip . . . I missed you a lot, and Jonathan brought his wife Valerie, at his own expense of course, but I saw how good it was to have a woman there in some of those situations. Dinners and meetings with dignitaries. I put it to Cabinet that any overseas travel of long duration should include our wives.'

I felt a dozen emotions at once. Tenderness, excitement, worry about the children.

'Would you like to come to Holland with me?'

'And leave the boys behind?' I had to say it. As much as I adored that he missed me so much he had asked the Australian government to pay for me to accompany him, I adored my sons too. I nearly said, *What about the shop?* but wisely held that in.

He put his hand over mine. 'By then, they will all be teenagers or close enough. At that age, I was away in boarding school. Tiny will stay with them . . . I've already spoken to her about it.'

I remembered now how Tiny had had trouble meeting my eye as I'd breezily bade her goodbye that morning. She knew something I didn't, and she felt guilty about it.

As I was trying to imagine it, the boys being here with Tiny and not me, Harry interrupted.

'Zara, I'm not really *asking* you,' he said, lightly, but I heard his meaning.

'I'm to say yes, no matter what I want?'

'I hope that you'll come to see it as an adventure for the two of us. Some time just to be Zara and Harry, not parents. And I need you. I'm to meet Queen Juliana of Holland about our migrant program, and from everything I've heard . . . she will respond well to me having my wife with me.'

I nodded, still not sure how I felt but curious about the idea of meeting an actual queen. 'And when will we go?'

Here he winced, and I knew – *I knew* – it would clash with the spring fashion parade.

'No, no,' I said softly. 'Harry, really?' I gestured around at the sketches. 'We've worked so hard. I have to be there.'

'Betty will be there. You're not the only person who works at Magg.'

'I don't *work at* Magg, Harry. I own it. It's my business, and this will be one of the most important weeks of my career.'

He fell into silence, and in that refusal to engage I knew my fate was sealed. I had agreed to this years ago, when we married and I first spoke to him about the possibility of running a business. I had agreed then, and I couldn't go back on my agreement now.

'Try to see it as a good thing,' Harry said, standing and patting my shoulder firmly. 'I know I'm looking forward to it.'

He left, and I remained gazing down at my drawings, wrestling with the desire to run after him and ask 'just this once' to sit at home and wait for him. But there would always be something. The way Magg was growing, there would always be something to miss while on a long trip away overseas. I resigned myself to my fate.

––––––

It was midmorning in The Hague, where Harry and I were staying at Hotel Des Indes. The receptionist had told us the hotel was built in the nineteenth century, and on seeing our room Harry had joked that it looked like it hadn't been updated since then. I didn't mind. It was a grand old building and I could easily imagine how glamorous it was in its heyday. Harry sat in a velvet chair under a fringed lampshade, drinking the tea they had brought us ('Too weak,' he complained) and reading a brief. But I couldn't settle. I walked from the window to the mirror to check my hair and lipstick, to the armchairs to pick up and sip my tea, and then around again. Waiting for the phone to ring. Because while it was a beautiful bright morning in The Hague, back in Sydney it was evening and the spring fashion parade had finished half an hour ago, and Betty still hadn't called.

'Pacing won't help,' Harry said drily.

'Neither will sitting still.'

He laid his paperwork aside and rose to join me, grasping me by the waist to stop me moving and silencing my protests with a kiss. 'Sit down and drink some tea,' he said.

'If she doesn't call soon, we'll be gone.'

'The car isn't coming for another twenty minutes. It will be fine. Sit down.' He led me to one of the velvet chairs, gently settled me into it, then handed me my teacup. At that very instant the telephone rang.

I leapt up, teacup clattering aside, and had scooped up the receiver in seconds.

'Betty?'

The operator spoke first, telling me in a thick accent that I had a call from Australia. Then she was off the line and Betty was wildly enthusing. 'It went *soooooo* well, and there were *soooooo* many famous people there, and your bridal gown got an encore.'

I let out a little squeal of delight, but I felt an actual pang for the fact I hadn't been there, listening to that applause, seeing those shining faces.

'Look I can't talk for long,' Betty said. 'There's a party now and I'm going to make friends with every woman who looks as though they have money. I so wish you could have been here, Zara. It was simply incredible.'

'Thank you for letting me know,' I said, but she had already hung up. I replaced the receiver in its cradle and turned to Harry. My face told him all he needed to know.

'Clever girl,' he said. 'Come and sit on my knee.'

I did a silly pirouette over to him and landed in his lap, where he stroked my thigh softly, then slid up the hem and found the soft flesh above my stockings. 'How much time did I say we have before the car comes?' he asked.

'Harry, really?'

He had been like this since the moment we'd said our tearful goodbyes to the boys. We had slipped into a two-person bubble that we hadn't really had the luxury to experience before. While our actual honeymoon had been short, and frankly a bit of a disaster with the plane delays and hotel mix-ups, the ship journey felt like the real honeymoon. Yes, Harry woke every morning at his usual ridiculous hour to spend his time reading and thinking, but I often woke with him or just after him, and so we had tea together in bed and I read a novel while he worked. We had time together every day to talk and dream and reminisce, and neither of us were too exhausted in the evening to strip each other slowly and make love by the soft lamplight in our cabin. The stops along the way were busy for Harry but not for me, so I wandered markets in Java, Colombo and Zanzibar, resisting buying knick-knacks that I'd have to lug around with me for weeks, but buying swatches of fabrics in exotic prints that caught my attention. It was a blissful few weeks, and sparked many conversations about us having some kind of getaway place – just for Harry and me – so we could enjoy each other's company this way more often.

Now we were in Europe and the fateful day had finally arrived: Harry's meeting with Queen Juliana of Holland. Today there would be no wandering in marketplaces for me.

The car was waiting for us outside the round porte cochère of the hotel for the long drive out to Soestdijk Palace, where the Queen lived and worked. We slid into the long back seat. Harry, who could read anywhere, immediately set about working through some papers.

I couldn't read in a car without growing nauseated, so I watched out the window as the city turned to countryside, to pastures and to woodlands and tiny villages and . . . windmills! I had always thought of windmills when I thought of Holland, but to see them standing over farmhouses and fields of flowers felt utterly magical, like a storybook come to life.

Eventually, we came to a huge set of gates that two footmen opened for us, and it put me in mind of a Georgette Heyer novel where rich people lived in grand houses that swarmed with staff. By my life wasn't a novel, even if it felt like one today. I *really* had designed a collection for a national fashion parade. And I was *really* about to meet a queen, in a palace.

The car took us straight up a long driveway, from where we could see the facade of the palace – a glorious tall white building with wings extending out and curving away on either side, and so many windows that the first thing I thought was, *I would not want to clean all of those.* But then I remembered the swarm of staff. I felt so lucky to have Tiny to help me with the housework, but took a brief few moments to imagine never having to pick up another person's socks ever again.

We were greeted by a handsome young man in a suit with a military sash and brought to the huge front entrance and down a hall to an anteroom. Our hats and coats were taken and bustled away to be hung somewhere. A smell of lemon and wax hung in the air as though everything had just been polished. The anteroom made me goggle. Elaborate moulded cornices drew my eye up to a painted ceiling frieze of cherubs playing among clouds. A heavy crystal chandelier hung from the centre of it.

'Impressive, isn't it?' Harry said.

'You've been here before?'

'No, but it's not the first palace I've been in. I wish I could take a photograph of your face.'

I smiled, and he smiled back. That boyishness. Those eyelashes. 'I'm nervous,' I said.

'Be yourself,' he replied. 'There's a reason I wanted to bring you.'

The door opened and a further two gentlemen came in. One was dressed in a grey business suit, and he clearly knew Harry and immediately began chatting to him about . . . oh, I oughtn't pretend to know. Something about immigration policy. The other gentleman, who was perhaps ten years older than me and already quite bald, engaged me on shallower topics. How was the car ride here? Did I think the weather would turn? They led us, talking all the way, down a long carpeted hallway and then opened a door.

'The Elephant Room,' Harry's companion announced. 'Her Majesty won't be far off.'

We found ourselves in a sizeable but not ostentatious room, with a large oak desk utterly heaving with disorganised papers, and a long sofa and matching chairs by a fire. A huge window looked out onto a terrace and down a long straight row of beech trees that led into a wood.

'Why is it called the Elephant Room?' I asked, having scanned the room and found no evidence of elephant statues, paintings or wallpapers.

My bald companion pointed to the rug beneath my feet. 'A gift from King George.'

I studied the rug but the patterns on it were abstract, and I could not make out the shape of any elephants until I turned my head and squinted a bit, then said, 'Oh, now I see the elephants!'

This was the precise moment the Queen walked in.

I knew she was the same age as me, and our hair was almost precisely the same shade of dark brown. But she was a striking woman, with hooded eyes and a very high forehead.

I don't know what I'd expected her to wear – a ball gown and a crown perhaps? – but she was in a pale blue linen dress with a deep V-collared neckline, short loose sleeves and a sapphire brooch.

A flurry of introductions followed, and the five of us made our way to the long couch and two armchairs. I felt quite left out of the conversation at first, but didn't mind at all as I was not particularly interested in politics. I took the time to observe the painting over the fireplace and admire the candelabra wheel that hung above us. After about half an hour, a trio of maids came in with a rolling cart and served us coffee and sandwiches, and that opened up the less formal part of the engagement.

'I have heard that you are a fashion designer, Mrs Holt,' the Queen said to me.

'Yes, in fact just this morning – tonight in Australia – we had our first national show. And we were a hit.' I was too excited to pretend to be humble.

Juliana smiled widely. 'I adore fashion. I was at Paris Fashion Week a month ago, and the Jacques Fath ball gowns were divine.'

'I love his work! As though he's defiant about the return to luxury and indulgence after all the rationing.'

We talked a little longer about clothes, and then about children – she had four daughters, two around my boys' age and two still very young – and finally Harry chimed in. 'Zara, why don't you tell Her Royal Highness about Willem?'

I turned to him, puzzled. 'Willem? The fellow who painted our house?'

'Yes. He was Dutch, remember.'

'Oh yes.' Still curious about where Harry was going with this, I was comfortable enough now with Juliana to prattle on. 'He was absolutely lovely and a delight to have painting our house, but do you know he wasn't a house painter at all. He was a scientist of some kind.'

'A chemical engineer,' Harry supplied.

'I'm afraid I don't know a lot about science,' I continued. 'But he had designed this very clever scientific object, like a still, that he believed would revolutionise the way we manufactured chemicals.

I'm afraid I can't tell you more than that. In any case, he wasn't allowed to bring it with him, and he was only allowed to bring forty pounds of cash. So this incredibly accomplished man slept in the park for five nights with his suitcase tied to his wrist until he found a job as a painter, and when we met him he'd been doing that for nearly two years.'

Juliana looked confused. 'So why wouldn't the Australian government let him bring his invention in?'

Harry cleared his throat. 'Your government wouldn't, ma'am. You have very strict rules about what your citizens can take out of the country. Forty pounds and no tools of trade. It makes it hard for us to attract skilled migrants.'

Juliana looked to my bald friend. 'Is this true, Jacob?'

'We do have quite a strict policy, Your Majesty,' Jacob replied. 'Would you like me to find the documents for you?'

'Have them on my desk by 9 am. He was sleeping in a park, you say? I can't bear the thought. One of our brightest fellows.'

'Yes, he did have it quite rough. Lovely fellow though. Worked so hard.' I helped myself to a ribbon sandwich, and let the conversation swing away from me to the details about immigration policy and the like, but a light bump on my leg and a wink from Harry told me I'd done what I needed to do.

The men all went outside after the meal to smoke cigarettes and the Queen and I were left sitting on the couch. Chatting to her was just as easy as chatting to any of the socialite ladies I met and we hit it off very well despite our different stations in life. I could see the men talking and comparing briefing notes on the terrace, and I sighed and said, 'Do you sometimes bore of all the politics?'

'I never bore of politics.' She laughed, 'But I admit I do despise social events where one must make small talk with all kinds of posh ninnies.'

I laughed at her choice of words. 'I think I know what you mean. Showing interest in things that are simply . . . not interesting.'

'After a few years in this role, Zara, it's possible for me to be standing at a ball, saying "how interesting" in nine different languages, while being asleep with my eyes open.'

We laughed together conspiratorially, then something caught my eye out on the terrace. One of the maids had joined the men outside to offer them top-ups for their coffees. She was in her twenties, attractive and blonde, and Harry was eyeing her with a look of such sexual hunger it almost made me gasp. My husband, a man of forty-two years, leering at a young and powerless woman. But then the look was gone, and he was smiling politely and holding out his coffee cup, and I wondered if I'd imagined it.

I returned to my conversation with Juliana, but it took the shine off my day. I didn't feel triumphant anymore – the successful fashion designer who converses with European royalty. I felt a frumpy, silly woman who probably talked too much.

Only Harry was able to make me feel so desirable one moment, and so utterly abject the next.

———

Four days later I received a telegram from Betty:

ORDERS COMING IN STOP TOO MANY STOP AGREE TO HIRE THREE NEW SEAMSTRESSES?

I sent back a one-word reply: *YES*

CHAPTER 23

'So you met a real queen?'

'Yes, a real queen. Betty, stand still.' Betty had an engagement party to attend, and I'd created her a cherry-red evening gown. While I was trying to pin the hem, she was reaching for the morning mail from the inbox on the counter. 'One thing at a time.'

'I've become addicted to opening the mail and seeing the orders.' Betty laughed, picking open an envelope. 'Though it's slowed down now, thank god. It's been a struggle to keep up. Zara, we doubled sales three months in a row this year.'

'There,' I said, 'pinned.'

'Lovely,' she replied. 'I'll run it up to the workroom so somebody can sew it for me.'

'About that,' I said. 'I'd like to invest some of what we've made. It makes no sense not to have a sizeable ready-to-wear collection here, if we have them in department stores in Sydney.'

'I don't want the place to look crowded,' she said. 'You know this. We've talked about it before.'

'Yes, yes, so we move the workroom offsite and refit the whole place. Have ready-to-wear down here for off-the-street browsers, and our couture upstairs. And maybe . . . freshen up the decor while we're at it?'

I glanced around the room, and already my imagination was flaring into life. Brass racks with a rich froth of skirts swaying below them. A glass counter wide enough for clients to sign their cheques on, maybe with jewellery inside on velvet display trays. And upstairs, mirrored walls. Velvet. A chaise longue with marble side tables. And all the noise and chaos of the workroom offsite – walking distance, of course, as I needed the workroom to ensure my designs would hold together as harmoniously in real life as they did in my imagination.

'You think we can afford it?'

'You said it yourself. Business doubled, three times, since the fashion show.'

'Our outgoings have gone up too.'

'You tell me. Is there a large-enough margin?'

She began to circle the room, barefoot in her cherry-red gown, slim as she ever was despite having had a baby within the last year. 'New wallpaper. Accessory cabinets. We'll make it so inviting that people will want to come in and never leave.' She turned. 'Yes, there's a large-enough margin, but should we talk to Roy and Harry? They might prefer the extra money come into our households.'

I paused, then shook my head. 'They've both made it clear it's our business and they're not all that interested in what we do. Harry made me leave it behind for two months! No. This is a business decision. *Our* decision.' I walked up to her and put my arms around her waist. 'Let's have the most beautiful boutique in Melbourne.' I paused, smiling. 'And from there, the most beautiful boutique in Sydney.'

'You're on.'

The next few months were chaos. We ended up with six society weddings to design for, which meant bridal gowns, bridesmaid gowns, mother-of-the bride gowns and going-away outfits for six different groups of people, all of whom had their own . . . let's call them *quirks*. I don't know how many times I had to explain to women that style did not mean wearing what everyone else was wearing – it meant borrowing and combining elements that suited them. I had dressed women for so long that I came to understand that every single female body was subtly different. There were the large-breasted with no hips. The small-breasted with short legs. The hourglasses and the triangles. The rectangles and the apples. No two of them were the same. I had learned so many tricks about seams, bias cuts, boning, asymmetry and balance that I could size up a woman and come up with three designs for wedding gowns in my head in seconds. I would talk through them with the bride, who was nearly always already convinced that she wanted a nipped waist, long sleeves and a lacy overlay with a Peter Pan collar like Elizabeth Taylor in *Father of the Bride*. Most could be convinced to entertain the idea of something different, but some could not, and I did design quite a few that I wasn't entirely comfortable putting Magg's name on. But I was often given more creative freedom with the other bridal-party gowns. I liked to imagine the set as they might look in a painting, thinking about colours and composition and how it all fit together as one perfect romantic tableau. A lot of work for dresses that were usually only worn once.

The important thing was that we had attracted a socialite set. Our clientele had always been Melbourne's exclusive ladies, mostly sourced from our own networks, but we discovered there were many more exclusive ladies in Melbourne than we knew. Sometimes a woman would come in with teenage daughters to dress them for balls, and then we had a new generation of clients growing up in Magg gowns.

While all this was happening though, we had to move all the sewing machines around the corner to a new workroom site, redecorating was happening upstairs, and as soon as that was finished, we moved everything up there so downstairs could also be redecorated. Added to this, we were getting our ready-to-wear collection manufactured, which meant more staff, more sewing machines and a lot of walking back and forth between the store and the workroom. I swear I never made that walk a single time in dry weather. It was a particularly rainy winter, and I eventually tired of ruining my shoes and bought a pair of gumboots for the journey there and back.

The busy-ness impacted every moment of my day. In the morning I'd wake up with a jolt, anxiety already tingling in my fingers and toes. Harry would be sitting up, reading his paperwork, and he'd reach over and pat my head and tell me I was working too hard. I'd be out the door by seven while the boys were still having breakfast with Tiny, and back in the door at seven, just as everyone sat down for dinner. One night I went to my bedroom to take off my shoes before dinner, only to wake up the next morning still in my shoes, Harry smiling down at me fondly.

'Do you need to hire somebody else to help you?' he asked for the dozenth time.

'I am Magg's designer,' I said. 'I'm the one who isn't replaceable. Even Betty will tell you that.'

'Well, you're my wife too. And you're irreplaceable in that regard. Don't forget about us.'

I simply never stopped thinking about the store, whether it was the designs, my ability to make enough time to consult with clients, the way the gold velvet curtains were hanging over the shop window or that damp walk between store and workroom to pin and drape and experiment. My poor sons had no luck at all getting my attention because I couldn't dress them up in gowns in my imagination, which was what I did with every woman I encountered, especially the boring ones at cocktail parties. I was obsessed, and it made me tired and anxious sometimes, and other times filled me with a sweet, feverish euphoria.

By September it was all settled. We celebrated the opening of the newly redecorated boutique with a small summer fashion show, and all the papers were there, as were dozens of the wealthiest women in Melbourne and their incredibly powerful husbands. Harry was there too, of course, shaking hands and making himself known to all. Even the boys came, dressed tidily and with their hair creamed down, and under the strictest orders to behave like gentlemen and not the rowdy teenagers they usually were.

After the show, the champagne flowed and the men spilled out onto the street to smoke cigarettes as I refused to let anyone smoke inside and ruin the smell of the clothes. Betty and I circulated, chatting to journalists and socialites alike, always keeping an eye on each other to make sure neither of us was stuck in an unpleasant conversation or had run out of champagne.

It grew close and hot inside, so as the crowd began to dissipate I went out to find Harry. He was talking with Roy and another gentleman I didn't know, and a tall blonde woman who was standing far too close to Harry for my liking.

'Ah, here she is. The woman of the hour!' Harry said, spreading out his left arm for me to tuck myself into. He kissed the top of my head. 'So proud of you, darling. Where are the boys?'

'They found some old receipt books upstairs and are drawing comics on the blank pages. You can take them home if you like. I can catch a taxi afterwards when everyone's gone.'

'No, no. I'll wait.'

The blonde woman leaned across and extended her hand. 'Zara, I'm Ellen Milton. I love what you do.'

I took her fingers briefly, then she pulled them away like a slippery fish.

'Ellen is Victor's wife,' Harry offered as an explanation, gesturing to the gentleman I didn't know. 'He's a client at the law firm.'

'Harry has not stopped talking about how clever you are,' Ellen said, but it didn't feel genuine. It felt . . . condescending. I couldn't put my finger on why. Perhaps it was the way her smile didn't quite make it to her eyes. 'I'm sure Victor has never spoken about me like that, have you, darling?'

Victor, a little round fellow in an impeccably tailored suit and waistcoat, muttered, 'Yes, well, you're not a successful business owner, Ellen.'

She pouted. 'See? You have no idea how *lucky* you are to have Harry.' Here she glanced at him sidelong, and it seemed to me that Harry pointedly did not meet her eyes. A tiny note of alarm sounded in me.

'We should get on,' Victor said.

'And I'd best find Betty and see if she needs me,' Roy said. He patted my shoulder. 'Outstanding work, Zara. I know houses better than I know dresses, but I can see imagination and good judgement in what you do. I'm proud of you too. Both of you.'

He disappeared back into the store, leaving Harry and me on the footpath.

'That Ellen . . . ?'

'Victor always brings her in with him. Honestly, I've only met her once or twice, but she seems to have . . . developed a notion for me.'

'That's very disrespectful. Right in front of me like that.' The words came out rather hotter than I'd expected them to.

'She's no threat to you, dear. Don't undermine your big achievement with such a petty reaction.'

I know he was trying to reassure me, but 'petty' was such a contemptuous word; it made me feel small.

Harry continued on, either unaware of or uncaring about the fact I felt slighted. 'So, now the reopening is all over, do I get my wife back?' As he said this, he drew me tighter against him, but I wriggled away.

'I don't say that every time you finish a parliamentary sitting. Why would you ask me that? This is my work, not a diversion from my "real" life.' I stopped myself before I reminded him that this month, I had actually out-earned him.

He let me go, but the tightness around his eyes told me he was annoyed. 'Ah well, I just meant that I missed you, but you seem determined to end the night in a bad mood, so perhaps I will take the boys home after all. See you when you come to bed. Perhaps you'll feel better by then.'

I watched him go, guts churning. I hated it when we fought, and I'd hoped we had left all the turbulence behind in our youths. I reasoned that perhaps I was tired. It had been a wild few months. I did wish that Harry understood that and could have been gentler with me, because in truth I *was* in need of a break, and perhaps even getting back into a domestic routine where life could be a little simpler for a while.

Harry was asleep when I arrived home, so I slid into bed next to him feeling sick with guilt about our tiff. It took me ages to drift off, and the next thing I knew it was morning and Harry was sitting up, working as always. The shuffle of papers. The scratch of his pen.

'Good morning,' I ventured.

'You need a break,' he said. 'I'm off to Canberra next week, but I'll organise something for the week after. Get time off from the store.'

'We can't miss Dad's birthday party.'

'We'll go a day or so after. Let me take care of it.' He kissed my cheek. 'I do love you, Zara. Don't ever doubt it.'

But it took me days to rouse myself out of my funk, which was a wretched way to spend my energy after such a brilliant night.

———

Vieve and I had taken charge of my father's seventy-seventh birthday party and we'd decided on a 'lucky seven' theme. We held it in my garden and decorated it with good-luck symbols and dozens of seven-shaped balloons, no doubt manufactured for a much younger person's celebration. Our brothers arrived early to 'help' but in fact it was their wives who ran about with us, setting up chairs and tables, making punch, frosting the two seven-shaped cakes and getting the savoury finger food in and out of the oven. Tiny was minding the boys and all their cousins, and was playing blind man's bluff under the cottonwood tree in the early dusk.

We had a moment to breathe before the guests arrived, so Vieve and I retreated to the front patio with a gin cocktail each while the others stayed in the garden to smoke and watch the children. Birds arrowed overhead on their way home to their nests across a watercolour sky.

'Cheers,' Vieve said, clinking my glass against hers. 'Haven't seen you since the big reopening last week. Are you happy with how it all went?'

'Oh yes. We had fantastic newspaper coverage. All the ladies pages had photographs and quotes from Betty and me. Even *The Age* had a tiny piece about us in the general news section. Though it didn't use our names. "Mrs Harold Holt and Mrs Roy Grounds".' That had stung – after all the work we'd done, to have our husbands take the credit. 'But it's lovely to have more people pop into the store just to browse. We hired two new salesgirls so I can concentrate on the couture upstairs.'

'So proud of you.' Vieve smiled and sipped her drink. 'Is Harry proud?'

'Yes, I think so. Some months I out-earn him, you know, though we never talk about that. My work comes second to his, and he made me promise that. But sometimes . . . it irks me.'

'Well,' Vieve said, shifting in her seat to pull her knees up beside her, 'I have some very good advice, if you'll take it.'

'Go on.'

'It was Mum who told me, actually. Don't quarrel if you can help it. But, if there must be a quarrel, make it an absolute banger. If it isn't worth shouting and throwing things, it isn't worth quarrelling about. Apparently, this is advice from Madame de Pompadour who was chief mistress to Louis XV, who as everyone knows had a slew of affairs and could have dashed off with whomever he wanted at any time. But he stuck with her for years because she didn't make things unpleasant. You want your Harry to stay. So let him win those little battles. You have Betty, you have great staff, you could have a much more casual relationship with the store. You don't need to devote hours and hours to it.'

I opened my mouth to try to explain it wasn't the time taken away from work that I begrudged Harry asking from me – it was the creative investment. The sheer joy of imagining something, which was so often suddenly interrupted by a gala or a ribbon-cutting somewhere. But then Mum and Daddy's car pulled up and I didn't feel like talking about it anymore.

Slowly the guests arrived and we showed them through to the garden. I was expecting Harry back from an afternoon engagement, but seven, then eight o'clock came and went without his return. The children were growing whiny, so we served dinner and cake and sang 'Happy Birthday'. By nine thirty, Daddy was obviously tired, so guests started to dissipate.

I was on the front patio kissing my parents goodbye when Harry's car finally pulled up. He hopped out, familiar briefcase in his hand, and strolled up to us as though it was perfectly normal for him to be home so late on an important night.

'Violet, Sydney, sorry I missed the celebration.'

He leaned in to hug Mum and I noticed she flinched in his arms, her nose wrinkling. Did he smell like cigars? Booze?

'Good evening, Harry. You missed a fabulous cake,' she said.

Daddy shook his hand. 'Sorry you couldn't make it, old chap. The busy life of a politician, eh?'

'Precisely,' Harry said. 'I'll take you both out to dinner in a few weeks to make up for it.' He slid his arm around me and that's when I smelled what my mother had smelled.

Women's perfume.

Something like shock settled on me. I managed to get through the goodbyes, the clean-up and making sure the children were in bed. When I came to our bedroom, Harry had showered and was already in bed, reading.

'All went well, then?' he asked.

I sat on the end of the bed, mute with rage.

He glanced up, puzzled. 'Zara?'

'You missed my father's birthday party and came home smelling of another woman's perfume,' I managed to spit out.

'Another woman's . . . ? Oh really, Zara. You do go on.'

'And my mother smelled it, so you made me look like a fool in front of her as well.'

'Oh, you are quite capable of making yourself look like a fool all on your own, my girl.'

I glared at him, a lump in my throat so rigid I couldn't speak.

'I was on legitimate business for my job, which, in case you've forgotten, is to serve the people of this electorate. The event brief neglected to mention that the meeting was followed by a dinner. I sat next to a woman who wore perfume so strong it made my nose itch all evening. I came home as soon as I could.'

Tears began to leak from my eyes. Relief, perhaps? Definitely some guilt at going off half-cocked. But also mistrust – was his story even real?

He leaned across and grasped my hand. 'Zara, where on earth has this come from?'

'Three times,' I choked out.

'What do you mean?'

'Three times in the last little while I've felt . . . you're looking elsewhere.'

'What were the other two times?'

'With that woman Ellen at my reopening. And with a maid at Queen Juliana's palace. You looked at her as though you wanted to eat her.'

Harry was shaking his head. 'And yet, for all your imagining, I've not touched another woman on any of those occasions.'

I fell silent. Embarrassed. The clock on my chest of drawers ticked softly in the quiet room.

'Zara, I love women. You know that. You benefit from that. I love looking at them, and that includes you. I'm intoxicated by them, and that includes you.'

'I wish you only loved looking at me,' I said, and heard my old teenage fears about his fidelity echoed in my 42-year-old voice.

He chuckled softly. 'That would be a very dull world. We're alive. We have blood in our veins. Do you mean to tell me your eye is never drawn by a handsome young man?'

I thought about it. Perhaps I had glanced passingly here and there. I didn't have the opportunities he did to meet handsome young men though, and I certainly didn't have the power and influence he had that drew women to him.

'I love you, Zara. Madly.' He reached for me and pulled me into his arms. 'You have been working too hard and trying to do too much. I have a surprise for you on the day after tomorrow. You'll need to pack for two weeks.'

'Really? Where are we going?' A little stubborn part of me didn't want to be roused out of my angry misery, but another part leaned towards the excitement.

'If I told you it wouldn't be a surprise.'

'The boys too?'

He was shaking his head. 'Tiny already knows. I talked to her before I made any plans. They'll be happy and safe with her, just as they were when we were in Europe.' He grinned his twinkling grin at me. 'We're going to take a special holiday. Just the two of us.'

CHAPTER 24

We flew all day. Three planes, all heading north. In the late afternoon, we disembarked in Cairns, and the difference between the air there and what we had left behind in Melbourne was stark. I didn't need my cardigan and scarf; it was balmy, with layers of sweet scents folded around me. It reminded me a little of India, but the humidity was gentler and welcoming.

'Cairns for a week?' I asked Harry, excited. I saw myself swimming in the sea or perhaps lying by a hotel pool.

'We're not finished travelling yet,' he said with a chuckle.

We picked up our suitcases at the bottom of the plane stairs and walked towards the road, where a rusty old green Chevrolet ute waited. A tall man climbed out and waved at us.

'Is that Johnny Busst?' I asked. Johnny was one of Harry's old university roommates, a man who seemed nothing like Harry's other friends. He was an artist and a conservationist, and last I heard he was living in a mud hut on an island off Mission Beach. 'Harry, we're not going to his island, are we?'

Harry just smiled at me and waved back to Johnny. Soon we were all exchanging embraces. Johnny was a lean, tanned man with sun-bleached hair who looked as though he hadn't shaved for a few days. He smelled like diesel oil and saltwater.

'So glad you could come to visit me and my new bride,' he said with a grin, then turned to me. 'Zara, I know you will love Allison, and she will love you.'

It was impossible not to like Johnny. He spoke as though everything he had to say was a special secret between the two of us. He helped us throw our suitcases in the tray of the ute, then we squashed into the cabin three abreast – I was in the middle – and began the long drive to Tully, where we would stay the night.

'Too late to cross to the island by the time we get down there,' he said. 'In the meantime, enjoy the view.'

I had to lean past Harry to look out the window, and was enchanted by the range of colours I could see. The road was red, the cane fields were gold and green, the hills were purpled by distance and heat haze. Trees – especially those around creeks and crossings – were deeply, rudely green and often enshrouded in flowery vines. And over the course of the three-hour drive, dusk mixed shadowy hues into the colours. My eyes feasted on it. We arrived at a hotel on the main street of Tully, with rooms booked for us upstairs. Harry and Johnny stayed downstairs in the public bar to drink and catch up, and I took a cold bath – the hot tap wasn't working – and lay down on the lumpy mattress to fall almost instantly asleep.

I woke up at dawn to the sound of birdsong. Birds I had never heard before. I left Harry sleeping and went to the window, pulled the curtain aside a little to gaze out. The house across the road looked as though nobody had lived in it for years, and a vine had wrapped it up like a birthday present, covered in yellowy-orange flowers. A sweet damp smell hung in the air. I gazed out at the trees, the birds, the mountain that seemed to rise directly at the end of the street, and then I heard Harry's voice.

'Up before me? Unheard of!'

I turned and smiled at him. Of course his briefcase was beside his bed, and of course he was reaching for it to do his hour or two of work before breakfast.

'Harry,' I said. 'Just this one morning, can you *not* work?'

'You do know who you're married to?' he asked, but he put his papers aside and patted the bed next to him. 'Come back to bed. See if you can sleep a little longer. We're heading to the island today.'

I slid into bed beside him, propped up on my elbow. 'You'll have to reassure me. He doesn't still live in a mud hut, does he?'

'He does! But "hut" is entirely the wrong word. It's a house, and he built it himself out of mudbricks. Johnny is very good at what he does. We'll be most comfortable, I promise you.'

By noon we were boarding Johnny's boat at Hull Heads, and then making our way out of the mangroves and across the sea. The day was clear and sunny, the water turquoise and teeming with life. I caught my breath when I first glimpsed Johnny's island, which was called Bedarra. It was like a painting: white sand, tall jungly hills, clear green water. Johnny brought the boat ashore and we took off our shoes and sloshed out, me getting the hem of my travelling dress wet, and took our wet feet across the sand and up the densely crowded path to Johnny's home.

His wife, Allison, who must have heard the motor on the boat, was already opening the door to greet us, and a happy Jack Russell terrier ran out and down the four front stairs to jump all over us, wagging his tail.

'Oh, don't mind Louie,' Allison said. 'He won't bite, he'll just lick you to death.'

I loved dogs, but having been so weighed down with children for years I'd never thought to adopt one. I crouched and let Louie scrabble up into my lap and lick me ferociously as I glanced up at the house. Harry was right – it was no hut. The brick walls were rough, but whitewashed. It had a covered front patio, a tin roof, louvred windows, and it stretched off in both directions, surrounded by tidy gardens.

I stood and Allison embraced me as though she had known me my whole life. 'Welcome, Zara. I've heard so much about you.

And here you are, in a travelling dress with a damp hem, and I can still see how stylish you are. So it must all be true.'

I pretended to preen like a movie star, dusting my shoulders, and Allison found this terribly funny. She was tall and lean like her husband, but dark-haired and with a slightly hooked nose that made her look birdlike. She grasped my hand and pulled me towards the house while the men managed the suitcases.

I was amazed at how much cooler the inside of the house was. It was dark too, but not unpleasantly so. Allison explained how they managed the light and the breeze with the louvres, and how even on hot days the house was pointed in the right direction to take in the afternoon wind off the sea.

'So if you're ever terribly hot,' she said, 'just wait a few hours. We only have a generator for the refrigerator so we don't run fans or have hot water, but I still think you'll be comfortable.'

Allison pushed open the door to a room with a high ceiling, cool mudbrick walls, and a large thick mattress on a high bed. 'Lots of ground clearance,' she said, 'in case of snakes. Do always check.'

I bent my neck to see under the bed. No snakes.

'We get a python or two, but we haven't had a dangerous one yet. I try to keep Louie away from them. He doesn't realise how small he is, and some of the pythons up here are . . . well, let's just say they'd have Louie for lunch and not blink.'

'I don't think snakes blink anyway,' I replied. 'No eyelids.'

'Well, you see. I've known you five minutes and already you've taught me something.' She sat on the bed companionably. 'Is it all right? Your room? You being a fashion designer and a society lady . . . I've been so worried.'

'It's perfect,' I said. 'It's so far away from Melbourne, from Canberra. It's warm and the sea looks glorious and I can't wait to swim in it.' I sat down next to her. 'How long have you and Johnny lived here?'

'We married in '49 but I only joined him last year. He wanted to have the house largely finished. He made every brick by hand.' She smiled. 'He's a remarkable man, and we are so happy. You and Harry? Have you been married long?'

'Ah, that's quite a story,' I said. 'Let's save it for when we have a few hours to fill. But we're also very happy.'

She put her hand on my knee and rubbed it, again, as though we had known each other for years. 'Two happy couples having a happy time on a happy island. Come on, let me show you the rest of the house.'

I found it astonishing that Johnny had built the place by hand. Certainly there was a rough-hewn look about the beams and the mudbricks weren't always finished smoothly – I'd already caught my jersey dress on a corner – but it was large and rambling and designed for the landscape it nestled in. Allison took me to the studio last: both she and Johnny were painters, and we were still in there chatting about form and colour when Harry and Johnny came to find us.

'We were hoping we could have some tea?' Harry asked.

'I'll get straight on it,' Allison said. 'Zara, come and learn the kitchen with me so you can help me cook this week.'

The big echoing kitchen opened out onto a back deck and a cleared area of garden about twenty feet across, then surrounded by dense foliage. Clouds had formed and it had started to rain lightly, making the day seem prematurely dark.

'Thunderstorm coming,' Allison said. As if the sky had heard her, a distant rumble of thunder sounded in the distance. 'They can be quite spectacular here.'

We made tea together and cut up a cake Allison had baked that morning, and served it in the louvred sitting room while the men smoked cigarettes. When the storm drew closer and the fat raindrops started finding their way into the house, Johnny jumped up and closed all the louvres, and lit a gas lamp in the stormy gloom.

The thunder rattled and thumped over the top of us, and the rain on the tin roof was almost deafening. It was a thrilling welcome to the tropics.

———

On the fourth night, Allison and I – now the very best of friends – decided we would organise a Hawaiian-style cookout. Neither of us had the faintest idea what we were doing, but we ran with the idea anyway. We took the boat across to the mainland, drove to Tully and picked up half a pig, then spent the rest of the day digging a fire pit and burying the meat in it to cook in the embers. In the evening, we made coconut pudding while drinking a little too much white wine. Johnny had taken Harry spearfishing, which I was terribly worried about as Allison warned me there could be both sharks *and* crocodiles in the water up here. I was most relieved when I heard their voices on the front patio, even if Harry was disappointed he had caught nothing.

I don't think I can express how unutterably *happy* I was to be there. Usually, being away from my sons was challenging for me, but perhaps that's because I usually didn't want to be where Harry took me for work. This was play. Swimming in the sea every morning. Harry could swim for miles and not tire of it; he was half-fish. Allison and I drinking wine in the garden every afternoon and drawing companionably beside each other. The whole mad idea for the luau. The giggly fun Harry and I had naked every night with the louvres open and the sounds of the night and the sea surrounding us.

Around seven, when dark was falling and dozens and dozens of fruit bats were making their way overhead, Allison dug up some of the pork and tried it. Fall-apart moist and delicious. We heaped our plates with it, and with the potatoes and peas I had prepared in the kitchen over the kerosene burner, and sat out at the big long table in the garden under the stars. I had decorated it with pineapples and flowery vines wound around candle holders. The smells of the food and fragrant flowers filled the air, and we ate and we drank, and we talked about art and trees and food and flowers and every little thing under the stars.

As Allison and I were clearing away the plates, Harry asked about dessert.

'Coconut pudding,' I said, reaching down to pat his belly, which had grown a little rounder of late.

'I have a better idea,' Johnny said. 'Wait here.'

Allison gave me a sidelong glance, a smile and a slight raise of eyebrows. I wasn't sure what she meant by it. 'Let me take these,' she said, relieving me of my load of dishes. 'I can soak them overnight and we'll clean up in the morning.'

I sat down in Harry's lap, gazing up at the stars. 'I wonder what could be better than coconut pudding,' I said.

Then Johnny came back and sat with us, pulled his chair in close. He placed a palm-sized tin on the table and flicked it open. Inside were two cigarettes.

'I don't smoke anymore,' I said.

'These aren't ordinary cigarettes,' he said. 'These are *cigares de joy*. I got them in the Philippines. Want to try?'

Harry picked one up and smelled it. 'What kind of joy are we talking about here?'

'The kind that's now illegal in every state but Tasmania, Minister Holt,' Johnny said with a laugh. 'But your secret will be safe with us.'

Allison had joined us. 'Oh, Zara, you must try it. If you think you enjoy colours and shapes now, you can't even imagine what you will see once you've tried a little of this.'

I exchanged glances with Harry. In Melbourne, not in a million years would either of us try marijuana. But here on the island, so far from the world, it seemed anything was permissible.

'All right,' Harry said. 'Show us.'

Johnny laughed and reached for the first cigarette. He lit it, showed Harry how to inhale it and hold it, then release it. I followed the same instructions, coughing like a fool as it was so harsh on my throat. Allison was next and then we all took another puff and Johnny gently stubbed out the cigarette on the end of the table, and enclosed it back in its tin.

'What now?' I asked.

'We put on a show!' Allison joked, but then her face grew serious. 'Oh, but what if we do put on a show for the boys? Can you sing, Zara? Come with me, let's find ourselves some silly costumes.'

I didn't feel any different, and it wasn't unusual for Allison to suggest something a bit wild, so I followed her to her bedroom and we started going through her drawers for things a cabaret performer might wear. I found a pair of bloomers – honestly, I don't know what they were or why Allison had them – but they were black and frilly and when I put them on they came midway down my thighs. Something about the frills made me giggle.

'Why are you giggling?'

'The frills. Don't they seem so funny to you?'

'Yes!' Allison agreed enthusiastically. 'You're right. There is something brilliantly funny about frills.'

We laughed about that for a little while as we sorted through Allison's clothes and pulled together cabaret outfits. Me in frilly knickers, a crimson shirt, and a yard of ribbon wrapped around me a few times to hold it all in. Allison in a voluminous half-petticoat and a bra that she quickly pinned a necklace of shells to. It felt as though we'd been gone only minutes, but when we returned, the boys were enjoying the next *cigar de joy* and told us we'd been missing for over an hour.

'We shall make it up to you!' I declared. 'For we have a show unlike any you have ever seen!' I gestured dramatically, then turned to Allison and said, 'What is our show?'

She descended into a fit of giggles. 'I hadn't even thought about what we would do.'

'Then I shall sing and you shall dance,' I declared. I wasn't naturally musical, though I had taken piano lessons all throughout my childhood. I launched straight into the first letter of '"A" You're Adorable', and the joy of it surprised me. I couldn't help myself hamming it up, sidling over to the boys and sitting on Harry's lap to stroke his cheek. Allison kept up her part by dancing along in something that looked like a cross between a hula and a foxtrot. Back, back, side, close, swaying her hips from side to side while making waves with her arms. All of it so terribly, terribly *funny*, but by the end of it I was *dying* for the coconut pudding, so I fetched it and four spoons, and we walked down the path to the beach to eat it on the sand.

'You can see so many more stars here,' I said.

'You already said that,' Harry replied.

'Did I? Well, it's true.'

'This is the best coconut pudding I have ever tasted,' Allison said.

We grew quiet, staring up in awe at the sky. I felt myself to be so small, and yet not insignificant. I felt as though I had found my place in the order of things, eating coconut pudding on a beach with friends.

'You know what we all are?' I said. 'We are humans, doing human things. Does that not make you feel so tender towards us?'

'Utterly so,' Johnny said. 'And tender towards the world that holds us.' He gestured around. 'To this beauty we are so privileged to witness.'

The breeze rattled the palms, laden with salt and ozone. I could smell every molecule. 'Do I feel this way because of the marijuana?' I asked.

'You feel this way because you're an artist, and a good person,' Allison said, taking my hand. 'Humankind has been seeking altered states since we were cavemen. Welcome to humankind.'

For some reason this struck me as funny, and I was off giggling again.

'Does everything feel better in this altered state?' Harry asked.

'Everything,' Johnny said. 'All of it. There's a rightness to things.'

Harry stood, brushed sand off his trousers and reached for my hand. 'Come on, Zara.'

Allison laughed. 'Goodnight, you two.'

I let Harry lead me to bed.

———

The next morning a boat landed on the beach and brought Harry some paperwork. I was so annoyed by this, especially after our incredible evening the night before. I thought I could have a few more days without having to watch him work. Allison distracted me with a tour around her gardens, and then a morning making a frittata for lunch with eggs collected from their chicken run down the side of the house. Harry emerged from our bedroom where he had been working at the little cane desk, but was clearly preoccupied during lunch. I watched him disappear back into the bedroom, cleaned up with Allison while Johnny went out to tend the vegetable garden, then sat at the dining table to draw with Allison.

Around two, Harry re-emerged, jolly and bright. 'All done,' he said.

'Good for you,' I said.

He came and peered over my shoulder. I was drawing dresses of course, playing around with hemlines that were long at the back and shorter at the front. 'Do you fancy getting outside in the fresh air?' he asked me.

I smiled up at him. 'I would love to. Allison, will you excuse me?'

She waved me away. 'Darling, do what you want. You're on holiday.'

I slipped on my sandals by the front door and Harry and I headed down towards the beach, clinging to the shade of the big trees.

'What was the emergency?' I asked him.

'Not worth talking about. All sorted out now.' He was watching the jungle alongside us closely. 'Johnny showed me something that I want to show you . . . I'm just trying to remember where it is. Aha!' He pointed ahead to where the outlet of a creek had carved a narrow valley in the sand. 'Up there.'

I followed him, curious. By this stage, all we wore were sarongs and sandals, and he was as brown as a berry. I tended to stay indoors more as I was more likely to turn pink. We walked down to the creek then turned to follow it in the shallow water, into the jungle.

'Is this safe?' I asked, Allison's warnings about snakes recurring to me.

'Quite safe. Probably.' He squeezed my hand. 'But very much worth it.'

We began to climb upwards, picking our way over rocks, still following the flow of the water. Here and there we passed shallow rock pools with leaves floating in them. I could hear the sound of running water nearby. Soon enough, around a bend, the trees parted to reveal a gap in the rocks where the water rushed over. Not a waterfall – nothing so grand. More like a cascade, or even a shower, wide enough for three or four people to stand under.

'Last few rocks to climb,' Harry said, taking my hand, because they really were big boulders now, then he hopped down onto a flat rock in front of the fall and helped me down.

'It's beautiful,' I said.

'Would you like to take a shower with me?'

I glanced around. 'In broad daylight?'

'There's nobody here, Zara. Johnny's nearest neighbour lives on the far northern end of the island. Johnny and Allison are back at the house. The only things in the world that can see you are the sun and the sky.' He reached for me, unpicked the knot on my sarong, then pulled it away from my body slowly and sensually. I shivered. Not because I was cold as it was such a balmy day, but because I was naked out in the wild. I slipped out of my sandals and he removed his own sarong and sandals. We folded them out of the way of the water, and stepped under. A huge blue and green butterfly skimmed past us, and I watched it with a laugh on my lips. Utterly perfect.

The water was clear, cool and gentle. Silken. In my mouth, it tasted softly of minerals. I sighed despite myself. Harry brought me into his arms and kissed me, and the water ran down our faces and into our mouths so it was as though we were drinking from each other. He ran his hands slowly over my body, caressing my curves, but it was sensual rather than sexual. We had both fallen under the enchantment of the cascading stream, the sun filtering through the leaves and rainbowing through the water, and the proximity of each other's beloved bodies.

This time, without the aid of Johnny's *cigares de joy*, I felt a great wave of wisdom roll over me. If Harry and I were here, raw and naked in nature, then the world could not get to us. The world would simply bustle and putter along without us – all the politicians and their wives and my business and the chaos of our children and the pretty socialites I worried about. None of it could reach us.

Harry would be all mine, here under the cascade.

CHAPTER 25

Back at Magg, Betty and I turned intensity and heat to building our business. I started with our ready-to-wear dresses, because they were turning over steadily but not brilliantly. I had the idea that I would design three themed collections a year, and then we could persuade the ladies pages to write about them, or even have a regular fashion parade at a hotel ballroom somewhere. Betty and I argued back and forth about the theme for our first collection, but then the King died and we decided that with a new, pretty young Queen in charge, we'd call our first collection the Coronation Collection (even though the actual coronation was over a year away). It featured whites and embroidered golds and red velvet and other things we thought looked 'queenly', and it sold very well.

The fifties were a marvellous time to be in fashion: an abundance of fabric and an abundance of creative spirit. I experimented with new materials – Swiss silk taffeta, sheer jerseys, fine shantungs – as much as classics like wool and silk chiffon. And in my drawings, at least, I placed no restrictions on myself. I drew pleated bodices, skirts that swung or skirts that clung, asymmetric hems, tiny waists, tulip shapes, trumpet sleeves, Magyar sleeves, checks, spots, bows, lace . . . I designed a whole July collection in autumn-shaded plaid wool, with buttoned straps and bows at cuffs and collars. The collections sold in our Toorak boutique but also shipped to four department stores around Australia. I did all this alongside my usual work of designing one-off pieces for wealthy socialites – the kinds of gowns that would get a photograph and a write-up in *The Argus* or *The Women's Weekly*. It was a time of immense and satisfying creativity for me.

My other job, being Harry's wife, didn't let up though. The boys were old enough and Tiny competent enough for the household to run itself, but Harry kept accruing power. He was minister for two portfolios and the chair of the Commonwealth Parliamentary Committee, so he never stopped travelling. I had to travel with him much of the time, including to New Zealand, Singapore, India, Zambia and two (or was it three?) Pacific islands. My passport acquired stamps rapidly, and I also rapidly became sick of boarding ships. But we also travelled a lot in Australia, by plane. I liked it when we met *real* people, like those at the immigration centre in Townsville who were so friendly and full of hope for their new lives in Australia.

But I grew tired of the interminable galas, with speeches about things I didn't understand or care about. I'll admit I enjoyed dressing for them, and then spending the first hour or so assessing every other woman's gown, then I would find sitting there at a table with people I didn't know so very boring. Harry seemed to thrive on it, coming home energised and working for a few hours before sleep, while I crashed the instant my head hit the pillow. Then he'd be awake before me, rustling papers, scratching his pen. He simply didn't need to rest like ordinary people did. But I needed it, and I was growing more and more exhausted.

———

Everyone was running late. The realtor, the shopfitter, even Betty. I had flown to Sydney for this meeting, inspecting a potential shop on New South Head Road at Double Bay. The location was good – Double Bay was not as expensive as Toorak but it was up-and-coming and home to quite an arty crowd. The rent was cheap on account of the store having once flooded in a rainstorm, but the water had only come over the lip of the front step, and it had the feel about it that I had dreamed of for our Sydney Magg store. High, moulded-plaster ceilings, pretty light fittings and floorboards in excellent condition.

Only I was the sole person standing there looking at all this. The realtor had let me in then dashed off to an emergency he said he'd soon return from; the shopfitter had left a message at my hotel that he might be ten or fifteen minutes late, and Betty? Who knew where she had got to? She had a million friends in Sydney and was probably right this instant having a champagne lunch with one of them and had completely lost track of time.

The problem was, I was due at the airport in ninety minutes to catch a plane to Canberra for an evening reception at the Lodge. A South African dignitary was in town, and there would be canapes, a string quartet, speeches . . . I would much rather have just sat here in my potential new shop and filled it with my imagination, but Harry expected me.

I paced about the shop, then to the door, watched a few trams rattle past. Grew indignant that I had been stood up by everyone. Grew humble as I remembered I wasn't more important than anyone else, and then finally scribbled a note to leave under the door.

We'll take it.

Out on the street, I hailed a taxi to the airport.

The day was grim and rainy, and I stared out the aeroplane window hoping that Betty agreed with my decision and the shopfitter didn't see any major impediments to a straightforward refit. I also hoped that at some stage – perhaps when the boys were finally grown men and left home? – I would somehow have enough energy to continue to manage these two demanding jobs of mine. I rested my forehead on the window. The water running down the outside created patterns – a stream with an arrangement of drops either side. It put me in mind of an embroidery pattern and I dug my sketchpad out of my handbag and drew it, knowing I would never have time to actually sew it. The pace of my life was so far beyond my control now, and such little things were the cost. Lost opportunities to simply sit and embroider. To contemplate. To take a deep breath. Only when we escaped to Johnny and Allison's, which we had only achieved on one other occasion, was there reprieve. I closed my eyes and imagined standing under the cascade with Harry. *Butterflies and sunshine.*

At the other end, I had the taxi take me to the apartment Harry rented in Canberra, a place I rarely visited. Harry was not there, as he would have gone ahead to sit and chat with Mr Menzies, his beloved mentor, who still referred to him as 'young Harry'. The place certainly lacked a woman's touch. Harry wasn't messy but he was spartan. Not a spare cushion on the couch, not a plant in a pot to be seen. I quickly changed into my gown for the evening – a blue cinch-waisted crepe dress with shoulder drapery that knotted loosely at the back – touched up my hair and make-up and pulled on my gloves. The telephone started ringing but I checked the time and ignored it. I did not want to be late.

I always found the Lodge to be such a gloomy place. The walls were panelled with darkly stained Tasmanian ash, reminding me of the setting of a Gothic novel with murder and mad sisters. But the drawing room had pastel curtains open to let the last of the afternoon sun in, and lamps blazed, and across the hallway the billiards room was equally brightly lit, and that was where the men smoked. I saw Harry, waved at him, then was subsumed by the ladies who wanted to talk to me, ask me about my gown, their gowns, fashion in general, and so on. Pattie, Mr Menzies' wife, greeted me as coolly as she ever did. There were ten years between us, and her natural reserve did not click with my ebullience in social settings. I always felt such an awkward, over-talking fool around her. In due course, we were all shepherded into the dining room, found the cards with our names on them (while glancing sidelong and hopefully at the cards next to us), and settled in for the evening of rich food and long speeches.

The dining room was barely big enough for the long table, with all of us bumping elbows around it, but I found myself engaged in good conversation with the young man next to me, who was the son of the dignitary we were here to welcome. He told wonderful stories about growing up on a farm where sometimes lions would find their way into the chicken coop, or hearing the thunder of an elephant herd in the distance.

After dessert, I went to the cloakroom to find my lipstick and touch it up. That's when I heard a woman's voice from behind me.

'Mrs Holt?'

I turned, smiling. The woman was about thirty, with wild curly blonde hair. I had seen her sitting at the other end of the table to me but not paid much attention. It took me a moment to realise she wasn't smiling back.

'I'm sorry, do we know each other?' I tried.

'I'm Corinna. I thought you should know . . .' She paused, took a deep shuddering breath, and I realised she was trying to hold back sobs.

I stepped forward, laid my hand on her shoulder. 'What is it, dear?'

'I thought you should know your husband is not faithful to you,' she said, her voice breaking a little and becoming breathy.

Cold electricity flooded me. My hand seemed frozen to her shoulder.

'And nor has he been faithful to me,' she managed, before shrugging me off and walking away.

I stood there, among the coats, lipstick still in my hand. My mind was scrambled. Up was down and down was up. Corinna had slept with Harry? And she was only one of . . . how many? Did it matter? One was too many. My stomach had started to cramp, and I dashed upstairs to the toilet and sat there and cried while my body evacuated itself. I took my time composing myself, adjusting my dress, my hair, patting mascara tears away with folded toilet paper.

Then I walked downstairs, out the front door and, in my fine evening gown, all the way back to the apartment.

———

I stripped off and stepped straight into the bath, sat in it naked and cold until it filled with scalding water. I rested my chin on my knees and tried to get my thoughts under my control, but they roamed everywhere. How it couldn't possibly be true. Could it? And if it were, what would Corinna's naked body look like compared to mine after three babies? When and where had they done it? Here in the apartment obviously, the apartment that I was partly paying for out of our joint bank account. Then the rage – the boiling, searing *injustice* of it – gripped me. Followed soon after by hideous, abject self-pity. I sat there until the water cooled, and then I heard the apartment door open.

Again, that feeling of cold electricity rocketed through me, and I realised I was terrified. Of losing him. Of losing the life we had built. Of being a single mother of three boys again.

'Zara?' I heard his keys drop on the couch.

I palmed tears off my face and hurried out of the bath, pulled my bathrobe straight over my wet body. I couldn't bear for him to see me naked at this moment. He heard the water gurgling down the plughole and pushed the bathroom door open.

'Where the dickens did you get to?'

'Here,' I said lamely.

'Yes, I see that, but . . . why would you walk out like that? You embarrassed me.'

The indignant fury fired up. '*I* embarrassed *you*?'

A look of caution crossed his face, and in that second I knew that Corinna had been telling the truth, and he had just realised she'd told me. But he held out. 'Zara? Care to explain yourself?'

'Corinna,' I managed. 'Who is she?'

'She's one of the aides in my Canberra office.'

'And you're sleeping with her?'

His eyes flickered, and I wondered if he thought about lying. 'I slept with her once,' he said, his voice quiet and guilty.

I made a noise of furious rage and pushed past him into the living room where his briefcase sat on the coffee table. I threw it onto the floor.

'Steady on, Zara.'

'Just once?' I rounded on him. 'Then why did she come to me crying?'

'The girl had a silly crush on me from the moment she started working for me. I ignored it for over a year, then . . . yes, one night I had a little too much to drink and I gave in. *She* pursued *me*. And afterwards I said, "We can't do this again, I'm married."'

I stood very still, my pulse thudding in my ears.

'Married to a woman I love very much.'

'Oh, rubbish, Harry. Rubbish. If you loved me you would keep your marriage vows. Which, I might remind you, are only a few years old.' I stepped up to him, drilled my finger into his shoulder. 'She said she wasn't the only one.'

'Well, that's just a lie.'

'Why would she say it if it was a lie?'

'For the same reason she would even speak to you about such things in the first place, Zara. She's trying to hurt me. She's angry that I'm having her transferred to a different office and she's lashing out. Believe me, I've learned my lesson.' He raised both hands, a gesture of surrender. 'You can be as angry as you like. You're entitled to be. But I'm a man, and I'm entitled to make a mistake every now and again.'

My heart wanted to believe him, that Corinna was the only one. But all the other things he'd said and done over the years and years I'd known him began to coalesce into a picture that was impossible to refute. A picture of a womaniser. I felt such a fool.

'Zara, my love, you're my wife. I'm not going anywhere. You and the boys, you're the world to me.'

On he went, but I was only half-listening. What were my options? To have a second failed marriage? To lose my society contacts in an ugly divorce? To have to take the boys out of the St Georges Road house? Oh my lord, *to give up Tiny*? I earned good money, but it was the money we earned together that made our easy and enjoyable life possible.

I raised my eyes to his, and I felt all the love I had ever felt for him. His dark, dark irises, looking at me hopefully. 'Do not,' I said with force, 'ever, *ever* fall in love with one of them.'

'Not possible, Zara, you are the only –'

'I don't want to hear romantic nonsense. Harry, you must only promise me this one thing. *Do not* fall in love with somebody other than me.' I dropped my voice. 'It would destroy me.'

'I promise you,' he said, hands reaching for mine. 'I promise, I promise. I don't want to destroy you. I want to lift you up. I want us to bring each other joy.'

I let him hold my hands for a few moments, then let them go and pointed to the couch. 'I won't sleep next to you tonight,' I said. 'Let me get my pride back.'

He seemed about to say something, perhaps more empty reassurances, then thought better of it. 'Of course,' he said. 'Sleep well.'

———

I flew home the next day and Harry stayed in Canberra on a flimsy excuse. I knew he wanted to avoid me, let my rage settle on its own. During those turbulent years of our early relationship, that tactic had always worked. But this time as I watched out the plane window, all I could wonder was if he was seeing Corinna, or another woman, and laughing at me behind my back. The wound felt fatal. How were we to be loving and easy with each other from now on? By the time Tiny brought me home in the car, I had grown very dark indeed.

The next few days I spent time with the boys, worked in the store, signed a lease on the place in Double Bay, but I was going through the motions as though I were two people, just as I had back in my youth, after the miscarriage. While I was a smiling, successful businesswoman with a loving household, I mostly felt like a tearful little girl watching her imaginary perfect life crumbling, with nothing at its centre to hold it together. And just like the last time, the feeling of being two people started to frighten me. I stood in front of a fundraising luncheon, full of women who had come to hear me talk about European fashion trends, and the sad little girl inside me watched it all in horror and dread. What was I doing up there? Whose were all those eyes trained on me? How did I think I could possibly do this without making a huge public gaffe? Somehow I got through; people even said they loved my speech. But I had to run off to the toilets shaking, heart thudding, feeling as though nothing at all was real.

The not-real feeling began to creep up on me at ordinary times too. Cutting vegetables. Hosing the garden. Making the bed. Every time it happened, my heart would pound and I'd wonder if I would die. I'd lie down with my eyes closed and listen to myself breathe until it passed. I rang Harry in Canberra and said he had to come home as soon as possible as I was really unwell.

I dreaded seeing him. I wanted to hold him so much, but I also wanted to kick his teeth down his throat. But when he arrived home, found me on my bed at three in the afternoon and took me in his arms solicitously, I cried with relief.

'What is wrong? What symptoms do you have?'

'I think it's my heart.'

'When did it start?'

'When . . .' *When you betrayed me*, I wanted to say. 'It happens when I think about the future.'

He sat back, drawing my hands into his. 'Then don't think about the future. Think about now. Here. My fingers.' He stroked my knuckles. 'The bedspread under you. Right here, right now, you're safe.'

His words made me feel better, but then I remembered what he'd done and the big wave of fear rose up again.

He must have seen it in my eyes because he repeated, 'Right here, right now, you're safe.'

I took a deep, shuddering breath and focused on his skin on mine.

'I have two pieces of news that I'd like to tell you, Zara. Nothing scary, I promise.' He smiled at me. 'Perhaps you could use the distraction.'

'Go on.'

'Your conversation with Queen Juliana? The Dutch government have eased restrictions on what immigrants can bring into Australia.'

'What does that mean?'

'By my office's calculations, about a million pounds a year for our economy.'

I couldn't help but smile. 'Really? Oh, but it wasn't just me. You all sat there and talked about policy afterwards.'

'It was the way you told the story, Zara. It was why I wanted you there.' He bent his head and made a little flourish with his hand. 'Australia thanks you.'

I giggled, and it was so strange to hear myself laugh after nearly a fortnight of dread and despair.

'The other piece of news is a little bit about the future . . . but not too far in the future.'

My chest tightened.

'Sh, sh. You'll be all right, I know, because I'm sure it will involve a beautiful new gown,' he said, stroking my hair. 'What are you doing in June next year?'

'The Sydney store will be opening at some stage, but we haven't picked a date yet.'

'Good. Keep June free. We've been invited to the coronation.'

I sat up, excitement thrumming through my body. 'Elizabeth's coronation?'

'Yes. We won't be in the fancy seats with Mr Menzies, but all of the Commonwealth Parliamentary Committee representatives are invited. There will be a special luncheon a day or so before, and then we'll be in the Abbey for the service. We going to see history made.'

I was already planning my gown when I realised that London was weeks away by ship. 'Harry, this is going to be difficult with the new shop. I can't be away for months, and we've already signed a lease.'

'That's the best part. We're flying this time.'

'Both of us? But that will cost the government a fortune!'

'You made the government a fortune, remember,' he said with a chuckle. 'And I'm not going without my wife.'

The word 'wife' felt like a smooth, beautiful stone in my hands. It anchored me in a way I hadn't been anchored in weeks. I leaned into him, dark curls resting on his shoulder, and let the tears fall.

'I am sorry I hurt you, my dear,' he said against my hair. 'So very, very sorry.'

'I forgive you,' I said, and felt his body relax against mine.

———

The sea air was welcome on a scorching late November afternoon. I sat with my sister and with Betty on the balcony of the beach cottage Roy had designed and built, hugging the cliff at Mount Eliza. Port Phillip Bay lay before us, silvery-grey under a leaden sky. A storm was surely on the way. We fanned ourselves with cane fans, and Betty poured us gin cocktails from a jug that left a condensation ring on the side table.

'It is so hot!' Betty said for perhaps the third or fourth time.

'We chose the right week to get out of the city,' Vieve said.

The escape from the city had been Betty's idea. I'd tearfully confessed to her that I wasn't coping at work or in life generally, and she had rounded up Vieve and said they were taking me away to the beach to recover.

Over the weeks, the terrible bouts of dread had abated, or at least I knew what to do when I had one. Find Harry, have him talk to me in his soothing voice. I interrupted him in his study more times than I could count, but never once did he grow impatient with me. Slowly I learned to soothe myself, to notice a detail or a sound and focus on it until the feeling passed.

But underneath it, a great weary sadness had been revealed, like a stain on a rug you don't see until you move a heavy table. That was proving more difficult to shake, and it infected every part of my life so that the thought of having to do anything at all made me tired. I still met my deadlines, helped my sons with their homework, turned up at my events, but it all made me exhausted. Some mornings, I would sleep until ten or even eleven, trying to beat the fatigue.

So here we sat, suitcases dropped and left unpacked in the cosy lounge room, hoping for a breeze.

Betty raised her glass. 'Here's to Zara's nervous breakdown for giving us an excuse to have a holiday.'

'I'm not having a nervous breakdown,' I said, though I wasn't entirely sure I was right about that. I had only heard the term in passing and it seemed to apply to much more fragile or hysterical women than me. 'And if it is, it's not my first and I recovered just fine last time.' I raised my glass anyway, as did Vieve, and we talked about our children and gossiped about our society connections for the first two gin cocktails.

By the third, Betty sensed I'd be ready to talk.

'So what brought all this on, darling? Why so tired and sad all the time?'

A welcome gust of wind rattled through the cypress trees that stood either side of the balcony. It cooled the sweat underneath my arms and breasts. 'I'm embarrassed to say.'

Vieve leaned across and placed her hand on my knee. 'I'm your sister. And Betty has been your friend for decades.'

'Yes, and nobody has done more embarrassing things than me,' Betty said in a cheerful but brittle tone.

'Harry . . . had sex with another woman.' I told them the whole story, growing tearful and feeling the hurt grow tender again.

'Oh, the bounder!' Betty declared when I'd finished, reaching for the jug to top me up. 'And you so beautiful and stylish. What an idiot. Men are so stupid.'

Vieve was more circumspect. 'Darling, are you really surprised though?'

I sighed. 'Yes he's an idiot, and no I'm not surprised. I was shocked, certainly. But no. Not surprised. I've known him years. This isn't the first time he's made me wild with jealousy.'

Vieve sipped her drink, fanning herself. Her eyes were on the horizon. 'Didn't you . . . Need I remind you that you were married to Colonel Fell when –'

'All right, all right,' I said. 'But I don't want Harry to leave me for somebody else, like I did.'

'But he's made it clear he won't,' Betty said. 'He only wanted to have a little thrill, not a whole new marriage. Zara, you're indispensable to him. He's not asking this Corinna woman to be at his side at galas and race days, is he? He's not asking her to attend the Queen's coronation with him. You're his wife, and don't think for a moment he doesn't love having a beautiful, successful and well-connected wife by his side. It's part of his grand plan. He's an ambitious politician; he's not going to throw away his reputation by running off with a pretty young lass from his office.'

I turned this all over in my mind. I knew it was true, but it didn't take the sting out of the jealousy. 'I get pictures of them in my mind,' I said.

'Your imagination has always got you in trouble,' Vieve replied. 'Here, when you get a picture of them in your mind, replace it with something else. A picture of you arriving at the coronation would be a good one. What will you wear? What will the weather be like? Who else will be there? It's terribly exciting to be part of history like that, and so much bigger and grander than where Harry put his you-know-what.'

I giggled despite myself.

'Vieve is right,' Betty said. 'You're not the first wife of a powerful man to face this, and you certainly won't be the last. Turn a blind eye.'

'But it hurts.'

'Yes, but you'll still have what you want. A few little hurts along the way aren't worth losing your mind over.'

Thunder rumbled in the distance and Betty muttered, 'Oh thank god. The heat is killing me.'

'The other thing we must talk about is how much you work, Zara,' Vieve said, and she exchanged a look with Betty that told me they had already spoken about this without me.

'It's a big year for Magg –' I started, but Betty stopped me with a shushing gesture.

'Yes, it's a big year for us,' Betty said. '*Us*. It's a joint business, and you working such long hours and refusing to hand over any of your workload makes me feel so guilty.'

'But it's not easy to delegate what I do,' I protested. 'I'm the designer.'

'There are many talented young women out there looking for an opportunity,' Betty said. 'You don't have to design every bridal party. You could draw up the wedding gown and then give notes or instructions to someone else. You can still oversee.'

'And for goodness' sake, hire somebody else to design the Double Bay boutique,' Vieve added. 'Give them a brief and let them go. I cannot bear if I have to listen to months of you deciding between apple-green and olive-green curtains. You don't have to make every decision.'

Betty threw her hands up. 'Truth!' she said.

'I like making those decisions. I like imagining things and making them happen. And I *love* drawing dresses. That's how I got into this business.'

'Then keep drawing dresses, but think of this as an opportunity to hand some of these creative decisions over to another woman who loves drawing dresses and matching curtains and so on,' Vieve said. She stood and came to crouch beside me, arm around my sweaty back. 'Darling, it's not making you happy right now. And you deserve to be happy.'

'You wouldn't be taking a step back from Magg,' Betty said. 'You'd be making room for it to grow.'

Another gust of wind, this one laden with the smell of rain. I turned my face up, letting the breeze cool me down. I felt myself at a crossroads, one I was not in any way expecting or prepared for. I had to see both my marriage and my work differently if I wanted to survive. Betty and Vieve were both right and I could see that, but it was terribly hard to let go of the life I'd imagined: complete control of the vision of Magg, a husband who didn't stray.

'Oh, here's the rain,' Betty said.

I opened my eyes and could see the rain sheet advancing over the sea. The wind picked up and the temperature rapidly dropped.

'Grab your gin, let's get inside,' Betty said, prodding me. 'You don't have to make a decision now.'

But I had. If what it took to keep myself sane was to hire a couple of up-and-coming designers, then I would. And if what it took to keep my husband was to ignore the occasional sexual indiscretion, then I would do that too.

CHAPTER 26

Seven thirty in the morning was a very strange time for Harry and me to be so finely dressed. He was in a suit with tails and a white tie; I was in a white satin embroidered evening gown and I had shown no restraint with jewellery. I sparkled at my ears, throat and wrists, and I even wore a tiara I'd borrowed from Betty.

'Ready, then?' Harry said, and I realised he was nervous or excited or both.

'I think so.'

There was a knock at our hotel door and Harry opened it. I'd assumed it would be our reminder that the driver was waiting outside the Savoy, but instead the waiter who had brought our breakfast stood there.

'It will be a long day in the Abbey,' he said. 'Many of the others going have ordered food to take with them.'

'Food?' I asked. But of course. The coronation ceremony would go for hours, right through lunch and beyond.

He held out two wrapped sandwiches and two bars of chocolate. 'Here, this should see you through.'

'Thank you, my good man,' Harry said. 'Zara, can you put these in your handbag?'

The door closed behind the waiter.

'Harry, no. I'm taking this evening bag. They won't fit. Here.' I took the packages from him and slid a sandwich into each inside pocket of his tuxedo jacket, and the chocolate bars into his pant pockets.

'We'll need something to drink too,' he said with a merry grin, and liberated his hip flask from his brief case and took it to the drinks cart to fill it with brandy.

'That can fit in my handbag,' I said, so that was what I took.

A black Rolls Royce waited for us outside in the rain, and we began the drive to Westminster Abbey. Although it was only about a mile, it took forever. So many shiny black cars carrying so many dignitaries from around the world. The streets of London were crammed with onlookers, yards and yards deep, waving flags and cheering despite the chilly, wet weather. My heart leapt from the excitement of being part of something so historic and thrilling. London had been through so much only a decade or so ago. On our walks around town, Harry and I had spotted many places that were still just piles of rubble left over from the Blitz. To see the English people so united in their love for their new young Queen made me happy. I squeezed Harry's hand and we grinned at each other.

Of all the trips we had taken together, this was my favourite so far. Flying the Kangaroo Route, as they called it, only took three days, rather than the three or four weeks aboard a ship we'd usually have to endure. We'd hopped from Melbourne to Sydney to Darwin to Singapore (where we'd stayed the night) then Calcutta, Karachi, Cairo (another overnight), then Rome and finally London. I was surprised by how comfortable and easy it was, and Harry and I spent our time on the aeroplane gazing out the window at amazing new landscapes, writing letters home or just chatting companionably. Harry was quite mad about the aeroplane, a 'Super Constellation', and told me lots of details about it. I was quite mad about the travelling dress I'd designed of beige silk jersey. I intended to have it produced in large numbers and sell it in our ready-to-wear collection;

it was so comfortable, stylish and easy to look after. The only thing wrong with it was that the belt wasn't holding its shape, so I would talk to Erna, one of our new young designers, about better belt linings for the final version.

And so we were in a happy, rosy mood when we attended the coronation. One by one, the cars ahead of us pulled up and well-dressed people emerged, hopped over puddles and entered the Abbey. Finally it was our turn, and on leaving the car I was greeted with the sweet overwhelming scent of the masses of flowers around the door. Stands had been set up all around the Abbey for the crowds of people, and more flowers lined the front of the stands too. It smelled like paradise.

Inside the Abbey was much colder than I'd expected, probably because of all the stone. We were ushered to our seats – covered in deep blue velvet to match the blue carpets rolled out across the floor – and watched (and snacked on chocolate) as the Abbey slowly filled. Seating was in tiers, some of them up very high, but we were sitting on the ground level directly across from the royal family, so there were many dukes and duchesses and so on in fabulous outfits that I feasted my eyes on. The opulence and the colours – velvets, ermine, satin gloves, scarlet trains, tiaras and collars of diamonds and rubies – kept me entertained for the very long time it took for everyone to be settled, and for the heralds to sound their trumpets.

Then the Abbey door opened and she arrived, with six maids of honour around her. I noted, of course, the white satin dress embroidered in silver and gold and sewn all over in pearls and diamonds, her long purple coat with the ermine edge and the blazing jewellery that seemed to make her glow from her head to her toes. But most of all, I noticed how young she appeared, how feminine and vulnerable. What a job she was taking on. It made my work problems seem very minor indeed. It had been straightforward to find two young designers who took direction well but had enough imagination to uphold Magg's reputation. I had reluctantly handed over the fit-out of the Double Bay store to a Sydney friend of Betty's, who did a magnificent job of interpreting my brief. So I had managed the transition with ease, and my mood had improved markedly. But this young woman could not delegate and step back in the same way *ever*. She was Queen of England, and of the Commonwealth, and such a slight young woman to have to take all that on. The moment I felt sorriest for her was when they finally placed the crown on her head and her neck seemed to bend with the weight.

I know little girls dream of being princesses and queens, but I don't think anyone would really want that much responsibility. I gave a little sigh and Harry and I passed the hip flask between us, discreetly taking a sip of brandy each. I wondered if he was having similar feelings to me, then decided not. Harry's name had been mentioned more than once as Mr Menzies' heir apparent, and from there of course he must dream of having the top job. I decided not to think about it. Being the PM's wife would be impossible alongside my business, and watching that young, fragile woman take on the weight of the world had made me feel tired.

When she finally walked down the Abbey and took her seat on the Throne of England, the organ boomed into life and we all stood and cheered and shouted, and we could hear cheering and shouting from outside too. The whole world was joyous noise, and then a huge bang sounded out, the first of twenty-one guns saluting Queen Elizabeth II.

That night, London was alive with joyous celebration. Every pub spilled out with people, and from our hotel room in The Savoy we could hear them calling and cheering and crying out 'God save the Queen!' until dawn. I slept late the next day, but Harry was up early as always, working on his papers. It was as though he were made of steel.

Tiny was rarely sick, but when she was it threw me into chaos. I never complained because I didn't want her to feel bad about taking a day off, and so it happened that one Thursday while Harry was away in Canberra, I peeled potatoes for dinner while supervising the work of three teenage boys and two young fashion designers who were at my kitchen table. Ordinarily, I'd be at Magg with the designers, but they'd been most gracious to come and join me at home. We were designing for a wedding party and, as it was a friend of Harry's getting married, I didn't want to take my eyes off the project. But also, Nicky – Nick, as he preferred to be called now – was in his final year of school and determined to qualify to study law like Harry, and Sam and Andy were not far behind. I hadn't a clue what their homework was about, but they seemed to work more efficiently if they knew I was watching them.

I sliced up the potatoes and dried my hands on my apron, and looked over for a moment while everyone worked diligently and quietly. The boys were nearly men, but I could still see their baby faces. Andy and Sam had a few spots on their chins, but otherwise seemed as liquid-eyed and soft-lipped as they always had (and they were the spitting image of Harry, but if anyone noticed they kept it to themselves). Nick had developed a seriousness around his eyebrows that I adored. He had such an expressive face and was so very clever. I found myself smiling just looking at them.

'What?' said Nick, glancing up at me.

'Nothing. Just thinking about how gorgeous and clever you three are.'

Sam rolled his eyes. Andy hid a smile.

'How about me?' This was Erna, one of my assistant designers.

I laughed. 'Oh yes, you are. Deirdre too. Here, let me see what you've done.'

I did the rounds of the table, checking everyone's work, then heard the phone ring in the hallway.

'Sam, if you're finished with your maths, can you fill the big pot with water and get it boiling?' I called behind me.

Allison Busst was calling.

'Darling, how are you?' I said. We had become close over four visits to their dream island now. There was a softness about her that made me feel calm.

'I'm so very well and also a little excited,' she replied.

'Go on.'

'First, the bad news. We're selling off Bedarra.'

'No!' My mind immediately went to standing naked under the cascade with Harry, the sunshine and the butterflies. I'd be bereft if I could never do that again.

'But hold your horses, not just yet. Over the next year or so because . . . we have bought another place on the mainland, right on the beach, and we have to build a new house. We bought acres and acres of land and, Zara, there are still acres and acres available.'

Allison knew of my desire to have a house up there. 'Really? Where is it?'

'Bingil Bay. Oh, it's delightful, Zara. Easily as beautiful as Bedarra but so much easier to get to. You must must *must* look into buying some land. It's very cheap! Shall I give you the chap's number?'

'Yes. Yes! Let me find a pen.' I scrabbled around in the drawer for a biro and some paper, and wrote down the number for a man named Charlie.

Allison explained how it all worked. 'The parcel of land includes a beach and nobody has ever owned it. It's still crown land and marked as such on all the maps, so you only need to call Charlie and he will put in an application for it to be publicly auctioned.'

'Auctioned? Then somebody else might buy it.'

'Yes, I suppose that is the risk.' I could hear a frown in Allison's voice. 'Lord knows what kind of neighbours we'd end up with. But imagine if it's you and Harry!'

I could imagine it. So easily. We could build a little house, and it would be room enough to take the boys with us, or Betty and Roy and their little girl Victoria, or Vieve or my brothers and their families . . . But most of all, I could live the fantasy of getting Harry *out*. Away from everyone. I hated the weeks he was in Canberra. I suffered stomach-aches the whole time he was away. I suspected he was seeing other women, or at least I imagined he was if I woke at 3 am. When he was home with us, or when we were away together, everything smoothed out.

It took several months, but finally the land at Bingil Bay came up for public auction. Allison's friend Charlie handled it all for me on the day, and we were the only bidders. And it was so incredibly cheap that I asked Charlie if something was wrong with the deal, or wrong with the parcel of land.

'Crocodiles,' he said cheerfully. 'Just stay out of the river and you'll be grand.'

Harry and I celebrated with champagne and made plans for a shack to be built there right on the beach. Three hundred acres of rainforest – our very own crocodile-infested paradise.

———

Once the skies opened up so ministers could travel internationally more readily, it seemed travel was all Harry and I ever did. My silk jersey travel dresses certainly saw a lot of service. I knew I should be grateful to see so many places in the world – places other people rarely go to or could never afford to go to – but I so often wanted to sit still. While Harry could fly from Melbourne to Ghana and stride off the plane and straight into a meeting, I always trailed wearily behind, forcing smiles and losing my thread in conversations. Crossing time zones barely seemed to affect him, but it hit me hard.

I endured.

The places we went in the middle years of the 1950s all started to blur together. I could only remember where we had been by remembering the frocks I wore. A white lawn shirt dress at lunch in Beirut. A marmalade-coloured chiffon evening gown at a gala in Singapore. A silk-tweed suit in Rome. A blue and white checked cotton sheath in Geneva. A beige and brown floral silk dress and coat in London. In and out of consulates and embassies, attending official parties, standing watching parades in the sun while my feet swelled, on and off naval bases, and one mad evening cocktail party in a nightclub in Bangkok where Harry and I both got so drunk I'm still not sure how we made it back to our hotel. I remembered a dancer at the party with the most incredible costume – a bodice of heavy folded silk, stiff with jewellery and gold embroidery – and I stayed up late and drew it while drunk. Reviewing it the next morning, it looked as though a child had drawn it.

Everywhere we went, I made the trip do double duty. I bought silks in Bangkok, jacquards in Seoul, chiffons in Paris, heavy cottons in Rome. And I took inspiration from everything I saw: the mad colour of bougainvillea in Singapore, or the shapes of sails on Chinese junks, or the gleam of a golden temple roof in Rangoon.

I rarely remembered names, I nearly fell asleep standing up sometimes, but I stood by Harry's side as a good wife should. He was raised up to deputy leader of the party and leader of the house, and he woke every morning at the same time, no matter how much sleep he had managed, and he worked. He worked and worked, and all I could do was watch on sleepily and long for my own bed.

I think the worst part was how boring it was for me sometimes. I would often be thrust among the other ladies, other wives in my predicament, and we chatted well enough and I was always pressed to talk about Magg (I always wore Magg designs at public events, and remained confident I was wearing the best couture in the room, except at one launch at the French embassy where everyone appeared to be wearing Dior), but I met so few kindred spirits. I could get along with anyone, but to make a dear friend seemed impossible in the situations we were in.

There were twenty men for every woman at these events, and the men simply didn't speak to us. They formed their little discussion groups and ignored us. We were decorations.

On rare occasions, Harry and I were sat together and could hold hands during long boring speeches. One of Harry's most disarming qualities was how much he derided very long and complicated official names for people's roles. They would start him chuckling softly, and if I heard him it would set me off and we would have to drive our fingernails into each other's palms to stop us from laughing. At one public address in Spain, when the host introduced a gentleman as the 'right honourable acting associate assistant to the minister undersecretary and acting deputy assistant secretary to the council of ministers', we nearly exploded trying not to give in to hysterics.

The bad days were more common, unfortunately, and the worst day was in Paris in 1957, at a luncheon of some kind, where I was the only woman apart from the French minister's secretary. I sat between the turned-away shoulders of two gentlemen, and I may as well have been completely alone. Harry sat across from me in deep conversation, ignoring me entirely. I picked at my meal guiltily – travel made me fatten up, unfortunately; it was all the rich food and the odd hours – and found myself growing angry with Harry. Why was I even here?

On the walk back to the hotel, he had the nerve to ask me how I had enjoyed the lunch.

'I didn't,' I said. We were walking across one of those gorgeous bridges over the Seine they have everywhere in Paris. The sky was grey, but the weather was warm enough that we carried our coats rather than wear them. 'Really, Harry, why do I have to be at such events if nobody there is interested in talking to me?'

'Just in case,' he said.

'Do you have any idea how boring it is for me?'

'That's the job though,' Harry said. 'Do you think I'm always having scintillating conversations? The job is smiling and making nice and creating goodwill. And that gentleman I was talking to has invited us both to the opera tonight to –'

'Harry, no. Not opera. Please, *please* don't make me endure opera! You know how impossible I find it.' My heart actually beat faster with anxiety at the idea of being stuck in an opera theatre, bored and completely lost, after having sat through that luncheon.

Harry stopped and turned to me. We had come to the end of the bridge, where a man sat in front of a cart stocked with vintage postcards for sale. He was spreading birdseed all around him and surrounded by what looked like a thousand pigeons.

'What is it?' I asked Harry, chin up in challenge.

'This is the job. Going to the opera is –'

'It's not my job. It's yours.'

'Zara . . .' A warning note in his voice.

'I don't mind attending things where there are other women, or where I can talk to somebody, or even where I can look at beautiful art. But you can't expect me to simply sit there like moss on a log in abject boredom. Don't you know what you have? A woman with spirit and humour and a wild creative brain. Why would you expect me to meekly wait, all wordless and dead inside?' I only realised I'd raised my voice when I noticed the postcard-seller turn to watch us.

Harry made a little 'hm' sound, then said, 'I see you need to cool down. I'll take the long way back and meet you at the hotel later.' With that, he gave a little nod and simply walked off back the way we'd come.

I was enraged. I wanted to chase after him and throttle him. Instead, I huffed and swore under my breath and stomped back to the hotel, walked right up to the concierge and said to him, 'I need to book a flight to Rome for this afternoon. Can you help?'

By nine in the evening, I was riding in a taxi from Rome airport to the Grand Hotel. I gazed at the street lanterns and lights in shops and restaurants as we zoomed past, but was too timid to go out by myself that night. I had left a note for Harry and I didn't care that he would be furious. Right now, he was stuck watching some interminable opera with people he barely knew, and I was sitting on a chaise that I'd pulled up to the window in my sumptuous suite, drinking champagne with ice in it, and feeling blissfully free.

CHAPTER 27

The hotel was a short walk to Via Veneto, where the rich and glam-orous sashayed in their high fashion. I strolled along it the next morning and found a cafe rich with the smell of coffee. I ate a *cornetto*, which was a half-moon-shaped pastry filled with pistachio cream. It was utterly delicious and I savoured every mouthful, washing it down with satisfyingly bitter espresso. I thought about Harry having tea and eggs on toast for breakfast, and it felt twice as decadent to be here in Rome instead.

I wandered. Stopped at the Trevi Fountain to sit and watch people. Made my way to Via del Corso to see the shops, especially the boutiques. Dodged Italian men on motor scooters. And then I approached a hairdressing salon and I paused. The hairdresser inside, a plump, dark-haired woman who was sweeping the floor, looked up and saw me through the shop door. She gave me a wide smile and beckoned me to come in, and I thought, *why not?*

Between my poor Italian and her poor English, we managed to work out what I wanted. Shorter and lighter. No more back-combing and hairpins and spray. I walked out feeling as though I would float away with my stylish new light-brown bob. I was so enamoured with myself that I stopped at a boutique and bought myself a pale pink silk Schiaparelli dress and a garnet-coloured velveteen coat.

I went back to the hotel when the day was warmest, drank more iced champagne, then decided to try the Via Veneto again at dusk.

It was infamous for bars and nightclubs, but I didn't want to enter any of them – besides, it was far too early for that. I simply wanted to soak up the atmosphere of this glittering strip of glamour and see if I could spot a movie star or two.

'Bella!' It was a man's voice, but I assumed it was not for me so kept walking.

'Bella!' he called again, and this time I heard fast footsteps approaching, so I turned and clutched my handbag a little closer to me uncertainly.

He was around my age, or perhaps a few years younger, with a thick head of black hair, silver at the temples, a square jaw and meltingly brown eyes. He spoke a long line of Italian to me and I hadn't the faintest idea what he was saying. But he didn't look as though he wanted to steal something, so I said to him in terribly pronounced Italian that I didn't understand, that I only spoke English, and he switched effortlessly to English.

'I said I haven't seen you here before and asked if you wanted a guide around town,' he said, accent thick but attractive.

I still wasn't sure if this was some kind of trick where he played the tour guide to part me from my money, so I replied, 'No, thank you.'

'Will you let me take you to dinner, then?' he asked, and finally the penny dropped. He was asking me to spend time with him. Romantically. He hadn't seen my wedding ring because I was wearing gloves.

I hesitated. I had to eat some time, and to sit in a restaurant in Rome with a handsome stranger was an attractive idea.

'You are considering it,' he said with a smile. 'Why not take the leap?'

'Yes, why not,' I blurted, regretted it instantly, but also felt the thrill of liberty. I imagined that I was single, that I was perfectly available to go to dinner with whomever I liked.

'This way, then,' he said, looping his arm through mine. 'My brother owns a restaurant just off the side street. What is your name?'

'Zara,' I said, then cursed myself for not making up a name. If I was truly free, I could be anyone: a Vanessa or an Annie. 'You?'

'Matteo,' he said. 'Zara is a pretty name. So unusual.'

'Yes, I've never met another one.'

We had turned off the street and down an alleyway, where over-grown windowboxes dripped water in the dark. But before I had a moment to wonder if he was taking me somewhere to kill me, he had pushed open the door to a dim little restaurant, lit by candles and with swirling yellow glass in the windows. Most of the tables were free, given it was still early.

'Angelo!' Matteo called, and a much older but still very thick-haired man emerged. There was much hugging and an exchange in Italian, where Angelo looked me up and down appreciatively, and honestly, I didn't know if it was the confidence my new hairstyle gave me but good lord, it felt wonderful to be admired.

Angelo led us to a secluded table, and I carefully removed my gloves so that my rose-gold wedding ring stayed inside the left one. I folded them away in my handbag. Matteo ordered us a carafe of red wine and took control of choosing the meal in Italian, then turned his attention to me.

'To meeting beautiful strangers,' he said, lifting his glass.

I tapped his glass with mine, thought about saying, *I'll drink to that*, but felt too guilty to do so. Instead, I just smiled.

'What brings you to Rome?' he asked.

I paused a moment. Some parts of the truth would do, but others I could definitely work with. 'I'm a fashion designer,' I said. 'I own one of the top three couture houses in Australia. When I travel, I look for fabrics and for inspiration. I was looking for inspiration when you called to me.'

He patted his chest above his heart. 'Ah, I knew you were no ordinary woman, just looking at you. We Italians have style. Well . . .'

He chuckled. 'Some of us do.'

'What about you?' I asked. 'What do you do for a living?'

'For a living? I work in the hospital. For my soul? I paint.'

'What kind of paintings?'

'Oils, though I love watercolours too.' He reached into his leather satchel, which he had hung on the back of the chair, and pulled out a tiny book to hand to me.

I flicked through it. The pages were stiff and swollen, but on each one was a gorgeous watercolour painting of some scene from Rome. 'I love these,' I said. 'They have so much character.'

'Ah, you make my heart glad.'

Together, we went through the little book and he told me about the places depicted, stories he had from those locations, and then asked me about my travels. We also spoke about our families – he had three daughters; I had three sons – our divorces, our dreams for the future of our creative ideas. Not once did I mention Harry – not during entree, main, dessert or with any of the four glasses of wine I consumed.

Perhaps it was all the wine, but I didn't feel even a little bit guilty. I thought of all the times Harry might have played this very game, sitting opposite somebody who openly desired him, and soaking it in. Maybe even acting on it.

Was I going to act on it?

The question threw a shock through my body and I pushed my chair back. 'I'm sorry,' I said.

'What is it, *bella*?'

'I'm so sorry. I don't . . . I can't . . .'

'You can't what?' He smiled an easy smile, indicated I should sit back down, but I knew what would happen if I sat back down. It was a version of saying yes to whatever came next, but I was a married woman, having run away from my husband in a fit of pique, and I couldn't turn a brief argument into an infidelity that would cause me remorse for years to come.

Did I want to stay and talk and wait for him to invite me home to see his paintings? Of course. Did I want his lips on mine? Without

doubt. Would Harry have shown such restraint? Unlikely. But I wasn't Harry; I was me. There was no joy in sex where there was no love. I seized my handbag and left without a word.

Matteo didn't follow me. Perhaps he did this every night. Easy come, easy go.

The next day I returned to Paris, but I refused to do it meekly. I held my head up, with my newly styled hair looking fabulous. I swept into the hotel room in my Schiaparelli dress and garnet coat, making Harry leap to his feet and grasp both my hands in abjection. I told him I refused to attend another event where there was no reason for me to be there or no other women to talk to. He told me he'd get Tony to go over invitee lists for all upcoming events and make it happen.

He also told me I looked beautiful, and raced me off to bed. Harry and I had always loved to make up.

———

When we were home in Australia, we visited John and Allison and finally went to see our own place, a very rudimentary shack overlooking the beach at Bingil Bay. The boys loved it . . . well, they were young men by that stage, and Nick had a girlfriend he brought with him from university. She adored fashion, so we hit it off famously and I promised her a job at the end of her studies.

In terms of travel, 1958 was a slightly quieter year, as Harry's roles on the Commonwealth Association and as immigration minister had come to an end. We headed north as often as we could, though Harry often brought Tony and kept working while we were away. Correspondence in the mornings. Phone calls until about two. Then he'd find Johnny and they'd go spearfishing, making me frantic with worry about sharks and crocodiles and other sea monsters. I worked on designs, drank cocktails with Allison, played cricket with the boys or read lurid novels about the scandals of long-dead kings and queens. I slept every night to the sound of the sea, my husband snoring lightly beside me, and it was a very happy year.

In November, Harry came home from Canberra one afternoon, a day earlier than expected. I had taken on the mammoth task of sorting all my design drawings into piles to keep or to throw away. Hundreds and hundreds of them had been kept in boxes in the back room at Magg, and Betty had finally said that either the boxes went or she did, as she was so tired of tripping over them. So I had them spread out across the dining table, and our home was in no fit state for a returning husband to see.

'Harry!' I exclaimed.

'This is what you get up to while I'm away,' he said, smiling. He kissed my forehead, removing his hat and dropping his briefcase. 'Sorry, I should have called you.'

'I will have this all cleared away by dinner,' I promised. I had had no plans to do so; I'd promised the boys to take them out for dinner at my parents' house so I could continue sorting drawings all night if necessary, to get the job finished.

'It's fine, it's fine. Please don't worry.' He sank into the chair at the end of the table and looked over the papers. 'How busy you have been all this time,' he said. 'You know I'm very proud of you. I'm sorry if I don't say it enough.'

'Thank you, love,' I said, but sometimes when he complimented me on his return from Canberra, I worried it was out of guilt because he'd been seeing other women. I could never fully enjoy his admiration. 'Why home early?'

'I cancelled tomorrow's meetings. I need to talk to you. I don't know if I want your advice or if I simply want you to listen.'

I nodded, reaching for his hand. 'I'm very happy to listen. And you know I won't hold back on an opinion.'

'It's not common knowledge yet . . . in fact, you will be only the fourth person to know.' He held up a warning finger. 'No gossiping.'

'I promise.'

'Arthur Fadden has spoken to Bob about retiring,' Harry said. 'And Bob has asked me if I'd consider stepping into the treasurer role. You have been a politician's wife long enough to know what that means.'

I certainly did. When a prime minister selected a treasurer, he was naming his successor. Harry would be a hair's breadth from becoming prime minister himself.

'Harry, that's enormous news. Did you say yes?'

'I said I'd think about it.'

I shook my head, astonished. 'This is all you've ever wanted, surely?'

'And yet, right when the grail is within my grasp . . .'

I tried to be practical. 'All right, then. What are your doubts?'

He rapped his knuckles on the table thoughtfully a few moments, then said, 'First, I'm not knowledgeable about or even interested in economics, and the years ahead promise to be some of the most challenging. Arthur has started the work of establishing a reserve bank for Australia, and the change to decimal currency is likely on its way and will need to be planned for. Added to that, inflation is running very high, and I . . . I'm good at people things, Zara, not number things.'

'This is all nonsense. If you surround yourself with people who do know and are good at these things, and take their advice just as you've done in every other role, you will thrive.'

'This role simply *matters* so much, Zara. If I get this wrong, Australia fails to prosper.'

'But you are up to it. I don't know anyone who works harder than you, and I don't know anybody smarter than you. Harry, you've been in parliament for nearly twenty-five years. There's nothing you don't know, and nothing you can't do.' I squeezed his hand. 'Though I must say this uncharacteristic bout of self-doubt is very endearing.'

He smiled weakly.

'So, what else?'

Again his eyes went to my drawings, and a dim feeling stole over me. I knew what he was going to say before he said it.

'You'd have to step back from Magg.'

'Why?'

'If I'm the PM-in-waiting, then you are the First-Lady-in-waiting. You'll have to increase your public duties, be available for more, and not just here in the electorate – all over Australia.'

'There are so many ifs before you become PM though,' I protested. 'If Mr Fadden resigns, if you say yes, if your party keeps winning elections, if Mr Menzies steps down . . .' But even as I said it, I could see all of those things coming true so easily. From the moment I'd met Harry, I knew he was destined for something like this. Now it was simply playing out as it should.

'I won't sell the business,' I said, a little too hotly.

'I don't expect you to. You can hire somebody to be a new you. Maybe you can get involved every now and again when an exciting project comes up. But I can't have you working full-time anymore. I'll need a full-time wife.'

The injustice stung. I may not have woken every morning at dawn and worked like he did, but I had certainly worked hard and I had built something out of nothing. To step back from it now when it was running like a powerful machine was so unfair. But then, I knew too that Betty had made noises about us both stepping back, being more hands-off, hiring young brilliant women looking for opportunities. She was tired. And sometimes I was tired too.

I sank back in my chair and gazed at my drawings laid out in front of me. Decades of work.

'Have a think about it,' he said, rising and picking up his briefcase.

'I don't need to any more than you need to think about becoming treasurer,' I said. 'You have been chosen, and I am your wife, and that's just the way it is. We both accept our fates.'

He leaned over, took my wrist in his warm hand and squeezed it tenderly. 'I know what this means, and I'm grateful.' Then he disappeared into his office.

I rested my head on the table, hands among my drawings, and tried not to cry.

———

Harry became Treasurer and the travel resumed its hectic pace. In Australia, it felt as though we were always on the move, while Harry talked to this group or that. The marvellous Tony, who always travelled with us, made sure I was never alone in a room full of men at any function and found other useful things for me to do, such as visiting veterans hospices or girls schools. I enjoyed talking to people and hearing their stories, so it went a long way towards making up the hole in my life left by handing the reins of head designer for Magg to Deirdre, and hiring Nick's fiancée Caroline to fill her job. I was still involved in the business, meeting with the team once a week, but unless I had a wild idea that I absolutely had to draw, I kept away from my sketchbooks and pencils. They only made me sad.

The international travel continued to wear me out, and there was so much of it. I remained fond of Calcutta, Rome and Geneva, but less fond of Paris and London, which seemed to me overrated cities.

On one of our Paris visits, in the first autumn of the new decade, we sat opposite each other at a formal lunch at the Australian Embassy. A dignitary had just been introduced to speak and he had an incredibly long title, and I met Harry's eyes as we both stifled chuckles. He launched into a speech in a very thick French accent about joint Australian–French economic relations, and I prepared to wander off in my imagination when a young woman, whom I recognised as one of the embassy staff, appeared at my elbow.

'Mrs Holt?' she whispered.

'What is it?'

'Please come with me.'

I gave Harry a bewildered look and rose, placing my napkin on the table next to my unfinished meal. My heart had picked up its rhythm as I followed the young woman into a small, quiet side office, with a window overlooking a courtyard of lime trees.

'What's going on?' I asked.

'Madame, a cable arrived at your hotel shortly after you left. They knew you were coming here and brought it to us. It's urgent.' She held out a piece of paper, and I noticed her hand shook and she couldn't meet my eye.

I took the cable as Harry burst into the room and asked, 'What is happening here?'

I read the message. It was from Nick, and it was a single line.

Grandpa died today, the 10th. Love Nick.

My knees wobbled underneath me, and Harry caught my elbow.

'Zara?'

'Daddy's died.'

'Oh. Oh, my darling.' He caught me in his arms and held me tight, and hot tears burst from my eyes. I'd never expected Daddy to live forever, and his mind had been slowly and gently deteriorating in the last year or so, but the shock took over my body and I began to shake. Harry squeezed me tighter, and we stood like that for perhaps three minutes before Harry said, 'Put it out of your mind and come back to lunch.'

I pushed him away, stepped back. 'What?'

'Try and think about something else. We're missing the speech. You can have a good cry back at the hotel this afternoon, and I'll take you for a special dinner to cheer you –'

'Good god, Harry! Is your heart a stone?'

He looked at me, and I could see the dawning realisation on his face that he had handled this very badly.

I turned to the young woman who had been hovering in the background awkwardly. 'Please call a car to take me directly back to my hotel.'

'Yes, yes, you're right. You should go back to the hotel and lie down,' Harry was saying. 'I'll stay here and make your apologies.'

But I wasn't listening to him, I was striding towards the hallway, leaving my coat and hat behind and taking my grief with me to wait for the embassy car to arrive.

Back at our room at the Ritz, I threw myself onto the bed, eyes on the ceiling, and cried and cried until my tears ran out. Then I poured myself a brandy and phoned Mum, who sounded very frail and distant, then Vieve, then my brothers, and finally Nick, Sam and Andy. I wanted to sound strong for them as I didn't want them to worry about me while they mourned their grandpa. All the phone calls made, I sat at the mahogany desk under the window with a second glass of brandy. Vieve had asked if I would give the eulogy at Daddy's funeral, which would be on the very day we arrived home from Paris. I wanted to write some notes down now, and then work it into something beautiful and memorable on the aeroplane on the way home.

A stack of Harry's papers were in the middle of the desk, so I moved them to the side and reached for a sheet of hotel stationery. And knocked over my brandy.

I leaped up, sweeping Harry's papers onto the floor so they didn't get soaked. I ran to the bathroom, seized a towel and came back to blot up the brandy. Harry's papers had become jumbled up on the floor, so I sat on the carpet to see if I could reorder them.

That's when I caught sight of Harry's neat handwriting on a lined page – rather than the other dozens of typed sheets – a part of a letter that appeared to have been stored in the middle of the pile. *Hidden.* That was the word that came to mind. I picked it up.

. . . whenever I can, and I hope you know that. When I can't, I think of you and your soft breasts and the way your mouth turns up when you smile. You shine a light into my soul and I am utterly in love with you. Perhaps even a little obsessed

with you: I only have to think of us standing naked under the
cascade at Bedarra to make my trousers go tight in awkward
places.

I smiled despite the terrible news of the day. Harry was writing me
a love letter? Had he started it while we were apart and never got
round to finishing it? I searched through the pile for the first page
of the letter, as this was clearly a subsequent page, and when I found
it my blood ran cold.

It did not say, *My dearest Z*, as he always started letters to me.

It said, *My dearest M*.

I couldn't concentrate to read it properly. My eyes jumped from
line to line, as my brain made the connections. He loved her. God,
he said it three times on the first page. And given that Johnny and
Allison had sold Bedarra two years ago, this affair had been going
on for a long time.

It was my nightmare come true.

At that precise moment, as I sat there on the floor with the letter
in my hand, shaking and crying, the hotel door opened and Harry
entered. He took in the scene in front of him with puzzlement;
I merely looked back at him, speechless with rage.

'Are you going through my government papers?' he asked with
a faintly accusatory tone.

'They fell off the desk,' I said, savagely sweeping them away from
me. 'And it's not a "government paper" I'm reading.'

He hung up his hat and coat slowly, deliberately, then came to
sit beside me. 'Ask whatever you need to ask.'

'How long have you been seeing her?'

'Four years.'

'Are you going to leave me for her?'

'No.'

'Does she think you're going to leave me for her?'

His eyes slid away. 'I don't know what she believes, but I've never told her that I would.'

'And you love her?'

'Not the way I love you.'

'You promised. You *promised* you wouldn't fall in love with somebody else.'

'I never intended to.'

'You took her to Bedarra, the cascade.' I let out a sob, the hot stab of jealousy too much to bear. 'That's a special place I think about when I'm sad or missing you. Why did you have to take her there?' Then it dawned on me. 'Johnny and Allison knew?'

'Yes.'

So many feelings welled up and overlapped within me that I was robbed of speech, so Harry took the opportunity to fill the silence.

'I know you feel terrible now. You have had two very significant pieces of bad news today, but I do love you, Zara, and I need you to focus on what I'm saying.'

I nodded despite myself, hanging on to him for comfort even though he had dealt this terrible blow.

'You are my wife. I am the Treasurer. This business cannot get out to the press. It will ruin us both.'

'Why would I tell the press? It's humiliating enough that Johnny and Allison knew. Who else knows? Is everyone laughing at me?'

'Nobody is laughing at you. Nobody. Allison most certainly didn't approve. Johnny has some . . . rather free notions about marriage so he didn't care. But neither told you because they didn't want to hurt you. I didn't want to hurt you either.'

'You've been having a relationship with this woman for years!' I blurted.

'Keep listening please, Zara. I know *you* wouldn't tell the press directly, but all would be revealed in a divorce court.'

His words finally cut through the fog of my pain. He was worried about his reputation. He would lose the support of his party for the top job if he had a divorce founded on adultery dragged through the newspapers. He had far more to lose than I did in that regard. The most that I would suffer would be the pity of the Australian public.

But if Harry was never to be prime minister . . . I realised I was as ambitious for him as he was. And perhaps as ambitious for me as the wife of a powerful man.

'Are you only staying married to me to protect your reputation?' I asked miserably.

He smiled tenderly. 'No, Zara. I have loved you my whole life. Madly. I will never stop loving you.' He spread his hands. 'This is just the man I am.'

I sat there for what felt like a long time. Dusk had crept up to the windows and the room was growing dim. Harry sat with me, not moving, simply waiting. And I thought about life without him, and decided I didn't want to live without him. I didn't want to miss him every day until I died.

I drew a shaky breath. 'What do you want me to do?'

'Look the other way. Like you have with all the others.'

All the others? But of course I had known there were others. I had known all along, and I didn't ask questions because I didn't want details that would lodge in my imagination and drive me mad. I didn't even want to know what the initial 'M' stood for. I wanted it simply to vanish from my mind, lest my thoughts got caught on it like prickles on a hem.

I pointed at him. 'And if I do this, you will treat me like a bloody queen.'

'I will,' he said. 'A bloody queen.'

We both chuckled weakly.

'Well, then,' I said. 'It appears we have struck a deal.'

PART 6

PART 5

INTERLUDE

BINGIL BAY, 1968

She cannot remember the drive, nor what route they took, nor how they kept Harry hidden along the way. A journey of fifteen hundred miles is not easy to hold in her head, so she concentrates instead on the details of their arrival. The long driveway carved through the rainforest at dusk, the back of the house appearing in the headlights, the fruit bats overhead crowding the sky, the hush-and-shush of the ocean, the stuffiness of the house, which had been locked up for over a year.

Harry sets about opening all the windows to let the fresh ocean air in. They had stopped in town for basic groceries, so she makes eggs on toast for dinner, and Harry finds a bottle of red wine in the cabinet by the door and sloshes her out an enormous glass while she scrambles and toasts.

They sit on the front patio with plates on their knees and glasses beside them on the concrete.

'Do you think you'll be happy here?' she asks him.

'I always was,' he replies. 'So I expect I will.'

'You're free here. There's nobody around. Well, except . . .'

'They may have seen us arrive.'

Johnny and Allison's property shares part of the driveway with theirs.

'Or they may not have.'

'They will eventually,' he says.

'We'll deal with that when the time comes.' She can barely admit to herself that she wants to be discovered by Johnny and Allison, to discuss this whole mad idea with somebody sensible. Somebody who loves her.

The palms rattle in the wind, and her eyes go up to the sky. The night is clear, dusted with stars. 'Do you remember the first time we stayed at Bedarra, and we were all high and talked about how small the stars make us feel?' I ask him.

'Yes,' he says, laying his plate aside and leaning back on the heels of his palms. 'I think it's the human condition to feel that way.'

'Does it bother you?'

'No. It sounds as though it bothers you though?'

She thinks about this for a few moments. 'Sometimes, when I think about how small I am, it makes me feel as though I don't matter. What is the point of anything I say or do?'

'I feel quite the opposite. Because our lives are small, we're obligated to make the biggest impact we can.'

She turns her eyes to meet him. 'Impact on what?'

'On our community, surely.'

'Well, you certainly had that. You were the most important man in the country. You did things that people will talk about for years to come.'

'It was a great honour,' he replies. 'The highest honour. I miss it.' He makes a fist and presses it under his breastbone. 'I worked my whole life for it.'

She watches him, desperately aware of how far this life they are living is from what he dreamed of.

'But if nothing else,' he continues, 'we have an impact on those we love.' His fingers reach for hers. 'What you have said and done for me is so far from pointless. Your adoration, your generosity, your sacrifices . . .' Here he drops his eyes. 'I'd like to think what I've said and done for you has made an impact too.'

'Yes,' she replies. 'Not always positive, it must be said.'

'Ah well,' he concedes. 'At least there's only the two of us now.'

'Do you miss her?' she ventures. 'She was with you the day you . . . you know . . . ran away.'

'No. I'm here only for you.' He smiles. 'It was never real love with her.'

She doesn't reply, but she's not sure she believes those words.

———

They are up early the next day, walking along the beach. The sky is blue apart from some pale grey clouds on the horizon and the sun is not yet hot. They hold hands, chat, let the sea wash in and out over their ankles. And she starts to think, yes, this will work. He's hidden but he's free. She can come and go as she needs to, but why oughtn't she choose a life as a recluse? Greta Garbo did it successfully enough. Zara could be an enigma like her, never talking to the press, avoiding all social situations, perhaps visiting family every so often but mostly living her life up here in the tropics with Harry. If people asked questions, she could simply tell them that *the incident* made her withdraw from public life.

'The water looks beautiful,' Harry says, 'and it's so warm. Should we swim?'

'We didn't bring our bathing suits.'

He gestures around to point out they are alone for miles in either direction.

She giggles, then unbuttons the front of her dress. He has his shirt over his head and his pants on the sand in moments, and they both wade into the salty water and dive under the waves.

The sunlit blue-green water engulfs her. Bubbles rush past her ears and then she bobs up to the surface, breaking into a lazy breaststroke. Harry is treading water nearby, lifted and dropped by the waves.

'It's colder than I expected.' He laughs.

She swims to him and his hands brush her breasts.

'You're like a mermaid,' he says.

'An ageing mermaid,' she jokes. 'These haven't sat where they started in a very long time.'

'You're too hard on yourself.'

Because you made me doubt myself, she thinks. But they won't argue here. Not in paradise. That would be mad.

'I'm going to swim out a little further,' he says, then sets off in a competent overarm stroke.

Anxiety grips her stomach. 'Don't go too deep,' she calls.

He keeps going.

'Don't go too far!' She knows he can't hear her. 'There might be a rip. You just don't know.'

Further and further he goes, becoming smaller and smaller. The clouds have moved from the horizon and edge over the sun. All of a sudden it looks like rain is coming. She flings herself onto her back, arms out and floating on the waves. Tears leak from her eyes. 'Come back,' she whispers. A raindrop falls on her cheek. She rights herself again, treading water. She can't see him. 'Harry!' she calls. 'Harry!'

'I'm right here.' He's beside her. He must have swum back from the other direction while she was floating, and now the rain clouds are parting and the last ten minutes seem as though she dreamed them. 'Zara, are you all right?'

'I don't like it when you swim out so far.'

'Then I won't swim out far,' he says. 'I won't swim at all if you don't want me to.'

'But you love swimming more than just about anything.'

He looks back at her, wordless for a long time, water clumping his long black lashes.

'I just want us to be happy,' he says. Or perhaps she says it. She can't tell anymore.

———

The closest grocery shop is at Mission Beach, and their supplies run out in days. Zara cannot rely on the cover of dawn or dusk to get past Johnny and Allison's place, so she drives out in the middle of the day and gives Harry strict instructions not to open the door to anyone. She intends to buy enough to last them a few weeks, but the shop is tiny and there isn't much on the shelves as they likely only receive a goods delivery irregularly. Perhaps next week she can take a longer drive to one of the bigger towns. For now, she has some lamb, a few vegetables for roasting, two loaves of bread and ingredients for baking. She attempts to listen to the radio on the way back, but can barely pick up a signal. An Elvis song flashes on and hisses out into static. 'Return to Sender'. She switches it off and winds the window down a little way. The smell of the sea is everywhere.

Harry greets her from the cane sofa he has pulled under the fan, where he is reading a book. 'Somebody knocked,' he says.

'You didn't answer it?'

'No. But they'll be back.'

She drops the grocery bags on the kitchen bench. 'What are you reading?'

He holds up *The Spy Who Loved Me*. 'Nonsense, all of it,' he says, but continues to read anyway.

She stacks away the groceries, stopping to give the refrigerator a clean. It smells yeasty and unused. There is vanilla essence in the pantry and she pours a shot into a teacup, and rests it in the bottom of the fridge to absorb the odours.

Then the knock at the door.

'Right, well,' she says, wiping her hands on a nearby tea towel. 'Here goes.'

But it isn't Allison. It's a young man with thick black hair, struggling with his English, who wants to know if they've seen a peach-faced lovebird. He is housesitting for Johnny and Allison and the bird flew out when he was cleaning the cage.

'How long are the Bussts away?' she asks.

'Until after Christmas,' he answers. If he has seen or recognised Harry, he gives no sign of it.

She promises to call in if she sees the bird and the man goes on his way. She closes the door, deflated. She has been looking forward to hearing Allison's opinion on their adventure, to share the burden of the secret finally. Though she can imagine what her protests would be. 'This will never work. He's the Prime Minister. What if somebody spots him on the beach? What if he gets sick or has an accident?'

The thought gives Zara pause because she can't believe she hasn't considered it before.

Weeks speed by and then summer is upon them, which, this far north, means rain. Storms roll over their shack most afternoons, and they watch them together from the floor-to-ceiling windows in the lounge room, arms around each other.

'You know it's nearly a year,' he says to her one stormy afternoon. 'Looks like we've gotten away with it. Thanks to your brain.'

'I always had a good imagination,' she says. 'I can conjure all kinds of scenarios.'

'You mean your imagination is always running away with you,' he teases.

'There are worse sins.'

———

The next morning she walks along the beach, looking for driftwood after the storm and finding mostly washed-up jellyfish. Barefoot, sand squishing between her toes. Seagulls overhead in a cloudless sky, which will be brooding and grey by mid-afternoon. The sea breeze takes the edge off the humidity.

She admits to herself that Harry must be getting bored. Of course he must be. He was Prime Minister. And now all he does is read spy novels, and he doesn't even like spy novels.

She stops, turns to face the sea and closes her eyes with a huge sigh. 'What are you doing here?' she asks herself aloud.

A deep, sad clunk inside her.

She feels as though she has put her foot out for a stepping stone and missed, and from that moment on she has been trying to regain her balance. She could have been firmer with Harry over the affairs, especially M. She could have stayed more active in her business and not travelled as much. She could have insisted on more time up here in the wilds, where they could connect and understand each other and deepen their love, deepen their commitment . . . She could have . . .

It hits her, and the idea is so utterly, perfectly correct that she almost gasps. The place she really wants to go is back in time.

But that isn't possible. None of this is possible, really.

She resumes her walk over the warm sand.

CHAPTER 28

MELBOURNE, 1966

The ballroom of the Southern Cross Hotel was noisy with chatter and music. One could almost mistake it for a party. The mood was jubilant, the band played upbeat tunes, and I could hear laughter from all sides. What I couldn't understand was why everyone wasn't anxious and on edge like me. It was election night, and some time this evening we would find out if the Australian people had voted for Harry to be their prime minister.

He had actually been in the role for several months, ever since Mr Menzies stepped down, but secretly he had told me he wouldn't relax until he had led his party to victory in an election and found out if Australia really wanted him. I understood. Officials had asked me several times about my plans for redecorating the Lodge, but I kept hesitating. What if we didn't win? What a lot of money would have been spent for nothing.

I sat at a table with my boys and their wives. They chatted animatedly, but I felt a little outside it all. I could see Harry across the other side of the room and wondered if he was as beset by doubts as me. Certainly most of the newspapers predicted he would easily win, but his party had been in power for eighteen years and criticism about the government sending conscripts to the Vietnam War grew more ferocious every day. I thought I could see the snares and traps more readily than anyone else in the room. It could all be taken away from us, and then what? How would I deal with a husband who got to live out his dream, but only for a handful of months?

I rose to walk across the room and refill my glass, too late noticing the journalist and television recording camera set up near the stage. I flinched. I would never get used to seeing myself on television, my face made shapeless in two dimensions.

The journalist pointed his microphone at me and called, 'Mrs Holt, Mrs Holt!'

I reluctantly approached.

'Mrs Holt, do you think you'll still be first lady in the morning?'

I didn't actually like the term 'first lady', as my role was not an official one like the wife of the United States president. But I accepted people used it. I put on a smile and said, 'I have so much confidence in my husband. He's doing a sterling job, and I know Australians are fond of him.'

'And are you looking forward to finally moving into the Lodge?'

That Gothic pile with its dozens of tiny pointless rooms. 'If I have the privilege of moving in, I'm sure I'll be very happy there.'

Moving to Canberra had been a terrible wrench at first. Leaving behind my house, my family, friends and my shop, only to wind up in the little apartment on Commonwealth Avenue – where I suspected Harry had conducted many of his extramarital liaisons – was deflating. But I was determined to recognise my privilege and find all the good in the situation I could. Waking up with Harry every morning, not just weekends. Being able to kiss him before he went to work every day and when he came home every evening. The view from the window into the garden, especially in winter when mist and weak sunlight wove around the trees and hedges. And the town itself, which had most of the amenities of a city but had sprouted in the middle of the countryside, so we were only ever a short drive from beautiful natural places. Every day I took a walk along the lake, feeling peaceful and settled.

Harry had swum the lake, once, in a publicity stunt leading up to the election. Nearly two hours it took him, but he'd emerged grinning and exuberant on the other side, and all the newspapers had covered it. We were both in our late fifties now, but he was still so youthful in his bearing, always smiling, eyes always sparkling.

Harry loved to swim, and we were a long way from the sea in Canberra. During his years as Treasurer, when that town had called him and held tight to him for weeks and weeks at a time, we'd bought a house on the clifftop at Portsea, about eighty miles from our home in Melbourne. It was much easier to get to than the shack in Queensland, and so we spent many weekends there swimming or spearfishing or just lying on the beach and listening to the waves.

I tried in vain to stop Harry working too hard during those years, but he wasn't made of the same stuff as the rest of us mortals. He had spent every moment cramming his brain with economic theory and policy. He rose at 6 am every day, seven days a week without fail, to work before breakfast. One time we were in Ghana; we had taken the most ridiculously circuitous route, all the way to London to catch the Ghanaian government plane back to Africa. We made it to bed in our hotel at 3 am, in a completely different time zone. I was muddled to pieces; Harry was awake and working at six, Ghana time.

Somehow, we still managed to have very good times together. The revelation about his mistress had shifted something between us. Perhaps, when he was only having one-off flings with other women, it was easier for him to forget them and forgive himself, but I imagine he had been feeling a great deal of guilt about this long affair, being in love with her. What a significant thing to be hiding from one's wife. Along with hiding the affair, he had been hiding part of himself, and that part came back now. He was open, warm and funny with me.

I hadn't even recognised those qualities dwindling until they came back with full force and he was entirely his charming self.

Just because the affair was out in the open between us didn't mean we ever talked about it. I didn't even let myself think about it. Sometimes I would hear him on the phone in his office, not loud enough to hear his words, but by his tone I could always tell if he was talking to her, and I would find the room furthest from where he was – whichever home we were in – and doodle pictures of fairy-tale castles until it was over. I comforted myself with the knowledge that he wasn't going to leave me. Not simply because his reputation would be in tatters and his political career completely blown up, but because he had started talking often about which place we would live in when we retired. He leaned very strongly towards Bingil Bay, while I leaned towards Portsea so we would be close to our children.

And grandchildren. Our first grandchild had been born in 1965, a dear little girl named Sophie, and she was the most perfect baby anyone had ever seen. Harry loved her to distraction, and Nick and Caroline often brought her and stayed with us at Portsea. Sometimes just Nick and Sophie came, as Caroline was busy running my shop for me. Magg continued to be a success. We won two Gown of the Year awards; Miss International 1962 was wearing something I designed when she won, and I was personally consulted on the designs for the Australian uniforms for the Expo in Montreal. The three shops did a healthy turnover, and we now stocked limited gowns from other high-fashion collections that our international buyer, Marie, sourced for us.

And I still out-earned Harry, even though he was Prime Minister. That was another thing we never talked about.

But the most fun we had was on our travels. As he was Treasurer, the travel demands were relentless. There was always an economic forum to go to somewhere, or a trade deal to hammer out, and sometimes we would arrive back in Australia for only two or three nights before setting off again. The constant sitting on aeroplanes, crossing of time zones, eating food at odd hours, made us both a little mad, and we found ourselves laughing at nonsense more and more, or doing nonsensical things to make each other laugh.

For example, in the bathroom on the Ghanaian government plane, there was a photograph on the wall of President Nkrumah, who was for all intents and purposes a dictator. I found it so hilarious that he was watching me while I was on the loo that I took my lipstick out of my handbag and drew a moustache on him. When Harry found it later he laughed until he cried. Photos of us when we travelled, which would appear in newspapers and magazines, always showed us smiling and laughing.

The long trips were punctuated with time at Bingil Bay with Johnny and Allison, who were such dear friends and knew exactly that kind of fun we liked to have. Dinner parties, followed by long days swimming and staring at the sea. Harry still worked relentlessly, but at least he was doing it to the sound of the ocean.

We were very happy in our way. I certainly loved him as madly as I ever had, although he drove me as wild with his behaviour as much as he ever had. But perhaps that was the nature of life and marriage and men and women.

Quiet had begun to descend on the hotel ballroom as I approached the bar, where they refilled my coupe with champagne and threw in a few ice cubes – they had been told how I like my champagne. I turned to see that Harry was approaching the stage. Everyone fell silent, and my pulse became distinctly audible in my skull.

'Ladies and gentlemen,' he said, beaming. 'Early numbers are in, and there is no way our opposition can form government now. We have won!'

Relief swept through my body and I thought, *You have won, Harry*.

The next morning, the front page of *The Sun-Herald* had a picture of Harry in his white shirt and tie, hands raised over his head, fingers in two victory salutes. The headline, in giant letters, read *Holt Sweeps Back*.

We arrived in Washington to meet President Johnson on a fine but brisk morning, coming in on a flight from New York. A shiny black car awaited Harry and me, and we were whisked off to Blair House, the official guesthouse where we were to stay for two weeks. Our baggage had been offloaded first and sent on ahead, and Tony – now elevated to senior press secretary – was following behind with Harry's secretary Pat in a second car. I had never been to Washington before – I usually stayed in New York if we were in the States – and I watched the passing scenery with delight. I suppose I'd seen enough movies and television shows set here to recognise the landmarks and it was strange to see them in real life. As though I was driving through a movie set.

Blair House was originally two terrace houses that had been combined into one and decorated and furnished with impeccable taste. An aide showed us through: Harry had his own study, panelled in red, and I had a dedicated drawing room and bedroom with a canopied four-poster bed. But it was the wallpaper in the reception room that caught my imagination – handpainted Chinese silk, hundreds of years old, with blossoms and butterflies and pheasants on it. I wondered if I could afford something like it for one of the rooms in the Lodge.

Harry was raced straight over to the White House and I was left with the unpacking duties. I had asked Harry several times if we could travel with a valet, but he refused. No Australian prime minister ever travelled with a valet (many other heads of state certainly did) and he wouldn't be the first and draw criticism about wasting taxpayer money. When I'd offered to pay for it myself, he'd said it wouldn't matter. 'The newspapers will run the story that sells, not the story that makes excuses, even if they are true.'

So I spent two hours unpacking and ironing ahead of a reception of honour for us on the White House lawns at eleven.

Then I showered and dressed in a rose-pink double-breasted jacket and matching pleated skirt, and was escorted over to the White House.

Harry was with the President and Mrs Johnson on the gravel driveway. An aide helped me out of the car and Mrs Johnson immediately gave me a hesitant hug, grasping my elbows and smiling deeply, and gestured to a woman who brought over a bouquet of roses tied in red, white and blue ribbon.

'Welcome,' Mrs Johnson said. 'I am so delighted to meet you.'

A well-bred lady from the Deep South. I loved her accent from the moment I heard it..

Harry put his arm around me and said close to my ear, 'He's wonderful. They're wonderful.'

I smiled up at him.

The sun was up full, but it hadn't quite taken the chill out of the air. Seats had been placed in a semicircle on the lawn in front of the White House, which was much whiter than I expected despite its name. Shady magnolia and cherry trees surrounded us, and a dais had been raised for the President and the Prime Minister to speak from. There must have been six inches difference in height between them, and I spent most of President Johnson's speech worrying that Harry would not be visible over the lectern. But the moment he took the stairs up to the dais, two men raced across and adjusted it, then disappeared as though they had never been there.

I admit I didn't listen to Harry's speech. I had stopped listening to speeches many years ago and used the time to run off in my imagination. I wondered how much say I would have over the gardens at the Lodge. Magnolia trees were so pretty. Would they grow in Canberra's climate? And so on . . . quite a long way away with the fairies. But I did hear when Harry finished his speech with the words, 'In Australia, and in me, you have an admiring friend, a staunch friend, that'll be all the way with LBJ.'

Applause and a couple of gentle whoops. *All the way with LBJ* had been Mr Johnson's election slogan, and the Americans seemed to warm to Harry for using it.

A moment later, Mrs Johnson was at my elbow. 'Mrs Holt? Zara? Our husbands are off to lunch now. Would you like a tour of the White House ahead of a tea I've organised in your honour?'

'Oh, please do call me Zara,' I said, rising from my seat. Then looked at her puzzled. 'Though I have no idea what your name is.' I had only ever heard her referred to as Lady Bird Johnson, which surely wasn't her name.

She laughed lightly. 'Well, my actual name is Claudia, but nobody ever calls me that. Lady Bird is fine, or just Bird, or Birdie.'

'Birdie it is,' I said. 'Show me the way.'

I honestly don't know how she found her way around the White House. It was simply enormous, with wide polished corridors leading to other corridors, vast rooms in different colours and priceless gleaming furniture and historical art. We chatted as we walked, starting with very anodyne topics such as the weather, but soon found more common ground.

'And how was your flight this morning?' Lady Bird asked.

'The flight was fine, but the unpacking . . .'

'Oh, yes. I know what you mean. When we travel, I find it so hard to stay organised. Once, we went on a tour with fourteen suitcases because we had so many public events and I couldn't be seen to wear the same dress twice.'

'But surely you travel with a valet?'

'We do, but he's more for Lyndon than for me. Didn't know how to iron silk until he marked one of my gowns, and since then I do the ironing myself.'

I sighed. 'I feel so lucky to see so much of the world, but . . .'

'But it is tiring. I do understand, darling.' She gave my hand a squeeze. 'I'm sure I'm probably one of the only people who understands. Let's talk more after the reception. It's in the Gold Room. You're going to love it.'

I did love the Gold Room. Decorated in pale yellows and limes, silver urns teeming with flowers, and portraits of all the first ladies around the walls. I was so surprised to see a room full of portraits of women that at first it was disorienting: usually, all portraits in official places were men.

Lady Bird had invited about forty-five women to this high-tea reception, and most of them were already in the room waiting for us. The tiers of sandwiches and treats were lined up on a long table with a white cloth, and she encouraged me to move about the room and 'meet everyone'. I quickly came to realise that she had gone to the trouble of inviting people who she knew I would have common ground with. Rather than the usual politicians' wives and socialites, the room was full of artists, women in fashion, interior decorators and businesswomen. The celebration of women even extended to the salmon sandwiches, which Lady Bird told me were made from the largest salmon caught by a woman this year. After an hour or so, when I was already stuffed, the chef brought out trays of ice-cream desserts named in my honour: the Bombe Zara, with a toffee sauce and flakes of almonds on top.

I ate one, of course.

The conversation was good for my soul. To hear other women talking about the way they used their creativity or savvy, the way they balanced work with family obligations, brought me such a sense of relief. And while nobody openly said that sometimes they simply broke down and got so anxious they felt like two people or cried all the time, the inference was there – all of us struggled with our duties and our guilt, in one way or another.

In all my years as Harry's wife, I had never attended a more stimulating public engagement.

Back at Blair House, Lady Bird and I sat on a long pale-green couch in the reception room, with a decanter of brandy and two glasses between us. Early evening had arrived, and the housekeeper came to draw the gold brocade curtains and switch on the lamps. The soft light reflected off the dark polished coffee table in front of us and glinted off the gilt frames of paintings. Harry still wasn't back, but I had seen him briefly in passing on the way over and he had taken me aside and told me that he and Mr Johnson had hit it off wildly, and were going to head off somewhere for dinner and drinks. It seemed only fair that Lady Bird and I should also have a little fun.

An aide – a tall man in a suit – hung about near the door.

'You can go now,' Lady Bird said to him. 'We'll be safe.'

'Ma'am.' He nodded and left the room, closing the door behind him.

Lady Bird immediately eased off her shoes and tucked her feet up under her. This casual gesture was so at odds with the rest of her appearance – the neatly pressed suit, the carefully coiffed hair – that it made me doubly fond of her. I did the same, and we clinked our glasses together.

'Tell me, then,' she said, 'your worst travel story. Then I'll share mine.'

'Uh . . . on the aeroplane between Karachi and Beirut. Food poisoning or something. I was throwing up every ten minutes, but we were at the front of the aeroplane and the bathroom was right at the back. So I just walked up and down, getting weaker and weaker, for hours.'

'Who looked after you?'

'Harry was sympathetic, of course, but he kept working. The stewardesses were very kind, made sure I drank lots of water.' I sipped my brandy. 'All right, then, what's yours?'

'I always try to learn a little of the language of the places we go,' she said. 'Just "good morning" or something like that, in case I'm called on to speak. I had memorised how to say "good day" in Korean, and after we arrived we were whisked to a function immediately, and I was saying "good day" in Korean to everyone and getting some very strange looks. Then Lyndon leaned over and reminded me we weren't in Korea, we were in Thailand.'

I laughed. 'Let's drink to that,' I said, and we both took a sip.

And then it became a game. Worst public speech. Worst gala event. Worst outfit choice for the weather. On it went, with us taking a sip of brandy after every round.

'Worst moment as a mother,' I declared.

'Forgot to pick Luci up from school. More than once,' she shot back.

'Forgetting Nicky's birthday because I was busy with a deadline,' I replied.

We drank to that.

'Worst fight with your husband,' she said in challenge.

'Oh, do we really want to do that?' We had both drunk a decent amount of brandy, and the giddiness of laughter and disclosure had made us reckless.

'Yes,' she said reaching across to squeeze my knee. 'We really, *really* do. I'll go first. Lyndon was lecturing me about how much money I'd spent on my new car, and I reminded him I earn more than him.'

'You do?' I asked.

'Yes. I have a company that owns radio and television stations. I was a millionaire in my own right before he even came to office.'

'Oh, we're drinking to that!' I said, splashing more brandy into our glasses. 'Because I earn more than Harry too but I would *never* say it. I think he's proud of me, but men have terribly fragile egos.'

'You're telling me? Lyndon hit the roof. Gave me another lecture about power and influence and how they were more important than money, which is likely true. But so are compassion and kindness, don't you think?'

'I do think that. I do,' I said. 'But those things are associated with women, so men never value them.'

'They ought to value them more,' she replied. 'Fewer wars. But speaking of wars . . . worst fight with *your* husband. Come on, you have to tell.'

'There have been so many. In our youth we used to fight just so we could make up,' I said, laughing. Then grew serious, and for some reason found myself saying, 'The fights about the other women.'

'Oh, darling. Once again . . .' she raised her glass, 'let's drink to that. Because I know exactly how you feel.'

'You do?' A beautiful clarity pushed through the drunkenness. I wasn't alone.

'Uh-huh. My husband once bragged to a mutual friend that he had slept with more women than JFK. And that's something. Why this mutual friend decided to report such a thing back to me remains a mystery. I like the truth, but I also like kindness.'

I swirled my brandy in my glass thoughtfully. 'So do all powerful men do this?'

'Have done since the dawn of time. All those kings of England had mistresses left and right, didn't they?'

'The one I can't stand is the long-term one. It's not just a silly fling, it's an affair.'

'A second relationship. Yes, Lyndon has one of them too. Alice.' She screwed up her nose. 'I don't know whether to punch her or feel sorry for her.'

'This is such a relief,' I said. 'I thought there was something wrong with me that I couldn't keep him.' I shifted in my seat so I could look directly in her eyes. 'Does it hurt?'

'Yes.'

'Do you look the other way?'

'Of course.'

'Do you wonder if you'll ever be happy?'

'Darling, I am happy and so are you. That man of yours loves you; I can tell by the way he looks at you. And mine loves me.'

She shrugged. 'Accept it and it hurts less.' She gestured around. 'Look at our lives. We are far too lucky to complain.'

I clinked her glass again. 'I'll drink to that too.'

———

From Washington, we went to London to meet with the Queen. While it was a great honour, the contrast with the warmth, light and openness of the White House was stark. Our lunch was to be at St James Palace, all dim corridors, uncarpeted floor and lead-lined windows. Somebody said it had once hosted a leper colony, and it certainly had a Gothic feel. The impression was only magnified when a tall, thin woman floated in, all dressed in pale grey with a veil. She looked like a ghost, though I was introduced to her later as Prince Philip's elderly mother. She sat next to me at the luncheon and I chatted away to her happily, only to find out afterwards that she was deaf and probably hadn't heard a word I'd said.

I only said a sentence or two to the Queen, but she was very gracious and so pretty with perfectly clear skin and liquid blue eyes. But after the openness and warmth of the Johnsons, the royal family seemed aloof and closed off. Mr Wilson, the English Prime Minister, was there, and he seemed to share their adherence to polite, banal conversation.

I decided what I wanted for the Lodge, for Harry as the Prime Minister of Australia and me as his wife, was the kind of light and warmth and good humour of the White House.

———

A rule existed for some reason that the Prime Minister couldn't stay in the Lodge when there were workmen in and out, so Harry and I went back and forth between the Lodge and the apartment for months. Our long overseas trip meant that much had progressed. I was particularly pleased to see all the dark wainscotting stripped back and painted white, and ready for us to hang paintings. I had ordered some colourful modern art pieces to offset the grimness of the unsmiling old men in frames all over the house. I set about to let more light in. Taking down pelmets in the hallway, we discovered fanlights over the doors, so I asked for curtains that wouldn't hide them. I had the drawing room and billiards room remodelled into one larger drawing room, which I had decorated with white shantung silk wallpaper and white voile curtains patterned with green ferns. Dark emerald carpet was laid right through the bottom floor of the house. The library was dark because of the plants growing outside – a big fir tree and some ancient wisteria – and I did consider having the plants removed, but decided instead to keep the room dim and mysterious, moving in some brown velvet furniture and a gold Chinese screen. I had to make every decision, as Harry simply wasn't interested. There were forty-four chandeliers that needed hanging, and I bought expensive ones only for the entrance hall, drawing room and dining room. For the rest I bought plastic chandeliers for three dollars each. I simply couldn't in good conscience spend that much taxpayer money on crystal when nobody would ever be able to tell the difference.

We had a tennis court, and I did ask about the possibility of putting in a pool, as Harry loved swimming so much, but most thought it too difficult an endeavour and Harry said he would be happier swimming in the sea anyway. The gardens were established and beautiful, and the gardener an absolute darling of a man named Bill. I had to have four other staff. One was the official driver, Roy, who took me absolutely everywhere, even to the supermarket. One was Tiny, who came back and forth to Portsea with us. The other two, I could not settle on. I'd hire a maid and she wouldn't work out. I'd hire a cook to find they were only in the country for another six weeks. It took a long time before we felt 'moved in' and could start hosting.

Because Harry showed no interest whatsoever in the decorating – he hadn't even blinked when I bought a new dining table and chairs

for an official dinner – I finished off by decorating the bedroom to
my own taste. Rosy pink linen and canopy, pale violet voile curtains,
brass Victorian lamps with lilac glass shades. Harry was unbothered
by waking up every day in a girly pink bedroom, probably because
he never noticed.

CHAPTER 29

I was reluctant to miss any opportunity to see my little grand-daughter, so when Nick asked if she and he could come stay at Portsea for a week, I booked my flight out of Canberra and headed down. Nick worked on some briefs out in the back sunroom while I entertained little Sophie, who was two years old and constantly on the move. I tried to enlist her help in making the minestrone soup we would have for dinner, but apart from happily dumping a tin of beans in the mixture, she was more interested in climbing up and climbing down on the little step I'd brought out of the pantry for her. With the soup bubbling away, I finally got her to sit still by fetching some paper and crayons. We settled at the dining table to draw together. She drew houses and suns; I drew ladies in dresses.

Just before sunset, Nick came inside and I ducked out to buy bread rolls, and have a break from Sophie. Her little spirit was very fierce, and I was not a young woman anymore. I had to pace myself if I was going to help out with her for a whole week. The sea air was brisk and blew my hair all over the place, so I pulled a scarf out of my coat pocket and tied it on.

The bakery was still open, but most of its shelves were empty by now. One other woman stood ahead of me: a tall, lithe woman who, like me, wore a scarf. I waited my turn, but noticed the man behind the counter looking from me to her and back again with some suspicion.

As the woman took her loaf of bread and turned to leave, we briefly met eyes. She immediately dropped her gaze, nodded at me and pushed past. She was familiar, so she was likely one of my neighbours up here.

Then it was my turn, and I got the last three bread rolls in the store and took them home, trying to make sense of the puzzling exchange between me, the woman and the baker. Sometimes people behaved oddly around me because I was always in the papers.

I was a hundred yards from home when it struck me. Mrs Gillespie, that's who she was. She and her husband had been at a function we'd attended up here . . . and now, as I racked my brain for her first name, a flush crept over me because I knew, I knew who she was.

Marjorie. *My dearest M.*

I stopped, a sudden urge to cry overwhelming me. I turned down the grassy pathway between two houses and stood on the clifftop, gazing out at the swirling grey ocean. I had never wanted to know, but now I did. Harry's paramour was our neighbour, Marjorie Gillespie, who was married herself, to a slightly overbearing man whose name escaped me. My heart thudded and I let the tears roll down my face. It was easier when I didn't know who she was, couldn't put a face – or a body – to the figure in my imagination. Of course she was thinner than me; I'd become such a whale that Harry had gone elsewhere and that was my fault. Was she prettier than me too? She was certainly younger. The self-loathing roared through me. How embarrassing that the baker had known and I hadn't. Who else knew? Everyone in Portsea? Had they not tried to hide it at all?

Had she been his lover before being our neighbour, or was it the other way around? Harry had found our place in Portsea after all. Did he see her every time he was down here? I had assumed his lover was in Canberra, had even told myself that now I lived with him up there, the affair must have fizzled out.

The sky grew dim and I realised I needed to get home to serve dinner to my son and granddaughter. So I pulled myself together, hoped my eyes weren't too swollen and set off home. I told myself to calm down, that nothing had changed. I just had more details than before, more than I ever would have wanted. But still I felt utterly crushed.

Harry copped a great deal of criticism for his 'all the way with LBJ' speech back in Australia. Too many people saw it as sycophantic towards the Americans, and in the context of the terrible war in Vietnam, which had been dragging on for years, everyone with an opinion liked to talk to the press about how foolish Harry was to follow Johnson so blindly. The nuance was different, of course, but the newspapers aren't known for nuance. Harry's ultimate goal was to see Australia as part of a stronger Asia and bring America along with him to fortify the whole region. Soon after my encounter with Marjorie, and certainly far too soon after our last trip abroad, Harry and I headed off on a long tour of Asia so he could advance this aim diplomatically.

Our first stop was Cambodia, a country of such thick green foliage that I thought it a wonder all the buildings weren't smothered in vines. We stayed at a guesthouse overlooking the Mekong, mirror-still and misty in the mornings. From Cambodia we went to Laos, which seemed very poor by comparison, with unsealed roads and thatched roadside stalls. But the people were so welcoming, and we attended a Buddhist ceremony for good luck then visited the King and Queen in their palace in the mountains. Both of these places were geographically close to Vietnam, and Laos in particular was in danger of being infiltrated by the communists. I know Harry's detractors – usually the younger set – were fond of saying that communism wasn't necessarily bad, but having lived through the rise of fascism and the terrible war that engulfed the world,

I understood how a stable democracy in Asia was so important to Australia.

Next we went to Taiwan, where I saw my first garment factory with buttonhole machines that would make my seamstresses weep: perfect symmetry. By the time we reached Korea I was starting to flag. While Taiwan had been hot and muggy, Korea was icy. I was wearing a fur coat when I stepped off the plane in Seoul, but it felt as though the wind could slice me in half. I dived for the warmth of the car as soon as I could, and our route to the hotel was lined with people waving Australian and Korean flags. The main square teemed with schoolchildren. The welcome was like nothing I've ever experienced; we may as well have been the Beatles. People were cheering for us as we climbed the steps to the dais for the welcome speeches and the band played the old convict song 'Botany Bay'. Under other circumstances I might have had my spirits lifted by all this, but I was bone-tired and endured through the official presentations in the freezing cold daydreaming about a warm bed and a long sleep.

In every Asian city we visited, the mayors or other officials had devised a relentless schedule to show off their culture – museums, temples, mountaintops, riversides, gardens and gala dinners with traditional dancers or parades of traditional dress. It was over-whelming, all starting to blur together.

When we arrived at our hotel room in Seoul that night, I said to Harry, 'Do you ever feel you're too old for this?'

'Not a whit,' he said.

'I do. Harry, will we have to go abroad again this year?' I collapsed on the bed and threw my arms above my head.

He came to sit beside me and stroked my hair. 'You don't have to, my love. Not if it's too much for you.'

For some reason his comment made me feel embarrassed. I was unfit and out of shape, and that was likely why I was finding this so hard. The thought of Marjorie flashed across my imagination, all lean and tanned. But before I could torture myself too much, somebody knocked at the door and Harry opened it to Tony.

'Sorry,' he said, seeing me flat out on the bed. 'Last-minute change to schedule I'll need to run past Mrs Holt.'

I sat up, weary dread on my heart. 'What is it?'

'You'll need to give a speech on Thursday afternoon at Ewha Womans University.'

'Need to? I mean . . . do I have to? I wasn't thinking I'd be speaking at all on this tour.'

'They're giving you an honorary degree in . . .' Tony checked his notes, 'the arts.' He smiled up at me. 'You know "ewha" is Korean for "pear blossom".'

Oh, Tony knew how to persuade me. An Arts degree from a university for women, named after the pear blossom . . . how could I say no? 'What do they want me to speak about?'

'Whatever you like.'

'Harry?' I asked, turning to him. 'What should I speak about?'

'It's a women's university. Speak about women's things.'

I don't know if he meant to sound dismissive, but he absolutely did. I thought about what Lady Bird would speak about in such a circumstance and decided I wasn't going to mention politics at all. I was going to talk about being a businesswoman and the kind of creativity and tenacity that took.

So I made my speech and received my honorary doctorate in front of six thousand young women and one tireless interpreter. I was given a gold ring with the university's crest on it and a black velvet academic gown. Shortly after, we flew home and I went to bed for two days to recover.

———

No American president had ever visited Australia before LBJ, and LBJ only came because of Harry. The two had become such firm friends – they were similar in age, they thought alike and shared a passion for the same kind of policies. I was excited because this meant Lady Bird would come too, but from the moment Mr Johnson's visit was announced there was uproar. Some were proud that Australia mattered so much to receive a visit from the most powerful man on earth, some thought Mr Johnson a warmonger and leading Australia down a dangerous path.

The security for his arrival was tight and we had extensive briefings beforehand. And yet when they flew into Canberra and we met them off the plane at the RAAF airport, it didn't feel any more remarkable than friends reuniting. Harry and Mr Johnson were laughing together within seconds, and Lady Bird and I hugged warmly and held hands while we waved at the gathered crowd. We were ushered into one car while Harry and Mr Johnson went ahead in another. The roads back to the Lodge were lined with people waving and cheering. I saw a few protest signs, but mostly the drive home went without incident. We were due to have dinner at the Lodge, so while the men talked in the drawing room, I showed Lady Bird around.

It was in one of the upstairs guestrooms that I saw the look on her face and recognised it instantly.

'Oh dear. You're utterly exhausted, aren't you?'

She forced a smile. 'No, darling. It was a long flight, but I'm sure I'll be fine.'

I looked around, even though I knew nobody was nearby and listening. 'Would you rather be back in your hotel room with a boiled egg and a pot of tea? And an early night?'

To my surprise a tear rolled down her cheek and she nodded mutely. 'Sometimes all the travel is fine, but sometimes . . .'

'You don't have to tell me,' I said. 'Let's get you out of here.'

I said nothing to our husbands, but had one of her security men take her through the kitchen, back into the car, then made sure they knew about the back entrance of the hotel they were staying in so they could avoid the crowds at the front. Most likely they would be wellwishers, but I didn't want her to have to face any protesters when she was so weary.

I guiltily crept downstairs to confess what I'd done, but the President seemed unconcerned. He was playing with a wallaby in our drawing room. Somebody had brought in two of the little fellows so our American friends would have a chance to meet some Australian animals, as their tour was so brief and only took in a few cities. I tried not to think about what I would do if one of the wallabies decided to relieve itself on my emerald-green carpet.

———

Two days later, the four of us plus our retinues headed to Melbourne. Once again, Harry and Mr Johnson went ahead while the wives were relegated to the second car. Once again the roads were lined with people, but so many more this time. Masses of them, and among them were many more protesters. Along with the happy cheers, I heard harsh voices shouting the same protest chant I'd heard Americans use: 'Hey, hey, LBJ. How many kids did you kill today?' Some held up placards on sticks. *No More. Stop The War* and *Vietnam Is Not Australia's War.* I was particularly affected by the signs held by middle-aged women that simply said *Save Our Sons.*

'How do you get used to the protesters?' I asked Lady Bird.

'By remembering that everyone is entitled to a view,' she replied evenly, though I could tell she was tired of the chanting. 'We may not like what they're saying, but this is what a democracy looks like.'

Her words gave me some comfort and I felt more forgiving towards the protesters then.

It was only when we got into the city that things started to get out of hand. Many more people crammed the footpaths and spilled onto the streets. At the crossroads of Swanston and Collins Streets, all I could see in every direction was a sea of people. Police were there with barricades, but when we slowed to negotiate our way between them, one young man jumped over and ran for the President's car.

A policeman tackled him; it looked so violent that I flinched. The crowds started making terrible noises, some cheering, some booing, and more people began to push against the barricade. The police were soon outnumbered, the barricades had been flattened and people surged towards the cars – and not the people who liked LBJ.

'Oh no,' Lady Bird breathed, closing her eyes.

I moved closer to her and clutched her hand, then leaned forward to ask our security man what we should do.

'Ma'am, just stay put. The doors are locked and the windows are unbreakable. We have security detail behind and in front and they will work with the police to disperse the crowd.'

I couldn't see through the crowd if Harry was all right, and now young men were climbing over our car too. One of them leered at the window shouting, 'Grab her by the hair!'

'Take deep breaths,' the driver said. 'We are well protected.'

But I was utterly frozen as feet thumped across the bonnet and roof of the car. Then the secret service started pushing through and grabbing the protesters. One young man was yanked by his ankle off the roof and thrown back into the crowd. I can't imagine that he was left uninjured by that throw. More booing and cheering. The security guards cleared the path enough that the cars could move again, the protesters still running alongside. My heart was thundering as I imagined us trying to get into the hotel unharmed.

We crawled along. Someone spat on my window. Men in the crowds were fighting now – supporters versus protesters. I realised I couldn't see any women among the throng and wondered if they'd all had the good sense to leave the moment things got tense. It seemed an age before we made it to the hotel, and of course there was a crowd out front there too. But the Victorian police had cleared a narrow alley from the car to the front door, arms linked as they were pushed by the crowd. Two of the big security guards threw open the car door and grabbed me by the elbows. I don't think my feet even touched the stairs. Right behind me was Lady Bird, similarly half-carried into the hotel. Then the door was closed behind us and I breathed out for the first time since we'd arrived in the city centre. In the foyer, while Lady Bird's secretary organised our check-in, I collapsed into a pale pink chaise and pulled out my fan. I felt flushed and unwell. Lady Bird sat next to me. Our husbands were in tense discussions with the secret service over beside the lifts.

'I had a plan, you know,' I said. 'If they'd got the doors open somehow. I always carry a cigarette lighter and I was going to set fire to their hair.'

She nodded. 'My plan was to strangle them with my belt.'

Then we both burst out laughing, partly because we realised that lighters and belts were not particularly good weapons, but partly from the relief that we and our husbands were all still in one piece.

After we farewelled our American friends in Townsville, Harry and I kept heading north and arrived at Bingil Bay to relax after all the tension and protests, which had followed us from city to city up the eastern coast of Australia. Tony and Pat came with us so it was more of a working holiday for Harry. Every morning Tony would drive to town and buy the papers, and Pat was always on the phone organising meetings for Harry. The three of them would spend the mornings in discussions and calls in the back room that doubled as our guest bedroom, and I would bake or draw or read novels and eat chocolates. Harry and I went swimming every afternoon and spent most evenings with Johnny and Allison.

But Harry only lasted a week on this occasion; he was needed back in Canberra. I reluctantly let him go and for the first time stayed on in Bingil Bay by myself. The house was very quiet when I woke that first morning, just the sound of the sea and the birds and the faint rattle of palm leaves.

I stayed in bed late then got up and made breakfast and ate it on the back patio, looking at the sea. The stark difference between how

I felt now and how I'd felt in the back of that car in Melbourne just a few days ago made me blink. Nobody for miles.

I enjoyed my solitude for most of the day, but then Allison popped by around three to see if I was lonely and wanted company and a cup of tea. She had brought a cake she'd baked, so I made tea and we settled at the kitchen table.

'Just a small slice for me,' I said as Allison cut the cake.

'It's a Vicky sponge. Your favourite.'

I patted my belly through my loose cotton dress.

'Oh, nonsense,' Allison said, but she narrowed my slice anyway. 'Harry back off to work, then?'

'An emergency in Canberra. I don't mind. Having the Johnsons here has been exhausting. All the protesters and the stress.' I poured the tea and ate a forkful of the cake. It was perfectly delicious, and I knew I'd be having a second slice because I had no willpower.

'I think you're doing marvellously, Zara. It can't be easy being the PM's wife, and throw in your business interests as well.'

'I don't do nearly as much as I used to. I have staff. I just float in from time to time and offer an opinion.'

'Do you miss it?'

I sighed and leaned back in my chair. 'I miss drawing dresses.'

'You can still draw dresses.'

'It's not the same. I like to design *for* somebody. I like it when I can see their figure and they say, *Oh, I want this for a party where there's going to be dancing.* Then I can imagine their body moving and think about how the gown will move with them. But I live in Canberra now and I'm always travelling, so I can't develop that relationship with clients and take that time.' I sipped my tea. 'Makes life feel a bit flat.'

'You do sound flat. Tired?'

I fixed Allison in my gaze and wondered if I would say it.

She drew her brows together, puzzled. 'What is it?'

'Why didn't you tell me Harry brought another woman to Bedarra?'

Allison's gaze skidded away. 'Ah,' she said. 'You know.'

A long silence unfolded between us. I finished my slice of cake and cut another. I felt guilty for asking Allison and putting her on the spot, but I suspected she felt more guilty.

She fidgeted in her chair, sighed, then finally answered. 'Johnny told me not to tell you.'

'So both our husbands are at fault,' I said wryly. 'Feels about right.'

'He said it would only hurt you, and as your friends we should protect you. I did point out to him that if you ever found out we knew, you'd hate us forever.'

'I don't hate you. I didn't hate you even for a moment when I found out,' I said. 'I felt betrayed, but it was nothing compared to Harry's betrayal.'

She nodded and reached her hand across the table. 'I'm sorry.'

'It's no matter,' I said. 'You're forgiven.' I grasped her fingers and our gazes met for a long time. 'What was she like?'

'She's not you,' Allison said. 'I didn't warm to her because I didn't like the whole situation. Johnny was very welcoming and he seemed to get on with her, but . . . I couldn't see why she had such a hold on Harry.'

'I think she still does,' I said. 'I think it's still going on.'

'Oh. That's a long time.'

'I ran into her down at Portsea. Didn't know who she was but it seems other people do. It's quite embarrassing. They must look at her and compare her to me and . . .' I pushed away the plate with the second slice of cake. 'This is why I simply *must* stick to my diet. I'm not naturally slim like you. Or her.'

'You're beautiful, Zara, and Harry knows it. Harry has never cared about a woman's size, he just likes women.' She took a deep breath. 'I'm resolved to be more honest with you, so I'm going to ask you this – do you know about the others?'

'Theoretically. I prefer not to know details. But . . . are there any other long-term ones?'

'Not that's he's mentioned. You see, he tells Johnny everything, and Johnny tells me, so I know rather more than I'm comfortable with. But I will answer any of your questions honestly.'

How much did I want to know? I considered this for a long time.

'Has he had more than ten lovers?' I asked.

She nodded emphatically, so I asked no further questions about numbers.

'Is it still going on with multiple women or is it just . . . her . . . now.' I didn't like to say her name.

'It's still going on.'

'But he's a grandpa!' I exclaimed. 'How?'

'He's powerful. And, you know, he's got that twinkle. You both have it. Johnny and I often speculated that the two of you must have had fireworks in the bedroom.'

I laughed. 'Yes, we certainly did have. Though I'm getting less willing and able some nights.'

'Do you want to know any more?'

'I think it's best if I don't.'

'All right, then. But you can always ask me and I will always answer you honestly.'

I put my head in my hands. 'Allison, am I a fool? Do you feel sorry for me? I don't want to be a pitiable creature.'

She shook my wrist to make me lift my head. 'You're not a fool. I feel compassion for you that his indiscretions hurt, but I also know how dearly he loves you because he tells Johnny that too. But most of all, the idea of you being a pitiable creature is such nonsense. I have admired you all these years. You are strong and clever and creative and successful. You fit more things into a year than some women fit into a lifetime.' She squeezed my wrist. 'If you could see yourself from the outside, you would never worry again.'

Her kindness made my eyes prick with tears. 'Thank you, dear friend.'

'And that's it, isn't it? You have dear friends. Wonderful family. So many people love you. If there's one little wrong note in your marriage, is that so bad? Not every tune can be perfect.' She pushed my plate back at me. 'Now eat the cake.'

I wiped away my tears and picked up the fork.

CHAPTER 30

The telephone in our bedroom in the Lodge rang early one morning, not long after the President's visit. Harry answered it. These calls were always for him, so I snuggled under the blankets in the Canberra chill and hoped it would be a short call so I could keep dozing.

To my surprise, Harry gently nudged me. 'It's for you. It's Betty.'

I sat up blearily and he passed me the phone. The long, curly cord cut across his morning paperwork.

'Betty? Is everything all right?'

'Yes and no. I think you should come down to Melbourne today if you can. The shop has been vandalised and the police will want to talk with both of us.'

'Vandalised? What? How?'

'You'll see when you get here, love. Earliest plane you can, all right?'

'Yes, yes, all right.'

I handed the phone back to Harry. He looked at me quizzically over his reading glasses.

'The shop's been vandalised and the police need to talk to us.'

'Oh, I'm sorry to hear that. Let's get Pat to organise you a flight. Are you all right?'

'I guess I'm shocked. Why would somebody want to vandalise a dress shop?'

Harry frowned. 'Don't forget who you're married to. It's not a secret you're the PM's wife.' He rubbed my thigh through the covers. 'I'll call Pat. You hop up and get yourself ready to go.'

By midday I was climbing out of a taxi outside Magg, and I could see the damage straight away. Somebody had splashed red paint over the entrance doors and broken the front window by throwing the paint pail through it. Broken glass and red paint were everywhere, inside and out. One of the dress racks had been knocked over and gowns were in a tangle on the floor, splattered with paint and sprinkled with glass. My stomach tightened and I gasped as though I'd been punched.

'Oh no!' I cried as Betty stepped out to greet me.

'I know, darling, isn't it grim? Come in. The police have questions.'

I followed her inside and felt such an ache under my rib cage seeing my beautiful shop this way. Drops of paint had splattered everywhere, even on dresses hung on the back wall. Nothing could be done to clean them so it represented thousands and thousands of dollars of damage. Two very kind police officers, who had already spoken to Betty, asked a lot of questions, especially about Harry and whether he ever came to the store. It was through their questions that I came to realise that the vandals were protesting Harry's policies and taking it out on his wife's business. The unfairness of this stung, especially as it hurt Betty too, and so many of the other staff who had invested so much care and talent in the garments.

When they had finished questioning me, the older, grey-haired policeman asked if he could use our telephone to call the station and I went to stand with Betty, careful not to get my shoes in the paint. Together we considered the damage.

'Do we have insurance for the window, or is that the responsibility of the lessor?' I asked.

'I'm not sure. I expect we'll have to spend the next few days making telephone calls and finding things out. We were lucky nobody came in while the window was gaping open to steal yesterday's takings.'

'Yes. I suppose we should call a glazier the moment the police are finished with the phone.' I looked over my shoulder and could see the policeman was in deep conversation, but his eyes kept flicking back over to us. 'Hm,' I said, 'he's listening more than he's talking. Maybe they already have an idea who did it.'

'Wretched long-haired young men who don't care a fig for anyone but themselves,' Betty scoffed. 'I am so tired of turning on the news and seeing them.' She gestured at the dresses on the floor. 'Where do we even start cleaning this up?'

'Rubber gloves and rubbish bags, I imagine.' Another pang as I spotted a gorgeous silver slip dress with hours of embroidery at the hip ruined by a huge splodge of red. 'Honestly, whose mind did they think they'd change?'

The police officer hung up the telephone and walked over to us. We both turned expectantly.

'We have three suspects already in custody at the station,' he said. 'The florist across the road was in early and saw them. He knew one of them and called it in.'

'Really?' Betty said. 'I say, that is quick work. We must thank the florist.' Then she laughed. 'How does one thank a florist? You can't send flowers.'

'Who would do this?' I asked.

'Yes, well, that is quite the surprise.' The policeman looked at his notes. 'Three women, all in their forties. Not the usual suspects for this kind of crime.'

'Women in their forties?' Betty exclaimed. 'What on earth did they think would happen?'

I remembered the signs in the crowd during LBJ's visit. *Save Our Sons.* Everything inside me softened. What if my boys had been eligible for conscription? What if they didn't have reasonable excuses not to go? Young men were dying every day, very young men, in a war that was a long way from home and – in the view of many – a war we needn't be involved in at all. If it were my sons, I might very well do something desperate as well.

'Will they be charged?' I asked. 'Can we request that they won't?'

Betty looked at me sharply. 'Of course we want them charged.'

'No, Betty, we don't. I'll pay for the damage myself if it's not insured. I'll stay here by myself and take care of getting it cleaned up and repaired, if you'll just let me make this decision.'

She sighed. 'You bleeding heart.'

'Think of how much you love your children, Betty. They were acting out of fear, a fear that we can understand.'

Betty shook her head and pressed her lips together, but I saw her eyes soften. 'Oh, Zara. Very well, then. Officer, can you let them go?'

'Please, officer?' I added, 'Tell them I understand and . . . I forgive them.'

He shrugged, sliding his notebook into his pocket. 'I can talk to my superiors, but I can't promise anything, ma'am. I must say, it's a very generous gesture. No wonder our PM is married to you.'

Who knew if Harry would think I was a fool, or if he would give me a hug and tell me I was a good woman? Either way, he'd deliver his opinion gently and warmly, if he wasn't so distracted that he forgot to ask.

———

Harry and I retreated to Portsea for some downtime after the midyear sitting of parliament. Tiny came with us, but this time even Tony and Pat stayed in Canberra. I was determined Harry would do no work for at least three days, and we managed to make it to two before somebody drove up in a car with a folder full of papers for him to read. Those two days were sublime though. We spent them having a leisurely breakfast in bed, wandering among the rock pools along the shore, curled up on the couch together listening to the radio, and drinking brandy in the garden before sunset, watching the sea.

'This will be what it's like when we retire, you know,' I said to him on the second afternoon as we sat on a bench in the garden. 'Doesn't it feel splendid?'

He curled his arm around me and squeezed me against him. 'Time with you is always splendid.'

'Just don't spend eighteen years in office like Mr Menzies.'

'I have no intention of it, my love.' He kissed the top of my head and caught a mouthful of my hair when the breeze stirred it up. 'I'll aim to be short and sweet.'

'You've already crammed in a lot.'

'I have more in me, but my ambitions aren't infinite.'

I sighed and leaned into him, feeling perfectly happy.

The next morning when his homework arrived, I left him in the sunroom and went for a swim. The water was chilly, so I didn't stay in for long. I patted my exposed skin with a towel, put my cotton shift back on over my damp swimsuit and slipped on my sandals, then had the idea that I might walk down to the village. Harry loved the cream horns from the local bakery and I thought I could bring one to him with a pot of coffee to keep him going. I had no idea how he would slog through such lots of paperwork, and for pleasure still read big, thick histories and biographies in very small print. It seemed his attention never faltered. Mine was always spinning off all over the place.

I was in and out of the bakery ten minutes later, a paper bag with a cream horn in my right hand, when I saw her across the street. Marjorie.

I froze. She hadn't seen me, and nor did I want her to. I looked a fright with wet hair and a dress with damp spots blooming on it. But then she was checking for traffic and crossing the road, and if I kept walking towards home we would walk by each other and there was no escaping it.

I thought of running, but then I decided I'd had enough of fretting and worrying about this woman and what she may or may not have done. As her shoe hit the footpath she looked up and saw me, and she too paused.

'Marjorie?' I said.

'Hello, Mrs Holt.'

'Call me Zara. Will you come and sit with me for a minute or two?' I gestured to a bench on the grass that faced the sea.

Fear crossed her face.

'I promise I'm not going to shout,' I said with a smile.

'I . . . all right.'

We walked awkwardly together, about five feet apart and with me a little ahead. Then we sat down. I tried to fix my hair but it was still quite damp so I told myself to let it go. It didn't matter what she thought of my appearance. She raised her sunglasses and perched them on her dark hair. In the full sunlight, I could see she was older than I'd thought, with deep lines around her eyes. Perhaps she was in her fifties too.

'Well,' I said. 'We meet at last.'

'We have met before. A long time ago.'

'I remember vaguely. You had a husband.'

'I still do.'

'And does he know about you and Harry?'

She blinked back at me, clearly not intending to tell me anything. I felt cut adrift, wondering why on earth I'd asked her to speak to me. What could I say to her without sounding like a petty jealous woman she could complain to all her friends about? I could hardly talk her out of having the affair. If she had a conscience, she'd have stopped it ages ago.

'What I meant was, we meet for the first time since I discovered your relationship with my husband. I wonder, Marjorie,' I said, and I tried to sound kind, 'where do you think this ends?'

'Where do I think what ends?'

'The affair. Harry's not going to leave me.' As I said these words I knew they were true. From the night we'd met, he'd said it. *We belong to each other now. Always will.* And that had borne itself out over forty years. Despite all our dramas, we always made our way back to each other.

There was a long silence, filled only by the sound of the waves and the seagulls.

'Look, Mrs Holt,' she said finally, 'I don't know why you're speaking to me. If you want to give me a piece of your mind, go ahead. But I don't have to answer your questions.'

Maybe I should tell her about all the other women. Maybe I should tell her Harry still made love to me as passionately as he ever had, if not as frequently. But she was shifting in her seat and I knew I only had her for a few more moments before she walked off, so I said, 'I want you to know something. You'll never love him as much as I do.'

'How do you know that?'

'Because it isn't possible for anyone to love him as much as I do.'

She nodded, rose to her feet. 'Is that it?'

'Have a lovely day.'

She left without saying another word.

———

In November, Harry asked me if I would please take on the role of working with a fundraising committee for a large charity that had been pursuing him relentlessly. This charity, which was called the Ladies Care Foundation, raised money for disadvantaged families in and around Canberra, and Harry was official patron. 'Please?' he begged. 'It will be two or three meetings and that's it.'

I relented because I felt so sorry for him. He had been getting constant back spasms and was taking painkillers that made him sleepy. He still woke at 6 am to work, but over those two weeks I think I finally saw him starting to flag. He swore all he needed was a week back at Portsea, to 'swim it out'. I was of the opinion that all he needed was a jolly long rest over Christmas. To get the charity off his back, I agreed to meet with them.

From the outset, the head of the Ladies Care organising committee, a Mrs Bainbridge, was clearly disappointed that she had to meet with me and not Harry himself. I really don't know what she expected – the man was busy running the country. But she was standoffish at our first morning tea while everyone else was welcoming and grateful. I'd invited them to the Lodge for tea in the drawing room and we chatted amiably among ourselves.

But Mrs Bainbridge was very keen to get the actual meeting started. She was only in her thirties, thin and nervy and precise, with very strong ideas that she absolutely battered us down with. The major fundraising event, which was to be held in the second week of December, was usually something like an art show or a music performance, and she launched straight into suggesting some arias sung by members of the Australian Opera Company, accompanied by a sit-down five-course dinner. She had worked out the budget – the proposed ticket price, everything – and rattled it off to us quick time, then said, 'If you all agree with this proposal, and I'm sure you will, we can kindly ask Mrs Holt to be the mistress of ceremonies for the evening.'

A few blinks and reluctant nods passed around the room, and I realised that Mrs Bainbridge had a hold over the organising committee and they were quite unable to say no to her. But I really, *really* didn't like opera. So I thought I'd have some fun with her.

'Or . . .' I started, and I swear there was an audible gasp in the room. 'Mrs Bainbridge, what kind of audience do you usually have for these events?'

'Women from Canberra's best families,' she said defensively. 'We had eighty last year and seventy-five the year before, so the numbers are growing. We must be doing something right.' She smiled at me, but it was icy.

'Wouldn't it be fun . . . given it's a female audience . . . I don't know, opera's not everybody's cup of tea, so wouldn't it be fun to have a fashion parade instead?'

'Oh yes!' the woman sitting beside me exclaimed. 'I *adore* fashion and was so excited when I heard you'd be at these meetings.'

Mrs Bainbridge flicked her a cautionary look but it was too late. Murmurs went around the room about how a fashion parade would be something different, might attract a bigger crowd.

'And then,' I said, 'rather than a sit-down dinner, we can have it earlier in the day and make it a high tea, where women can circulate and meet and talk to each other.'

'Oh, I don't know about that,' Mrs Bainbridge said. 'People don't like to walk and eat.'

'Lady Bird Johnson hosted just such a high tea for me a few months ago,' I said. 'It was a roaring success. Then we don't have to charge as much and more people can come. In fact, I'll provide all the clothes for the fashion parade, source the models, organise the whole show, if you like. It is rather my special ability.'

'Will they all be clothes from your shops?' she asked, and I caught her inference, which was, *Is this just a big advertisement for Magg?*

'We will mix it up,' I said. 'Shall we put it to a vote? All those who want opera and five-course meal raise your hands.'

Mrs Bainbridge and one other woman's hands shot up defiantly.

'All those in favour of a fashion parade and high tea?'

The other six hands went up, including mine.

'What a pleasure it will be to work with you on this,' I said to Mrs Bainbridge. 'And I'm a terrible emcee. I'll get lost and ruin it for everyone. But I can provide a speech. You just let me know what you want me to talk about.'

I'd like to say Mrs Bainbridge warmed to me, but she didn't. She never quite got over what she saw as Harry's snub of her foundation as he had barely engaged in his role of patron. Also, she thought fashion not good enough for the crème de la crème audience she wanted to attract as donors for her foundation. She was polite and respectful, but she seemed to relish disagreeing with me on the most tiny details. As I didn't care about details, I often let her have her way. It mattered nothing to me if the tickets were on blue card or yellow card, so I often let her win, thinking this would be the last petty argument. But it never was.

Even after we sold 130 tickets in the first week they were on sale, she didn't concede the fashion parade was a good idea. She grumbled about having to move the event to the bigger ballroom, but this was brilliant for me, because it meant the models could stride right down the centre of the room and the clothes could be seen from all different angles.

Finally, a week before the event she gave me a brief for my speech. I was to talk about what it was like being the wife of the Prime Minister. I shrugged when I got off the telephone from her and sat down to write a speech.

———

We hired a professional emcee who had commentated for fashion parades before. The Grand Ballroom at the Rex was festooned with Christmas lights and a huge tree in the corner gleamed with gold decorations. Chattering women arrived and found their seats. The curtains were drawn and stage lighting turned on and a hush fell over the room. Then the first model walked out.

I sat in the front row with the rest of the organising committee, the folder that I kept my speeches in flat on my lap. The lights on the ground caught shimmers and shadows in the flounced skirt of the gown, and I swelled with pride. I may not have designed this particular dress, but I designed this empire that Magg had become. As the models kept coming, I thought of all the women who had been part of that success: Betty, of course. Mum and Vieve.

Tiny, who had looked after the home front so I could get on with things. Caroline, who had stepped into my shoes and ran the business with such passion and care. The junior designers and seamstresses, and even humourless Miss White, our bookkeeper. In among the Magg dresses were some Schiaparelli, Pierre Cardin, Mary Quant and Chanel – all designs we stocked. But they were mostly ours, and it was an explosion of colour and modern cuts and classic styles, all ending with a gorgeous long-sleeved column bridal gown with a high embroidered waist. The audience clapped furiously, and I looked around to see my fellow event organisers all smiling. The curtains were opened again to let in daylight and the emcee invited Mrs Bainbridge to the lectern to say a few words about the foundation, and to introduce me.

She gave a quick history of Ladies Care, which I discovered had grown out of the early twentieth-century temperance movement, but now devoted itself to helping schoolchildren afford uniforms and books so they wouldn't be left behind. It was a touching speech, much more so than I expected from her, and I clapped enthusiastically.

Then she said, 'I'd like to invite to the lectern now our guest speaker for this afternoon, ahead of our high tea. Please welcome the Prime Minister's wife, Mrs Harold Holt.'

The audience applauded as I climbed to my feet and approached the lectern. Perhaps it was something about the way she'd introduced me. I loved Harold, but I didn't enjoy having my name subsumed by his. Perhaps I was tired of her being disappointed that I wasn't the PM and was only going to be able to tell second-hand stories about him. Or perhaps it was the roomful of women's eyes upon me. But when I opened my folder, instead of reading from the speech I'd written that week, which was sitting on the top, I leafed through until I found the speech I had given at Ewha Womans University in Korea.

'Good afternoon. Today I want to speak to you about women. About their innate qualities – their creativity, their good sense, their compassion – and how all of these things can be harnessed for their success.' I glanced at Mrs Bainbridge, whose eyes were burning a hole in me.

'But first,' I said, going off-script briefly, 'if you come up to introduce yourself to me over tea – and I hope you do – please don't call me Mrs Holt. I'm Zara.'

———

I told Harry about it that night as we lay in bed. I massaged the stiff left part of his back with my thumbs and related how well my speech was received.

'And do you know,' I babbled, 'a young woman of about seventeen was there with her mother, because she wants to be a fashion designer and she absolutely hounded her mother to buy the tickets. And I was reminded of being that age and dreaming of a life as a designer and, well, I made it, didn't I? All my dreams came true. When you dream them though, you don't think about the bumps along the road, but it's by living through the bumps that you learn and grow.'

'Mm-hm,' he said, wincing as I went a little too deep with my thumbs.

'Oh, I'm sorry, my love. Am I driving you mad with my prattle?'

'Not at all,' he said, his voice muffled by his pillow. 'I'm always proud of you. I'll never stop being proud of you.'

I leaned down and kissed his back. 'I'll never stop being proud of *us*. We didn't do too badly for a couple of mad young things.'

He reached behind me with his right arm and patted the side of my bottom fondly. 'I love you, Zara.'

'I love you too, Harry.'

———

The lead-up to Christmas was frantic. We had to buy presents for so many people. While I took care of family and friends, I had to hire somebody to go and fetch presents for all the staff and work contacts that Harry needed to keep onside.

At the same time, Allison arrived from up north because she hadn't seen a dentist in years. She was frightened and needed a friend to go with her, so I'd offered for her to come and stay and see my dentist, who was a very gentle chap and opened his office on a Saturday especially for her. He gave her four fillings, removed a tooth at the back, and sent her home to the Lodge with painkillers and a terrible headache.

We had all hoped to head to Portsea that afternoon, but Allison was in no fit state to travel, and I was a long way behind with my present-wrapping. Harry and Tiny went off together, and I watched television with Allison and got her to promise me to help wrap presents in the morning.

It was around midafternoon the next day that Tony arrived. Allison and I were knee-deep in wrapping paper and string, and already had one Christmas brandy under our belts.

I let him in. 'Tony? You know Harry's not here.'

'Yes, I do, I . . .' He trailed off, and I realised he was pale. That's when the feeling of dread came over me.

'What's happened?'

'They can't find Harry.'

'What do you mean? Who can't find him?' My stomach felt loose, as though I was falling.

Allison, who might have heard the note of alarm in my voice, emerged to stand beside me.

Tony glanced from me to her and back. 'He went for a swim off Cheviot Beach and didn't come back.'

A swim. Harry's element was water. I felt a momentary relief. 'Ah, I don't think we should worry, then. He's probably found a rock somewhere to sun himself, and he'd have a good chuckle knowing he's caused us all so much stress.'

Tony looked down at his hands then back at me. 'If it's all the same, Mrs Holt, I'd like to transport you immediately to Melbourne.'

That falling feeling again. Allison put her arm around my waist.

'Right,' I said. 'Right, then. But we won't worry too much yet, will we? Somebody will call any moment and say he's turned up.'

'I have a RAAF plane ready to go, and a car out front.'

'I'll just get my jacket. Can Allison come too?'

'Of course. Of course, whatever you need.'

I fussed about readying myself and getting in the car while I reasoned it through in my head.

Harry will be all right. He's a strong swimmer. He's always all right.

(But his back, that spasm, those painkillers that make him tired.)

The man is made of iron. He is fit as a fiddle. Has barely been ill a day in his life before his back problem.

(He's getting old. Nearly sixty.)

He's swum off Cheviot Beach dozens of times. He knows it well.

(And so do I. It's unpredictable and turbulent.)

Within an hour we were taking to the skies. Allison tried to distract me with chatter, positive words and so on. But Tony still hadn't received the phone call saying Harry had been found.

'Don't give up hope,' Allison said. 'Use that wonderful imagination of yours to imagine the very best outcome.'

So I closed my eyes. The aeroplane hit turbulence and rocked me up and down. My stomach lurched, and my imagination conjured only a bleak, white nothingness.

EPILOGUE

Every day of the last year, she has wished for something different. If she could go back, that is when she would go back to. Back to the day he left. She would say, 'Wait a day or two and travel with Allison and me.'

Or maybe she would go back to when she found out about Marjorie, and tell him he either ended it with her or she'd drag him through divorce court and ruin his political career. Because it was Marjorie who was with him on the beach, and he was likely showing off to her by entering such dangerous water.

Or maybe she would go back to when they bought the place in Portsea and say, 'Let's save our money and have Bingil Bay as our beach house', because the water never sucked and boiled in front of our shack up there.

There seem to be too many intervention points, moments where fate could have turned, and she could have avoided that draggingly long drive to Portsea, the clatter of helicopters overhead, the looks on her sons' faces, the growing desolate horror of knowing he was probably dead, and the equally painful hope that kept spearing through her. All while cameras caught her fallen face, her shaking hands.

But nobody can go back in time. She needs to stop imagining these wild scenarios, these situations where she and Harry somehow escape the jolt and press of the world and live happily ever after, retire to Bingil Bay and spend their days with their legs entwined on the settee.

Zara opens her eyes. She is at her son Nick's place, sitting on the back patio with little Sophie, recently turned three and no longer the tiny baby she and Harry had cooed over.

'Look what I drew, Grandma,' Sophie says, brandishing a picture all drawn in red-coloured pencil.

'Well now, let me see,' Zara says, putting on her reading glasses. The picture is of a girl under a shining sun, wearing a triangular sundress. 'It's very good and the dress is pretty, but if she's in the sun she'll need a hat.' She taps the little girl's nose. 'Always design for context.'

Sophie wrinkles her nose, with no idea what Zara means. But she earnestly returns to her little art table to draw a hat on her girl anyway.

'Come draw dresses with me, Grandma,' she calls.

Zara kneels beside her, stiff knees cracking. 'Oof,' she says. And reaches for paper and a pencil.

ACKNOWLEDGEMENTS

It has been a long time between books for me, as I've dealt with a range of challenges, both global and local. The support of many people has been crucial in getting me back on my horse, so to speak. To Vanessa and all at Hachette: thank you for holding a space for me – both literally and metaphorically – and for your continued belief in my writing. To my big sister Mary-Rose, whose love and off-colour jokes keep me going when things seem impossible. To all my other writer friends (Lisa, Helen, Isobelle, Kathleen, Jo, Kate) and all my academic friends (Beth, Alex, Sandra, Other Lisa, Other Kate, Heather), for top-notch fellowship, a place to vent and sometimes karaoke. To my beloved children, Luka and Astrid, whose judgement, wisdom and hilarious expressions of withering scorn I take full credit for. To my mother and brother, for unconditional love. To my Champion, David, for tending the hearth so I can tell stories there.

Special mention to the blessed felines who have warmed my lap while writing for the last few years: Samwise, Frodo, Onyxia (may they rest in peace), Pangur and Norna. Frodo: I will never stop missing you.

Thank you to Dame Zara Holt/Bate, whose life was the spark for this novel. I read Zara's autobiography, *My Life and Harry* (1968), and it inspired me to create a work of fiction that drew on the experiences of this impressive woman and build the imagined world you are reading in these pages. We owe so much to the women who have come before us, who pushed against barriers and lived passionate lives. Zara did that.

But most of all, my loving gratitude to my beloved literary agent of nearly thirty years, Selwa Anthony. It has been an extraordinary adventure, not without its plot twists, but always tending towards a happy ending.

Kimberley Freeman is an Australian author of historical fiction about and for women. She has published more than thirty novels and is translated into more than twenty languages. She is also a Professor of Writing at the University of Queensland, and lives in Brisbane with two unruly cats.

hachette
AUSTRALIA

If you would like to find out more about Hachette Australia,
our authors, upcoming events and new releases, you can visit
our website or our social media channels:

hachette.com.au

f HachetteAustralia

⬛ HachetteAus